For my family

Unburied

Heather Critchlow grew up in rural Aberdeenshire and trained as a business journalist after studying history and social science at the University of Cambridge. Her short stories have appeared in crime fiction anthologies *Afraid of the Light*, *Afraid of the Christmas Lights* and *Afraid of the Shadows*. She lives in St Albans.

Also by Heather Critchlow

The Cal Lovett Files

Unsolved
Unburied

UNBURIED

HEATHER CRITCHLOW

First published in the United Kingdom in 2024 by

Canelo
Unit 9, 5th Floor
Cargo Works, 1–2 Hatfields
London SE1 9PG
United Kingdom

A CIP catalogue record for this book is available from the British Library.

Print ISBN 978 1 80436 260 0
Ebook ISBN 978 1 80436 259 4

This book is a work of fiction. Names, characters, businesses, organizations, places and events are either the product of the author's imagination or are used fictitiously. Any resemblance to actual persons, living or dead, events or locales is entirely coincidental.

Cover design by Andrew Davis

Cover images © ArcAngel, Trevillion

Look for more great books at www.canelo.co

Printed and bound in Great Britain by Clays Ltd, Elcograf S.p.A.

1

PROLOGUE

WESTER ROSS, SCOTTISH HIGHLANDS

BRYONY, 2007

Bryony tilts her face to the weak sunlight, trying to catch some warmth to stem the chill snaking through her veins. It's not the worst place to wait, but it is cold, sitting slumped on the doorstep. She lets her fingers fall to the slab of remorseless stone, worn smooth by centuries of farming feet. Her hands are sticky and warm, the blood congealing. Panic stirs inside her. Will someone come? Did they hear the shots? If so, they'll be here soon, with their false concern and judgement.

Her mind spirals, sending thoughts in loops and swirls. It would have been different if Robbie hadn't wet the bed. They wouldn't have been at home, and this wouldn't have happened. The moment her son slipped shamefaced into their bedroom this morning, gears slid into motion and darkness smiled.

Her fingers close tight, hands convulsing so that her nails pierce the skin in crescent moons. She was going to be better. She tried, but she failed. Since Robbie was born, she's had something else inside her. An ugliness that lay beneath the surface, undiscovered for so long, rearing up with motherhood. She shuts her eyes for a moment but the bloody image is imprinted on her brain, the smell in her nostrils. She's let everyone down. Her sons most of all.

Her breath sounds loud in the quiet.

Today was going to be a good day. They were going to go out. She was going to make an effort and take the boys to the green-watered lochan through the pine trees. She wasn't going to rush or scold them.

The bag she packed last night is just inside the doorway. Even with her eyes closed, she can see it: small swimming shorts and rash vests with dinosaurs on them; a box of Tunnock's teacakes tucked in beside the good intentions. Sean loves the marshmallow. It was going to be an Enid Blyton-worthy adventure. *Making memories*, the way those Facebook bitches are always on about. She was going to let the boys throw stones, get muddy, climb trees. She was going to be the kind of mother she once had so much faith she would be.

The sun slips behind a cloud and she shivers at the sudden cold, can't clutch the wisps of thought that pirou-ette in her brain.

She could tell by the look on Robbie's face that he'd wet the bed again. She didn't need him to confess or to run her hand over the bottom sheet and find the damp patch, its penetrating odour nestling in the mattress, the room, his skin.

She should have been kind. Felt what normal mothers feel. The ones who can tuck a baby into the crook of one arm and wipe a kitchen surface with the other hand, all the while smiling like their life isn't the biggest heap of shite around. But she wasn't. She lost her temper. She ripped the sheets from the bed and cancelled their plans.

It wasn't that she didn't see the tears in her son's eyes, so much as she couldn't feel them.

Does she sleep? Her eyes jerk open and, against the greenery and the gravel and the hardness of the doorstep and the carnage in front of her, she sees *his* eyes. Haunting her. Blue and staring. Shock painted onto them. Robbie. Her oldest. Her complicated one. The child who deserved so much more.

'Robbie,' she whispers, her lips dry and cracking. 'I'm sorry, love.'

And she is. She really, really is.

She feels a sudden pain in her chest that burns so fiercely, it makes her fingers numb.

'Mummy's here,' she wants to say. 'Mummy's got you.'

But she doesn't, because nothing ever comes out right when it comes to Robbie. He's gone now. She can't go where he's going. She just hopes his brother will be waiting for him and they can hold tight to each other. Robbie and Sean. Her boys. Her poor, darling boys.

Is it later, or is it now? She keeps sliding into what feels like the deepest sleep, but then she's back again, in the cold of consciousness, unable to remember her dreams. She can hear a man shouting and the horrible crunching noise feet make on the gravel but she can't resolve the wailing into words. She thinks about putting her hands over her ears but she's just too damn tired.

She's always wishing for life to go faster, for the boys to grow, the drudgery to end. Time interminably slow and awful. But now, just at the moment she's changed her mind, it speeds up. Of course it fucking does. She just wants a few more minutes to sit here, to feel the wind on her face and hear the rush of the sea in the distance. To linger in regret.

But it's all louder now – the sirens, the feet, the slamming. She's finding it harder to stay calm. She can't breathe. They're all going to know. They're going to know how bad she truly is.

CHAPTER ONE

WEST MIDLANDS

CAL

Cal stands on the street corner, hesitating – or at least pretending to. He made a promise that he keeps on breaking. *Go home, Cal, go home.* Even muttering the words doesn't help. Where is home, anyway? Living back with his mother in a house he swore he would never return to, his marriage over. That's not home; it's necessity. Something stirs inside him, a compulsion that he can't shake. Even as he rehearses the arguments against it, he finds himself looping through the streets towards his prey, compelled to scratch the impossible itch.

The cafe is only open for another hour. There are few patrons left inside, just the dregs of the post-school pick-up crowd. Fractious kids and tired mothers, a spaniel slumped on the floor, head on its paws in despair.

He orders a coffee – black, because it's quick and he isn't bothered about drinking it – then chooses a seat at a table with an abandoned highchair, dodging the scattered crumbs and half a banana squashed onto the floor.

His hands shake a little with adrenaline as he uses a napkin to wipe a spot clean for his laptop and he pulls it from his bag, no intention of logging in, only of hiding behind it. He grips the hot mug between his hands and focuses his gaze on the garage over the road, where a recovery truck is unloading a dented car. A man in a luminous vest unclips cables, lowers a ramp. Then the man he's talking to rounds the vehicle and Cal's breath constricts. His sister Margot has been missing for thirty-six years and, though there isn't even a scrap of evidence, he is sure this is the man who killed her. He just can't prove it.

As he watches ex-convict Jason Barr, something tightens inside Cal's chest, making it hard to breathe. He shouldn't be here. If the police knew what he was doing they'd be furious. He made a promise to DI Foulds when she gave him privileged information in a moment of sympathy. He's abusing that trust. But he can't look away.

The man is thickset and walks a bit like he's sitting astride a horse, his thighs great trunks of muscle under jeans. The roll of fat on the back of Barr's neck, beneath his shaved skull, is one of the few changes that dates him from the pictures of him as a young man. The predator may have aged, but he's still ox-strong and muscular.

Cal's attention is absorbed by the tattooed arms that are now propped on the roof of the broken vehicle. Old patterns and declarations of love swirl and ripple there, an inked history of changing loyalties. Barr has altered them since doing time for assaulting women, hiding the man he was before.

As Cal stares at the hot metal beneath Barr's hands, he pictures the paleness of his sister's neck, the fragility of her collarbone, the red silk of her hair. He runs his fingers over the small tattoo of a swallow on the inside of his own wrist. A tiny memory of her.

'Excuse me.' Cal is wrenched back into the present by a woman bending forward to insert herself into his vision. 'Is this chair taken?' He can tell by the tone of her voice that this isn't the first time she's asked.

'Oh,' he says, his voice shaking. 'No. Sorry. It's not.'

By the time Cal looks up after he has helped her lift the chair, Barr and the battered car have gone. He feels a turn of wretchedness, a queasy sort of regret after giving in to his compulsion. He comes here often, and for what? Watching, waiting, unable to do anything.

It bothers him, how close to his childhood home this garage lies. How close to where Margot was set down in the countryside after an argument with her boyfriend. Left to make her own way back. Never seen again. It's almost like Barr is taunting him with his proximity, blatantly getting on with his life.

DI Foulds promised that the force were investigating, yet it has been months. Impatience nags at Cal as he slugs back a few mouthfuls of the now-cold coffee and slides his untouched laptop into his bag. He should go to his mother's now; it's getting late. But as he pauses on the pavement and inspects the dark clouds at the edge of the sky, Jason Barr steps from the dark cavern of the garage. His arms are stiff and swinging, a pack of cigarettes in his hand, phone bulging in his back pocket.

Barr saunters down the street, and even though Cal knows he shouldn't – Barr may well recognise him from the articles in the papers – he can't help himself. The devil inside takes over and he trails him down the road, hurrying to match the length of the other man's stride.

Dark fantasies descend: the going-home traffic beside him is steady – a bus heaving with people ready for their tea. What if he pushed Barr in front of it? He can almost

7

see the ensuing scene: the blood, the wailing, the *peace*. He feels his fingers twitch and his arm jerk slightly: a shadow movement of his deepest desires.

But then Barr halts, turning and peering back along the road as if looking for someone. Cal feels adrenaline tear through him, followed by shame and a fear that makes him feel every bit the nine-year-old boy whose older sister never came home. He bends and fiddles with the laces of his trainers. In a head-to-head between the two of them, it is easy to see who the loser would be.

When he glances up, Barr has moved on. The bus has stopped, disgorging passengers. People stream around him, tired and ready for home. He straightens and scans the distance, frantic to see over their heads. Barr, the ex-bouncer, turns into a side street, vanishing from sight.

Cal should go home. Instead, he finds himself jogging along the street, desperate to reach the corner before Barr slips away from him. He skids into the side street, surprising a black-and-white cat, which darts under a car. Bright blooms spill from window boxes on his right, and on the opposite side an overturned bin has spewed last night's curry onto the pavement. The residential street is quiet, deserted. But as he jogs past the terraced houses, he sees the lumbering form in the distance. He slows his pace, cursing his recklessness.

Cal falters when Barr turns, but the man is just extracting and lighting a cigarette, barely pausing as he exhales. He follows the scent of the smoke in the air. Tailing him here is so risky. If Barr looks back he will see Cal, but he follows anyway, realising with a chill that he is mirroring the man's crimes: the way he stalked women in the early hours as they wound their way home after evenings out, late nights working or arguments with their boyfriends. The thought makes Cal uneasy – makes him wonder if he is in some way becoming the predator he is shadowing.

But he shoves the misgivings aside because, as they thread their way through the streets in the direction of the river and the green swathes of willows dipping in the flow, he understands where Barr is going.

It seems too audacious, too insulting to be true. It's only when Barr pauses on the bank and stretches to peer over some bushes that Cal knows for sure he is right. The scrapyard is just across from where the bulky mechanic is rocking from foot to foot: rusting hulks of old machinery clothed in weeds. A place usually still and silent, remnants of the past decaying into the earth.

This is the place where serial killer Marc Dubois hinted that Cal's sister is buried – information he and DI Foulds believe came from Jason Barr. At least, Foulds *used* to believe that. Who knows, now?

Dubois and Barr only shared a cell for a short time, until Dubois was moved to a secure hospital setting, but it was enough time, Cal is sure, for a bored and manipulative serial killer to extract information for fun. The final piece of the puzzle, as far as he is concerned, is the discovery that Barr once worked in this scrapyard. How many coincidences do you need before something becomes meaningful? Cal asks himself this question all the time.

The truth is, he knew the moment Dubois uttered Margot's name that there was a sick honesty behind the words. It is impossible to explain properly – he tried so many times with Allie before the divorce and she still saw room for doubt – but there was a gleeful kind of satisfaction in the way Dubois had dropped his crumbs.

The pleasure of knowing something Cal didn't, and the plan to stretch it out and watch him suffer.

Cal drops back to the shadow of a bridge to watch, biting his lip as Barr circles the same patch of ground, grinding his cigarette butt into the grass with his heel, fists clenching and unclenching. When Barr moves off, Cal slips from his hiding place, tempted to follow, though he is increasingly uneasy at the man's erratic behaviour.

Then Barr spins to face him, turning back along the narrow river path, his face thick with twisted thunder. There is no time to move, or hide. Nothing to do but keep walking. A sense of terrible inevitability rises up inside Cal. His sister's laugh echoes in his mind as the man bears down on him.

Cal takes his hands from his pockets as Barr draws near. His heart shouts so loudly inside his chest that all he hears is the blood pumping in his ears, distant traffic fading away to nothing. Without choice, his gaze is pulled to the wide face, like metal to a magnet. As they meet on the path, Cal readies himself for a blow – the world slowing, the suck of river water suddenly loud in his ears, and the dank smell of mud and weeds filling his nostrils – but instead, the man he hates like death catches his eye and nods to him like he could be anyone.

Instinctively, Cal nods in response, though everything in him screams in protest at the bland, automated movement. As he steps to one side, too shocked to act, to block the path, to hurl abuse, he registers Barr's pale face and clammy expression: a million shades from the devil-may-care mechanic he's been watching for weeks.

'Cheers, mate,' Barr says as he passes, but even the voice is off-kilter.

Something is wrong.

Rooted to the spot, Cal lets out an agonised breath, furious with himself for bottling this moment. He whirls round, fists clenched, suddenly suicidally determined to have it out, but Barr is fifty metres away, jogging in the other direction, as if fleeing for his life.

Bewildered, Cal folds at the waist, bracing his hands on his knees and taking in shaky mouthfuls of air. Gradually, his pulse steadies to a normal rate, his hearing returns. Sounds filter through the haze. The crunch of metal, the whine of a motor, a shout.

He stands, edging towards the sound, the thing Barr saw that made him turn tail and run.

The police. They're digging in the scrapyard.

CHAPTER TWO

Cal fits his key into the lock and steps into his mother's home, his mind pounding with thoughts: wonder, relief, excitement, fury. He saw a forensic van through the hedge and a PC standing sentinel at the gate. Why hasn't Foulds told him they are digging? He has tried her mobile several times now, but she isn't answering.

'Where have you been?' His mother's voice, high-pitched and thready, drags him back to the present. His teeth clench at the sound.

'Just had a walk down to see Margot's bench,' he lies, resting his bag on the floor and slipping out of his shoes, setting them neatly on the mat, toes pointing out, heels to the skirting, as his mother prefers. Christ. It's happening already. Like the automatic nod to Barr that he will forever despise himself for.

'At this time?'

He hangs his jacket on the allotted peg and follows her voice into the spartan kitchen. Her back is to him and she is washing up at the sink, her bent figure leaning against faded mustard-yellow cupboards. He catches a glimpse of pink scalp through thinning white hair and it sends a rare twist of tenderness for her through him. There is a plate of food on the table: a grey pork steak, mashed potato and soggy green beans, covered by a stretched piece of cling film. It's well past six. Dinner is at six.

He sets it in the microwave and turns the dial.

'It'll need more than a minute,' she says.

Cal waits for the ping, then drowns the green beans in ketchup. The food is bland but filling, a snap back to childhood. Clods of meat stick in his throat.

He's tired: adrift and homeless. At the best of times, being here makes him feel desperately sorry for his younger self. And these are not the best of times. But he and his ex-wife agreed she would stay in their old house for now. It's in a good location for Chrissie going to sixth form, and Allie needs the studio for her art. He spends half his life on the road investigating cold cases for the podcast, anyway.

Cal's mind is whirring. Besides Foulds, he hasn't told a soul about the Jason Barr theory. The possibility is a cork wedged tight. So he has no one he can talk to now. No one who understands. Desperate to be alone, he tells his mother he will bring her cup of tea through when he is done, then concentrates on finishing every insipid bite of his dinner.

While he waits for the kettle to boil, he sends Chrissie a quick message; he's missing his daughter's lightness. Then he lingers over a message that Shona, so far away in Aberdeen, sent earlier. Their fledgling relationship is one of the only good things in his life, but it's been over a month since he saw her. Will she recognise this even more fucked-up version of him? Time will tell, and soon. They're going away together in a few days – a week-long break on the west coast of Scotland.

He types a message then deletes it, unsure of what tone to take, what he's feeling and if it's a good idea to reveal it anyway. The end of his marriage happened so gradually, and his wife's disappointment was so persistent, that he has lost confidence in himself.

The switch on the kettle flips and he slides the phone back into his pocket. He'll message Shona tomorrow.

By the time he takes the tea through, his mother has nodded off in front of the television, one hand on the remote. Not for the first time, Cal wonders if finding Margot would be too much for her. He draws the curtains against the dark and tucks a blanket over her knees. Then he moves down the hallway to the door and unlatches it quietly, leaving the snib on and stepping outside. He stands at the front of the house and watches the silent street.

There is no glow from the direction of the scrapyard, no noise, no light.

He thinks of his old home – Chrissie, Allie and the dog – and wishes he could turn the clock back, find a time when life was better, and cling to it. But if he could shift time, how far would he go? How far is far enough?

–

Foulds has been ignoring Cal's calls. When he tries the station again in the morning, he is told she is unavailable but will call him back as soon as possible. It's all he can do to stop himself going down to the scrapyard to see what's happening. Every time he tries to settle to work, he finds himself on his feet again, pacing the small room, the boards creaking at his movement. He trusted the detective. She's letting him down.

He walks his mother to her friend's house and then stops by a small supermarket to pick up some supplies so he can cook for her tonight. He wants to feed her up.

She doesn't seem to eat properly anymore, just picks at food like a bird. As he gets back to the house, he pays little attention to the unfamiliar car parked outside. Lost in thought, he only half-hears its door open.

'Cal.'

He almost drops the shopping when he sees it is Foulds and a male officer in uniform. She looks dishevelled, pale – haunted, even – but he barely registers that. His heart rate accelerates.

'Finally. I must have called you seven times yesterday.' Foulds opens her mouth to reply, but Cal barrels on, letting her have the full force of the nightmare that's his life. 'You're digging. In the scrapyard. And you didn't have the courtesy to let me know it was happening. I have to find out because Jason sodding Barr walks past there...'

'Barr?'

Shit.

Foulds' voice is whip-sharp, her face turning from tiredness to thunder. 'What the hell? Cal. You promised.'

Now he's the one on the back foot. 'You weren't doing anything about it! I mean, I thought you weren't...'

The shopping bags are cutting into Cal's hands. His fingers throb with the weight.

Foulds' body has tightened like she wants to take a swing at him. She half-turns away as if she can't bear to look at his face. 'Never should have breathed a word,' she mutters, glancing to check where the uniform is standing.

When she turns back, her tone is urgent. 'So he knows that we're digging there?'

Cal nods. 'I followed him. I didn't mean to, I just...' It seems a wholly inadequate explanation. 'He walked down to the river and he saw.'

Foulds walks over to the other officer and Cal sees him pulling a radio from his pocket. Her voice is low, the words lost.

When she comes back, he feels shamed but petulant still, hears his own voice from a distance. 'Why are you here?'

'Can we talk inside?'

He shrugs and unlocks the front door, leading the way to the kitchen and dumping the shopping bags on the floor. The other officer has stayed with the car.

'Tea?'

'Thanks.'

He fishes the kettle from the back of the worktop and sets out cups while it boils. Foulds waits, standing, silent.

When he sits down at the table, he can see the tiredness jostling with sympathy on her face. She's trying to hold it together for him. He takes a breath.

'Tell me.'

'I'm sorry you've been kept in the dark. We *are* looking at the scrapyard, using dogs and scanners to detect areas of disturbed ground, but it's not going to be a quick operation, Cal. The place is a total mess, been abandoned for a decade now. It's like looking for a needle in a haystack. We have to go slow or we'll miss things.'

He nods. 'And if you do find something?'

'We have to cross that bridge when we come to it.'

Cal stares into his cup of tea, as if answers can be found in the steam rising from the murky liquid.

'How are you?' Foulds gestures around them. He knows she's asking about the end of his marriage, his dire personal circumstances, but he chooses to misunderstand her because work is easier to talk about.

16

'Ever since Layla Mackie,' he says, thinking back to the last case he worked, 'I can't find the next podcast. The story I want to tell. There are so many of them out there, but I just can't do it. It's because of this. *This* is the story I want to tell. Margot's.'

It's not for lack of opportunity. Since Layla, he has been inundated with desperate pleas from families who want answers to lifelong questions about missing and murdered loved ones. Going through their emails, knowing he cannot help most of them, is heart-rending.

'You can't tell it. Not yet.'

'I know.' Cal drops his head into his hands and lets out a groan of frustration. 'But what if we don't find her? Then what?'

Foulds doesn't answer. They sit in silence, drinking their tea. Cal studies the table and wonders for the millionth time what Jason Barr is doing right now.

'I'm supposed to go to Scotland at the weekend,' he says. 'For a week's holiday. Maybe I should cancel. Just in case.'

She shakes her head. 'I think you should go. I'll call you the second we find anything. I promise.' She drains the last mouthful of her tea and pushes back her chair, fixing Cal with a look. 'Besides, that might keep you out of the way of temptation when it comes to this amateur surveillance hobby of yours.'

'I'm not going to follow him again. I know that was stupid.'

She raises an eyebrow at him. 'Jason Barr is careful and cunning, and we cannot fuck this up. Understood?'

'Understood.'

'I mean it, Cal. No more following Barr.' The message is clear. He cannot jeopardise this. Everything has to be by the book.

'I hear you.'

Foulds lowers her voice. 'I'm looking for witnesses from when he was a bouncer, as I suspect he worked off the books at a club Margot used to go to. We aren't sitting on our arses; we're putting this together piece by piece. You need to be patient.'

'I'm trying.'

'I get it,' she says. 'I really do.' Her usually calm expression creases into something even harder than her stern warning to Cal. 'And if it's him, I will take great satisfaction in making him pay for it.'

Cal sees her to the door. He watches as she strides down the path and gets into the waiting car. It moves away as soon as she shuts the door and he is alone, shivering in the empty street.

CHAPTER THREE

WESTER ROSS, SCOTTISH HIGHLANDS

BRYONY, 2007

Bryony wipes scattered cornflakes from the table and rescues a plastic toy drowning in a puddle of milk, discarded by the boys who fought so hard over it only moments ago. Exhaustion drags like heavy weights in her limbs and her eyelids droop. Sean has been waking at five, refusing to settle properly after that, so she is constantly battling fatigue and a sense of despair.

She presses the heels of her hands into her eyes and takes deep breaths, trying to ignore the dark feeling, reminding herself that today is different. For the first time, both boys will be at school. She will be free; she can breathe.

How did she end up here, in this farmhouse perched on the edge of nowhere? It doesn't seem long since she was dressing in her smart business suits, puffing her hair and tottering down Glasgow's Buchanan Street, feeling like the world was hers for the taking. Being an up-and-coming lawyer in a firm of solicitors made her chest swell with importance; she met girlfriends for drinks, fended off the unwanted attention of the senior partners, fell for the rising star.

All that changed when she married that star. Not immediately. But as soon as she held Robbie, it was over. Her place in the world no different than her mother's. When it came to it, someone had to look after the boys, and that wasn't going to be her husband.

From the sink, she watches Angus drinking his coffee in the garden, his concession to domesticity before he gets into his car and drives back to the life she used to have. In his shirt and tie, he looks like a stranger, kicking a ball to Sean, who pelts across the grass, their long lawn startlingly green and her youngest son burbling like the water that rushes from the hills when it rains.

From the end of the garden, Robbie calls to his father for attention, swinging so high that she sees the soles of his trainers flashing to the sky. She looks past the three of them to the wilderness beyond the fields: purple hills in the distance and the dripping darkness of the pine forests before them. It looks idyllic. It is idyllic. So why, two years after moving, does she feel this darkness spreading over her? Why does she feel so trapped that she would do almost anything to get away? Why does she long to feel pavement under heels instead of mud under wellies?

The gulf between her and Angus is growing wider. She feels powerless to stop it. His weeks are filled with meetings, brain work, lunches from the sandwich shop she used to love. She feels so dreary in comparison, her anecdotes domestic, revolving around her sons and their discovery of the world – the impossibility of having anything impressive to recount. Maybe it would be different if she'd forged new relationships in the village, as Angus is always urging her to do. That was the plan. But somehow it hasn't happened yet. Folk are pleasant enough, but she hasn't got to know anyone, doesn't feel comfortable, accepted. Angus says this is all in her head.

She's counting the years until she can start work again. When they decided to have children, they said she could if she wanted to. *You can go back any time.* Angus said that, she's sure he did. But that was before they moved here, and now it's dawning on her how difficult that would be. Who would pick the boys up from school? It's not like there's childcare in the village. Angus spends three nights in Glasgow most weeks.

They were always equals before, she thinks as she loads the dishwasher, and he appears at the door, a harassed look on his face as if he's already late. He hands her his coffee mug and she pours the dregs down the sink.

'I'll have to leave them to it. I've got to be getting on.'

She nods, accepting the kiss on her cheek that has become perfunctory.

'Bye, boys!' He barely looks back at them. 'I might be a bit late Thursday. Don't wait for me to eat.'

Bryony wants to wail. There are so few things to anchor her week and his return after those long nights away, the ten minutes while he does bedtime stories, is a respite in her otherwise excruciating routine.

He doesn't know what a privilege it is to be the one who gets to walk out the door. What Bryony wouldn't give to have those days to herself, or even just the car journey.

The door slams and there is a moment of quiet, a vacuum of thought, time and responsibility.

It's punctured by a sharp cry from the garden.

'Muuuum! Sean's hurt himself.'

She puts her hands on the counter, sucks air in, holds her breath a moment. She just can't. Can't, can't, can't.

'Mum! Sean's crying. Mum!'

Bryony pushes away from the counter, surfacing back into her life. She takes three quick strides to the doorstep, then runs down the garden to where Robbie is crouched over his little brother. The dew soaks through her slippers; the ground squelches beneath her feet. Sean stretches little chubby arms to her, his face tear-stained, Robbie's an anxious mirror.

She scoops her younger son into her arms, hefting his solid body until she can press her nose into the soft bit on the side of his neck, smother it with kisses. Make it all better. Feeling dead inside.

—

Three hours. That's how long she has to herself. Sean is starting mornings at school, building up to doing a full week. If it wasn't for that she'd be going mad. She wanted Angus to stay a little bit longer today, to be there for a photo when Sean goes in through the door. But he said she was being sentimental. *I've got a meeting; I can't be late just for this.*

It's funny, she thinks as she searches for Robbie's school shoes in the mess by the back door, how she keeps being told how important her role is, that what she's doing is crucial. Only, it's never crucial enough to be the actual priority, is it? It's only important for her to do. For anyone else it's a waste of time.

'Robbie, where did you take them off?'

'I don't know.' He dithers on the mat, hopping from one foot to the other, tears building.

Bryony can feel a hot pressure inside her head, the utter lack of control over her life. Robbie wet the bed again last night. There's always the feeling that she's doing all this utterly wrong. It's her fault. She glances at her watch: they're going to be late and the sense of her precious moments of isolation slipping away makes her frantic.

They eventually locate the shoes under the sofa. Robbie is velcroed in, Sean waiting in his anorak by the door. It's raining, it's always raining. Late August downpours.

'Bloody hell,' she mutters under her breath, taking their hands and towing them through the rain and down the drive. Why do things never go to plan? 'Come *on*.' She yanks at their hands to make them go faster, half-dragging them to match her pace.

They screech into the playground and she squeezes Robbie, kisses him on his rain-soaked head while the teacher hovers impatiently under a large umbrella.

'Have a good day,' she says, belatedly. Trying to impart some love, to make up for her sharpness and impatience, her constant failings.

She's shit at this. And that makes it all the worse. She's letting everyone down, and for what?

She turns back to Sean, who is standing in a puddle up to his ankles. Thank God for the frog wellies. He looks up at her and beams. She feels a rush of regret. Wishes she could go back and start this morning all over again.

She reaches out a hand. 'Come on, Seanie. Time for school.'

–

After a squeeze and a kiss, Sean trots into the classroom with barely a backwards glance. Too late, she remembers she didn't take a photo. As she smiles sympathetically at another mother trying to prise a screaming girl from her neck, Bryony finds herself grateful for her robust son – his desire to play with the toys has eclipsed any reluctance to leave her side. Or, the unwanted thought creeps in, maybe it's because she's terrible at this and he's glad to get away from her. Maybe that other mother is harder to leave.

She mentally shakes herself, says goodbye to the teacher and retreats into the playground, where the rain is slowing somewhat and the clouds have parted slightly to suggest that there might be sky beyond.

And it strikes her now that she has no idea what she is going to do. A sort of panic fills her mind. How is she going to make it all worthwhile? How is she going to use this time to become a better person for them all? A calmer, nicer person. One who bakes cakes and smiles indulgently when her sons traipse mud across the kitchen floor and her husband rolls in late after stopping at a pub on the way out of the city after days away from them. Actually, strike that. She'll be so calm and wonderful, he'll be racing home to her.

She can see how ridiculous this is and lets out a snort of bitter laughter, tilting her head to the sky to allow a few drops of cleansing rain to spatter on her face. It is cold and sobering. At that moment, the other mother stumbles out of the building next to her, the dampness on her face tears rather than rain.

The woman wipes her cheeks with the back of her hand and looks curiously at Bryony, who has the sudden and unusual inclination to build a bridge. Maybe this woman could be a friend, a way into the community Angus keeps banging on about.

'Second child,' she says, nodding her head towards the school. 'Yours will be fine.'

'Oh, Emma's my third,' the woman says. 'My middle one is in a class with your other son – Robbie, is it?'

The woman looks at her kindly, but Bryony thinks she sees a flicker of calculation in her blue eyes, judgement masked with a hasty smile. Just because she has failed to engage with this community, to find a place in it, it doesn't mean that they don't know all about her, who she is.

'Oh, yes,' she says, like she just remembered and is laughing at her own forgetfulness. All the while the walls are closing in around her.

'It's just so hard, isn't it? You have them with you for such a short time. She's been my wee trooper, my baby, I guess. Not sure what I'm going to do without her. Before we know it, they'll be in school full-time, won't they?'

Bryony can feel that this woman's hand has reached out for some kind of connection; it's what she wanted a moment ago but it's all so slippery and she can't really feel how to grasp it. Floundering, she turns to what she knows.

'So, will you go back to work?'

The woman's lips widen in surprise. 'Oh, no. By the time they need picking up it's just not worth it. I do the coffee morning at the church on a Friday for the pensioners. They'll miss Emma being there too, mind.' The woman's eyes mist over and Bryony thinks with horror that she's going to start bawling like the child did a moment ago. 'By the time I sort everyone out, there just isn't time.'

There's an awkward silence, while Bryony tries to think how to reach back, how to formulate all the questions she has racing around in her head, the desperate need to feel unburdened and understood. *Don't you want something for yourself?* she wants to scream. *Don't you want to be someone, too?*

The woman looks at her watch. 'Right, well, better get on. See you later.'

'See you,' Bryony says. Her words drift through the air as she watches the woman stride away. Hope for the future withers a little, panic growing in its place.

Bryony takes a deep breath. It's just one woman, one opinion. She's being silly.

The cafe, she thinks suddenly. She can go and get a coffee, maybe even buy a newspaper to read to feel like she's using her brain. The idea is warm and real in front of her: the fuggy calm of the old smithy with its steamed-up windows, the comfort of a hot cup of coffee, maybe even a piece of cake. She hasn't had time for breakfast and her stomach rumbles at the thought. As if to nudge her, the rain increases again, blowing into her face as the wind whips off the field next to the school. What is with this weather?

As she turns the corner, she realises she has been unintentionally following the other mother from school, sees her press her hand to the door of the cafe and step through. It doesn't matter, she reasons. The old smithy is large – she can just sit at the other side of the room, smile and wave.

But when she reaches the door, Bryony sees that the woman is not alone – she's joining at least ten others at the large communal table in the centre: some have toddlers in pushchairs, one a newborn baby in her arms. Faces turn to the woman who is everything Bryony isn't, smiles greet her, someone gestures to a waiting coffee.

Somehow, the sight of this woman's apparently fulfilling and accepted life makes everything so much worse, breaking something inside her into little pieces.

She hovers, one foot into the porch that's crammed with umbrellas and children's scooters.

'Are you coming or going, lass?' Bryony jumps as a man nudges her from behind.

She steps back, her face contorting. 'I'm on my way out,' she says.

He opens the inner door, and a waft of warmth and the smell of baking and fresh coffee drift out to her, filling her with longing. But the spell is broken, her confidence punctured, and she just can't.

She retreats, feeling foolish and lost, the spectre of the empty farmhouse in her mind. She can't go back there.

Above the village, the hill is obscured by mist, and she feels an unexpected kinship with it, drawn to the empty space and the desire to be free. Decided, she ducks into the newsagent on the corner and buys a pastry in a bag and a bottle of water. She zips her anorak up tight and strides to the end of the street, to the forest path and the only escape she can think of.

CHAPTER FOUR

CAL

He doesn't know whether to tell his mother about the police search or not. When she comes back from her friend's house, he can feel irritation pouring off her as he tries to take her coat, and she bats him away like an insect when he offers a cup of tea. At times like this, the small terrace feels like it's closing in on him. He can't face the conversation, so he delays, telling himself that the search may come to nothing. It does little to stifle the feeling of being on edge.

Only when she is in bed does he allow himself to call Shona. His hands are sweaty, his nerves teenage in their insistence. But when she picks up, he relaxes a little. Her voice is a comfort. He presses the phone to his ear, wishing he were sitting beside her, not hundreds of miles away in a house that feels like a mausoleum. His shoulders unclench as he listens to the story of a lost beaker in a lab.

'He wasn't wearing his glasses,' she finishes. 'Almost drank the solution instead of his Irn-Bru!'

Cal chuckles, so revived by the conversation that he almost forgets where he is.

'Anyway,' she says when he doesn't fill the pause. 'What's new with you, stranger?'

He hasn't called for days, knows she is testing the waters.

'I'm sorry I haven't been in touch.' He rushes on before she can say it's okay, when it isn't. 'But they're digging in the scrapyard,' he tells her. 'For Margot.'

A sharp intake of breath. 'Oh, Cal.'

'I know.' His voice is shaky now. 'I should have called sooner, I just…'

'And you let me blether on? God, I'm sorry.'

'No,' he says. 'I needed to hear about something else. Just for a minute. Cliff's biohazard near-miss has cheered me right up.'

'I'll tell him he's useful for something.' But the lightness has left her tone. 'How long will it take?' As a forensic anthropologist, Shona doesn't need to be told how difficult a search of this nature is and what state any remains would be in.

'They said a couple of weeks.'

'I hope they find something.'

'Me too.'

They are both quiet for a moment. Cal pictures the rusting hulks of scrapyard metal tangled in thorns, roped by grasses to the ground.

Her voice hauls him back to the present. 'Do you still want to come up this weekend? I'd totally understand if it's not good timing.'

'DI Foulds told me I should. I think she wants me away from it all.'

'How come?'

Cal takes a breath and tells Shona everything – his compulsion to follow Jason Barr, the fact that the suspect knows about the search, the detective's instruction not to interfere.

'On top of it all, my mum and I aren't getting on. Everything I do annoys her; it's like walking on eggshells. I'm not sure why I thought moving in here would work. It's just that after the fall last year she seemed so weak...'

'Maybe you just need some time away from each other.' Shona's voice is strong and soothing. Cal closes his eyes and leans into her words. 'Look, if you do want to come, you can always rush back if anything happens. I'll drive you straight to the airport. You can be home in a few hours if you really need to be.'

'Thanks, Shona. I really want to see you.' He should have known she would understand. It's just that he wishes she didn't have to – that he was more pulled together and impressive. It's hard to believe anyone would want him like this.

–

Shona meets him at arrivals in Aberdeen. Her short blonde hair is tucked behind her ears, and she's wearing her trademark DM boots and holding two takeaway coffees – props that make it easier for them to hug quickly and then busy themselves with bags and drinks. The dance of desire and anxiety spins through Cal as he kisses her. Her perfume is intoxicating.

As they walk, Shona chats about where she's parked and how many hours it will take them to drive to the west coast. Her chatter makes him think that maybe she's nervous too so when they've lifted his bags into the boot of the car, he takes a chance and pulls her towards him, studies her face, ignoring the bite of the wind against his skin.

'Good to be here,' he says.

Shona meets his gaze, deadpan. 'It's the weather, isn't it? You missed the weather.'

'Oh my God.' He rolls his eyes and hugs her tight to him, feeling their laughter mingling. 'I missed you.'

When he pulls back, Shona kisses him and he relaxes into her embrace. At least one thing in his life isn't a disaster.

CHAPTER FIVE

On the west coast, Shona has booked a cottage in a line of identical terraced properties facing the sea; theirs is a fetching shade of mint green. When they get out of the car, Cal stands and faces the foaming waves, raindrops hitting his face, already the most relaxed he has been for ages. DI Foulds, his mother's anger and his failed marriage all feel a million miles away.

They spend their days taking long walks in the hills, dodging harsh April showers that segue into bright flashes of warmth. They eat fat wedges of cake and drink pots of tea in coffee shops that pepper the wilderness and are often attached to little art galleries, then at the end of the day fall into cosy pubs, with roaring fires and wet dogs. Wandering through one of the coffee-shop galleries, legs aching from the hills, he pushes down thoughts of Allie and how she would love this. It's such a hard habit to break after being together so long. Her affair was just a symptom of them growing apart, he sees that, though being without her is like missing an arm sometimes. Now, their calls are limited to practicalities and chats about their daughter. He misses her friendship.

But then he looks over at Shona, poring over a map to work out where they went wrong on the path, and he feels the warm glow of desire inside him, hope sparking through his veins.

The week flashes by – much-needed relaxation that is like a long exhale. They plan to spend their penultimate evening in the Tide Inn, the pub along the shore from their cottage, which has become their local. Before they leave, he calls his mother to check in on her. He's been planning to tell her about the dig but every time he calls, her terse one-word replies put up a barrier he cannot cross. Tonight is no different. When he hangs up, Shona takes one look at his face and slips her hand through his arm.

'What happened?'

He sighs. 'The usual. Everything I say is wrong. I spend all my time trying to work out the right words, but I just couldn't tell her.'

'Maybe there aren't any,' she says, reaching up to cup the side of his face. 'You're pretty good with words, you know. If they were there, you'd find them. It's really more about her, isn't it? You can't control how she reacts. None of this is your fault, Cal.'

He turns his head and kisses her hand. 'How come you're so wise?'

'I'm actually a witch.' Shona's eyes glitter with laughter and he feels the tight elastic band inside him loosen, his shoulders drop.

'Well, I'm really glad that you're my witch.' He kisses her softly, afraid that she'll pull back at the words that just slipped so easily from him. Is she his? Is he hers? They haven't had that conversation. Yet. But Shona leans in and he feels his muscles relaxing further, sending a message to his brain to stop second-guessing everything.

'Come on,' she says, taking his hand and tugging him to the door. 'You need a drink.'

They scuttle through the start of a rainstorm to the warm entrance of the pub, hanging their dripping jackets on pegs by the door. The building is long and tables line the thick walls, so the patrons can watch the changing moods of the sea from the comfort of their seats. Books and trinkets line the windowsills and a fire burns in the hearth at one end of the room. Cal and Shona slide into a couple of high-backed armchairs at a table near the fire. Everything in here is mismatched, and yet it all goes together perfectly.

They've eaten here several times, but tonight there's an interest in the air, even a hostility, a lingering to the glances. Cal can't understand it.

'Do you feel like we're being watched?'

'You're being paranoid,' Shona says, but he's sure the man at the bar is staring at him.

'Just your witchcraft, then,' he jokes.

Cal busies himself studying the menu, which is filled with the kind of fare that can get you up and down the hills. As his hands tingle in the warmth, he peers at steaming bowls of soup that have been set down on the next table over.

Shona ruffles the front part of her hair, which is tousled where it's not been covered by her hood and has been whipped about by the wind. Her face is red and her eyes have the outdoor sparkle Cal can feel inside himself, or how he *had* felt until he sensed the watchful atmosphere.

He looks up now and finds that the staring man is talking to the barman. The two glance over but look away when they see Cal watching them. His skin starts to itch under the scrutiny, anxiety prickling along his arms.

'Stop,' Shona tells him, her eyes kind. 'It's just small-place curiosity.'

'Sorry.' He fixes his gaze back on her. 'It's silly. I know. I'm being silly.'

But all the same, he wishes they were up on the hills with nothing but the sky and the occasional sheep to notice them. He's unwound and been himself this week, and he thinks it's the same for Shona. A spark flares when she touches him, like his skin coming back to life.

Outside, he can see that a storm has blown in from the sea, initial drops turning heavier, making it even cosier inside. But even once they've ordered food and acclimatised to the warmth, the buzz of noise and the stamping of feet as people enter from the wet road, Cal still can't settle.

When Shona goes to the bar for more drinks, he buries himself in his phone and tries to shut out the world outside their table. He's texted Foulds twice this week and both times she's replied to say there is no news. It's hard to stop his mind straying to the thought of diggers and dogs, white-suited searchers by the riverbanks.

He smiles when Shona sets down two pints and licks foam from her fingers where beer has slopped over the side.

'My magic powers failed. You were right, I was wrong.'

'About what?'

'They do know who you are. Guy at the bar asked if you were *that podcaster* and what you were doing here. They're speculating that you might be doing a series on a crime that happened in the village. I've set their minds at ease. Told them you're on a thing called a holiday.'

She reaches for her pint and takes a long swig. Cal feels a pleasant twist inside that comes partly from Shona's rosy cheeks and partly from the confirmation that he isn't going crazy. There *was* an atmosphere. Cal sometimes forgets how much coverage the Layla Mackie case had in Scotland. It makes sense now. Already he feels the weight has been taken out of the air: things are moving more easily around them and he no longer feels the pariah.

'What crime was it they thought I was looking into?'

Shona shrugs. 'He said "that bloody shooting" – something about "those poor kids". Didn't seem keen to elaborate.'

'Well, they're safe from me. All I want is food and bed.' He raises his eyebrows and Shona grins.

They're tucking into heaving plates of pie and mash when the door flies open and a wild-eyed youth in skinny jeans and a checked shirt bursts into the bar. Everyone stills a moment as the wind and rain squall in after him. The youth turns on the spot, pushing back his wet shoulder-length hair so he can eyeball the patrons. His gaze doesn't land on anyone for long. Even from their corner, Cal can feel his distress and a nervous energy like electricity.

In seconds, the barman is by the boy's side, cajoling, placating, pulling him behind the bar and into the back of the pub. The older man returns and shoves a glass under the optics, waiting for a double measure of amber liquid to empty into it. The quiet that has fallen is broken by murmurs and laughter at the far end of the pub. The lights flicker a little and then everything returns to normal. Cal could almost believe they imagined the moment.

'What was all that about?' He watches but the young man doesn't reappear.

'Maybe there's a full moon.' Shona laughs.

'Did you see his eyes? Looked like he was on something. Not sure a whisky is the thing he needs.'

Cal mops the last bit of ketchup from the side of his plate. All of a sudden, he wants to be alone with Shona, away from this strange place that feels like a stage where everyone is playing a part and he doesn't know what his should be.

They zip up their coats, and he leans forward and kisses her in the tent their hoods make together. Their breath mingles and warms his face. Shona tucks her arm in his.

'Ready to make a dash for it?'

'Guess we'll have to.'

It's only a few hundred yards to the holiday cottage, but the wind is up, and the waves are crashing on the remaining sliver of beach and sending spray into the road. Clouds are moving fast but he can see a glimpse of moon before it vanishes behind them.

They follow the road along the shore, buffeted by the power of the ocean and the rain. It's exhilarating. Cal feels like there are strange voices carried on the breeze, like the dead fishermen of the depths calling them in. He's drunk way too much. But then the voice gets louder and Shona tugs on his arm, like she can hear it too. He spins and sees it's the wild-eyed young man from the bar following them and calling out, his words caught by the wind and whipped out to sea.

'Wait!'

Cal glances at the light in the window of the cottage, only a short distance away. He grabs Shona's hand and tugs, pulling her into a brisk walk, making it clear they aren't interested. His heart is pumping blood fast around his body. When he looks back, he sees that the man isn't giving up – he's still coming after them. It's late, and he was tired, but now his senses have been jerked to attention.

'You go ahead.' He has to raise his voice for Shona to hear him over the weather. She shakes her head, and he can see the alarm he feels echoed in her eyes.

'Cal, wait! Please, wait. Cal Lovett!'

The man knows his name. They're only a few doors away from the cottage now and Cal is fumbling in his pocket for the key, but something in the man's voice makes him stop and turn. He puts his body between Shona and the approaching youth.

'Cal, come on.'

Shona takes the keys from his hand, and he can hear the urgent scrape and jangle as she fits them to the lock.

But he halts. Now that he can see the man's – the boy's – face in the glow of the light, somewhat sheltered in the lee of the building, he can see there is no threat, only desperation. The rain has wet the youth's face and, in a flash of recognition, he finds grief in his features. *There you are, my friend.* It floors and disarms him, makes him want to reach out and take this stranger in his arms. *I know*, he wants to tell him, *I know.*

'I'm sorry.' The boy is a step away, panting. His hair keeps flying into his eyes so he uses a forearm to pin it to his head. 'But I need to talk to you. It's about my mother. I need your help. Please. I really need your help.'

And maybe it's the wind and the weather – the sheer impossibility of conducting a conversation in what is becoming a storm – but Cal is swept through with pity. Though Shona's face is guarded, uncertain whether this is wise, he bundles the boy off the road and into the building with them, closing the door against the storm.

'I'm sorry.' The youth says it over and over again, until even Shona's tense face relaxes. He is clearly no threat in this state.

'Aye, well. Come in,' she says. 'Take your shoes off.'

The boy follows Cal into the kitchen, sinking onto the chair pulled back for him. He's left the pub with no coat, and is wet and shivering, so Cal fetches him a towel. All the while she is making tea, Shona throws questioning glances his way. The boy has his head down now, and he is crying quietly. Cal pulls out the chair next to him, leans forward with his elbows on his knees, trying to get into his line of sight.

'What's your name, son?'

The boy looks up and Cal experiences a lurch of vertigo when he sees the haunted edge in his eyes.

'Robbie,' he says. 'My name's Robbie Campbell.'

CHAPTER SIX

WESTER ROSS, SCOTTISH HIGHLANDS

BRYONY, 2007

As she walks, Bryony feels something loosen inside her. The water is making runnels in the path, like a rushing stream. Her boots splash in the run-off and, to her left, she can hear the swollen burn flowing fast and furious towards town.

She hasn't been up into the hills in ages. When they moved, this was the kind of thing she and Angus thought they were going to spend their weekends doing – taking their children into the wilderness, walking, camping, biking.

Those dreams just haven't been realised. Instead, she's been harnessed to two small children, with no energy left at the weekends to devise plans and fun family outings. It's too much even to cope with the mounds of washing and the endless mess in the farmhouse.

They aren't a team anymore, she and Angus. The fun they envisaged has dissolved in the practical sniping of daily life.

Angus comes up here on his bike most weeks. Sometimes, she'll suggest he takes the boys with him, but he always finds a reason not to. She knows the reason – she lives with it every day. Two small children aren't compatible with the things he wants to do: they have intrusive needs, and it means going slow when his brain and soul are set to fast.

She powers upwards, relishing the pace. She's never able to move this fast, usually held down by a small hand and the accompanying whining. She's so light she could float off the hill.

The rain has stopped now, and she turns and admires the view. Below her, the village looks unthreatening. It's just a collection of houses, a church, a school, a handful of shops and farms scattered in its orbit. Nothing to be so scared of after all.

She glances at her watch, determined not to be late for pick-up on Sean's first day. She has time, she thinks, to eat her pastry, then she will have to turn back. Sitting on a felled log, she drinks in the view, stretching within herself and finding the corners to her personality again. It's exhilarating. When she's done, she licks the sugar from her lips and tilts her head back to chug from the bottle of water. This is better than a cup of coffee in a stuffy cafe.

'All right.'

Bryony sloshes the water down her front.

A man in a waxed jacket is standing over by the trees. He's holding a shotgun. Her reflex is to jump to her feet, adrenaline firing, heart thumping.

The man holds up a hand.

'Steady. Didn't mean to frighten you.'

He breaks the gun open and slides fat red cylinders from it, then sets it down against another log and puts the cartridges into his pocket. Bryony presses a hand to her chest and the man, who can't be more than ten years older than her, seems to grimace behind his close-cropped beard. It's only then that she notices the spaniel by his side. The man makes a noise in his throat and the dog moves towards her, wagging its tail. She ruffles its ears of black silk before it zooms away.

'Bonny day.' He takes a rolled cigarette from the massive pocket on his side while she ingests the sarcasm. When he lights up, the sweet smell of the smoke tickles the inside of her nostrils, strangely pleasant against the freshness of the rain-drenched hillside and the clean sap of the felled trees in the clearing.

Bryony adjusts her posture to face the view, realising she's been staring at him too long. He's broken her isolation and she wishes he would leave, but there's *something* about him. He's so different from her clean-cut, office-bound husband. There's something masculine and feral in the air. What would it be like to slide her hands beneath that waxed jacket?

She blushes, feeling her cheeks flaring. What is with her? Desperation, that must be it. And loneliness. She toes a torn piece of timber on the ground. Its pale flesh is ripped and raw, and she is shocked at the image that springs into her mind of fucking this stranger on the shredded wet ground.

'You on holiday?'

'No. I live down there. Just having a walk while my son is at his first morning of school.' There. She's mentioned her child. Has done something to throw her mind back onto the track of her life. Something like sadness flashes into his eyes.

He takes another drag of his cigarette. 'Not in the coffee shop with the other mums, then?'

The way he says it is dismissive. It's a bolt of relief to hear the accepted group derided a touch.

'No, not today.'

'You haven't seen a wounded pheasant on your travels, have you?'

'No. Is that what the gun's for?'

'Not squeamish, are you?'

Bryony thinks of her main client in Glasgow, the things he was rumoured to have done. The tiny, illicit thrill it gave her sometimes.

'No,' she says, suddenly bold, meeting his gaze. 'I'm not.'

Something passes between them, or his view of her alters a little, because she can feel him take notice of her properly for the first time.

'Guest on a shoot bungled his shot. The bird flew off but there was blood and feathers all over the shop. Can't have gone far.'

This man must be from the estate over the hill. It has lodges for shooting parties, a luxury spa.

'And you're looking for the bird?'

'Aye. We always track down the runners.'

He takes the cartridges from his pocket and slots them back into the gun, clunking the barrel into place. He's about to leave and Bryony wants to claw him back for a moment but she can't think of anything to say. It's ludicrous. A craving for attention that she hasn't felt since she was a teenager. He raises a hand in farewell and strides from the clearing, the dog at his heels.

Pigeon wings flap loud and violent in a tree above her, breaking her daze and forcing her back into herself. She could almost believe that she hallucinated the man. But the taste of smoke still floats in the air.

She glances at her watch almost absentmindedly, then swears into the empty space, despair rushing in. She's late.

Sean is the last of the wee ones left. The other mothers have cleared the playground by the time Bryony stumbles through the gate, sweat running down her face and pinning her T-shirt to her beneath the airless prison of her jacket. She has pelted down the hill and through the streets like a madwoman, her hair streaming behind her and her legs aching.

She curses herself as she sees his brave face, the tears that come to his eyes only now he can see she's coming. He's clutching a picture in one hand. The teacher stands beside him, her smile fixed and her jaw tight.

If only Bryony was a normal mother, one of those meeting in the cafe, waiting for their little darlings, actually focusing on her child instead of haring up the hill because she's too afraid to show her face. Sean deserves that. If she was that kind of mother, she'd have someone to call to collect him if she was running late, so he didn't have to be left behind, like an afterthought.

'Sorry,' she puffs. 'I'm so sorry.'

'Mrs Campbell. The children finish at twelve this week. You need to be here on time.'

Sean looks from the teacher to Bryony, small features pinched with worry. She hates this woman for making a scene in front of him. It was one fucking time. Big deal. She reaches for his hand and he presses against her, creasing his picture in the process. Realising what he has done, he leaps back to protect it and his face crumples. Panicked, she grabs it and smooths it out.

'Wow, Seanie. Great picture…' She stares at the blobs of purple and green. Maybe she has it the wrong way up. 'What is it?'

'It's my family. We drew our family.' His voice sounds injured, like it's obvious. She swears the blasted teacher rolls her eyes.

'Oh yes. So it is. Look at us.'

She waves apologetically as the teacher shuts and locks the door. Taking Sean's hand, she tows him towards the gate, realising that she'll be back here in a couple of hours to get Robbie. Stuck on a treadmill that never ends.

CHAPTER SEVEN

WESTER ROSS, SCOTTISH HIGHLANDS

BRYONY, 2007

She needs to talk to Angus about it. He's always late home and there's never a good time, but when he finally shows up on Thursday night, after the boys are in bed and they've eaten the remains of a shepherd's pie, she pours two generous glasses of red and builds up her courage.

Angus is stoking the fire, trying to get it to send some heat into the farmhouse. That's another thing she failed to see when they swapped city-living for the rural idyll. The people they bought from now have a new-build across the fields by a small loch – with walls of glass that bring in the view, insulation and modern heating.

She and Angus were swayed by the picturesque farm-house, with its thick walls and tiled floors, but God, it seems to absorb heat without giving anything back to them. She hands Angus his glass of wine and bundles herself into the blankets they keep on the sofa. When she's warm and snuggled, the room does look pretty. It's just hard work; she feels rigid with cold sometimes, hanging the boys' pyjamas on radiators to keep them warm, tucking hot-water bottles into their beds.

'Sean's almost done his first week at school,' she reminds Angus pointlessly, cross that he hasn't asked and that he didn't make it back in time to bathe the boys and play with them, but also trying to start a conversation, to help them find their way back to each other.

'How has it gone?'

'Good, I think. He seems happy. I was a minute late to pick him up on Monday, though, and the witch on the door was horrible to me.'

Angus barely seems to be listening, the glass of bloody liquid tilted between his fingers, his gaze distant and his mind clearly elsewhere. 'Oh, aye.'

Bryony shuffles round to face him, cupping her glass in her palms as if it can warm her. His gaze flicks up to her warily, as if he can sense an argument or a request he's going to want to turn down. When did he start looking at her like this?

'Now that they're both at school...'

'Well, Sean isn't really at school yet, is he?' Angus slugs at his wine as if realising that finishing it is what's trapping him here. 'Not full-time.'

'No, but almost. I was thinking...' Bryony peers at him. 'Maybe I could go back to work. Part-time, even. To start with.' She buries her nose in her glass and waits for a response.

Angus smiles indulgently, as if she is making a joke. 'We don't need you to do that.'

'But I *want* to go back to it, Angus. It doesn't suit me, being at home. I miss work.'

'You're serious.'

'Yes.' She waits, glad he has cottoned on. They're a team; they need to work together for everyone to be happy.

'But you must see that could never work. How would you pick up the boys?'

'Well, I was thinking we could share the pick-ups, maybe find a childminder,' she says patiently. 'It must be possible, other people must do it.' But even as she says the words, Bryony racks her brains to think of a local example and comes up short. Angus snorts.

'Bryony, there's no way I could do that. It's enough of a challenge working one day a week from here. What sort of message would that send? What sort of impact would it have on my career, my earning capacity?'

What about my career, my earning capacity? she wants to shout at him.

'But Angus, I'm not happy.'

'We can't all be happy all the time, Bry. That's chasing rainbows.' Oh Christ, she's going to get the hard-work lecture again. 'It's just hard while the boys are wee. Maybe in a few years, when they're both properly settled in school, you can find a job here. We've just got to get through it until then.'

He pats her knee and everything inside her recoils from his touch. She doesn't want the sort of job she could have here. She wants to be the solicitor she was. His life hasn't changed but hers has been torpedoed. And the worst thing is that she agreed to it, went along with it, and now she can't unravel it. She thinks of their old cramped flat, with the narrow stairs that you couldn't get a buggy up, and is astounded at how much she wants to go back there. It's not fair.

'Anyway,' Angus says. 'Can you imagine? Going back to that?' He shudders.

'What do you mean?'

'The kind of people you used to represent, Bryony.'

She rubs at the tears on her cheeks, all the while feeling like she's in a glass jar, banging on the sides to be heard.

'They were colourful, that's all.' She feels defensiveness sliding down over her like a cloak. Angus is right, some of her clients sailed a bit close to the edge and there were a couple of incidents, mainly around one man – Sal Ellis. A battle-scarred former con with a lot of cash and a desire to establish himself as a legitimate property mogul. Bryony got used to his rough-and-ready ways, the old and dingy pubs he liked to meet in. Yes, some of his associates were less than friendly, but she'd always felt he acted paternally towards her, that she had his protection.

He snorts at her. 'That's not all. We had to check under the car for bombs for three months, remember?'

'That was a misunderstanding. We were never really in danger.'

A memory of being six months pregnant and kneeling on all fours to look under the vehicle springs back into her mind. She's stunned to feel a sense of nostalgia for what was, on paper, a shit and scary time.

Angus always looked down on Bryony's work. She knows he saw his clean corporate clients as a cut above hers. It never bothered her before, but now she feels protective of her past. Did they ever have the conversation about her giving up work for good? Or did they both just make assumptions along the way?

She can't remember. When she looks back, everything after Robbie's birth is foggy and muted.

Angus tilts his glass and the last fat drops of wine slide into his mouth. He sets it down on the coffee table and yawns.

'I'm going up – you coming?'

Bryony stares into the dying embers of the fire. One log glows a luminous red but it's the last one, the others are charred black heaps.

'In a minute,' she says, unable to find the energy to get off the sofa.

'Lock the doors, will you,' he says. Before she can complain, he rushes up the stairs and she hears the ping of the bathroom light pull, the sound of the taps. Bryony stares around the dull and dusty room. The romance has left it now that the fire has died and their glasses are empty. She sighs and pulls back the blankets, slips her stockinged feet from front door to back, checking the locks. At the back door, she pauses, pulling it open on impulse.

Waves of green and purple are undulating in the sky, shimmering and pulsing. She steps onto the ice-cold slabs at the back door, not caring when the damp penetrates her thick socks. She wraps her arms around herself and turns her face up, transfixed by the unearthly beauty in the sky.

Once, she would have run through the house to get Angus to share the experience. But tonight she has no such desire. She pads forward onto the lawn; her feet are soaking now but she doesn't feel the cold, drawn hypnotically to the otherworldly lights, the beauty in the distance.

CHAPTER EIGHT

The air in the room is still; the absence of sound echoes in Cal's ears now they are out of the physical assault of the weather. Robbie opens and closes his mouth but the attempt at words is halting and his skinny frame wracked with shivers. Shona sets a cup of tea on the table next to the boy and then backs away, standing next to the door with her own cup. She leans against the wall, apparently relaxed, though Cal senses she is ready to go for help, if needed.

A whistle of wind threads into the chimney and the rain against the window sounds like gravel. There are houses either side but the walls are thick and he doesn't think anyone would hear them if they called out.

Robbie tips his head towards the tea to feel the steam on his face and wraps his hands around the cup for warmth.

'I'm sorry for chasing you,' he says again. 'I just need… Someone said you were in the pub. Is it you? Are you the man from the papers? The one with the podcast? I saw you on the telly once… but I'm not good with faces, so…' He squints at Cal.

Cal nods. 'Yes, that's me.'

He thinks of Chrissie, back home, most likely sketching. This boy, Robbie, can't be much older than she is. Now he can see him closely, it's obvious he is just a kid.

'I need help. My mother was shot. She died.'

Robbie's face is an odd blank as he says the words, like he can't let the pain through or everything will fall.

'I'm sorry,' Cal murmurs. 'That's terrible.'

The shooting the barman referred to.

'I just can't rest, with whoever did it still being out there. Living their life.' Robbie's eyes are pleading now.

Cal makes his words as gentle as possible. 'I'm sure the police are doing everything they can. Sometimes these things take so long, but it doesn't mean…'

The boy shakes his head from side to side repeatedly, agitated.

'They didn't. They've given up. It happened fourteen years ago. I was five. She was on the doorstep.' He swallows, his face a mask, memory behind pale, spotty skin. His words break on entry to the world. 'She died on the doorstep. The ambulance came but it was too late. Me and my wee brother… we were in the garden when it happened.'

Robbie rubs at his eyes like the child he was then.

Unable to stop himself, Cal reaches out and touches his hand, but Robbie leaps as if scalded. 'Sorry.' Cal pulls back. It's like handling a wild animal: nothing is rational; all he can see is fear.

The touch dissolves whatever composure Robbie was hanging on to. Tears drip down his face and the look of desolation overwhelms Cal, making his own eyes smart.

'Can you…' Robbie's body heaves with sobs. '…help find who… did it? Please.'

In-person pleas are even harder to hear than the steady stream of plaintive emails he receives.

'Robbie,' he says gently. 'I'm so sorry about your mum. Really, really sorry.' How do you put enough feeling into words when you're saying no? 'It must have been awful to lose her so young. But it's just not something I'll be able to help with. I'm not here for long, just a few days on holiday. I'm not the right person.'

'No, you have to,' he says. 'You have to. No one else will. They've all forgotten her, they've moved on, and I can't.'

Cal exchanges worried looks with Shona. Robbie's voice is rising, his face fevered. He keeps garbling at them, back to being the unhinged man in the bar.

Shona glances at the clock on the wall and he catches her meaning. It's late, too late to have a rational conversation about such an emotional issue. He never should have invited the boy in. How can they hurl him back out into the storm in this state?

'Robbie, what was your mum's name?'

The boy halts at Cal's words. 'Bryony. Bryony Campbell.'

He lets a moment's silence filter between them. Lets the name stand, the woman slip in.

'Look, Robbie, I can't investigate your mum's death. I'm so sorry. But, tomorrow, if you want to meet for a coffee and tell me about it, maybe I can suggest some ways you can look into it, if you want to try and get the case reopened?'

Robbie gapes at Cal, his eyes red-rimmed, but with the tiniest flicker of hope. 'Would you, really? I can tell you everything…'

'I know you can, Robbie, but it's late tonight and I'm not thinking clearly. I'm tired. This is important, isn't it?

It needs to be done properly. You'll need a pen and paper to write things down.'

Robbie nods at him.

'Right. So, for now we need to get you home, and then we can meet up tomorrow, yes?'

'Okay.'

'Where is home, Robbie? Where do you stay?' Shona has stepped closer to them now the bargain has been struck. He looks up at her as if he didn't know she was there until this moment. The only one he was looking at was Cal.

'It's a little way out of the village. But Tom lets me crash at the pub after a late shift. I can go back there.' He looks eager to please, waits for Cal's approval. Something in this kid unsettles him, stirs his heart.

'Would you like us to walk you?'

Robbie shakes his head. 'I'll be fine. What time will we meet tomorrow?'

'How about ten in that little coffee shop along the way?'

'Annie's?'

'That's the one.' Cal isn't sure if it is the one he had in mind but the place is small, they'll find it.

'You'll no forget?' Cal recognises the expectation that people will let you down, that hopes will come to nothing. He is trying to get the kid to leave, it's true. But he isn't going to ghost him.

'Promise. And you know where we're staying now, don't you? You could find me if you needed to.'

Robbie nods, seeming mollified by the suggestion. They guide him to the door and watch as he slips out into the night. The wind is calming now. It's still raining but the violence has gone; the waves seem less angry than

54

before and the spume that was frothing in the road is dissolving.

The boy looks back at him and Cal fancies there are fathoms of darkness in his eyes as he raises a hand, the fight gone out of him. It's like looking at a shell of a person. He knows all too well how that feels.

They watch for a moment until the silhouette melts into the darkness, then he closes the door and lets loose a long breath. A moment later, Shona's arms reach around him and he turns to meet her, presses her tight against him.

'I thought you promised me a peaceful holiday,' he says when she tilts her face up to his.

'This is all on you. I'm not the celebrity. It's like holidaying with the bloody queen,' she says.

Her lips are a relief after the drama and the weirdness that Robbie exuded. He was like a broken doll. Cal shuts his eyes and banishes the thought, feels himself falling into Shona, their hands snaking beneath each other's clothes, bodies pressed tight. The feel of her skin against his makes Cal realise he's cold, and Shona is shivering too.

'Come on.' The fire in the little sitting room is laid so he pulls the curtains shut, striking a match and coaxing flame onto the firelighters. Heat flares into the room and he kneels beside it with her.

They are in another world in this tiny room on the edge of the west coast, the wild sea at their backs and an orange protective glow around them, blocking out everything else in his life. Just for now, he surrenders all thought, lets himself get lost in kissing her, in the feel of her hands on him, the way the blazing heat seems to be melding them together, the magnetic join of their hips and the loss of control that he so desperately needs.

CHAPTER NINE

In the morning, the air is clear and sharp as a blade. The sea is glass, with all the hurt thrown out of it: pieces of driftwood and seaweed scattered high on the rocky beach. The events of the previous evening seem a distant dream. Cal has volunteered to go out for bacon rolls, leaving Shona in a tangle of sheets, warm and sleepy.

He texts DI Foulds, then scuffs along the shore, occasionally bending to pick up a shell. The water looks enticing, but when he dips a finger in the stillness it has an icy bite and he shivers at the deception in its beauty.

Armed with bacon rolls dripping in fat, and large cups of coffee, he takes the quicker pavement route back along to the cottage, the beach below him. A gull calls out greedily, seeming to know what he has in his parcel. They have a trip to a coral beach planned today but it will have to wait. Though their night-time confrontation with Robbie doesn't feel real, his meeting with the boy is in only an hour. It's possible Robbie won't show, but he isn't going to be the one to let him down.

Back in the cottage, all is still. He grabs a couple of plates and heads upstairs.

'Hey, sleepy.' He prods the lump in the bed. 'I'll eat your bacon roll.'

The edge of the cover flips up and he sees Shona struggling to open her eyes, yawning so he glimpses the pink inside of her mouth.

'Don't you bloody dare.'

'I've got coffee, too.'

'Oh, it's love,' she says, and then falters. 'I mean…'

'It's okay.' He laughs. 'I know what you meant.'

He kisses her as she emerges, feeling a swell of wonder at how light and easy this seems, how normal. When is it going to go wrong?

Shona grins and takes the cup from him, lifting the lid and drawing a long gulp of coffee. He settles back beside her and they eat their bacon rolls quietly, leaning in against each other. Satisfied. Propped on pillows, from here they can watch the sea reflecting the sky, over the dark hulks of purple islands in the distance.

'Any message from Foulds?'

'Nothing.'

She puts her hand on his. 'Is it driving you mad?'

'Can you tell?'

'You're doing an okay job of hiding it, to be honest. If it were me, I'd be climbing the walls.'

'It's silly,' he says, shifting to face her. 'I've been waiting my entire life. What's a few more weeks?'

Shona leans forward and kisses him. 'Everything.'

'You're amazing, you know?' Cal whispers, and then turns to face the view again, the heat rising in his cheeks.

Two kayakers are cutting through the mirror surface of the water, leaving a line in their wake, making the rest of the sea seem even more still and strange. Once more he's struck by the constant awe-inducing beauty of the landscape. The colour and the light are different. And they change something in him too.

Or maybe that's Shona.

'I've got to have a shower,' he says reluctantly as her hands sneak beneath his T-shirt. Their lips meet again, still greasy from the breakfast roll, still hungry. Everything inside him is calling out to stay here and bury himself beneath the sheets. He pulls back for breath, in danger of getting carried away and forgetting his promise. 'I'm meeting Robbie, remember?'

She groans and presses her head against him. 'How could I forget our midnight visitor?'

'I'm sorry. It's part of my personality. I bring chaos wherever I roam.' He's only half-joking about that.

Shona laughs. 'It's fine. I like your chaos most of the time. I'll take my time getting up and then I need to call the lab anyway. Check Cliff hasn't burned it down or done anything else stupid.'

'Doesn't Cliff have, like, three PhDs?' Cal finds their relationship, which they play up like mother and teenage son, an endless source of amusement.

'Aye, he's got all the letters, but nay common sense,' she says, shaking her head. 'None whatsoever.'

'He's probably having a right party, with you out of his hair.'

'He wouldn't dare.'

'I'll bet.'

'Nah… he'll be pining for me. Just like you will be in a minute.' She sticks her tongue out at him.

'I won't be too long,' Cal tells her, extricating himself. 'So don't go back to sleep – I want to see that coral beach you promised me.'

'Well, I might have bent the truth about it being actual coral… it's actually maerl, which is what happens when seaweed calcifies and… You've glazed over, do you have somewhere else to be?'

He wishes he could dive right back into the bed with her mischievous grin. 'I do, actually. But can I have my science lesson later, please? You're very sexy when—'

A pillow hits him on the head.

Cal's still smiling when he's had a quick shower and is closing the cottage door behind him. A brace of cyclists with chunky panniers on their bikes wobble along past him and turn up the road into the hills. He carries on to the coffee shop where he and Robbie agreed to meet. The bright blue-painted frame is pristine around the polished window, where a display of mouth-watering and doorstop-sized cakes stands proud, with comfortable tables and sofas scattered beyond.

He pushes open the door on the dot of ten to find Robbie already there, lurking by the till. Cal sees he has a notebook and pen in his hands, the price sticker still on the front. Hurt twinges inside him. He struggles sometimes, with surviving family, not to plant himself too fully in their shoes. When you know, you can't undo that knowledge.

'I wasn't sure what you'd want.' Robbie gestures at the pastries and the coffee machine, his voice high, his face flushed.

'Ah, no worries. It's my treat, anyway,' Cal says, pulling his wallet from his jeans. Robbie looks relieved, though he keeps shifting from foot to foot. Cal wonders if he is always this jittery. But then he becomes aware that the two women behind the till are staring. When they see him notice, they come to and busy themselves. It's hardly subtle.

'What will I get you, then, Robbie?' The first woman is neat in a pressed apron with blue swirling letters across it: *Annie's*.

'I'll just have a tea, please, Annie.'

The woman tilts her head to Cal. 'Morning.'

It's not unfriendly, but he can feel the question in her greeting. As Cal absorbs the interest in them both and realises how uncomfortable Robbie is, he understands this was a mistake. He's put the boy under the spotlight by choosing this place. Everyone knows him; everyone knows what happened to his mum.

'Tea for me too,' he tells Annie. Then to Robbie: 'Would you mind if we had them on a bench outside? It's such a beautiful day...'

Some of the rigidity leaves the muscles in Robbie's face. 'No, that would be fine, there's a bench on the grass over there.'

Cal searches the direction he's pointing, finds the wooden bench overlooking the sea. No one will overhear their conversation. 'Why don't you go make sure no one else takes it,' he says. 'I'll get the teas, I'll just be a minute.'

Robbie bobs his head and darts out the door, leaving Cal and Annie face to face.

He waits for a question, but she just purses her lips and rings the teas through the till. Cal's stomach protests at the array of cakes in front of him. The smell is incredible and the bacon roll has barely touched the edges.

'Hang on, I'll take a couple of these as well...' He pauses, taking in the display, unable to choose from the selection.

'That's his favourite,' Annie says after a moment, pointing to an iced bun with swirls of raisins. 'He's liked

60

them since he was a wee boy.' She says the words carefully, looking at Cal, and he grasps the meaning behind them.

'I'll take two of those then, thanks,' he says.

It makes him feel slightly better, the fact that there is a layer of local protection over the lad fidgeting on the bench in the distance. Sometimes it's good that people are watching.

But then as Annie hands him the drinks, she fixes him with a look. 'It's not always a good idea to dig up the past. You're looking for a podcast, but we have to live here.'

Cal knows there's little point in trying to explain. He can feel a quiet from the couple of occupied tables in the cafe, a stillness in the patrons that tells him they're listening. He inclines his head. 'Thank you,' he says. He means for the drinks, but lets her think what she likes.

Crossing the road, he tries to push away the hostility, handing Robbie the tea and a paper bag with a bun in it. The youth peers in and looks at Cal, surprised.

'I don't get the credit, I'm afraid,' he says. 'Annie told me they are your favourite.'

Robbie smiles ever so slightly, just for a second. He fishes in the bag for the pastry, tearing off bites and devouring the bun. He seems ravenous. He's thin, too – bony wrists, dark hairs on scrawny arms and a nervous energy that doesn't dissipate. His hair is damp. Grazing his shoulders, it protects him from view as he fixes his gaze on the sea.

Cal waits for him to speak.

'I'm sorry about last night,' Robbie says, looking down into his cup after a slurp of tea. 'I'd had a drink and when I heard you were there… I wasn't thinking.'

'Tell me about your mum,' Cal says gently.

Robbie sighs. 'I don't remember that much about her. Not really. I think I remember her singing to me, once, but when I told my dad, he said she didn't sing.' He looks up at Cal. 'So maybe I imagined it.' His voice drops to a whisper. 'It just seems so wrong that no one has ever been put away for it. How can no one know what happened? It's not fair.'

'Have they ever arrested anyone? Declared any suspects?'

Robbie shakes his head. 'It's like I'm missing something and I don't know what. I feel it all the time. It's getting worse. I think I'm going mad. But people round here don't like to talk about it.'

Cal knows that the adage about time and healing is an oversimplification. Sometimes things rear their head and burst through the surface of your life.

'And what about your dad? Do you get on?'

The youth rubs his face with the back of his hand. 'Aye. I live with him and my brother and my stepmother. They're great, but they don't seem to feel like I do. Sean isn't like me. It's not that he's not bothered or anything – it's just like, it doesn't consume him. He disnae think about it all the time. He was only four when it happened.'

'Are you close to him?'

Robbie shrugs. 'Used to be. He's been really moody for a while now, though.'

'Typical teenager.'

'Aye.'

They sit for a while, Robbie talking and then lapsing into silence. The murmurs of comfort Cal can offer are nothing against the extent of Robbie's grief. Listening to him is agonising, and yet there's something in there that's activating Cal's inner journalist. That and the atmosphere

62

in the shop, the sense that there's something here. He shakes off the temptation. This is not his investigation. He'll make sure the boy has some avenues to follow and that's it.

All the same, the case plays on his mind as he waves Robbie off to his shift at the pub, with a promise that he'll think about the details, and makes the short walk back to the cottage. How can someone approach a house in broad daylight, shoot a mother in cold blood while her sons play nearby, then vanish without a trace? It's unfathomable.

Getting involved would be a terrible, terrible mistake, of course it would. But when he reaches the cottage, Cal realises he hasn't thought about the search for Margot for over an hour, or the way his mother shuts down when she answers the phone to him, or Barr's thick fingers and his cold eyes.

CHAPTER TEN

'Uh-oh.' Shona studies him as they drive over the headland in search of the coral beach. They have a rucksack filled with sandwiches, cake and midge spray. The sky remains clear and washed out from last night's rain.

'What do you mean?' Cal has to keep his eyes on the twisting road, with its terrifying corners and occasional surprise sheep, so he can't turn to look and see her facial expression, but he can picture it. 'I'm not getting involved, if that's what you're suggesting.'

'Sure you're not.' She chuckles.

'I'm not! I can't.' His hands grip the wheel, guiding the car around a hairpin bend. 'I feel bad for him, that's all. He's so lost.'

Shona slides a hand onto his knee and squeezes his leg. 'I can see it's bothering you.'

'I'm sorry, am I being awful?'

'That's not what I meant.' Her voice is light and he believes her. There's no hidden agenda. He breathes freely, trying to dispel the sense of connection he feels with Robbie. One lost boy to another.

'I'm not the right person for this. It's a close community. I get the feeling they aren't going to accept outsiders.'

'Maybe you're exactly the right person.'

'You remember the hostility in the bar the other night? Well, it was just like that in the cafe today. I don't know. All the Margot stuff as well… it's making it feel too close, too hard.'

'I understand, I do.' The warmth of her hand on his knee makes him breathe more easily.

'I'm going home tomorrow, anyway. There isn't time.'

'True. You could be here for longer, though. What is it you're going back for? More stalking?' She's joking, but he feels the serious point beneath it all.

He has confessed to Shona that he was following Jason Barr, has ranted to her about the glacial pace of the police investigation and the disintegration of the already-fragile relationship with his mother. What is there at home?

Chrissie.

Shona directs him to the parking spot when they round the next bend. The coast is out of sight, over a rise of heather and rocks. They lock the vehicle and he hugs her tight before they set off in silence, each one lost in their own thoughts.

'Down there.'

She points to a path that feeds its way around the headland, flanked by a drystone wall on one side and rocks slippery with orange seaweed on the other. The tide is out, exposing a small island close to shore, a gnarled tree clinging to the rocky outcrop. Then they round the corner and emerge on a lush green plateau leading to a pure white beach, where the ruins of a croft overlook crystal waters. He pauses.

'I wish I *could* stay.'

Shona leans against him, pulling his arm around her. 'I'm sorry. I shouldn't have pushed you. It isn't fair. It will all still be here if you want to come back. Foulds is going to have answers for you soon. One way or another.'

Cal sighs. 'If finding nothing is an answer.'

'It may not come to that.'

He looks down at her. So strange and different. At once his equal and yet vastly superior. With Allie, this kind of conversation would have ended in arguments and tears. Shona is the definition of being on an even keel.

'I need a podcast if I'm going to get Sarah off my back. She's pushing me to pick something but I just can't. All I've been able to think about for months is Margot. And him.'

His producer is nothing if not persistent. Since their last case in Aberdeen, investigating Layla, they've formed an understanding, but they still work in entirely different ways.

'You just need to get through these next few weeks. This isn't normality. It will get easier.'

He nudges her, desperate to hold on to the sense of peace he experiences by her side. 'This week has been wonderful.'

She smiles, and the rays of it catch his breath. 'Maybe you could come back here sometime and investigate. I could drive over and see you at weekends.'

He pictures it. Being alone here in this isolated place, so far from home and the raging tempest of his life. Could he do it? It's been a while since Layla's case and yet it still tugs at him. He's coming to realise that each investigation he plunges into takes a little of himself that he can never get back. And there is Chrissie to think of – though her May half-term holiday and reading week is coming up. He allows himself to envisage her here, the wind ruffling her hair and the coral crunching beneath her toes.

He shakes his head. 'I can't make Robbie any promises. He's too fragile.'

Shona throws down a picnic blanket and reaches a hand to pull him down beside her. As Cal folds his arms around her and they watch the tossing waves, he tries not to think about the woman bleeding to death on her doorstep, while her children played close by.

–

They stay on the beach until they are chased off by the rain. Cal rolls up his trousers and wades into the waves, gasping at the cold, which is so intense it bites his legs, and he has to retreat and advance several times, until he loses all feeling entirely. Shona hovers patiently over apparently empty rock pools, pouncing triumphantly on unsuspecting molluscs and casting them back when she's peered at them.

'None of these things have bones,' he jokes, taken with her delight. 'Is that the attraction?'

'I never thought of that.' She laughs. 'Nothing like the day job. Thank God.'

Her face clouds at the thought of her forensic anthropology work – a cluster of bones have been found buried in the grounds of an old children's home. She and Cliff are among the team excavating them. The suspicion is that more will be found. Lots more. Cal's not the only one running from reality.

They walk back to the car, physically tired but mentally lighter, salt-swept and planning to pick up fish and chips and eat them in bed. Cal feels released from responsibility, giddy with tired happiness.

Until he sees the car.

A line gouged into the side, along every panel. Shock brings him up short.

Shona, humming to herself and swinging her coat, looks to see what's stopped him.

'What? Oh, you're kidding.'

Cal spins on the spot, but the surrounding hills are empty. The road is wide at this point; there's no chance a passing vehicle grazed their car accidentally. Shona trails a finger along one of the ridges, which are deep and filled with anger.

'It looks deliberate, like it's been keyed.'

'Kids?' But that seems unlikely out here in the middle of nowhere − the nearest house isn't even visible. The thought rises inside him that this could be related to his discussions with Robbie and the hostile eyes on them this morning, but he pushes down the paranoia.

Shona has drawn closer to his side, her face pale. He stretches out an arm, hugs her tight.

'I'm sorry, what a pain.'

She shudders. 'It's probably one of those random things.'

'I think so.'

'Because it's not like someone would go out of their way to give us a message.'

He imagines them being tracked, followed while they thought they were alone and free. Has someone been watching them as they walk, lie on the beach, kiss? Shona runs her hands through her hair and he can see she's rattled.

He takes the keys from her and unlocks the car. 'Come on, we've got fish and chips to get, remember? Then we'll go back and report it to the police and the insurers, and get it sorted.'

The journey back is filled with disquiet, despite his attempts to make light. When they park outside the cottage, he takes her hand.

'Are you okay?'

She nods. 'I'm being silly. I just…'

'What?'

'I had a horrible boyfriend in my twenties. He used to mess with my head and when we broke up, he did a load of twisted things. This is exactly the kind of stunt he would pull, and it's brought it all back.'

'I'm so sorry that happened to you.'

'It's fine, it was a long while ago. But I wasted too many years on him and it just takes me back to a place where I do not want to be.'

Cal leans across and kisses her softly. 'You are not there anymore. Promise.'

He feels her relax slightly. Outside, the sun has dipped below the horizon, adding an instant chill to the world.

'How about I get the food and you light the fire?'

She nods. 'Thanks, I might have a bath as well.'

He sees her into the cottage, turns on the lights and closes the curtains, even though it isn't dark yet. The room feels like a haven, away from the reality outside.

'I'll be back soon,' he tells her, locking the front door when he leaves.

He walks along the shore and stands in line at the fish and chip van, then settles onto the wall to gaze at the sea while he waits for their order – it comes quickly, a fat warm parcel that he clutches to his chest as he returns, a sense of calm descending as the afternoon's disruption fades in his mind.

But when he reaches the door, he startles at the unexpected surprise that lies on the step, almost dropping the parcel he is carrying. The smell reaches his nostrils a second later, thick and pungent, designed to repel. A large rotting fish carcass. He stares up and down the street, his heart beating a rapid pace.

There is no one – just a couple of people out walking their dog in the distance. Lights glow from the surrounding cottages. He doesn't want Shona to see the festering remains, so he sets their food parcel to the side and finds two sticks to lift the rotten fish up and across the road, crab-walking it down to the shore, where he casts it into the sea for the waves to claim.

He walks back to the cottage quickly, unwilling to linger in the gathering dark, unable to banish the prickling sensation of scrutiny. He thinks back to the conversations he has had with Robbie and the swirling chaos of his life outside. He is nervous about going back home, waiting for news on Margot and having to accept that it may never come, plus he has his mother to deal with and no Shona to make him smile. On the other hand, he misses Chrissie desperately, and she is coming to see him at the weekend.

He pauses at the front door, taking one last look around, saying goodbye to this place. The waves are playful, but this is the spot where they stood talking to Robbie and he can't stop the image of the damaged boy leaping to the front of his mind, his eyes filled with a pain that Cal understands all too well. Pushing away the guilt, he shivers and turns back into the cottage.

CHAPTER ELEVEN

WESTER ROSS, SCOTTISH HIGHLANDS

BRYONY, 2007

Bryony goes back again and again to the hillside. Compulsively. Unwilling to try the coffee shop and the other mothers again, she allows herself to grow more and more isolated. Shame swims inside her at her failure to make connections with other people. It's like being coated in an ever-present darkness, a sort of desperation that acts like a siren, warding others away.

No matter how she looks at it, there isn't a way to get her old life back. The boys are becoming trickier by the day – Robbie spends most of his time clinging to her like a limpet and his constant need for reassurance makes her want to scream at him to leave her alone. He isn't making friends and is always the last to trail out of class at the end of the day. She knows the flash of despairing anger she feels at the sight of his dejection isn't rational. Why is she like this? What is wrong with her?

Even Sean, reliably bouncy, isn't his usual self – tired out by the classroom routine. He's grumpy and short-fused, provoking Robbie until his brother retaliates. Then everyone ends up in tears, even Bryony. Especially Bryony. Every time she thinks she's at the end of her tether, something else happens that pushes her further.

So she gets away in the only way she can – exploring the myriad paths that claw the hill, stumbling on peat-stained streams with startlingly clear waters, leaping from rock to rock, faster and faster, daring herself to fall. Fantasising about injury – going to hospital, being able to sleep in clean sheets with tight white corners tucked in around her. She roams the landscape within orbit of the school, going further and higher as her legs get stronger, losing weight, forgetting to eat. As autumn sets in, the weather worsens but she doesn't care. It feels appropriate.

If she's honest, there's another reason for the walks too. She's always on the lookout for *him*. The estate manager with the shotgun and the sense of something about him. She clings to that memory as the one bolt of excitement that has hit her all year. It turns into something else in her mind in the process. The connection that she doesn't have with anyone else, that she craves.

Then, one day, she almost steps on him. As she rounds a tight bend on a narrow path, he is there, beneath her feet, crouched behind the roots of a tree that has fallen across the path, torn out of the soil in a giant disc of earth.

He reaches his hand up, pulls her down next to him and then instantly they are there together, the sweet scent of hand-rolled cigarettes and some other musk that is intoxicatingly him. Blindsided, Bryony follows the direction of his gaze over the line of the tree trunk to where a group of young deer are grazing. Dark wet muzzles and liquid eyes. She hardly breathes as they crop the grass, darting their heads up nervously to listen for predators.

She slides her eyes to the right, trying to get a glimpse of his face. Then a sick feeling invades her. The gun is propped against the log beside him, its barrel hard and gleaming.

She won't let him, she decides. If he reaches for the weapon, she'll leap to her feet and scare them away. The thought gives her comfort. He can't kill the deer; he won't.

'Are you going to shoot one?' She whispers the words, barely breathes them. He is close, so close that she has the sense more than the sight of him.

He shakes his head, leaning forward to speak into her ear. 'Too young.'

Bryony relaxes against the log, turning her face once more to watch the herd.

She can feel him there beside her, the awareness in her skin dialled up so high, like the alertness she sees in the deer in front of them. She wants him, so badly and so irrationally. Isn't this one more way to fail her family? An absolute betrayal instead of the scores of tiny ones she makes on a daily basis?

Then, for no apparent reason, one of the deer spooks: it raises its head to listen and finds fault, bounding away across the rocks and the heather, followed by the other three animals leaping so fast that their white tails are flashing blurs across the hill. Their presence only a memory.

The man next to her grunts. His arm presses against hers as he reaches into his pockets for his tobacco pouch and rizlas. She leeches comfort from the warmth and solidity, the strength of him. Waits while he lights the cigarette.

'What are you doing?' She nods to where the deer were grazing, the impression they left behind.

'Counting them.'

'Why?'

'They're part of the estate over the hill: Rillgowan. They're bred and they'll be venison on plates eventually, I'm afraid.' His gaze slides sideways to her.

She shrugs. 'I'm not usually sentimental about things like that. It's just they looked so…'

'Aye,' he says, his gaze seeking the distance again. 'I know.'

They stare out across the hill to the sea, the village hidden by the curve of the land. She can't think of anything to say.

'Why do you have the gun?' she asks finally.

He shrugs. 'Keeping the rabbit population down.'

She stares at it, reaches a finger out and slides it along the smooth polish of the wood, transfixed.

'Do you know how to shoot?'

She shakes her head. 'No.'

'I could teach you. Never know when you might need to know.'

She laughs, genuinely amused that he would think her life interesting or dangerous enough for that. Or maybe he just means keeping the rabbits out of the garden.

There's another length of quiet between them, a strange combination of coiled spring and contentment.

'You have a wean to go and get, don't you?'

Bryony glances at her watch. 'As long as I set off in ten minutes, I'll make it.'

One side of his mouth pulls up in a smile as he looks down the hill. 'Long way.'

'Well, I'm fitter than I used to be.'

'I see that.'

His face is only a few inches away from hers, in this intimate shelter between fallen tree and hill. If she turned, their lips would touch. Is that what he's waiting for? Is she?

'I have coffee,' she says, reaching for the Thermos in her bag. She pours a cup into the lid, holding it out to him as an offering. They take it in turns to drink, then she scrambles to her feet. Her bottom is damp and cold from sitting on the ground.

'What's your name?' he asks as she shoulders her ruck-sack.

'Bryony.'

'Duncan. Let me know if you want that shooting lesson,' he says.

'How about next week?'

The words come naturally, without her thinking.

He peers at her, and she wonders for a moment if he will backtrack. 'I'm usually over this way on Tuesdays.'

'That's perfect.'

He takes her number, then turns and strides away without another word. Setting one foot on the trunk of the tree and springing up, over and away, like the deer before him.

A single bright laugh escapes and she claps her hand over her mouth. As she jogs down the path, jumping patches of scree, landing on smooth flat rocks or springy turf, she tells herself it won't mean anything to him. At least not as much as it means to her.

CHAPTER TWELVE

Cal's only been back one night. One night of his mother's disapproval, of missing the Highlands and Shona so badly it aches. He keeps thinking of Robbie, picturing the familiar desolation in his eyes, but pushing away the guilt and the attachment he felt.

The doorbell rings just after his mother has gone to the shops and he and the house have exhaled in relief. Cal trots down the hallway and opens the door, knowing she will have forgotten some direction she wanted to give him, or has decided to check the gas isn't on or the windows unlatched. But it isn't his mother. It's Foulds. When he sees her, the truth threatens to knock his feet from under him.

Her eyes are full of sympathy, but more than that, grim determination.

'You found her.'

'Can I come in?'

She hasn't denied it. Cal wants to punch the air. And he wants to cry. He leads her into the small sitting room and they stand in the centre of the room, staring at each other. At this moment, he feels like he and Foulds are the only people in the world.

'Do you want to sit down?'

He shakes his head. 'Tell me,' he says. 'Please.'

'We've found bones wrapped in a tarpaulin beneath one of the cars. They're in a bad state, Cal, I don't know how much evidence we'll get. But with them we found this.'

From her pocket she pulls a clear plastic evidence bag and, through mud and dirt, he sees the dull gleam of gold, the curve of a swallow's wing. His mouth goes dry; he can't breathe properly. The last time he saw this, it was hanging round his sister's neck, swinging as she bent over him, glimmering in the light like liquid sunshine. When he was small, he would catch the bird between his fingers, press it to his eye and peek out at her. There is a photograph of them together like that. Involuntarily, his fingers twitch, his hand reaches for it.

Foulds draws back the bag. The movement brings Cal to his senses. Dazed, he swivels his wrist to display his tattoo – a perfect replica of the swallow she is clutching. He drew it from memory. She nods and slides the necklace back into her pocket. 'I think it's her, too. I'm sorry.'

Cal is and he isn't. He can't cope with the conflicting emotions. Sinking onto the sofa, he holds his head in his hands. Foulds waits.

'What happens now?'

'We bring Barr in for questioning,' she says. 'Tomorrow morning. We need today to prepare.'

'Does it mean we've got him? Will he admit it?' Maybe she sees the bleakness in his eyes. He knows she can't answer that.

'I was a PC back then. I door-knocked after Emilie Pardot was found.' Foulds fixes her gaze on him, her voice fierce. 'She wasn't found until the binmen started their shift. The pavements were covered with ice that morning. It was so cold. The bastard left her there all night.' Her fists curl, and by the shake in her voice Cal can tell she's struggling to keep control. 'She'd just been promoted at work and was having a night out to celebrate. She can't feed herself now. Her parents have to do it.'

Cal nods. He's intimately acquainted with the case history and the devastating consequences that rippled through the community like fractures in bones. He has pored over accounts of the assaults, the victims, looking for evidence and similarities, sickened by the fact that four of them have red hair. Like Margot. Like his daughter.

He's been waiting for this moment for forever. And now he doesn't know what to feel. His hands shake as he says goodbye to Foulds and closes the front door. Around him, the house is heavy, the air stifling. There are so many people to call, to tell, to warn. He closes his eyes and he pictures his sister, driving her image into his mind. Red curls, strong arms and fierce cuddles for her younger brother, the age gap too wide for him to be a nuisance. An arrow of pain fires through him. So intense that his knees buckle and he thinks maybe he'll never be able to draw breath again.

–

Cal holds his mother's hand, the skin thin and translucent like paper, so light that a breeze is apt to whisk her away. She stares into the distance. A small muscle in her cheek twitches and goes still. He's not sure she's taken it in. Is she too old to cope with this? He looks anxiously for signs of a heart attack, a faint, a stroke.

'Do you understand what I mean, Mum?' He leans forward after a few moments.

'I'm not senile,' she snaps back, coming to life like a switch flicked. He jerks upright, almost laughs in shock. In his mind, Margot rolls her eyes then casts him a wink.

'Of course not.'

'And this came about because of you?'

'Not exactly. The officer I spoke to after the Dubois interview I did last year – she had a hunch that he'd got Margot's name from someone. She's tracked it down to a man who shared a cell with him. Jason Barr.'

His mother's face whips to his, eyes startling in their intensity. 'The bouncer.'

Cal swallows. Wrong-footed.

'Um. Yes.' He stumbles over the words, many questions competing with them. 'Some of the things he's said in the past made her think it could be him.'

'But they can't tell for sure it's her.'

'Not yet. But… they found a necklace.'

'The swallow.' He has to strain to hear the words. His mother nods once. Closes her eyes. Inhales and exhales. It's like she's gone to another place, a place he has never been granted access to. Her inner impenetrable world.

When she opens her eyes, they are still shuttered. 'I think I'll go and have a lie-down.'

'Okay,' he says. 'There will be food when you're ready for it. It will keep warm.'

She rises painfully, slowly, batting away his outstretched hand as if he were a moth trying to nest in her cashmere.

He sits very still, listens to her making her slow way upstairs, picturing her hand gripping the bannister. The level of comfort she has offered him is consistent, if nothing else. It was the same when he was nine years old. Seeing it fresh through adult eyes is revelatory. It's not totally her fault, he knows, but he deserved more. He still does.

The door to her bedroom closes softly, the clock on the mantel ticks. It's exactly six o'clock.

–

To take his mind off things, Cal makes lasagne. He sits up late but his mother doesn't emerge from her room. He calls Allie and Chrissie, tells them the news in halting tones.

'I wish you were here, Dad,' Chrissie says. He knows what it is to worry about a parent and he doesn't want her to have that burden.

'I know, love. But Gran and I are fine, and you're coming for the weekend.'

'I was going to get the train tomorrow from college. Mum is going to drop me at the station with Rocket. Is that still okay?' His chest squeezes at the thought of his daughter and his dog coming to see him.

'Of course it is. I can't wait. Text me when you have a time and I'll meet you on the platform.'

As he hangs up, he realises he hasn't actually asked his mum if the dog can stay. He meant to, but there's been so much going on and he's fallen into the trap of waiting for a good moment that never comes. He has a horrible feeling she's going to react badly, but he pushes away the thought – he'll have to deal with it later.

At ten he extracts the dried-out lasagne from the oven and dishes out a portion; he toys with it with a fork while the sky grows even darker outside. He can hear the sound of a television through the wall, an inkling of life carrying on around them. He's trying to think about Margot but he can't. It hurts too much. Instead, the image that keeps sliding into his head is of Robbie. He keeps seeing the sheer grief and desperation in the boy's eyes. It's as if this is the only way he can understand his own feelings. He can't feel it for Christopher Longacre – the child he once was. He can only feel it for a lost boy, who played in the garden while his mother bled to death a stone's throw away.

CHAPTER THIRTEEN

Barr is arrested in the early hours of the morning. The news hits the breakfast shows at six and the press hit the doorstep thirty minutes later, the brief statement from the police media relations team giving them more than enough to go on.

Cal is lying awake in bed, staring at the breaking news alert on his phone, when the doorbell goes. His heart leaps and he jolts upright. He throws back the covers and pulls on his jeans, grabbing a T-shirt and yanking it over his head as he plunges down the stairs to the front door. The bell rings again before he can get there. Silhouetted people through frosted glass, the lightning flash of a camera.

He waits at the door for a moment. Hand to the latch, head on the frame. One deep breath. He has to open it, if only once to say, 'No comment.' But he's groggy, puffy-eyed and unshaven. Not the best look for TV, and yet another reason he loves being a podcaster. One more breath and he opens the door. A chorus of voices. *Barr*, he hears, over and over again, the only distinguishable word in the racket, when it should be *Margot*. There aren't that many of them, ten people maybe – one TV crew, the rest hacks and snappers – but all the same, it is overwhelming. His mother will hate the intrusion on their lives, the disruption to their peaceful street.

Cal holds his hands out, waits for the shouts to stop.

'We're letting the police do their job,' he says. 'I'm not going to be able to comment. Sorry.'

He's turning away when a woman at the back yells a question.

'The police have your full confidence, then? Despite everything? Don't you want to make a statement and get out in front of it?'

In front of what? He swivels, trying to see who asked, but the faces blur in the crowd. He feels his brow crease and his face tighten, betraying him as he's trying not to give anything away.

'No,' he says. The word a tiny squeak. A scramble to realign his features. 'I don't want to make a statement, and yes... they do have my support.'

He clears his throat. Do they know something he doesn't? The way she's asked the question is strange. He wants to ask for clarity but he can't. He's being paranoid, that's all.

'What about the defence Barr will mount?' The same voice cuts through the noise. 'Do you think it will be successful?'

Cal feels his palms sweating under their voyeuristic attention.

'You need to get back.' He gestures at the gate. 'That side.'

As he retreats into the house and shuts the door, they continue bombarding him with their nonsensical bollocks questions.

'What would Margot want you to do? How much do you miss your sister? What would you say to her if she were here?'

The sound of their grumbles dulls in the cocoon of the hall. He rests his head on the wall and closes his eyes.

The voice, close to his ear, sharp and accusing, makes him jump.

'We need milk. You didn't get milk.'

He did, but he used it up in the cheese sauce for the lasagne she didn't eat.

'I'm sorry, Mum. I'll go out for some in a bit.' He gestures at the door. 'When they've gone.'

She gives him a look that is loaded with resentment; the words *I told you so* hang in the air between them. This is exactly what she didn't want. Cal opens his mouth to apologise, but the words falter on his tongue. The resentment in her eyes changes to distaste and the flashback to his childhood makes his stomach drop. Is there something wrong with him? It's no less painful, but easier to see now that even if there is, there's something wrong with her too.

–

Cal knows the police can question Barr for twenty-four hours and that they will ask for more time if needed, so he doesn't expect any news for a while. Nevertheless, it's impossible to concentrate. Even though he feels his mother is constantly irritated with him, he doesn't want to go out and leave her with the pack on the doorstep. He alternates checking his phone with watching her, waiting for some show of emotion, but there is none, only distance.

She gets up to make a cup of tea and he tries to step in and help, but she snaps at him to leave it, then realises they have no milk anyway. Anxiety builds in his veins, bottled and trapped when it wants to be set free. Cal wishes he could be in the interview room, see the strain Barr must be under, watch him sweat and avoid the questions, struggle to contain the rage he knows is in there.

In the afternoon, his mother goes to the lounge to watch *Countdown* with a piece of paper and a sharp pencil, a cup of herbal tea and two plain Hobnobs biscuits on a plate beside her. He can hear the fizz and babble of the television. At the kitchen table, he flips open his laptop and attempts to concentrate. He doesn't think he'll be able to, but then he starts searching for articles about Bryony, and the intricacies and fathomless mystery of the case send him down a dark and obsessive rabbit hole. He has headphones in so he doesn't hear his mother's footsteps in the hall, doesn't know she's there until she reaches out and touches him.

Startled, he whips the AirPods out of his ears, gazes up at her pinched expression.

'Mum, I didn't know you were there.'

She huffs at him. 'He's about to make a statement. I thought you'd want to know.'

'What? Who is?'

He's still in the Highlands, on a blood-drenched door-step outside a coastal village. His brain swims slowly through the fog of confusion, but his mother just turns on her heel and heads back to the lounge.

Barr can't make a statement. He's under arrest, in a cell or an interview room. He follows her through into the darkness. The curtains are drawn as protection against cameras. He turns his attention to the television. It shows the front of Lloyd House police headquarters, a pack of expectant reporters in front of the glass canopy that fans out above the entrance, something scheduled, planned. Foulds is in that nick; Barr is in there too. Cal watches, his thoughts colliding stupidly. What are the media waiting for?

Then the doors to the station open and a group of people stride out. Barr, in a suit and open-necked shirt; two, maybe three lawyers; some police officers holding back the media scrum – a far larger crowd than had gathered outside his mother's door this morning. Someone has tipped them off that this is happening. Ordinarily, he'd say it would be someone in the police, but the group now positioning themselves at the top of the steps look prepared.

One of the lawyers steps forward – he appears crisp and laundered, with his hair neatly styled, grey at the edges in a distinguished way. He hands an expensive-looking leather briefcase to a lackey and pulls a set of note cards from his pocket. The man looks like he has his shit together. 'Good afternoon. I would like to make a short statement on behalf of my client and then we'll be happy to take questions.'

Beside him, Cal's mother leans forward until she is perching on the edge of her armchair, her eyes fixed on the screen.

'Our client, Jason Barr, was taken from his bed by the West Midlands Police in the early hours of this morning in an unnecessarily dramatic and threatening manner. Since then, he has been co-operating with their inquiries into the disappearance of Margot Longacre, a woman my client had met only briefly at the time of her disappearance thirty-six years ago.'

He knew her? Barr's admitting he knew her. Cal's body trembles and his mind fires with vindication, followed by disbelief that they are announcing this so plainly. Why aren't they hiding it? It also doesn't escape his notice that the lawyer has failed to use the word 'arrest'. And where has Barr got the money for these sort of lawyers – the slick, expensive, winning type?

'We would like to express our sincere sympathy to Ms Longacre's family but emphasise that my client had nothing to do with her disappearance, and he is the victim of prejudice and poor policing. Today's intrusion is nothing more than a witch-hunt and, we contend, part of a worrying trend in our society to deny men the right to rehabilitation. Jason Barr has paid for mistakes he made as a young man…'

'Mistakes? He assaulted five women!' Cal's words explode into the stillness of the room and his mother tuts.

'…I am confident that my client will be found to be completely innocent of any wrongdoing and expect the West Midlands Police to be issuing a full apology in due course. We have taken the unusual step of speaking to you today, as we are shocked and disappointed that Jason's attempts to build a new life for himself are in danger of being derailed by spurious accusations. Mr Barr is here to prove to you that he has nothing to hide.'

The man turns to one side, speaks into the ear of a woman next to him that Cal hasn't previously noticed. She's well-dressed, late forties maybe. Her hair is neatly styled with shoulder-length blonde waves. As they turn back to face the media, the woman steps closer to Barr, laying her hand on his arm and leaning into him like she owns him. Cal wants to recoil on her behalf.

'Who's that?' His mother's voice in his ear, sharp and wary.

'I don't know.'

His mind scrambles to catch up. He's been researching Barr for weeks now but he's never seen that woman before. Who is she? Standing next to the ex-con, she makes him look better, less intimidating somehow. He hates that.

'Jason, Jason! Why do you think the police have asked to speak to you? What evidence do they have?'

Barr leans forward into a microphone. He slips an arm around the mystery woman and Cal feels bile rising in his throat. 'As far as I can see, they don't have anything concrete. I was living in this area when the lady went missing. As she came to the nightclub where I was a bouncer at the time, and I'm told she was a troubled character on the scene, I guess they're looking for an easy answer.'

Cal feels nausea building – is he right that Barr has just subtly undermined Margot, making it sound like she was out every night drinking? Surely the man isn't smart and calculating enough for that? And surely these days nobody will buy that sort of blatant manipulation?

Another reporter is asking a question about Barr's life now. Cal tries to focus on the answer. 'I'm a different man than I was all those years ago. I go to church, have been working in the community and' – here he tightens his grip on the woman next to him – 'I'm getting married to a wonderful woman who has supported me through the last few years.'

At this, the cameras strobe the scene and the questions come thick and fast, creating a fog of noise. The woman simpers in front of the attention, but Cal feels like he's watching a performance by a coiffed and polished puppet master. She holds her hand up for the cameras and a diamond glistens in the light of the attention.

When a nearby reporter brandishes a microphone, she leans forward to speak. 'I just wish you could all know the man I know. Jason is gentle and kind; he'd do anything for anyone.'

He's going to vomit. How has Barr managed to turn the investigation into Margot's death into some sort of engagement party?

A stifled moan escapes his mother's lips and he drops to a crouch beside her, fumbling for the remote, which has fallen to the floor.

'Don't watch it, Mum. Let's turn it off.' Her lips are white, and she turns a furious gaze on him, reaching for his wrist, her grip surprisingly tight.

'You see what happens when you stir things up? She was gone and she was safe and now...' She squeezes his arm, biting into it with her arthritic fingers, and then lets her hand flop back to her lap, lifeless. His skin stings.

'But he can't be allowed to get away with it, Mum,' Cal pleads. 'Even if it's hard for us. Now we can get justice, for Margot.'

She stares at the television. The party in front of the police station is disbanding, the group of lawyers shielding Barr as they stroll down the street to waiting cars. He doesn't look frightened or harried: swinging his fiancée's hand, he seems barely inconvenienced by the events. As Cal watches the man he hates slide into the back of a car, his mother's voice cuts through his thoughts.

'Maybe that's not what's going to happen,' she hisses. 'Did you ever think of that? Maybe we're going to have to watch him get away with it.'

CHAPTER FOURTEEN

Cal is at the station long before Chrissie is due to arrive. He buys a coffee and waits, observing people rushing back to families, some of their faces relaxing after leaving the city and others looking more stressed for being home.

He is trying to ignore the newsstand across the concourse but can't help his eyes flicking to screaming headlines and the bold print. Barr has thrown all the cards in the air, rewriting the script in an awful and audacious way. Without intending to, Cal edges closer to the things he is determined not to read.

Chrissie's train is now five minutes late. He feels a sick sort of desire to know what's happening. Maybe it's better to be informed than to be wondering. He crosses to the display. One of the papers has got hold of some childhood photographs of Barr. A grainy 1970s shot of a boy playing with a kitten. The headline – *Barr: I'm no killer* – makes a metal taste form on Cal's tongue and his vision blurs as he stares.

How has this all been created so quickly? It hasn't been, Cal realises. Barr has known this was coming since he saw the police at the scrapyard. He knew they would find her. It's a planned campaign.

He lifts the paper and for a moment he forgets where he is. The announcements fade into the background and the clip of feet on the concourse recede, as he flicks through the pages and sees how one-sided the story has become. There is nothing on Margot, but not only that: there is nothing on Barr's other victims. The ones he did time for. There are no quotes from their families, no childhood pictures of them, no mention of lives upended. He blinks a couple of times to be sure.

The narrative is so skewed that it is about something entirely different. The team around Barr were slick and prepared. They're making this about redemption and rehabilitation, the undercurrent being the maligned nature of the hard-working white male in a 'woke' world… something that would make Cal laugh if it wasn't being done so subtly, so insidiously. If people weren't going to believe it.

None of this can come cheap. It's sophisticated. So who is paying for it? Cal closes the paper and his eye falls on the picture of Barr's fiancée. Naomi Middleton. Maybe she's more than a prison pen-pal obsessed with a dangerous man. If he digs behind the headlines, what is he going to discover about her?

'Dad!'

Cal drops the paper on the rack and spins to find Chrissie bearing down on him, a rucksack on her back, her red curls gleaming and Rocket trundling at her heels. He grabs his daughter and hugs her tight, then crouches to accept the dog's joyful licks and nudges, feeling the thump of his powerful tail.

'I've missed you guys so much.'

Chrissie hugs him again. 'I'm so sorry, Dad.'

He pulls back so he can look into her eyes. 'Don't be sorry. They found her. After all this time, we can put her to rest.' Tears fill his eyes as she nods.

'But the things they're saying. The things he's saying on the news...'

Cal draws her close again, closing his eyes as they hug, her head tucked under his chin, the smell of her favourite strawberry shampoo taking him immediately home. 'Things have a way of coming out in the wash,' he says. 'We won't ever stop fighting for her.'

Chrissie bites her lip. 'Is Gran doing okay?'

He sighs. 'She's refusing to talk about it. Might be best not to bring it up. She's excited to see you, though. Shall we go?'

For a few moments, as he takes Chrissie's bag and the dog's lead, and they link arms and leave the station, everything is simple and real, and the monstrous unfairness in the way Barr is being treated fades away.

But on the way home, he realises he never did ask his mother about the dog coming to stay. Mercifully, the reporters have gone. He unlocks the front door and waits for his daughter to go in first, while he holds back with Rocket. But when the Lab hears his mother's gasp of delight at seeing her granddaughter, he takes Cal by surprise, jerking the lead from his hand and bounding down the hallway in a blur of yellow fur and excitement.

He isn't sure which comes first, the shriek or the smash, but when he finally makes it inside, Chrissie is holding the wriggling dog away from the scattered shards of a broken vase and his mother is staring at him with a look of accusation and horror.

'I'm sorry,' he says. 'Watch your feet, Mum. Chrissie, take the dog into the garden. I'll get this cleared up.'

Chrissie hauls the penitent dog through the kitchen to the small courtyard garden. Cal picks the biggest shards of the vase out of the mess and sets them to one side, rifling in the understairs cupboard for the same dustpan and brush they've had since he was a child.

His mother hasn't moved, but as the china pieces clink into the dustpan, she recovers her voice.

'What is that animal doing here? It's not staying?'

'I'm sorry. I thought I'd mentioned that Allie is away this weekend while Chrissie is here. There's no one to look after him. I meant to ask you and everything just ran away from me. We'll take him out most of the time. He won't be any trouble…' Cal falters on the words, looks up from his crouched cleaning position to find his mother staring down, her displeasure burning holes in him. 'I'll replace the vase. It's really very out of character. He's just excited to be in a new place, I think.'

Chrissie has left Rocket in the garden. When she speaks, they both swivel to her stricken face. 'I'm sorry, Gran. He can be such an idiot. It's my fault.'

His mother's face softens and she pats Chrissie on the arm. How does she do that, his daughter, smooth the edges of people so naturally?

'Well. I'm sure we'll manage this weekend. He can just stay out there.' They all look to where Rocket's face is pressed against the glass of the back door, his breath making circles of condensation and his nose smudging it into streaks. He wags his tail once and Cal tries not to smile.

–

The hardest part of Chrissie's visit is arranging where she's going to sleep. Once they've had a cup of tea, taken Rocket for a long walk and then turfed him back into the garden with his dinner and a chew, Cal knows he cannot avoid it any longer.

'I'll help,' Chrissie says, following him upstairs. Overly solicitous. She knows.

'You go in,' he tells her. 'I'll just get the bed stuff.'

In his own room he pauses and takes a breath. Then he picks up the pile of new bedding he's chosen.

When he returns with his arms and heart full, the door is open and Chrissie is bent over her aunt's old chest of drawers, her fingers trailing over a mother-of-pearl jewellery box. He knows she's not Margot but, with her hair draped over her face and her slim frame in profile, she could be. He stands a moment on the threshold.

Then Chrissie looks up at him and he steps forward, into the place he used to feel the most welcome.

'Well,' he says, looking around.

The room is clean – his mother dusts and hoovers in here every week, shines the window and the mirror – but the air is stale and close, and no one has slept in here since his sister died. It's not been so much a shrine to his family as an unpleasant reminder. That suddenly feels wrong.

Cal walks to the window and loosens the catch, tugging at the frame to pull it up and wincing at the squeal the warped wood gives as he heaves. It gets halfway before it sticks, but that is enough to allow the clean smell of outside to filter in. Below, Rocket tilts his head to look up, then goes back to gnawing the bone he is holding between his paws.

'Look,' Chrissie says. Inside the lid of the jewellery box is a little faded photograph. A red-haired teenager about Chrissie's age, with five-year-old Cal on her lap. They are both beaming at the camera but there's a mischief in Margot's eyes. 'It's you.'

'I think we got in trouble right after that was taken,' he says. 'I was ticklish and we got the giggles. We were supposed to be sitting nicely.'

He knew it was there but he hasn't looked at the picture for an age.

'I've never really seen pictures of you as a baby. You were so cute, Dad!'

'What do you mean, *were*?'

Chrissie laughs and the sound sparkles around the room, bringing it to life. 'Bit old and grizzled now...'

Cal shakes out the sheets and together they make the bed. When the new duvet is arranged, it looks warm and welcoming. While Chrissie retrieves her rucksack from the hall downstairs, Cal tugs open the chest of drawers, suddenly afraid he will find his sister's clothes in there and will be unable to cope with the sight, but they are empty.

He expects to find the same when he opens the door to the built-in cupboard in the corner, but instead it is an Aladdin's cave of junk. His eyes catch on a box he half-recognises, shoved into a corner at the back. Leaning over, Cal manages to loosen a flap and, with a jolt, he realises the box contains all the family photo albums – he didn't know his mother still had them.

He can hear Chrissie chatting to her downstairs so, before either of them can disturb him, Cal leans into the cupboard and wrenches the box free of the other detritus, hefting it until its squat heavy form is cradled in his arms. Quick as he can, he trips across the hallway into his room and shoves the box far under the bed.

He's breathing hard, guilt coursing, but Cal manages to wipe the dust from his hands in time to make it back to Margot's – Chrissie's – room. His mind is churning with desire to look at the contents of the box as an antidote to the newsprint coverage of earlier. But the thoughts subside for a moment as he looks up to find his mother behind Chrissie, a small vase of sweet peas in her hands.

'I thought these would be nice,' she says, setting the vase down on the bedside table, then hurrying away.

–

When Chrissie and his mother go to bed, Cal settles Rocket on a blanket in the kitchen and turns off the lights, checking the locks on the doors. With Chrissie upstairs and all the bedrooms occupied, the house feels full and warmer than usual.

He's been waiting for this moment all evening – his ears on the conversation but his mind on the box beneath the bed and its dusty, forgotten contents. Now, he presses his door closed quietly, clicking the bedside light on and drawing the curtains to make a cocoon. He pulls the box out into the light and gently opens the flaps. A handful of loose pictures are scattered on the surface – old school ones of his, taken after Margot had gone. He can tell by his expression.

He takes the top album out of the box and tilts open the cover. The pages make a sound like Sellotape pulling as they unpeel from each other, revealing neatly lined-up pictures with labels written in his mother's flowing hand.

Just seeing the elegant curls of the letters sends a loop of nostalgia through Cal. Over time, his mother's handwriting has become spiky and uneven.

There she is. Margot as a small child. A shock of red curls as she ran in a park; stood smiling for the camera, her feet encased in small green boots and a duffel coat buttoned to her neck. In one, she's pulling a wooden dog along a path he doesn't recognise. Smiling back at whoever was taking the picture. His father, he thinks, though he doesn't know why.

Cal sinks to the bed and turns the pages, dropping deep into the past.

He isn't in the first couple of albums – made when Margot was the only child. But then, midway through the third, he appears in his mother's arms: a wrinkled face peeking from a hospital blanket. On the next page, at home, lying on Margot's lap as she looks proudly up at the camera and shelters him with her arms.

The tears come now. Seeing the pride on her face. He can feel the love seeping from the page. This is what was taken from them. This is what people don't see when they praise Barr for his 'community service', when they look into the eyes of a harmless boy holding a kitten. Cal wants them to see. How can he get that through to them?

He wipes his eyes, reaching into the box for more, greedy to remember. Time rolls back as he works his way through them all. The later albums have fewer pictures, the ages more spaced out. But just before the end, Cal finds one that takes his breath away. Margot is grown – maybe eighteen or so, a year before she vanished. Yes, he sees it confirmed in another picture: her eighteenth birthday, a cake with pink frosting. He remembers suddenly the knife plunging into the sponge, the sweet sickly buttercream on his tongue, a blast of laughter in his ears.

But it's the first picture in the set that he returns to. A rare image of his father – more often to be found behind the lens than as the subject of the photograph. It's been a decade since his heart attack; dying young is a common side-effect of losing a child. In this picture, he's standing with his arm around Margot but he isn't looking at the camera. The thing that surprises Cal most about the image is that the man he remembers as bitter and argumentative, even violent at the end of her time with them, is looking down at his daughter with the kind of love that Cal feels for Chrissie plastered on his face. Adoration.

He exhales a long breath of air and tears. He'd forgotten. Didn't realise that deep down he'd harboured a horrible fear that his father never loved her, and that meant he never loved any of them. It doesn't negate the things that happened. Nothing can. But there is a dark hole in Cal that closes the tiniest fraction. He can see it now. Captured for all time.

—

Cal is too tired to undress or brush his teeth. He sets the albums carefully down on the floor next to the bed and lies back just for a moment. His mind mixes then and now, flitting between Margot and Robbie in strange snapshots.

But then his eyes drift back to the pile of albums. What if he begins his own campaign for justice? What if he doesn't leave it to chance?

Groaning, he rolls to a sitting position on the edge of the bed. Before he can change his mind, he chooses five different shots of Margot, trying to encapsulate her character, her verve, her smile. He peels back the plastic and unsticks them, making a tidy pile beside a paperback on his bedside table. Then he repacks the box and returns it to its hidden cave beneath the bed.

He digs in the pocket of his bag for the crushed card one of the lurking journalists pressed on him and smooths it out next to him on the bed. Without stopping to think about it, he uses an app for scanning pictures and emails them to her. As well as a rash queasiness, Cal feels a grim fire kindle inside.

CHAPTER FIFTEEN

The pictures are in the Sunday paper when it flops through the letterbox. Cal intercepts it and tucks it away in a drawer. It was the right thing to do, he's almost sure of it, but he shivers to see Margot's face staring out from newsprint. He'll explain to his mother later.

He and Chrissie go for a walk and a long coffee that bleeds into lunch, before he sees her and the dog onto the train. Every time the article crosses his mind, he shoves it away, steering Chrissie past the concourse newsagents.

'Thanks for coming,' he says. 'I know she can be tricky...'

Chrissie looks up at him. 'She's fine with me.' He can see the subtext from the frown line in the middle of her forehead.

'I've made my peace with it,' he says. 'To be honest, it's a relief that you can see it too. I used to think I was going mad.'

His daughter shakes her head slowly. 'I feel kind of bad getting on with her when...'

Cal cuts her off. 'No way. You have nothing to feel guilty about, Chris. You've missed out on so much family on my side. I want you to have fun with her. And it's good for her, too. It helps me to see it, honestly.'

Her expression clears. 'Thanks, Dad.'

As they say goodbye, Cal squeezes her tight.

'Have a good week, love. Call me when you get in.'

Chrissie tugs on Rocket's leash, smiling in a flash of white teeth, her hair flying out behind her as she jogs to the platform. 'See you soon.' The words drift back to him.

He takes the long way home, past Margot's bench. There's no one there.

'Wish you could be here,' he tells his sister, relieved that the park is empty so they can talk. 'She's so like you. But Mum *likes* it!' He can imagine Margot laughing. 'Maybe she has mellowed more than I realised.'

He pauses briefly. 'I did something stupid,' he says, kissing his fingers and pressing them to the plaque in the centre of the backrest. 'She's going to hate it, but I had to do something, M. I hope you'd forgive me. I think you would.' Cal sighs. 'But to be honest, I don't know.' He looks around for a sign – what is it people always say? A robin? A white feather. There's nothing.

Sitting in the cold, quiet park with her in his head, he plucks up the courage to check the online reaction to Margot's pictures. He scrolls social media feeds, afraid of what he will find. And rightly so. There is a vocal presence online that supports Jason Barr and his apparent attempts to clean up his act. It's not just one section of opinion either. There are liberal posters opining the need for rehabilitation, while the right wing, misogynistic crowd rail against Margot's imagined promiscuity. Barely noticing the cold bench making his trousers wet, Cal sinks into a bile-filled world, where madness and misconception are turned into reasonable argument.

Even now, the focus is still on Barr and his fiancée, the life they are planning to lead together. All these compliments about his community service, as if that was his choice. There are neighbours attesting to his generosity in fixing their cars, pictures of him leaving church, a new narrative – one that makes raking over the coals of the past a sin, conveniently forgetting the need for justice.

Meanwhile, Margot is being erased or discredited. Her life is reduced to a handful of details, all that is left because it was taken from her. She hasn't had the chance to build a life that would impress other people; she was denied that luxury. Cal can feel fury bubbling inside him, chased by despair. The ducks on the pond set up a furious squabble and he takes it as his sign to go.

–

Cal is still thinking of the foul comments, dwelling on one troll's view that 'the slut's family should be over it by now', when he gets back and finds his mother waiting for him.

'How could you?'

They will never be 'over it'.

She's standing in the kitchen doorway, holding the paper, and he quails at the look on her face. It's more than dislike, anger or despair. Something deeper and ingrained. Something there is no coming back from.

'Mum, I…'

'You had no right.' Her voice is low and her words rush out at him in a dangerous torrent; she is close to losing control and he has rarely seen her do that. 'Those were not your pictures. Those are *mine*. She was *my* daughter. You had no right at all.'

Something about the way she speaks makes Cal feel he is losing Margot all over again. But this time losing even more. The ground shifts.

'Mum, listen. We need to show our side of the story, we need to fight back, that's how the media works these days. If you say nothing then the other side just fills the gap. Barr will get away with it.' Cal tries to conceal the shake in his voice.

'Wake up!' she shouts. 'You're not a useless child anymore. He *got* away with it. Here we are, thirty-six years later. It's a lifetime without her. He *won*, Cal. No matter what happens now. Even if it was him, he won.'

'That's not fair…'

'None of this is fair. It isn't about fair.'

'But we can have the last word,' he pleads. 'We can fight. We don't have to leave it like that. She deserves…'

'Don't tell me what my daughter deserves. What about what I deserve? You have no respect, no consideration. Do you really think you're the only one grieving her? That you get to decide what to do?'

Cal's keys clink in his hand. He grips them so tightly that they dig into his palm.

'I'm sorry – I know we disagree, and I should at least have told you what I'd done.'

Her mouth purses and the frost deepens. 'You don't understand. I know that. I've always known you don't understand.'

Cal opens his mouth to argue. But what's the point? 'No. I don't understand.'

There are two pink spots on his mother's cheeks.

'I want you to leave,' she says.

Cal's mouth goes dry. 'What do you mean?'

'Go,' she says, turning away from him. 'I want you to move out. Just go away and leave me in peace.'

Cal stands very still while she walks upstairs and into her room, shutting the door. He stays there, fixed in the same position, for many minutes more. Because maybe, if he doesn't move, the pain won't rush in like the tide.

He's not sure where he's going, until he pulls his car into the long track. Cal knows he shouldn't have come here, but he has nowhere else to turn. He parks in the familiar spot and turns off the engine, already regretting the decision. This is no longer his home. He can't just show up here like this.

It is late and most of the lights are off. He's about to restart the engine and leave, when the front door opens and Allie appears on the porch, barefoot, a giant cardigan wrapped around her. He knows how the wool feels – has hugged that scratchy, cosy fabric so many times.

She raises a hand in greeting, a question on her face, and he opens the car door slowly. He needs to explain what he's doing here, but now she is in front of him, he can't find the words; he just feels himself disintegrating further. What a mess.

'Chrissie's asleep,' she tells him in a loud whisper, the door pushed closed behind her.

'I'm sorry. I shouldn't be here, Allie. I'm not sure what I'm doing. I'll go.'

He half-turns, but she descends the porch steps, her hands dropping to her sides. 'Wait. Cal. I've been watching the news. The ridiculous things they're saying. None of it is true. It's all about selling papers.'

She knows. It's easy to forget in the aftermath of a marriage, how well the other person knows you. Just because they stopped getting along doesn't mean they never did.

'I've fucked up, Al. I didn't tell Mum about the pictures.' He rubs his face, trying to stop himself breaking down in front of his ex-wife. 'I was so mad, I just sent them to a journalist. She's angry – the worst I've ever seen her.' There's a pause, while Allie digests this. Then she holds open her arms, and he steps forward and into them, tears coming now. 'I thought it would be different, Al, when we found her. I thought it would change everything.'

'I know,' she soothes, rubbing his back like she used to do to Chrissie when she was small. 'I know.'

Safe in her arms, he sobs. This was his life, his home. His daughter and his dog are inside, and he's on the outside. It feels as if his world is caving in on him. He belongs nowhere.

'Come on,' she says when the tears subside, squeezing his shoulders, pressing him together. 'I'll make you a hot drink.'

He follows her inside and is hit by the comforting smell of home. For a moment, he doesn't think he can go any further. But he forces himself forward. In the kitchen, she puts the under-cupboard lights on so the room glows just enough to see. Rocket grumbles from his bed and he scratches the dog's belly, then sits at the table and waits while Allie makes him a cup of tea. He can't help but notice that she's moved the mugs to a new place.

'What happened tonight?'

'Mum asked me to leave.'

Allie nods. He doesn't need to explain the complexity of the relationship and the coldness at the heart of it, not to her.

She tilts her head at him. 'Chrissie said she was being awful to you. It was a nice idea moving in with her, but it was never going to work, was it?'

'Seems pretty obvious now.'

'I'm not sure any of us have been thinking straight.'

He studies her in the low light. She looks better. The worry has gone from her features. In this strange twilight it is easy to open up to her, and so he does. He tells the whole sorry story: following Barr, his obsession with finding a resolution, his inability to work in the meantime. Then, because the words won't stop falling from him, he tells her about Scotland – about Robbie and Bryony, and the fierce connection he feels with the damaged son of the murdered woman.

'I don't know what to do, Allie. Tell me what to do.'

'I think you do know.'

He shakes his head emphatically. 'I wish I did.'

'You need to work, Cal. You have always found yourself that way. It's this waiting and obsessing over Jason Barr that's killing you.'

'You think?'

'Yes. That and living in your bloody mother's house.'

His mouth twitches at the last comment. She's right. There, madness lies. It always has.

'But how can I go away now? I'd be abandoning Margot.' His voice cracks. 'Just at the moment when it's most important.'

'No,' Allie says, emphatically. 'This is not a fast process. It's going to take years. You need to keep yourself safe. Margot would understand. You're a father, Cal. Chrissie needs you to be okay. You have to give the police the space to do their job. I think going away would be the absolute best option, not the worst.'

'Really?'

'You have to let go of her, Cal. It's going to hurt. It's going to hurt so badly, but you have to let go. You can't stop the pain; you can't bypass it.'

Her words strike him, find their way into his addled brain.

'I keep thinking about Jean and Tam,' he says, remembering the Aberdeenshire case, the bones of the long-missing woman he helped to locate. 'When Layla was found. It all got worse for a while.'

'Exactly,' Allie says. 'Have you spoken to them?'

'Not yet. They left me a message, though.'

'Call them. They know how you feel.'

'I will.' Strangely, they feel more like parents to him than his own mother. 'I'm sorry for showing up here, Allie.'

She shrugs. 'It's okay. I mean, don't make a habit of it, but it's okay this time.'

'It's hard to know...'

'I know.' It is Allie's turn to look tearful. 'We did the right thing, but I still miss you.'

He grips her hand. 'I'm still here. I'll always be here.'

'Thanks,' she whispers.

He looks at the clock. It is two in the morning. They've talked for hours. 'God, I'm tired. You must be too. I should go.'

'Stay,' she tells him. 'The spare-room bed is made.'

'Are you sure?' The thought of waking in this house one more time is so comforting. It's an illusion, he knows it is, but he wants to cling to it, just for a moment.

Allie nods. 'Just this once.'

CHAPTER SIXTEEN

WESTER ROSS, SCOTTISH HIGHLANDS

BRYONY, 2007

The day of her shooting lesson dawns clear and Bryony hustles the boys into school as early as she can, anxious to get started. She still hasn't mentioned it to Angus and it felt a bit late to say anything when he left yesterday – maybe it's unfair but she wants to keep something to herself.

They're going to a clearing where they can practise with clay pigeon traps. She waits on the corner of the road outside the village for him to pick her up, huddled in her coat against a stiff wind coming off the shore. An oil rig that is being decommissioned sits on the horizon and a small boat, taking tourists to see the seals, chugs out of the harbour. It won't be long until the trips stop for the winter. Already, visitors to the village have reduced to a trickle. On the far side of the bay, a castle that now houses an exclusive secondary school peeks from between the trees, but she turns her back to the view, creating a tiny shelter of warmth between her and the high-sided bank.

Finally, a mud-spattered Land Rover screeches in beside her and, feeling guilty, she scans the area before she climbs up into the cab. A pair of black spaniels are in the back this time, wriggling like eels. She pets their silky heads.

'Two dogs.'

'They'll bring back anything you manage to shoot.'

'I thought we were shooting clays?'

Duncan shrugs as he turns the 4x4. 'We'll see.'

Bryony squirms in her seat. It's weirdly intimate being in his car. All of a sudden, she has nothing to say. The silence stretches on as she stares out at passing fields, until he makes a sharp turn onto a pitted track.

'I've never been up here.'

'Shortcut,' he says. 'Not open to the public.'

'What's the Laird like?'

Duncan snorts. 'Him? Why do you want to know?'

'Just curious.'

He's silent for such a long time that she's convinced he isn't going to answer. She leans back and feels the dogs' hot breath against her ear, is suddenly tired from all the effort everything in life seems to take.

'He's out of his depth, really,' Duncan says, spinning the wheel to take a bumpy road into the woods that line the right-hand side of the track. 'He's trying to make the shooting holidays pay for the upkeep of the estate. He means well.'

The short way he answers makes Bryony think that perhaps he has to put up with a lot from his boss, but that maybe he likes him.

'Does he have a family?'

Duncan takes his eyes off the road and stares at her. 'Why all the interest?'

She shrugs. 'Just making conversation.'

'The fact that you don't usually do that is one of the things I like about you,' he says, shortly.

Bryony isn't sure how to take that. She turns her head to look out of the window so he can't see the smile that's sprung to her face.

After ten minutes or so, they draw into an isolated clearing and he pulls the car onto a patch of grass, then opens his door to leap out and let the dogs free. They criss-cross the area, noses to the ground and tails going nineteen to the dozen, while he pulls guns from the back of the car. He hands her one to carry. She takes it tentatively, alarmed at the coolness of the barrel and the responsibility for holding it.

'It's not loaded,' he says, seeing her face.

She feels like a child as she follows him, unsure and inadequate. What is she doing here? A stay-at-home mum on a school day, in the middle of the woods with a strange, uncommunicative man in a waxed jacket. Then she pictures herself sitting alone in the coffee shop, or the housework that awaits in her empty home, and feels glad she is here.

Duncan teaches her how to load, position and fire the gun. The report is earth-shattering, making her jump and startling the birds resting in the trees around them. They flurry into the sky and Duncan swings round gracefully, picking one off. It falls to the ground in the distance, landing among the trees with a dull thump. He gestures to one of the spaniels. 'Cora, go.'

Bryony watches as the dog pelts off in the direction he pointed. The other spaniel whines beside them, its eyes fixed on the spot in the bushes where Cora has vanished. A few moments later, she is back with a pigeon in her mouth, red-stained feathers and glassy eyes.

Then it's Bryony's turn to try and her hands turn clumsy, her face flushes with awkwardness.

'Slow down,' he murmurs. 'You've plenty of time.' The dogs are still, poised at their feet, the birdsong returning after the silent outrage of moments ago.

He stands behind her, shows her where to hold the weapon, how to line it up, initially shooting into nothingness. At first she's only aware of how close he is to her, acutely conscious of his body: the strength of him, the fresh pine-needle smell. But then she concentrates on the feel of the trigger beneath her fingers and the outside world clears.

Instead of confusion and doubt, she feels only focus and concentration. The sound of her own breath is loud in her ears; she feels, rather than sees, the slightest hint of movement around her. Her body prickles with attention and she can smell distinct odours from the clearing – the base notes of soil, fresh crushed grass beneath the Land Rover's wheels and the dogs' wet fur. Everything is crystal clear.

When she squeezes the trigger, she is surprised by the violence of the kick in the gun, intoxicated by the physicality of it. She looks at Duncan in shock and wonder, and he laughs.

'Maybe this time, you should try and hit something.'

He loads the clays into the machine and calls a warning as he releases them. Bryony squints along the line of the gun, missing on her first few shots. He spends some time correcting her, showing her how to line the gun up and follow the movement. But he doesn't interfere too much. Just stands back and lets her experiment.

She misses again and again, but he waits patiently, ignoring her exasperation with herself. His calm has an effect and she stops swearing, lets the external world fall away until it's just her breath down the barrel of the gun and her heartbeat sounding in her head. On her next shot, she swings her arm gracefully and decisively. When her shot shatters the clay, she isn't surprised.

Afterwards, she's sweating and exhilarated. He hands her a water bottle, swapping it for the gun.

'Thank you,' she says, turning to face him, breathless. 'That was so much fun.' He meets her eyes and for a split second she sees something raw and needy inside him, before it closes over. For that moment it felt like she was looking at herself. Involuntarily, she steps towards him.

She doesn't mean to be, but now she's close to him. Closer than she intended or can cope with.

He reaches out and touches her face. His face is moving towards her, blurring, turning out of focus.

Bryony shivers and she wants to cry. She needs him. But she absolutely can't have him.

She steps back. 'I'm sorry...'

Emotion flashes in his eyes and she can't tell if it's surprise, sympathy, derision or anger. As fast as she glimpses it, the moment has gone, and he's shutting down and stepping back like he expected nothing more. She wants to reach out and make it better, but that won't help.

'We should get you back,' he says, whistling for the dogs.

Bryony can't speak. All of the conversations she imagined having with him vanish in her mind, become impossible. She doesn't know him at all and he certainly doesn't know her. Exhausted, she clambers into her side of the car and leans against the door as he shuts the dogs in the back. When he settles behind the driver's seat, he pauses for a moment as if there is something he wants to say. Whatever it is, he thinks better of it.

They drive back to the village in silence. The car is laden with something that wasn't there on the drive out.

She thanks him again and he says goodbye, turning the car and accelerating fast away from her. Bryony watches until he is out of sight. On the surface it's all so straightforward, but underneath she's seen something else, something she can't unsee.

CHAPTER SEVENTEEN

EPISODE ONE: IN COLD BLOOD

The driveway to Gulduigan Farmhouse is flanked by rhodo-dendron bushes: invaders to the west coast of Scotland that have spread like weeds and would take ten years and millions of pounds to eradicate. When the interlopers bloom, the air turns purple and you can almost forget how toxic they are to native species. Through their glow, I can just see the wide stone doorstep where mother-of-two Bryony Campbell bled to death fourteen years ago.

A neighbour found Bryony not long after the attack, but by the time paramedics reached the isolated West Highland property, she had lost consciousness. She was pronounced dead at the scene. Five-year-old Robbie and four-year-old Sean were playing in the garden, oblivious to the danger close by.

In the days and weeks after Bryony's death, investigators probed every corner of her and her husband Angus' lives and rifled through the affairs of all the villagers in the close-knit coastal community. To this date, they have been unable to find a motive for the attack, or to identify a suspect. The weapon used, believed to be a shotgun, has never been found.

Bryony and her family were relative newcomers to the village, having left Glasgow for a rural life that would give the boys fresh air and freedom in the Highlands. Locals say Bryony kept herself to herself, and was often seen heading into the hills while the children were at school. The secret of who killed her that day *has gone to her grave with her — a simple stone in a crowded churchyard overlooking the sea.*

Over the years, many theories have been put forward. There were suspicions that Bryony's legal career back in Glasgow had thrown her into the path of nefarious characters, or that her husband's alibi was not as iron-clad as claimed, or that the tragedy was a case of mistaken identity — but nothing has ever been proved.

Whoever shot Bryony Campbell has evaded justice for fourteen years. Robbie Campbell is now nineteen and remains haunted by his mother's death. He believes the time has come for whoever knows something to break their silence and end his misery.

This is Finding Justice *and I'm your host, Cal Lovett.*

CHAPTER EIGHTEEN

It takes fifteen minutes to walk to the farmhouse from the village. The property is backed by fields but when he looks back down the way he has come, he sees the sea – today slate grey, with icing caps of foam – peeking between the curves of the valley.

Once more he checks his phone but there is nothing new about Barr – no fresh revelations. Robbie's gratitude and the relief in his voice have reinforced Cal's belief that this is the right thing to do. It took Allie to make him see sense. He can't be near his mother or Jason Barr right now. He's managed to rent the same seafront cottage he and Shona stayed in. The tight band around his chest is loosening. He can breathe again.

As Cal rings the bell, he realises he is standing on the doorstep on which Bryony died. He looks down at his feet. The wide slab is scrubbed and clean, no hint of what happened all those years ago. All the same, he feels it in the air as a kind of heaviness. He steps back down onto the gravel to wait.

Long minutes pass before a woman comes to the door, a look of apprehension or suspicion on her face, he can't tell which. Either way, the expression is quickly replaced with a smile. Robbie has spoken fondly of his stepmother, but she is younger than Cal expected, can only be in her thirties. That someone so young has taken on the mothering of two grieving boys is impressive. He suspects there are few who would be willing or able to step into that role.

'Cal?'

He remounts the slab of stone and stretches out a hand, struck by how delicate hers seems beneath his grip. It's foolish fancy to imagine Bryony's spirit watching them, because the wisp of cold air on his neck is just the breeze, but he shivers anyway.

'You must be Katherine? Thank you for speaking to me. It can't be easy having this brought up again after so many years.'

Her face clouds slightly and one hand flutters to her throat. He can only imagine how strange it must be to have your husband's first wife brought back into public consciousness for a podcast. If Bryony hadn't died, Katherine wouldn't be here, after all.

'Not at all. It's great that someone is willing to try. Come in.'

When he crosses the threshold, an older man with traces of Robbie's face in his long cheekbones and strong jaw comes into view. He is holding back, hovering in the doorway to what must be a lounge with wine-red sofas covered in cushions.

'Angus?'

The man forces a smile and thrusts a hand out to meet the one Cal offers, but the businesslike shake pastes a thin veneer over obvious discomfort. Cal shifts the bag holding his recording equipment to the other hand. There is such a swirl of emotion and woodsmoke in the narrow hallway that it's making it hard to breathe.

Katherine has twisted one leg around the other like a stork. She looks anxiously at her husband and Cal, before unfurling and gesturing down the hall.

'It's warm in the kitchen, let's go through there.'

Cal follows her slight frame, reaching the foot of the stairs at the moment Robbie emerges from above, his hands tucked in his jeans pockets and his face pinched. Cal smiles, tries to telegraph reassurance.

As Robbie starts to descend, he sees there is a second boy peering out from behind him. The boy's hair falls over his eyes so Cal can't see his face fully, only the jut of an acne-pitted jaw. He wears dark baggy skater clothes, and his limbs seem too big for him, like he doesn't know where to put them.

'Hi,' Cal says, lifting a hand.

The boy dithers for a moment, stutters a word of greeting and then falls back. A second later, Cal hears a door close.

'Sean!' Angus calls.

Katherine puts a restraining hand on his arm. 'This is hard for him too.' Then, to Cal: 'He's at a difficult age. Come through. I'll put the kettle on.' He watches her smooth things over, settling them all at the table, squeezing Robbie's arm as she passes.

While Katherine bustles at the Aga, making tea, putting some biscuits on a plate, Cal pulls recording equipment from his bag.

'What's that?' Angus sits up straight.

'Oh, just a couple of microphone packs – they make the sound clearer, particularly when there is a group of people.'

'I didn't consent to being recorded.'

Silence pierces the room.

'Oh, right.' Cal stills, flicking a glance at Robbie, trying to gauge the reality against the picture that was painted. Does Angus even want him in the house?

'Dad.' Robbie's fingers press into the table – Cal can see the whitening pressure beneath his nails, can hear the shake in his voice. 'You said we could do this.'

'I know I did, but if the police couldn't find anything years ago then what good is a man with a microphone going to do now?' He looks at Cal. 'No offence. I just think you're getting your hopes up, Robert. Officer Cauldwell did a sterling job back then and I won't have anyone say otherwise.'

Cal watches a wildness of feeling ripple across Robbie's face and through his body. He feels a duplicate wave inside himself in sympathy.

'Dad, no one's saying…' The words are spat out through gritted teeth. Katherine has stopped midway to the table, cups in her hands, looking between them.

'No, you're right,' Cal says, addressing the older man, making his tone smooth and reasonable, a mask for the depth of sympathy he feels for Robbie – the mirror experience of having a parent who is ready to shut the door on open grief. 'It's a long shot. I'm sure the police were extremely thorough back then. But sometimes we find the passage of time loosens things a little, nudges people who might know something but have been afraid to speak out in the past. Relationships and loyalties change, and sometimes all that's needed is a fresh attempt at the right moment. Secrets are a burden. Sometimes people want you to ask.'

The air stills again. Father and son stare at each other. Cal looks up at Katherine's pale face and pushes back his chair. 'Here, let me take those…'

By the time he sits down again, things have thawed a little.

Angus inclines his head. 'Very well.'

'Thank you.' Cal glances at Robbie and sees his grip on the edge of the table loosen a touch.

His father is still handsome, Cal sees as he watches Angus sip his tea in tight uncomfortable movements. But there's a cragginess, a worn-away appearance that makes him seem older than he is. There's probably only twelve or fifteen years between him and Katherine but she seems so young in comparison. It's a different kind of grief to the rush of despair running through Robbie, but the effects are noticeable, all the same.

Cal opts to put a microphone on the table instead of clipping individual ones in place. The entente feels precarious and Angus flinches at the burst of loud music from an upstairs bedroom. Is this a reflection of how Sean feels about their endeavours?

'I'll go,' Katherine says, flitting from the room.

'So how do we do this?'

'It's really up to you,' Cal says. 'But maybe you could tell me a little bit about your... about Bryony, first.'

'Like what?'

'What were her interests? What was she like? How did you meet? Anything, really. It helps me to get a sense of who she was.'

Angus grips his cup between long fingers. 'We met at school. We went to different universities, but we stayed together and when we graduated, we did our solicitor training in Glasgow.'

Cal nods, desperate for the man to unwind, give him more than facts and statistics. Now that he's here, he regrets the idea of a group interview. This uncomfortable scene has the air of an interrogation, far from the collaborative detective work he envisaged.

'What was she like as a person?'

Angus stares into the distance and Cal is struck by the rolling emotion on his face, like waves hitting the shore.

'She was fun,' he says and his words come out huskily. 'She was always laughing… back then. She used to wear these skyscraper heels and run about town going to meetings; she had so much energy to her. We lived in this flat in Glasgow with high ceilings and massive windows that she covered with fairy lights. She threw these parties that made the neighbours furious.' Angus seems unaware of his surroundings.

Robbie is leaning forward, his eyes wide and his mouth open. His dad doesn't talk about Bryony, Cal realises, with a stab of pity. Robbie doesn't know any of these details about his mum. He thinks of Margot's pictures hidden away in his mother's cupboards.

'And then you moved out here,' he prompts, forcing himself back to the present. 'Before you had the boys?'

Angus shakes his head. 'No. Sean was one. Robbie would have been nearly three. We wanted to bring them up in the countryside, where they could have more freedom.' He looks at Cal almost defiantly. 'I wanted that for them. A fresh start.'

Cal notes the choice of words, wonders what they could have needed a fresh start from.

'And so you commuted all the way to Glasgow?'

'Still do.'

'Wow, that's quite a journey.'

Angus tilts his chin. 'I work from home a lot, only really go down once a week. I stayed over more back then, went down on a Monday and came back Thursday.'

'That must have been tough, though?'

Angus swigs at his tea. 'I don't mind the driving.'

That wasn't what he meant. Cal pushes a tiny bit more. 'How did Bryony find it?'

'She was fine.' Angus sets his cup on the table with a loud clunk. 'She had the boys, this house, this beautiful place and enough money. What more could she want? What else could I have done for her?'

'Nothing. Listen, no one is suggesting you did anything wrong. I just want to get a picture of her life, so we can try to find out what happened to her.'

Angus was quickly ruled out as a suspect back then, had an alibi from one of his Glasgow colleagues. Out of the corner of his eye, Cal sees Robbie pulling back, his expression shuttering. He becomes aware that Katherine has come back down the stairs and is standing in the doorway, listening to it all.

'Was Bryony unhappy in some way, before she died?'

Angus glares at him and seems to struggle for control, his mouth working angrily.

'Bryony didn't… take to motherhood. She found the boys difficult.' Cal can see the understatement and the calculation behind the bitterness. 'She struggled to meet their needs. She wanted to go back to work.'

He remembers Allie's loss of self after they had Christina, how the only thing that seemed to tether her to herself was her art. She had to cope with snatched moments while the baby slept or evenings when Cal walked the fields with Chrissie in the sling, just to give her a break to be herself.

'And did you discuss her doing that?'

'It would have been utterly impossible,' Angus tells him. 'She agreed to move here, to make our lives here, and she needed to get on with it.'

He thinks of the utter wildness and beauty that surround them, sees that, for Bryony, it could have been a trap.

'All the same,' Cal says, leaning towards Angus. 'Sometimes we make decisions that we end up regretting. It's human to make mistakes.'

Angus jerks away from him, his chair clattering backwards. 'If you could ask Bryony, I'm pretty sure she'd tell you everything in her life was a mistake. She should never have been a mother.'

The table rocks from the violence of Angus pushing away from it, sending his mug onto its side, spilling the dregs of tea in a puddle on the wood. The man exclaims angrily and strides from the kitchen, out into the garden and away from them all.

Cal can feel Katherine's inhale of shock even before she rushes forward to grab a cloth.

But the spilled tea isn't what's on his mind. He's still and horrified, staring across at Robbie. Looking into the crumpling face of a teenager who's just heard the message that his mother didn't want him.

'Robbie, it doesn't…' he starts, but the youth shakes his head, wards Cal off with his hands as he, too, scrambles to his feet, backing away.

'I can't,' he says, breathing heavily, his chest rising and falling. 'I need a minute…'

'It's okay, I understand.'

All Cal can do is nod and try to stem the pain he feels inside in response to Robbie's anguish. The suspicion that you are an unwanted child. The stain it leaves on you that you can never, in all your years, wash away. He isn't sure Angus even registered what he said. But it can't be taken back.

'Rob,' Katherine says softly. 'Wait.'

Her words break the stasis, and Robbie shakes his head and strides from the room in the opposite direction to his father, leaving Cal and Katherine in the debris of the conversation, the recorder on the table still running.

Katherine sinks into the chair next to Cal.

'That didn't go how I expected it to,' she says shakily.

'Me neither. I'm sorry, I hadn't planned for Angus not being keen to talk – or realised that there might be things that would be hard for Robbie to hear in this first conversation. I should have known better.' He curses himself for rushing into this.

She clutches her hands together. Cal watches as tears come to her eyes.

'Robbie's always been sensitive, but in recent years it's been like watching him crumble away. He should be going off to university, starting his life, but he just can't settle to anything. That's why Angus agreed to the podcast. He's… We're hoping it might help Robbie move on.'

'You're very understanding,' he says, carrying the half-drunk cups of tea to the sink as she dries the table with a tea towel. 'It can't have been easy coming into a family with this history. And you must have been very young… Sorry, I don't mean to be personal.'

He stops, unsure how she will take his comment. She's leaning against the worktop now and he sees a glimpse of the sort of sadness that could suck you under, though it is quickly replaced with a smile.

'It's okay, you can say it. I *was* young when I married Angus. Not that much older than Robbie is now. Had no clue what to do with two little boys who'd lost their mum. My parents didn't approve.' She fixes Cal with a look. 'But I fell in love with him, I'd have done anything to be with him, so you just… get on with it, don't you?'

He smiles. 'I guess you do.'

She scans the room, throws the tea towel onto the draining board. 'Do you want another cup of tea before you head off? I didn't really get to drink that last one.'

'If you're sure.'

'Definitely. I'd appreciate the company.'

He watches as she takes clean cups from an old wooden dresser. Her brown hair twists in loose waves past her shoulders, gleaming strands of blonde mixed in, but natural, he thinks. She's wearing skinny jeans and a mint-green jumper, a silk scarf twisted at her neck and gold studs in her ears.

They sit at the table together, the house quiet around them, no trace of the thumping metal music Sean blasted down before. Cal thinks again of ghosts, of living your life in the footprints of another woman. Doing the things she did, sleeping under her roof.

'Is it hard, living here, where it happened?'

Katherine eyes him for a moment.

'I was going to say no,' she says. 'Because that's what I always say when people ask. But the truth is: yes, it was at the start. It's only in the last couple of years that we've started using the front door again.'

'So why didn't you move?'

'By the time Angus and I got married, the boys were settled here again after everything. They went to their grandparents for six months after Bryony. But they died not long after, and there was just so much change and sadness.'

'I see.'

'It seemed wrong to uproot them again.' She looks around her, murmuring almost to herself, 'But maybe that was a mistake. Everyone in the village has a theory – even now you can feel it when Angus walks into the pub. They notice us in a different way.'

He sips his tea, letting the heat furl its way around him. Outside, a passing shower smatters the ground but he can see clear skies in the distance, following the rain.

'And you never had any more children?'

She blinks and he feels voyeuristic even asking.

'I'm sorry, it's another intrusive question.'

'You wouldn't be the first to wonder.' She sighs and again he sees brief shafts of sadness that she closes over as fast as they appear. 'No. Angus would have. But the boys… It just wouldn't have been right for the boys and so… we didn't.'

Cal doesn't know what to say. 'That's a pretty selfless decision.'

Katherine smiles weakly at him. 'If the boys have families, I'll get to be the young, cool grandmother one day. I'm not missing out.' Her gaze turns fierce – a glimpse of stone beneath the softness, like rock under moss on the hills. 'I love Robbie and Sean. As if they were my own.'

'I can see that.'

'Angus doesn't think you'll find anything new,' she says.

'And you?'

'I don't know.' She closes her eyes briefly and the pose makes her look even younger. 'I just wish they could find peace. That we all could.'

'It's a terrible thing to have happened.'

She sighs and turns to look out the window, so he can only see her in profile, shadowed against the light. Her voice is pensive. 'Sometimes I picture them in the garden, out the back on their own, while...' A tear slips down her cheek and she presses it away. 'I'm sorry. That thought hurts so much. I don't often get to talk about it. No one does in this house.'

Cal thinks about the pain that is spilling from Robbie; the dark silences in his own life; and the impossibility of forgetting such a loss. Papering over the cracks and moving on doesn't work. This is why the boy is imploding. What Cal needs to do is to bring the past into the light. But it's like turning over a rock. You never know what you'll find crawling beneath.

He hopes they're ready for it, that this isn't going to make everything worse.

CHAPTER NINETEEN

WESTER ROSS, SCOTTISH HIGHLANDS

BRYONY, 2007

Bryony normally does her shopping at the supermarket twenty miles away. She has become superstitious about picking things up in the village store, feeling judged. But today, she enters the main store in the village and scans the aisles, clutching her basket. She imagines that everyone must be staring at her but, when she looks, the other shoppers are intent on their own purchases.

The exception is an old man who, she thinks, has one of the fishing boats on the pier. Bill, she thinks, his name is. *How does she know that?* He catches her eye.

'Morning.'

'Hi,' she says, forcing a smile.

'It's a braw day.'

Then he reaches for the pack of bread rolls next to her and trudges away.

The air clears and Bryony exhales the breath she has been holding, realising her hands are clenching the basket handles so tight that they're digging into her flesh. Just being friendly. That's all it was – so why does she feel so constantly afraid?

She pulls herself together and picks up a pack of the little cakes Robbie and Sean love, the ones with rice-paper stickers of cartoon characters on the top. She'll treat them after school if they eat their tea properly, she decides. Maybe that will sweeten the long late-afternoon and early-evening hours, when she is desperate for Angus to come home and help her, when the twilight feels like a kind of madness closing in on you. For the last three days, Sean has resolutely refused to let a vegetable pass his lips.

The rush of people who were in the shop when she arrived gradually thins out and she contents herself with trawling the aisles while two women take an age chatting at the till. She tunes out their words and instead marvels at the range and variety of goods crammed into the store – lines of midge repellent, fishing tackle, medicines, colouring books, gloves. It's a treasure trove of essential items, an attempt to cater to every need and whim. Upstairs is a similarly crammed hardware section, with cooking pots and utensils, nails and chicken wire.

Finally, she makes her way to the till.

'Morning.' The woman smiles as she scans the purchases and Bryony tries to shove them quickly into bags.

'Take your time,' she says softly. 'I'm no going anywhere.'

Bryony jerks her mouth into a smile, wishing every movement she made didn't have to feel so clumsy and forced. The thought that there is something seriously wrong with her swells like a balloon inside her, then sets itself loose, drifting on her anxiety.

'It's Bryony, isn't it? I'm Morag.'

The woman points at the badge pinned to her cardigan and when she looks up and nods, Bryony has time to take in the kind creases by the side of her eyes. She judges that Morag must be in her fifties, strong and fit like many of those in the village – used to physical tasks and the constant presence of real weather. There are a few strands of grey in her brown hair, tied back in a ponytail. Her skin is smooth and fresh – almost like a child's. Morag doesn't wear a scrap of make-up and there is something so reassuring about her – Bryony feels the tension in her shoulders ease just a tiny little bit.

'Your husband,' Morag says as she scans a bag of peas and passes them over, 'he's a lawyer, am I right?'

'Yes.' The sound of her voice is alien in the store. In Glasgow Bryony was never mute or tongue-tied. 'A solicitor.'

'It's just that we might need a bit of advice at the next community meeting. The new Laird over at Rillgowan has been blocking off footpaths on the hills.'

Bryony's head jerks up at the mention of the estate. She thinks of Duncan, traipsing over the heather, his waxed jacket flapping in the wind and his cap pulled low over his eyes. She thinks of the deer bounding free, the way she feels when she's up there.

'Angus is a tax solicitor,' she says. 'He doesn't really do land disputes.'

'Ach. I thought it might be something like that. Could you ask him anyway? He might be the best we have to start with. We're hoping it won't come to having to take anyone to court.' Morag passes Bryony the bunch of bananas, helps her slot it on top of the bag. 'Maybe he can recommend someone at least.'

There's a moment where Bryony hesitates, her mind racing but her body standing still, lips parted so that she must look like a fish just waiting for a hook. Morag tilts her head slightly, narrowing her eyes. 'If it's difficult to ask...'

'No, it's not.' She stumbles a little on the words. 'It's just that I used to be... I am a commercial property solicitor. Well. I gave it up when we moved here. Maybe I could help? It would just be informal, though. Point you in the right direction.'

Why is she offering? What is she doing? Bryony wants to whip the words back into her mouth as soon as she's said them. She plugs her PIN number into the machine, extracting her card quickly and slotting it back into her wallet.

But Morag's expression has already resolved into what seems to be a trademark smile.

'That would be a real help, if you could. Can you find the time? Those boys must have you run off your feet.'

She can't detect any judgement in the words, only sympathy: a momentary connection that brings tears to her eyes.

'I've got the time,' she says, reaching for her bag and straightening a little, realising only now how hunched over she's been. 'I'd like to help.'

She's only saying it because it's polite and that's what you say, isn't it? But as she leaves her number and waves goodbye to Morag, hefting her bag from the checkout, Bryony finds it's true. She does want to help. It's only the smallest chink of light but it's the closest she's felt to useful for such a long time.

As she steps from the shop, she allows herself to look around. To scan the horizon, drink in the choppy waters beyond the calm of the bay in which the village is nestled. For a very brief moment, it doesn't feel like an alien landscape. As soon as the sense of hope and peace enters,

Bryony can feel it leaving her again, but as she starts the walk home carrying the heavy bag of shopping, she clings to its memory like one of the sharp barnacles on the rocks.

–

Bryony loses confidence while she sleeps, thinks maybe she won't advise on the footpath issue after all. It's not exactly her specialty and they probably aren't going to follow up anyway – Morag was just being polite. If they do, she can just explain that she doesn't have time. But the phone goes early the next morning as she is corralling the boys to leave for school.

She grabs the receiver in the kitchen.

'Bryony, hi, it's Morag from the shop.'

'Oh, Morag.' She waggles a hand at the boys to keep quiet – they're shoving each other on the mat and, though it's good-natured now, she knows it could easily slip into argument. The sight of them causes her to feel that her tentative grip on control is slipping, the usual hopelessness gliding in. She has to make a real effort to tune in to what Morag is saying.

'We've a committee meeting next week in the village hall and I mentioned your offer – we wondered if you might be able to pop along, even for a wee bit?'

Caught off guard, Bryony starts to formulate the words to refuse politely, explaining that she isn't the right person after all, but the older woman ploughs on, her voice warm and wheedling.

'We're really grateful to you – who knew what talented people we have in our midst? Those hills have been open to all forever and they should remain so. It breaks my heart what he's doing.'

Scotland has no laws of trespass, but Bryony knows this can be manipulated and circumvented by malicious landowners – moving paths, erecting fences and making it impossible for others to use the land in the way they should be allowed to and have been doing for generations. She loves those pathways herself; these days she's fit enough to reach the estate during her school-hours roaming.

'I'll come,' she finds herself saying.

When she hangs up, she strides to the door where, sure enough, Robbie and Sean are squabbling. She thrusts it open and pushes them both through.

'Enough!'

Bryony reaches for her rucksack, shoves her flask and phone into it, and then at the last moment adds a couple of bananas and a packet of biscuits she picked up in the shop. She's been meeting Duncan regularly, is routinely taking snacks for two.

As they walk along the driveway, past the dripping rhododendrons, she strides fast, forcing the boys to run to keep up with her, wishing she could outpace everything in her life just for a few moments.

–

When she tells Angus, he looks at her with incredulity. 'What have you done that for?'

Bryony loses her grip on the bulging rubbish sack that she's just hauled from the bin. Little bits of eggshell spray across the floor and she swears under her breath.

'She said they just need some initial advice. About their rights.'

'But you aren't a land lawyer. And you shouldn't be giving anything that could be seen as advice, you know that.'

'I can look into it, though.' The indignation threatens to pour out of her. 'It's not like I've got anything else to do with my brain, is it?'

Angus crosses the room. 'Sorry. That's not what I meant. You'll be brilliant at it.' He kisses her forehead. 'They're lucky to have a mind of your calibre helping for free. There's no way they could afford your old hourly rate.'

'Thank you.'

He takes the rubbish sack from her and finishes tying the handles together. 'Just don't take on too much, that's all I'm saying.'

Bryony feels deflated. She was excited about the idea of helping, but at the same time, she wonders if Angus is right. Is she biting off more than she can chew? Surely, it's just doing a bit of research – looking into the case law for them and checking the statutory position?

Angus lifts the bag and traipses across to the little boot room, setting it on the mat and reaching for his raincoat, for the promised downpour has set in and he'll have to dash across the wet to the bin store. It's dark and late: the boys have only just got off to sleep because they were playing 'horsey' rides with him when he got back. Bryony suddenly feels inexplicably tired and lost, like she can't quite find her place in the world. Why would anyone listen to her? She can't even get her own life in order.

She walks to the hob, stirs the bubbling casserole dubiously.

'I just want to use my intellect for once,' she says, looking over to where Angus is pulling on his wellies.

'I know,' he says.

Then he wrenches the door back and steps out into the rain.

CHAPTER TWENTY

WESTER ROSS, SCOTTISH HIGHLANDS

BRYONY, 2007

She glances at her watch, then crosses to the window to see if the car has turned down the drive yet. How sad that this is the biggest night out she's had in forever. She's not dressing up – that would be silly for a community meeting – but minimal make-up and the earrings do make her look a little better than usual. Just not quite as put together as she used to be.

Looking in the mirror, Bryony tugs her long jumper down over her jeans and experiments with a smile. She looks nervous, even to herself, and there are butterflies in her stomach. Still, it's too late now. She's told Morag she's going and that's that.

She checks her watch and the window again. Angus knows about the meeting and she asked him to be back on time. The boys are bathed and in their pyjamas, tucked on the sofa watching cartoons far later than they are usually allowed.

She grabs a scarf and pounds down the stairs, sticking her head around the doorway to check they're where she left them.

They are: Sean, for once still, has snuggled into Robbie and they've pulled one of the blankets over themselves so only slack eyes and damp tufts of hair stick out. They're transfixed by the screen and don't even look over, so she leaves them to it, relieved to have a few moments of peace.

But the relief doesn't last long: ten minutes pass and he still hasn't come home. She tries calling but the reception is bad through the glens and it goes straight to voice-mail. She waits in the kitchen, chewing her nails, resisting the urge to scream at the unfairness of her life being so beholden to everyone else.

The file containing the few documents she has printed off sits on the table. If she left right now, she could do the twenty-minute walk and only be a few minutes late. Her fingers stretch for her keys, overpowered by the tempta-tion to just walk out and leave them to it. But she can't leave the boys, even if Angus is going to be back in a moment. Can she?

They wouldn't move. She'd only be gone for an hour or so, most likely, and their father will be here soon. Why not? She slides her arms into her jacket and grabs the file, turning to say goodbye to the boys. But then car headlights turn down the driveway and she snaps back into herself. Of course she wouldn't.

She crosses the driveway in a crunch of gravel, leaving the front door open so it spills its light across the wide step. The sound of the boys' cartoons follows her.

Angus is halfway out of the car when she reaches him.

'Evening…' He sighs the word out as if he's had the hardest day. She feels anger curdling inside her, alongside the stress of being late.

'I've got my meeting,' she says, holding her hand out for the keys.

He freezes for a moment.

'Oh. Yes. The village-hall thing. Sorry.' He's clearly forgotten all about it. 'Where are the boys?'

'Watching cartoons. They're ready for bed. Just need stories.'

Angus tilts his watch to the light and she's ready to really let him have it now. *Yes. It's late and they should be in bed already but that's your fault, not mine.*

She swallows the words instead, feels them sink down in her stomach alongside the rest of the bile. She takes the keys from his hand and slams the car door, as he wishes her good luck, doesn't watch him cross the driveway to the house as she turns the car in a circle and leaves them behind.

–

Bryony parks on the seafront and sucks in great lungfuls of salt air, steadying herself before she trots along the pavement to the hall. It feels strange and illicit being out after dark, which strikes her as sad and ridiculous. Her life has folded into nothing in the past few years. How did that happen? How did she let it?

There is a circle of chairs arranged in the hall and they are nearly full. Clutching her file, Bryony feels the swing door whoosh shut behind her and the assembled faces turn, curious. Her mind stalls and her hands are clammy; she is anchored to the spot until Morag beckons her forward.

'This is Bryony,' she tells the others, patting a chair that she pulls up beside her. 'Bryony, this is John, our chairman. Come, sit.'

Bryony nods to the grey-haired John. Wearing a checked shirt and an olive V-necked jumper, he is peering at a document on a clipboard.

'Ah, yes. Our land expert.' The chairman looks at her over the top of his glasses. The gaze, though assessing, isn't unfriendly.

'Well, not really. But I've looked a few things up.' She sets the file on her chair and wriggles free of her coat, wondering what Morag has promised. As she sits, she studies the rest of the group, which consists mainly of men of all ages. She recognises the old man from the shop the other day and gives him a tight smile. A sausage dog in a tartan coat is nestled under his chair and she warms to its bright-eyed gaze, its pointed reddish-brown snout.

There are a couple of younger men, too – one in a suit, as if he's just come straight from the commute. Maybe he has. She pictures the gaggle of mothers that meet in the coffee shop and wonders if he belongs to one of them. Morag and another older lady are the only women in the room. She feels again the unfairness that their lives are largely being decided by men, coupled with the relief that there aren't more of her peers here.

'We're just finishing the previous item,' John says. 'Help yourself to tea and one of those biscuits Bill made, and we'll pick your brains after that.'

Bryony pours tea while they discuss the repair needed to the cattle grids that protect the main section of the village from marauding sheep. She likes it in the hall – it's warm, and the sound of the discussion is calm and predictable, like a business meeting rather than the chaos she deals with at home.

She takes a biscuit and bites into its melting sweetness. Bill is the old man with the sausage dog. Her friend from the shop. She's seen him on the pier with a small boat, going out in all weathers. It seems a funny choice for a fisherman; a sausage dog doesn't seem very seafaring. Now that she's here and the anxiety of getting to the meeting has dissipated, she realises how tired she is, stifling a yawn in the warmth of the room.

When the topic changes to the new Laird's management of the estate, she forces herself to sit upright and widens bleary eyes, trying to seem professional.

'Way markers have been torn down, signs have gone up saying the land is private and now they're even planting saplings across the footpaths,' Morag says.

She holds her phone out and Bryony sees a series of stills showing places that she recognises. She roams the hills freely, without a care to where she should and shouldn't be going. If there is an obstacle, she does what the deer do: weaves around it. Perhaps that isn't something she should be doing. But the idea of anyone owning the wild is an alien notion to her. Clearly, these deterrents are enough to put others off.

When it's her turn to speak, she pulls out her documents and evidence, talks them through the case law.

'The best thing to do would be to open a dialogue with the Laird or his agents in the first instance,' she says. 'These things are far better resolved informally.'

She thrills a little inside at the way they are all listening to every word she says. Paying perfect attention, like she matters. *This*, she thinks, *this is what I miss. This is where I find meaning.*

'And if they won't play ball?' John asks.

'Well, there are things you could do. Talk to the press, appoint legal representatives… but you may find that just knowing the legal situation and your rights is enough to get things back on track.'

'That's been very reassuring,' John says once she's outlined her recommendations, and other members of the group murmur agreement. 'I don't suppose you would have time to help with some of this?'

Bryony darts a look at Morag, who raises her hands in a show of innocence.

'I haven't promised you.'

'I can't really give advice,' she says quickly, thinking that Angus is going to disapprove but is just going to have to deal with it. 'But if you were going to write a letter, I could look over it?'

Helping the community. That's all this is. It may not be a job, but it's a step back towards what she wants to be doing. A step that might just stop her climbing the walls in the meantime.

As the meeting draws to a close, and she stays to help tidy up and stack the chairs, she feels almost part of a team. She doesn't want to drive back to the house on the hill, with its atmosphere of grievance and tension. Where the pressure of responsibility is greater than the joy.

So she calls goodbye to the others, rubs the sausage dog on the head and walks slowly to her car, letting the wind whip open her jacket and turning her face to the spray of high tide. It's a welcome pause from the merry-go-round of motherhood. For once, she doesn't feel dizzy.

Only when she's shut herself back in the car, and the roar of the waves has dulled, does it occur to her that the Laird is Duncan's employer. He might even be the one planting the trees. She has been so focused on what Angus thinks about her taking on this fight that she hasn't stopped to wonder what Duncan is going to think.

CHAPTER TWENTY-ONE

EPISODE TWO: MENTAL STATE

'I'll be honest. I thought she'd killed them.'

Hamish Galvin lives in a property half a mile away from the farmhouse where Bryony and Angus lived. On the day Bryony died, he was working in his garden when he heard gunshots. He was the first person on the scene, an experience that has haunted him ever since.

'There's shooting on the hills, so we're used to hearing the guns, but it wisnae the right time for it and it was too close, like. The first shot went out and it made me pause, but I thought I'd been mistaken. Then I heard another. I went back to the weeding but there was something no right about it. I had a set of shears to take back to Angus so decided I would just walk along the road and take a wee look. He'd asked me to keep an eye out, so there was no harm in checking.'

'He had? Did you think that was strange?'

'Well, he'd told me she wisnae doing so well with the boys. Said she was struggling. We could all tell she wisnae quite right. She never really talked to anyone in the village since they came to bide. It's a lonely place when you've no pals. I used to hear her bawling at the loons sometimes too so I kent she wisnae that happy a person, though maybe that was just the way she was.'

This is a theme repeated by so many in the village. That Bryony was different. She didn't fit in and she didn't seem to be making an effort to. It makes me wonder if Bryony was suffering from postnatal depression. After the birth of her first child, Robbie, family and friends say she withdrew. Some of her closest Glasgow friends didn't know that she was moving to the Highlands until the week they left. After that, Bryony's state of mind seemed to deteriorate further and when she stopped getting in touch, they assumed she was busy with her new life on the coast.

'What did you find when you got there?'

'I saw her from a distance. From down the drive. I couldnae work out what I was seeing until I came close. The door was open and she was lying on the step with something around her. I realised it was blood and, I'll be honest, my first thought was that she'd done something to the kiddies. That she'd snapped. When I got there, she was saying their names and the blood was just… sorry…'

'It's okay, take your time.'

'I thought, Christ, she's killed them. The blood was gushing out of her, like. It was spattered on the wall and the door. There was so much of it and the smell… I ran into the house and rang 999, and I was calling for the laddies but I couldnae see them. I went up the stairs to their room, shouting, but it was so quiet. I was scared of what I was going to find with every door I opened. And then I went back out to the front and I tried to put pressure on her chest, and I was trying to ask her where they were but she was fading in and out, and she wasn't making any sense.'

'What did you think then?'

'I didnae ken what to think. I was holding a scarf I'd found in the hall against her but it was soaking and everything was red. It took so long for the ambulance to arrive. They told me later it was only twelve minutes – they'd been on the way back from another call, so they werenae far, but I'll never forget those minutes, watching her get weaker, drifting.

'It was only when the paramedics arrived and asked me where the gun was that I realised it wisnae there.'

'Hamish, did you see anyone leave the property when you arrived? Anyone on the road? Any cars?'

'No. Whoever did this was a ghost. They just vanished.'

CHAPTER TWENTY-TWO

Shona laces her fingers through Cal's as they stand and look out across the valley after a steep climb. In the distance, clouds coat the Cuillin Hills on Skye, dark and threatening.

He glances at her. The wind is blowing her short blonde hair out from the roots and her eyes are bright in the force of the wind. She grins back. It's so good to have her here for the weekend. Though there have been no other instances of vandalism since he returned to the village, there is a watchful feeling – a sense that he's being observed and discussed. When he enters the shop or one of the three cafes, silence falls so briefly it's almost as if he imagined it, and then talk resumes. It's nice to have someone here with him, someone firmly on his side.

'You're quiet,' Shona says.

He stretches his arms round her waist and brings her close. 'I don't want you to go. I've got the Sunday night blues.'

Shona kisses his neck. 'We've got one more night.'

'I know. This weekend has gone too quickly, though.'

'Aye, way too fast.' Shona's tone shifts and he can tell she's thinking of the work that waits for her, too.

They huddle inside a stone cairn circle, out of the wind, drinking coffee from a shared Thermos.

'Sorry, I've brought you into my blues too.' Cal nudges her.

'No, it's just hard sometimes, isn't it? Jobs with death attached.'

'I never thought of it like that.'

Shona holds her hair back and looks into his eyes. 'Never wish you worked in town planning or a travel agency?'

'I suppose it's normal for me. With Margot. It's always been like that. I can't imagine anything else.'

She reaches for his hand and squeezes it. 'How are you feeling about your new project? Sarah must be happy?'

Cal remembers the exclamation of relief from his impatient producer. 'She was relieved more than anything. But she seems to think I can magic a solution up and I'm not sure it's going to be like that this time. It seems so random, like a mafia hit on the least likely mafia target ever. There must be something in Bryony's past that explains it. I just need to find it.'

'Or the husband?'

'Angus, yes. Or maybe it was nothing to do with them and it was just a case of wrong place, wrong time. Then we'll never know.'

'You'll figure it out. I know you will.' She leans in and kisses him. Cal feels warmth spreading through him, even though the wind is bitter now. 'Thanks for coming all the way over here this weekend. It's so good to see you – everyone here looks at me like I have an agenda.'

'You do.' Shona laughs.

They get ready to trace their way back through the rock field and along an exposed ridge. He loves the way the clouds change up here, cloaking them in damp greyness one moment and breaking to reveal blue skies and intense views the next.

The journey back down the slopes is arduous, and not in the good way it felt on the top – the path is difficult to follow and the clouds come in for real this time, obscuring the view and making them feel cut off from the world.

They descend a steep, rocky section and Cal looks back, sure he sees a flicker of movement in the mist – a sheep perhaps, or a deer? Nothing. He's spooking himself, that's all. They huddle against the wall of the cliff, taking shelter as the rain begins, cold needles striking them in the face.

'Amazing how it changes so fast,' he says, remembering the clear view on the top, finding it hard to get his bearings.

'Aye. It catches folk out,' Shona says, splitting a Mars bar and handing half to Cal.

As he bites into the sweet chocolate and caramel, he feels it again: a sense of something above them moving and the sound of rocks shifting, scree sliding, like someone is walking above. It's unnerving.

It's nothing, he tells himself. *Relax.*

'We need to get down the hill,' Shona says, shoving everything in the bag, oblivious to his jumpiness. 'This weather isn't getting any better.'

He eases himself to his feet and looks cautiously around the hillside, as far as the mist allows him to see. There's no one. Sound is deadened in the close weather and they start to gradually pick their way down the path until they reach the treeline. Out of the intense weather higher up the hill, he feels calmer, amused at his overreaction.

They start to chatter again, making plans for the evening and for seeing each other again soon. His tension unwinds at the ease between them. The trees feel friendly and protective, compared with the bleakness and sense of menace up on the hill. His mind was playing tricks on him, like a traveller lured by strange lights or wisps into a bog. All he wants now is a hot shower and a warm pub, a last night with Shona.

But when they struggle, exhausted, onto the road and along to the lay-by where they left the car, Shona's face turns to his, pale with dismay.

All four tyres have been slashed.

CHAPTER TWENTY-THREE

Shona's bags sit by the cottage door in the morning. The cottage feels so much emptier now that she's packed, less welcoming when he's the only one staying in it. Cal walks her to the garage and they check out the new tyres that have been fitted, the scratch in the paintwork still a glaring reminder of the unseen animosity.

'My insurance company is going to wonder what the hell is going on,' Shona says, and he can see that she's still shaken by thoughts of her unpleasant ex.

'I think it could be Barr's people,' he says to reassure her. 'Or maybe someone's trying to put me off this podcast.'

'What are you going to do?'

He shrugs. 'What can I do? Keep a wary eye out.'

'Be careful.' She pulls him close and rests her head on his shoulder.

'I will. I'm going to miss you, but I'm kind of glad you're going home, away from this.' Even so, he feels flat and tired at the thought of the village without her.

'Maybe you should come with me, Cal. It could be dangerous.'

Cal swallows. It's so tempting, but when he thinks of Robbie, he knows he can't allow himself to be deterred. If someone is trying to put him off then there's something there that he can uncover. If it were that serious, they wouldn't be messing around with rotten fish.

'I'll be careful, I promise. Robbie would be heart-broken if I gave up now. I can't do that to him.'

Shona tilts her face to his. 'It's not just for Robbie, though, is it?'

'You can be annoyingly perceptive.'

'I know. Cliff says the same.'

'You take it easy, though – don't let the case consume you. Take some breaks.'

'You're sounding like Cliff again.'

'Well, thank God for Cliff. Tell him he has my full support.'

Shona chuckles. 'I'll do no such thing.'

He watches until her car turns the corner at the end of the village, feeling lost as soon as she is out of sight. For a moment he wants to call her back, to prolong the lightness in his life, but he forces his hands into his pockets and tries to ignore the two women on a nearby bench, who are not-so-subtly watching him.

As a distraction, he heads into the shop to pick up supplies for the next few days. The elderly woman behind the counter studies him openly as he picks out bread, milk, cereal and some ready meals. In a way, it's a nice change from all the people watching but pretending they aren't. Small, bird-like, with silver hair in a messy chignon, she's perched on a stool behind the till.

When he carries his basket over, she peers at him, her manner assessing rather than unfriendly.

'You're *him*, aren't you?'

She scans the first item and the beep sounds loud in the empty shop.

'I might be. I'm Cal,' he says, relieved that someone has the confidence to confront him and engage. 'Nice to meet you…'

'Morag.'

He opens his reusable bag and starts packing his shopping.

'You're the one helping Robbie out.'

'Yes. Well, I'm trying to. Do you know the family?'

She tuts in a way that suggests he's foolish for asking.

'Of course you do. Everyone knows everyone in a small place,' he says.

She hands him the loaf of bread. 'Everyone thinks they know everyone.'

'But they don't?'

'Sometimes people only see what they want to. Like with Bryony.'

Her tone snags Cal's attention. 'What did they want to see with Bryony?'

'She didn't behave the way people expected her to. The other mothers at the school gate didn't have a lot of time for her.'

'But you did?'

She shrugs. 'She wasn't as bad as they liked to think. She just wasn't settled here, that's all, and that got some folks' backs up. Said she was harsh with the boys. I don't know. Maybe she was. It was a big change, moving here, for her more than him.' She waggles a hand. 'What's his name?'

'Angus.'

'Angus, that's right.'

Morag fixes her gaze on him and he has the distinct feeling she's forgotten who he is. Her hands remain frozen.

He looks around the shop, wondering if he needs to seek help, but then she seems to reanimate.

'Angus isn't the only one, though.'

'He isn't?' Cal notes the slide into the present tense.

Morag looks from side to side, leans in towards him as if ready to impart a secret.

'I saw her, on the beach. She doesn't know I saw. I don't want to make trouble for her. She and that husband of hers need a night out. That's all it might take, you know. Get them back on track. No need to kick up a fuss over it all.'

'You mean she was arguing with Angus, her husband, on the beach?'

'No, no, no. They could have done that indoors, couldn't they? Now what was his name? I'm not good with names these days. It escapes me... it'll come back in a moment.'

He nods, not wanting to divert her, unsure what he's being told and about whom. Morag carries on talking, seemingly moving in a different direction.

'She struggles with those boys. Not that they're bad laddies, mind, sweet little things. She could just do with some help.'

'There's not a lot of childcare options round here.'

'Well, exactly, and with him working such long hours. I have been thinking about seeing if the lassie up at the farm can help out. She must be old enough now – she could do with some cash in hand.'

He puts the last microwave meal into his bag. 'That's thoughtful of you.'

She beams at him. 'Well, maybe I'll do that, then.'

Cal hands over a twenty-pound note. She's fast pulling coins from the drawer, her fingers flying automatically.

He pockets the change, and has just thanked Morag and picked up his bag, when she calls out.

'Duncan! I knew it would come back to me.'

'The name?' He halts, waiting for more.

'Aye. Would you believe? And her helping us with the footpath problem as well – maybe she's a double agent.'

She cackles and her eyes slide out of focus a little. At that moment a door behind the woman opens and a younger version of Morag, pink-cheeked and fair-haired, bustles in. She stops in her tracks, looking surprised when she sees Cal.

'Is Mum bending your ear? I'm sorry. I just popped out so she was watching the till.' The woman lowers her voice. 'She's having one of her days and I thought it better to have her here with me. Sometimes she's all right at home on her own.'

He smiles. 'We've been having a nice chat.'

The woman doesn't return the smile. 'You mustn't mind everything she says. She gets a bit confused sometimes, don't you, Mum?'

Morag rolls her eyes at Cal and he has to stifle a laugh. He understands the need to live in the past, the way it can swoop down and feel as real as anything in the present.

'I was just going anyway,' he says.

–

Cal hurries back to the cottage and opens the box of papers that has been couriered over by DCI Cauldwell – a retired officer who has agreed to speak to him for the podcast. The box contains neat photocopies of notes that the man has kept at home and says he still pores over, looking for the one detail he's missed, the clue that will crack the case and end the tormenting mystery of it all.

Despite how idyllic it seems, the longer Cal stays, the more he realises the village lives ever so slightly on the edge, as if it has been poisoned by the unsolved events of the past and can't move on without resolution. If it isn't somebody, it could be anybody. He can feel the tension in the conversations he has, whether the person is hostile to the idea of raking things up or, like Morag, seems grateful that someone cares enough to do so.

He leafs through the pages, looking for mention of a Duncan, but he can't find anything and the name isn't ringing any bells. What was it Morag had said? *The footpath problem.* What could it refer to? He scans the statements made to the police at the time of the investigation and finally finds something in one that Angus made a week after Bryony died.

The officer had asked Angus if Bryony had made any enemies. If there was anyone she'd fallen out with.

> *No. Bryony didn't make enemies. She wasn't like that. She'd been down since we moved here but she would never... She was doing better, I thought. She'd even been helping the village committee with some legal advice.*

Cal can feel the pain and confusion oozing from the page. Angus' lack of comprehension. The need for answers. Grieving while looking after two young sons. If he'd known, back then, that there weren't going to be answers, could he have coped with the thought?

Ignorance is bliss in that sense. Cal looks back at the years since Margot vanished and finds it hard to fathom that she is not avenged. No justice done. He feels such impatience. The clock is ticking and Barr is free to enjoy his life. Experiencing years that can't be taken away from him. It's the same for Bryony – no one has paid for what they did.

One of the popular theories in the press back then was that Bryony was killed by a hitman. How else could the killer have vanished so effectively? They had to be experienced, professional, and able to melt into the background. Cal would have agreed with this notion before, but the longer he stays in the community, the more unlikely he finds it. Visitors to the area stand out. They'd be noticed by someone. How would they get in, get out? Unless they were a commando and took to the hills? And that's just ridiculous. Or is it? As unpalatable as it is, Cal thinks the answer more likely lies in the community itself, in someone who could walk unnoticed among them. One of their own.

He makes a cup of tea and settles back at the table, digging further into the documents. Eventually, he finds the minutes of a community meeting. They're long and involved, with dry topics such as the volunteer rota for cleaning the public toilets, but the document must be in here for a reason and at the end he finds it. Discussion with the Laird of Rillgowan over footpath closure is the last item on the agenda.

This must be what Morag was talking about. Was there some sort of dispute? He digs back in the box for more minutes and eventually finds them underneath a pile of other papers, languishing at the bottom as if they are the least interesting thing in there. But then he sees the name that Morag mentioned, on the files, and he starts to think that maybe there is something worth following after all.

–

He's just leaving the cottage, fumbling to lock the door, when his phone rings. Chrissie. Cal scrambles to answer it – she's so busy these days that he has to take his opportunities when they're offered to him. He loves that it's that way now. She has friends and a thriving social life at college, after being bullied at school during her GCSEs. There's even a boyfriend – though she's tight-lipped on that subject.

'Hi, love!' He crosses the road as they talk, ambling down the pebbles to the shore. Further along, a group of lads is hanging around on the patch of grass between the sea and the road. They have six-packs of beers and a youthful shrieking bravado that's trying to be harder and bigger than it really is.

'Dad – how's it going?'

His radar sounds when he hears the flatness in her greeting. 'What's up?'

'Oh, no, I'm good, it's just… have you seen Twitter today?'

Cal's stomach drops with a heavy sense of inevitability. 'No. Is it Barr?'

'I'm sorry to tell you, I just didn't want you not to know… Apparently, he got married yesterday.'

Cal feels the air rushing out of him, along with a small, bitter laugh. He looks out to sea and the landscape wobbles. He checks his social media feeds every evening to see if there is any news, but there was nothing last night.

'Wow. Okay.'

'I guess it will hit the papers tomorrow.'

Margot never got to get married. Yet another life stage denied her. It's like Barr is laughing at him. He's been doing all he can to find out about the man's fiancée, now wife. Naomi Middleton lives in an expensive Manchester suburb and started writing to Barr when he was in prison, as part of a pen-pal scheme. She's a decade younger than Barr and divorced from a wealthy businessman. He guesses this is where the funds are coming from for the defence. What she sees in Jason Barr is beyond him.

'Maybe he's getting it in before he goes away for a very long time,' Chrissie says.

'Let's hope so.'

They both know this might not be the case.

'I feel like I should warn you that there's a picture,' she says. 'Of him feeding her cake.'

'Bloody hell.'

'I know. It's put me off cake for life.'

Despite himself, Cal laughs. He's missed Chrissie these past few weeks. She's the best part of his life. No one else could make him see any humour in this moment.

'Let's not talk about him,' he says, hating that the man is in their thoughts like this. 'How are you? I miss you.'

'Well, I might be able to fix that. The reason I'm calling is that I've got half-term and a reading week coming up, and I was wondering if maybe I could come and spend some time with you?'

Sunlight dances inside him.

'Isn't reading week for reading?'

'You can read books in Scotland, I've heard. It is allowed.'

'Very funny. What does Mum say?' He knows, in navigating the co-parenting quagmire, that this is the essential question. Chrissie is not above playing one off against the other. But he desperately wants to see her.

'She said it's fine, if you say yes and if you have space for me.'

He turns to look at the lonely little cottage behind him, feeling a burst of excitement that Chrissie will be here to share it with him.

'Then book your train.'

'Amazing! Thanks, Dad.'

'And bring waterproofs.'

'I will.'

'Thanks for telling me about Barr, Chris. I know it isn't easy being the bearer of bad news.'

'That's okay. I don't believe what they're saying, Dad. Other people will see it too, in the end.'

When they've said goodbye, he continues along the beach to where the group of boys is drinking. As he passes, Cal's eye alights on one of the youths, who is sitting on the edge of an upturned boat, bent over with his head between his knees. The boy looks up, flipping greasy hair out of his eyes, and he sees that it is Robbie's brother, Sean.

Sean's eyes are vacant, zoned out, like he's on something. Does Angus know what he's doing? Katherine has told him that Angus and Sean are close in a way that Robbie and his father are not. Maybe that's what's kept him going while his brother falters. But he can't help but be struck by the reports of Sean as a cheerful child – he seems so far from that now. Cal pushes the door to the pub open, soothed by the warm air and the crackle of the fire. Needing to remain sharp for scripting the next episode later, he forgoes the temptation of a pint and slides into a chair with a soda water to wait for his fish pie. From his seat he can see Sean and one of the lads on the grass – jostling now with a piece of driftwood. If you half-closed your eyes, they could be children playing, carefree. Like so many things here, it's an illusion.

CHAPTER TWENTY-FOUR

WESTER ROSS, SCOTTISH HIGHLANDS

BRYONY, 2007

Angus doesn't ask her about the meeting, and the atmosphere between them festers all weekend. They are unnaturally polite to each other when they have to interact, but otherwise they stay out of each other's way. Bryony hadn't realised it was possible to feel even more lonely than she already did.

When he leaves for work, the Thursday lunchtime meeting is the one thing she has to look forward to. As a result of her letter, the Laird has offered to come and talk to the committee, and Morag says John wants her there. She makes it there early, trudging down to the hall through the rain. It feels colder inside than out, so she keeps her coat on and helps to set out cups and a plate for biscuits. Morag, John, Bill and the sausage dog are all present, plus a woman called Sue who wasn't at the last meeting.

Bryony and Angus bought their house from Sue and her husband, Kevin. She's always thought Sue looks guilty whenever they meet – or maybe that's just how Bryony thinks she should feel, because she and her family are now happily ensconced in a warm new-build with vaulted ceilings and huge glass panels situated across the valley. Angus and Bryony, having fallen for the romantic notion of an old farmhouse with history and original features, are left with cold floors, blooming damp stains and leaky pipes.

Just one of the many ways in which reason and sense left her when they made the decision to move here, Bryony thinks. If she was smart, she'd have seen past the image of the coastal idyll, to the hard graft it takes to live and thrive in places tourists coo over. But as they cluster together in the hall, she feels ashamed of herself for being resentful. It's not their fault she's an idiot who went along with her husband's plan while in the fog of depression and now finds herself unable to live the life she intended.

She arranges chairs, waiting in the background while the others chat about other committee issues: the upkeep of the public toilets, which are cleaned and maintained by volunteers; the lack of meeting places for local teens; the annual Burns Night plans.

'Bryony.' Morag beckons her over to where she is talking to Sue. 'I was wondering if you had any babysitting needs? Sue's daughter is sixteen and she could do with some cash, if you and that dashing husband of yours wanted a night out at any point?'

'Oh. That would be…' It would be amazing, though her husband would have to be speaking to her for it to be an option. 'Do you think she'd want to?'

'I'll get her to pop down and say hello,' Sue tells her, and Bryony feels a loosening of the bonds. If she can get a babysitter for nights out, maybe she can get one for other times too, if Angus lightens up.

She's saved from dwelling on her relationship by a sudden gust of wind as the door to the hall is pulled back and a man enters, sloughing rain off his jacket. The long-awaited Laird. There's a slight commotion and others step forward to help him find a peg for his coat, so at first Bryony can't see him. She cranes her neck, curious to get a glimpse. But when he turns and lifts his chin, she's disappointed.

The Laird hasn't come, after all. He's sent a representative. Someone Bryony really should have talked to about this when they met and shared a flask of coffee in the hills earlier in the week. Her face flushes at the memory of them sitting together on a large flat rock, sipping coffee and crumbling shortbread biscuits. The press of his arm against hers is a shuddery memory. Now she is split between disappointment that the Laird isn't here in person, excitement at seeing Duncan, and apprehension that he's going to be angry that she kept this from him.

He scans the room and his eyes alight on her. She smiles but he looks startled. His dark eyebrows come together in a frown. It's strange seeing him here, out of context, interacting with others. She feels a desperate pull of longing for him.

'Ah, yes,' John the chairman says, apparently noticing the look of fierce curiosity Duncan gives Bryony. 'Most of us I think you know, but this is Bryony Campbell, our "legal adviser", so to speak.' He chortles, hamming up the words, but Bryony sees Duncan bristle at the implication that they are legally prepared and that it's Bryony who's preparing them.

John takes a step towards her. 'Bryony, this is Duncan Buckie, the Laird of Rillgowan.'

Bryony has stretched out her hand but when she hears the chairman's introduction, it falls to her side. 'Laird?' Her voice betrays her shock, she's sure it does.

Duncan just nods. 'Aye. Pleased to meet you.'

His tone bites and he intends it to, she can tell.

Bryony's name wasn't on the letter that was sent, detailing their concerns. John put it together and, though he emailed her a copy, she has been too distracted to open the message, so she hadn't seen the full name of the person to whom it was addressed.

Her mind twists itself in knots, trying to remember their conversations. What's been said between them? Has he lied to her at any point? Or has she simply assumed? Either way, she hasn't been the only one concealing the truth. Her face reddens at the memory of her questions about the Laird, humiliated now she can see the evasion in his answers.

She thought she mattered to him. It's a cold blast of sea water to find that he's been hiding himself from her. Has he been laughing at her too?

Stomach churning, she takes her seat in the tight circle of chairs.

'Well,' John says, slapping his knees. 'You've had my letter and you asked to meet, so the floor is yours, as they say.'

'My land agent was supposed to attend but he's unwell.' Duncan's words are clipped and sour. Bryony sees the others bend away from him in their minds.

'So will you be reinstating the footpath?' Morag leans forward. Bryony has learned that her late husband's ashes were scattered on the path.

'I'm managing the land for the good of the wildlife,' Duncan says. 'It does no good to have folk traipsing across the areas where the deer like to congregate, making a noise and leaving a mess.'

He has never shown the slightest annoyance at Bryony's treatment of the landscape, her constant 'traipsing'.

'But we've always had access through the land,' John says. 'Your predecessor never had any issues.'

'Well, with respect, it isn't his land anymore. It's mine.'

Bryony feels her fingers flex with frustration. She wants to speak, but feels she needs John's permission before she launches in. She's stung by the duplicity in Duncan's relationship with her. How can the one person she saw as a lifeline in her godawful existence turn out to be a deception?

She shifts in her chair and John looks at her for assistance.

'It's not really that simple,' she says, an authority she doesn't ever experience these days running rusty through her voice. His face swivels to hers, those eyes too familiar. She wonders if the others in the room can see the effect he has on her. 'The previous landowner accepted public money – grant funding and money raised by the local community – to surface some areas of the footpath. It's such a waste of time and money, not to mention sad to close off what is a historic route for walkers, dating back hundreds of years.'

His face darkens, and she feels sorry for him, here alone in front of a hostile crowd. Even the friendly sausage dog has retreated under Bill's chair. Bryony's still trying to reconcile the man she knows in the cloud-riven hills with the one sitting in front of her. But she carries on regardless, the legal terminology flowing more easily from her lips the longer she continues to speak. With each word, she feels more energy run into her veins. She bandies the correct terms, the legal red tape he could tie himself in, the trees that would later have to be uprooted if a ruling went against him.

The others are all quiet, though she pauses several times to allow any of them to jump in and speak if they would like to. A couple of them nod in approval, but no one steps up. She has the floor.

At the end of her speech, Bryony pauses and Duncan meets her eyes. She can see the challenge there – the desire to push back because it's her and he feels betrayed by her silence. She understands: it's how she feels as well. Her chest is heaving, and all of her anger and emotion has congealed together.

'I can offer an alternative route.'

'But we'd need a formal agreement for that and it could be a nightmare.' She keeps her voice soft, trying to find the reason she's sure is inside him.

An alternative isn't what the community wants – the valley he's shutting off to them is a part of this village's history, as well as a place of natural beauty, studded with rare heathers and orchids. This isn't about the route, now, she can see that. It's becoming a competition.

'That particular path is significant,' she says. 'The community feel a change would be a betrayal of their heritage.' Murmurs of agreement sound around her.

'A betrayal? That's what they think?' He growls the words at her.

She raises her chin, defiantly. 'A betrayal.'

'Sometimes,' he says, 'there are reasons for things, and it would be nice if there was trust.'

'There has to be trust on both sides.'

There's silence in the room, apart from the insistent rain on the skylights in the kitchen.

'Right.' He sets the cup of tea he has barely touched down on the floor. 'You've made your position very clear. I'll discuss this with my agent and come back to you. Thank you for your time.'

The meeting hasn't gone as well as everyone hoped. There's an awkwardness as he leaves. Bryony stands back, shame and defiance swirling inside her.

When she leaves the hall a few minutes later, calling goodbye to the others, the wind is up and there's still half an hour to kill until she needs to collect the boys. At least Sean is finally on full days. It's not worth going home, so she decides to walk along the shore, needing the cleansing, buffeting power of the elements.

She sets off for the end of the bay, where a cluster of rocks mark the path round the headland. She's found fuchsias growing in mossy caves round there before, their dark pink petals stark against the wet rock and ferns.

Pulling her hood up, Bryony marches, leaning into the wind and watching her feet on the stones. Against the wind and the waves, she doesn't hear him, so when Duncan catches her arm and spins her round, she almost falls and he has to hold on to her to keep her upright, despite the fury in his face.

'Why didn't you tell me?' he shouts.

'I had no idea it was your land – you know I didn't.' Tears spill down her cheeks.

He makes a noise of frustration. 'Don't fucking cry. I can't take it if you cry.'

'I'm not.'

She turns on her heel, tries to make it to the shelter of the headland, but he follows her. It's not like she doesn't want him to.

'I'm managing that land the best I can.'

Bryony walks faster, fired by the conflicting feelings she has towards him, tripping on the slimy rocks. 'So let them walk across it. They have the right. What's it to you?'

'People. I don't want to see people.'

'You see me. Every week.' She spins to face him. 'You never said you didn't want me there.'

'I do want you there.'

'Why? I'm still people.'

'It's different. You know that.'

'Why is it different? You didn't tell me who you were, even when I was asking all those questions. I feel like such an idiot.' The tide is coming in and the waves are crashing on the outer rocks, sending great spurts of spray into the sky. She directs her words to the violent sea, shouting them into the abyss and throwing her arms out. 'I spend my whole life feeling like this. I'm a joke to everyone. It would be better if I wasn't here at all. It would be better if I was dead!'

The wind takes her words and whips them out to sea.

'Don't say that.'

He moves right close to her, blocking out the spray, sheltering her. She turns away but he grabs her arm again, wrenching her round to face him.

She knows what's going to happen, because it feels preordained. They've been on a collision course. He presses his lips to hers and it's not soft and gentle, it's harsh – the punishment she needs. She feels a hungry desire right through her body. Every part of her aches for him. So she kisses him back. Violent, bruising kisses, lips clashing and worlds colliding. Her hands roped in his hair.

He pulls her tighter against him and that's the moment when the image of her sons springs into her mind. Their trusting faces, their shitty mother, their compromised lives. They were perfect and she's ruined them. She's ruined it all. It would be better if she was dead. She can see that now.

Bryony slides her hands down his chest and shoves so hard that he stumbles backwards. 'No.'

He looks at her aghast. 'I thought that's what you wanted.'

She feels her face twist as she answers him. 'I can't have what I want. I don't deserve it.'

Then she wraps her arms tight against her sodden body and backs away from him, waiting until she is a safe distance before she starts to run, slipping on the wet stones, threatening to turn an ankle and not caring. She looks back when she reaches the hall, but the beach is empty, like he's vanished into the air or stepped into the sea.

By the time she reaches the school door, her mask is back in place – all of the hurt, confusion and worthlessness buried deep. Sean rushes out and she opens her arms mechanically to receive him. They wait for Robbie to emerge from his door, and then they each take a hand and she leads them back to the house. She even manages to nod to another mother as they go. If you looked at her, she thinks, you'd never know.

CHAPTER TWENTY-FIVE

EPISODE THREE: NO RHYME OR REASON

'It gets under your skin. In all my years of policing, this is the case that keeps me awake at night, wondering. It just makes no sense. No sense to me at all.'

Retired Detective Chief Inspector Derek Cauldwell and I are walking along the shore of an isolated bay in front of his white-painted cottage. The squat building is weathered and hardy, like Cauldwell himself. It overlooks the sea, and in the winter it is battered by spray that drives up and over the rocks. On calm days, he takes his little motorboat out to a small island in the distance and fishes, kept company by the occasional seal or dolphin visitors to the bay.

'By the time I got there, she was gone. They'd been working on her, trying to revive her; you could see that from all of the debris scattered around the step – swabs and the like – all bloodstained. There was so much blood – it had soaked into the gravel. I'll never forget it. The neighbour was covered in blood – and in shock, I think. He was white as a sheet, panicking about the boys. It took me a minute to get it out of him that they were missing, and how old they were.'

'What did you think you were going to find?'

'I thought they'd be dead. That it must be the husband. When the house was clear, I thought it was a domestic and he must have abducted them. But they were in the garden all along. The neighbour had been too shaken to look there.'

'What were they doing?'

'The younger boy was on the swing. All of a sudden, there he was. In these little frog wellies, just laughing and swinging. His brother was watching him. They had no idea.'

In this episode of Finding Justice, I talk to Cauldwell about the original investigation on a case that has mystified police ever since that day.

'What do you think happened?'

'That's just it. I have no idea. In most cases, even if you can't prove it, you have a fair idea what's gone on. I'd have expected it to be the husband. But he was at a client's office, had an alibi. We searched all of his correspondence for evidence that he'd paid someone to kill her – nothing. I worry that I missed something, you know?'

Cauldwell has been kind enough to arrange for Police Scotland to share copies of some of his files with me to help my investigation. In my view, he's being too hard on himself. The investigation appears to be exhaustive.

'What do you think happened to Bryony?'

'My best guess is mistaken identity. There's no reason for her to have been killed. None at all.'

CHAPTER TWENTY-SIX

Cal has to go the long way round to reach Rillgowan House. Although the village is close as the crow flies, the drive is an hour. He takes the time to listen to music, trying not to think about Barr and his marital bliss, though the doubts have crept in since he checked online and saw reams of congratulations messages. It's like entering a pre-feminist nightmare. He can't believe these people exist in the droves they seem to.

The driveway to the estate is long and winding. Cal turns off the main road, bumping over a cattle grid, and enters a deeper level of wilderness and isolation. In the snow, the road must be impassable. This is going to be a wasted trip if the man is out, but he hasn't called ahead because he doesn't want to miss his chance to catch him unrehearsed.

It takes fifteen minutes to drive to the house. He catches a glimpse of it between the hills at one point – positioned at the top of a silver-grey loch that looks like a scrap of sky that's fallen to the ground. The house seems modest in the distance but when he gets up close, the scale changes and it towers above him, magnificent and imposing. Cal parks and steps out of the car, stretching his cramped legs and arms as he looks up at the turrets and thick stone walls.

A line of holiday cabins are dotted along the river leading from the loch. Positioned to offer privacy, he's seen from the estate's website that they are exclusive and expensive – the preserve of wealthy visitors who want to fish or shoot. From the small amount he has been able to glean from locals, the Laird keeps to himself and is rumoured to be difficult. Rarely seen in the community, he does employ people to clean, cook and attend to his guests, so there appears to be some loyalty towards him. Cal's attempts to elicit gossip haven't really yielded anything other than, he suspects, disdain for such stereo-typical journalistic dirt-digging.

He heads for the grand front door and rings the bell. It echoes in the house beyond but no one comes. Cal sighs, wondering how long he'll have to wait for his ambush. He takes a couple of pictures and then sets off round the side of the house. He's hardly made it to the corner when he hears barking, and three spaniels in different shades of mud appear.

They're wagging their tails, so he assumes they must be friendly, but the noise is intimidating. He's bending down to try and pet one when he hears the sound of someone clearing their throat loudly. Cal looks up to see a man bearing down on him. The only detail he takes in as he straightens to greet him is that the man is holding a gun. The riot the dogs are making fades into the background as he stares down the gleaming barrel.

The thought of Bryony, bleeding out on her doorstep, makes fear and bile rise in his throat. The blood rushes in his ears, and his mouth is dry as he tries to speak. Why the hell did he come alone? He wasn't thinking. He pictures slashed tyres, the scrape of metal where a key gouged an angry line in Shona's car.

But slowly, his mind clears enough to see the man breaking the gun, setting it over the crook of his arm in a non-threatening position. His heart rate slows, though the man's expression is forbidding.

'What do you want?'

'My name's Cal Lovett. I'm researching for a podcast.' He's too far away to shake hands, so Cal settles for a wave of greeting, unnerved by the ongoing racket the dogs are making.

The great hulking figure in a waxed jacket doesn't seem disposed to be friendly, so Cal concentrates on taking in as much of an impression as he can. The man's hair is tousled and his face is weathered in a tanned, craggy way, and there's an edge to him. Cal is still acutely aware of the gun.

'Quiet!' The man raises his voice and the dogs fall silent at the command. 'This is my home. You need to leave. I don't want to talk to you.' He gestures to where Cal has parked.

'It won't take long.'

'I said no.' He turns away.

'You haven't asked me what it's about,' Cal says, quickly. 'The podcast.'

Duncan keeps walking. 'I don't need to know.'

'But you knew Bryony Campbell?'

The man's steps falter at the name and when he looks back, Cal's sure he sees fear in his features, quickly masked.

'You did know her?'

'I had nothing to do with this. You have no reason to be here.'

Cal takes a breath and hopes he isn't going to end up regretting his words. 'Bryony was shot. And the gun has never been found.'

'What's that got to do with me?'

He lets his gaze slip to the weapon in the Laird's arms.

'If you're looking for people with shotguns in the area, I can point you in the direction of a dozen. I'm not interested in your ridiculous podcast and your muck-raking theories. I've asked you to leave.'

'If I could just—'

'Leave!'

The menace in his voice tells Cal that he's pushed it far enough for today, even before the man starts reassembling the weapon in his hands. He backs away, pulling his keys from his pocket.

'I'm going. But I'm staying in a cottage in the village, if you change your mind.'

'I won't.'

Duncan glares at him from under bushy eyebrows. A shiver runs down Cal's back, though maybe that's the rain squall blowing through, the first drops smiting the ground around them like shells. Safe in the car, Cal locks the doors and starts the engine, unsettled by the encounter. As he pulls away, he looks in the mirror and sees the imposing figure still there, unmoved by the rain, gun in his hand as he watches Cal go.

CHAPTER TWENTY-SEVEN

It's lazy, but he eats in the pub again – too tired to cook, but also not wanting to be alone in the cottage with his thoughts. The pictures of Barr doing the rounds online are nauseating, but he's also disturbed by his run-in with Duncan and the decision of how to cover the alleged relationship in the podcast. He's unearthing things about Bryony that her family might rather not know. Cal's acutely aware that the man gave nothing away today – but he didn't deny knowing Bryony either.

This is why, he thinks, staring moodily into his pint, spur-of-the-moment podcast decisions are a terrible idea. He orders a curry, and then takes his phone outside and dials his producer Sarah's number, pacing the stretch of grass between the road and the beach.

'Cal? How's the west coast?'

'I don't know,' he says. 'A bit of a mess, to be honest.'

She sighs.

'I know, I know.' How does she make him feel like a child? She's half his age.

'How can I help?'

'Ethical dilemma.'

'Great. Shoot. Sorry, bad choice of word.'

'I think Bryony may have been having an affair with a local landowner. Someone let it slip that she saw them arguing, but the family don't seem to know anything about it. I don't know if I want to be the one to tell them. He's refusing to speak, other than to tell me to get off his land. He's not exactly friendly.'

'Is it relevant to the case?'

'He runs shooting holidays and he was holding a shotgun while we spoke.'

She lets the silence stand for a moment. 'Right, then. I'd have thought the answer to this was pretty obvious.'

'When you put it like that, it is.'

'Glad to have been of service. We're getting some good reviews and initial listening figures, by the way.'

'Great. No pressure, then.'

'What are you talking about? Loads of pressure, buckets of it. Shitloads.'

'I'm not sure why I bother calling you.'

'You're welcome.'

Back in the pub, Cal tucks into his meal. She's right, and he bloody hates it when she's right. He's going to have to bite the bullet and break his suspicions to the family. As protective as he feels of Robbie, it isn't his job to hide the truth.

As he eats, he becomes aware of a commotion in the kitchen, behind the bar. The pub isn't that full, and everyone else is at tables and seems unaware, but the landlord – Tom – keeps going back into the kitchen and Cal thinks he can hear him remonstrating with someone. Since he returned to the village, Tom has been one of the only friendly faces – kindness well hidden beneath his craggy appearance and the hard lines on his face.

'You okay?' he asks when Tom returns, looking flustered.

'Aye. It's Robbie, like. He's had a bit too much to drink. Or something.'

'Do you need a hand?'

The landlord looks like he's about to say no, but then the front door of the pub goes and a family tumble in out of the rain, and he nods at Cal. 'You can have a try. Just see if he'll calm down, will you?'

Cal slides behind the bar, crossing the divide from the smoky darkness into the glaring lights and bustle of the kitchen.

Robbie is leaning against a wall at the back and a chef is holding his arm.

'Tom sent me,' Cal says when the chef looks up. 'To see if I can help.'

Robbie turns and Cal is shocked to see how unwell he looks. His eyes are wide and bloodshot, his skin clammy, and he smells stale. It's only been a few days since he last saw him, and the deterioration is stark.

'Robbie,' he says. 'What's going on?'

'I can't.' Robbie shakes his head back and forth, his lank hair swinging. 'I can't sleep, and I keep seeing it over and over in my head. I need it to stop.'

'Have you been to the doctor?'

'No,' he says. 'I don't like doctors. I don't trust them.'

'Tom said to get him to go upstairs for a sleep,' the chef tells Cal. 'But he won't go.'

'I can work,' Robbie shouts. 'I'm not useless.'

The chef rolls his eyes at Cal and returns to the stove, where various pots are steaming and bubbling, small slips of paper lined above with orders.

'Let's go and have a cup of tea, and then you can come back down,' Cal says to Robbie. He takes him gently by the arm and guides him to the stairs, ignoring his protests and relieved to feel him capitulating.

By the time they reach the upstairs landing, Robbie is crying, apologising over and over for being a mess and fucking things up again.

'Tom's going to fire me,' he wails.

'No. He just wants you to have a rest, Robbie,' Cal says, adopting the strict tone he used when Chrissie became too tired and overwhelmed as a young child. 'That's what you need, so stop fighting it.'

Robbie shakes him off and then starts wailing again. It takes another five minutes to persuade him to sit on the bed, then drink the water Cal fetches and, finally, lie down. He's the embodiment of misery.

'I just think it would be better if I wasn't here,' Robbie says, his eyes pleading with Cal.

'That's not true,' Cal says, leaning forward and gripping Robbie's arms. 'Your family need you. You're important to a lot of people.'

'I'm not. I'm just not.'

Robbie rolls onto his side, curled on the single bed in what looks like a frequently used guest room. There are clothes scattered at the foot of the bed and some old tissues on the floor.

'All right, Robbie,' Cal says when the kid's eyes start to close and he jerks them open again. 'Don't fight it. It'll all seem better in the morning.'

'Will you stay?' Robbie says, grabbing his arm. 'Just while I fall asleep.'

'Yes. Close your eyes now.'

'I don't know what I'd do if you weren't here. Thank you for doing this. The podcast, I mean. It's the only thing...'

Cal quietly leaves the room and slides to the floor in the hallway, from where he can see Robbie. He watches as the boy drifts into unconsciousness and jolts awake several times. His limbs are stiff by the time Robbie's breathing evens out. Tiptoeing into the room, he tucks a blanket over him, then quietly takes the stairs back to the kitchen and the bar.

'He's asleep,' he tells Tom, back in the bar, which is now heaving.

The landlord makes a frustrated noise in his throat. 'He's always been a bit disturbed and who's to wonder at that, given what happened, but he's really starting to worry me, you know?' Cal nods. 'Here. This pint's on the house.'

'Thanks.' He accepts the drink and takes a long draw of the smooth beer.

'I want to help him, you know, but if this carries on... I think I'm going to have to let him go.'

–

Cal lies awake that night, unable to feel peace after seeing Robbie in such a state. He knows the exposure to Robbie's pain is only opening his own wounds, but he's committed now. The sound of the waves prods and pokes at him when he closes his eyes, insistent and invasive. Is he missing something? How on earth is he going to tell Robbie about his mother's connection with the Laird? If only the truth were an easier one.

It's late, but he knows Shona works long hours at the lab when needed. He sends her a text, then throws back the covers and stands in front of the window, looking out to the grey coastline, which is lit by a faint moon that illuminates the hulking black rocks at the headland.

There is a light shining from a boat and he stares at it, his eyes swimming with tiredness, until he can't be sure if there is one light or two. His thoughts turn to the malignancy of the slashed tyres, the line carved in the car's flank and the rotten fish. It all adds to the sense of driftlessness he has felt since he and Allie split – he is welcome nowhere.

He opens the window and lets cold night air spill into the room, shaking his head a little in a bid to still the free flow of his imagination and properly wake himself, until he is saved by his phone buzzing on the bed. He lunges for it, grateful.

'You're up late.' Shona is clearly still at work.

Cal finds himself whispering, though there is no one in the cottage to hear him. It's the witching hour and he's unnerved himself by dwelling on the strange happenings.

'Can't sleep. It's not as much fun here without you.'

'What I'd give to be there now.' Shona sounds shattered – not just tired, but affected by the work she is doing and the horrors of the past she is helping to uncover.

'Do you want to talk about it? Are you still in the lab?'

'Yes. I sent Cliff home. I was just doing one more thing, but that was…' There's a pause while she checks the time. 'Shit. Three hours ago.'

'Have you eaten?'

'Do Kit Kats count?'

'Shona! No, Kit Kats do not count.'

'Even if you have four?'

'Even then.'

'Really? Damn. Lunchtime then.'

Her humour warms him, even though he is standing, shivering in his pants, in a frigid bedroom miles away.

'You have to promise me that when we hang up in a minute, you'll go home, and you'll eat something and sleep.'

'Promise.'

'I'm worried about you.'

'I know. But it's better if I don't talk about it yet – it's too much to get my head around. I need to just be a scientist for a bit. Microscope, not wide lens.'

'I understand.'

'You haven't told me why *you're* still awake at this stupid time.'

Cal sighs. 'Robbie.'

'What's he doing?'

'Something's wrong. I know that's a stupid thing to say. His mother was shot. But it's like he's spiralling. He's even worse than the night we first met him.'

'Really? That's pretty bad.'

'Every time I see him, he seems to have deteriorated. He's repeating himself, looks so washed out I think he might keel over, just seems agitated.'

'Do you think he's on something?'

'Maybe. He's saying some very strange things about not being needed.'

'That's not good.'

'I think I know what I need to do, but I don't want to do it.'

'Talk to his parents?'

'Yes. It's betraying his confidence but I feel so responsible, like I've come blundering in and messed everything up.'

'Robbie asked you to investigate. He came to you, remember?'

'I know. I just can't work out why he's breaking apart so fast. He knows the investigation will take time. The worst thing is that today I discovered that his mother might have been having a relationship with someone else.'

'Damn.'

'Yeah. Not the ideal thing to have to tell them.'

'You're good at this. You'll find a way.' He presses the phone to his ear and closes his eyes, imagining she's near. 'There's something else, isn't there?'

His words rush into the darkness. 'Is it going to help? Even if I get the answers, is it going to help him? Is it going to help me…?'

'So this isn't just about Robbie and his family?'

Cal tries to laugh but the sound is shaky. 'I'm like a broken record sometimes.'

'You're too hard on yourself.'

'It's frightening. The idea of answers for Robbie *and* for me. He's staking everything on this and I can see how bad that is for him. But then, I've spent my whole life waiting for justice for Margot. How does that make me any different? And even if Barr is charged, is there going to be any peace at the end of it? I don't know what will be left of me if that goes. I won't know how to *be*.'

Her voice is calm and he clings to it. 'You just need to take it one step at a time. You'll build it when the time comes, the new way of living. You will.'

'You're right. I know you are. I don't know what I'd do without you right now.'

'I'm here, whenever you need me.'

He thinks he hears the stifled sound of a yawn. 'Enough counselling me. Right now you need to get home and go to bed,' he says. 'It's late. Too late to be in the lab.'

'Will you be okay?'

'Yes. You've helped. I'm going to speak to the family tomorrow about Robbie and then I'll take it from there. One step at a time. For both of us.'

'Good. You're right. I should leave this tonight. It will still be here in the morning. I can't take away the families' pain by doing it faster. I can see it doesn't work like that. So maybe you're counselling me, too.'

'We're both as bad as each other.'

She chuckles. 'I wouldn't go that far.'

'Shona,' he says. 'I love you.'

There's a pause long enough for him to think: *fuck*. But when she speaks, he can hear the smile in her voice.

'I love you too.'

He stares out at the distant light on the water for a long time after their call, listening to the susurration of the waves and not noticing how cold the air is around him. Back in bed, he pulls the covers over his head and breathes a fug of hot air underneath to warm his limbs. In a few moments, he slides out of consciousness.

CHAPTER TWENTY-EIGHT

WESTER ROSS, SCOTTISH HIGHLANDS

BRYONY, 2007

Angus is early. Bryony, up to her elbows in the sink in a bid to clear up a bit before he comes home, hears the car and thinks she must be mistaken. Her insides are still twisting with pain over her argument with Duncan on the beach. It will be lost tourists turning in the driveway again, or stopping to pose for pictures against the view. But the engine comes closer. She pulls the rubber gloves free and flops them onto the counter. When she walks through to the lounge at the front, she sees the familiar car, and her husband emerging from it. Her heart skips a little with anxiety. Why is he home this early?

Then he leans into the back of the car and lifts out a bouquet of flowers and a carrier bag. He looks light, happy. She watches as he scans the horizon, drinking in their surroundings, then scuttles back to the kitchen, checking out the back to make sure the boys aren't getting into too much trouble. They are chasing each other, locked in a private game.

A few moments later Angus opens the front door and strides down the hallway, so she wipes her hands on a tea towel, bracing herself, pushing down the guilt. He is all smiles.

'These are for you.' He hands the flowers over and scoops her into a hug, planting a kiss on her cheek. For a second they are who they used to be. She pulls back, mystified.

'What have I done to deserve these?'

Does he know?

'It's not something you've done,' he says, scotching the notion. 'We're celebrating.'

'We are?'

'Guess who's just been made partner?!'

'What? Really? But...'

Angus looks the happiest she's ever seen him. She feels an unexpected rush of pleasure.

'Wow,' she manages. 'Congratulations!'

'I know. Youngest partner they've ever had.' He kisses her on the head emphatically. 'Where are the boys? I've got them a present.'

He crosses the kitchen to the back door, beaming with success, giving Bryony a moment to try and work out what this means. Late nights, partner dinners, client drinks and important meetings. This explains why he's been so late so often. He's been working towards partnership. Part of her feels left out of a secret, not consulted on what really is a family decision, or should have been. The hours, the daily strain, the squeeze on quality of life. He's effectively ambushed them.

But the money will be better. A lot better. Maybe that means there are options for her. Maybe this will free her to restart her own career somehow.

Outside, the boys have run to Angus, and he is pulling a toy dumper truck and digger from the bag. She can hear their shouts of delight. Sean bounces up and down, pulling on Angus' sleeve. She watches them, emotions racing through her.

'Have you started cooking?' Angus appears at the back door, face glowing.

'Oh, no, not yet. I was just...'

'Great. I've promised the boys fish and chips.' He turns his head without waiting for her reply. 'Fish and chips it is, boys!'

'Chish and fips, Daddy, I love chish and fips.' Sean bounds towards them, shouting so loud they must hear him down in the village. The arrival of his dad with gifts has infected him with excitement.

Bryony looks beyond and sees Robbie watching her, a careful smile on his face as he waits to see how she reacts. She changes her pensiveness to a smile, presses down the myriad questions sparking inside her.

'Can we eat them on the beeeach? Can we?' Robbie asks, running to Angus.

'Yes!' Angus lifts him and swings him up in the air.

This is what she wants, Bryony thinks, what she has always wanted. Angus to come home and fully participate. The irony of it happening because of partnership is not lost on her. Partnership works when there is a wife at home: supporting, organising, running everything. There are a handful of female partners, too, but the ones Bryony knew either didn't have families, or had husbands or partners willing to take the strain. It nags at her that partnership could create an even greater strain but she pushes the thought to one side, determined to try and be positive for once.

She lets herself get caught up in the excitement, bundling the boys into the car, going back for gloves and scarves in case it's chilly on the beach. Angus is talking about driving to a cove where the water is clear as glass and you can see the spiky black sea urchins clustered on the rocks.

Bryony waits by the car while Angus and the boys go into the shop. Sean wants to choose his chips on an individual level, and Robbie is worrying about whether he will like the batter and if the fish have eyes left in. She doesn't have the patience to deal with it. She folds her arms and looks out at the sea. It doesn't look welcoming tonight. Steel waves whip the beach, cold and harsh. She thinks of Duncan, and her eyes stray to the rocks.

'Bry…!' She hears her name shouted and swivels. Just for a second, life falls away and Angus looks young and handsome, like he used to look to her. 'What do you want?'

She throws her arms out to the sides and bellows back a Sean impression. 'Chish and fips!'

He laughs and bats his hand at her, then darts into the shop. She watches them, her three boys. The same tousled fair hair, Robbie's a little darker than the others'. A moment of satisfaction. Is this what other people feel? All the time? Even some of it?

They drive across the headland and scramble down to the sandy beach. The boys are desperate for their chips so she nestles them in a sheltered spot between rocks and opens up the fat parcels, shows them how to balance them on their laps so they won't fall.

'That's my one, Mummy,' Sean says proudly. 'I choosed the chips.'

'Did you?' she says. 'Clever boy.'

'You can have one of mine if you like, Mummy.' Robbie holds out his parcel, his face serious.

She's going to say no, but then she looks at him being so kind and grown up, and she feels an overwhelming blast of love like she has never felt before. It's like the earth shaking beneath her.

'Thank you,' she says, reaching for one.

Robbie looks at her like Christmas has come and she wants to cry, because this is what some children have from their mothers all the time. He should be able to take it for granted but he can't.

To hide the tears that have sprung to her eyes, she looks for Angus and finds him coming up the beach towards them with an armful of driftwood, his hair blowing in the breeze.

'Let's make a fire!'

He arranges some rocks in a circle and stands the little pieces of kindling up in a pyramid. Bryony screws up some chip paper and passes it to him and, after a couple of goes and some coaxing, the driftwood catches, the bright flare making the rest of the beach seem darker. Twilight is coming and the children's greasy faces and bright eyes shine in the glow of the flames.

'I love 'motion day!!!' Sean shouts suddenly, leaning forward and putting his whole body into the sound, then bursting out laughing at himself.

Robbie giggles beside him. 'Me too!'

'I like promotion day too,' Angus says to Bryony quietly, shuffling next to her so their faces are close. She waits while he searches her features, not sure if he finds what he's looking for, or if he can see that she's lacking and she always will be.

'Well done.' She leans against him, testing the truce between them, feeling like a visitor to a foreign land. Something has been cast away by this break to their routine. They didn't have a holiday last year, stayed home and did jobs instead. She can see that was a mistake.

They haven't had the chance to see each other in new surroundings, to challenge the boys to try new things and watch them thrive. This one moment feels more like a proper break than a whole summer.

Maybe, she allows herself to think as she dips chips in a pool of ketchup and watches Sean and Robbie running around the beach, maybe this will be good for her, too. They could get a nanny or some extra help. She could work part-time at least – until the boys are bigger.

A bright shiny path of possibilities opens up to her.

'I was talking to Morag today,' she says. 'She mentioned we could ask one of the local teenagers to babysit. So we could go out one night.'

She feels shy, like she's asking her own husband on a date and he might say no.

Angus grins. 'I like that idea.'

'She suggested the girl from the farm. She must be sixteen or seventeen and they totally owe us for selling us a house without any insulation.'

'I've had an idea for you, too,' Angus says, nudging her. 'I know you haven't been happy recently.'

Bryony swallows, unable to articulate how much it means that he's noticed, that he cares. 'You have?'

Maybe they are on the same page.

'Yes, let's talk about it when the boys are in bed, though.' He leans in and kisses her, his lips greasy and salty as the sea beside them. For the first time in a long time, Bryony relaxes into the kiss, opening her lips and tasting him. In the firelight and with the waves hushing the shoreline, it's magical.

'Yuck!' Sean and Robbie have run up the beach and are looking at their usually warring parents with a mixture of disgust and fascination. 'Yuck, yuck, yuck, yucky, yuck.'

They pull apart, laughing, and Bryony balls up paper as Angus chases the boys down the sand to the sea. They scream with delight at being chased, until it tips into a mixture of anticipation and hysteria, and he scoops them up, one under each arm, and ploughs into the waves, threatening to drop them in.

She watches him stagger out of the cold water and drop them on the sand. The three of them collapse, laughing, sprayed by salt, the boys incandescent with glee. Sean and Robbie pile on top of Angus.

She walks towards them. It's a shame to break their happiness.

'Come on, time for bed. Angus! You're soaking.'

Robbie is the first to break away and trot up the beach to her. He takes her hand. For once, she doesn't want to pull it back.

Angus puts out the fire and they walk back to the car in the gathering dark. Both boys are flagging now, their eyes heavy. They fall asleep on the short journey home and Bryony watches them in the mirror, awed by their flushed and happy faces. She and Angus carry them to bed, taking off their shoes, coats and trousers, and tucking them under the covers. In the morning, their beds and ears will be full of sand.

Bryony stands and watches them for a moment. Perfect eyelashes closed on red cheeks. She never normally notices these details. Tonight, it's as if someone has brought the world into brighter relief. As she watches, she makes them a silent promise. When she is working again, she will sort herself out. This is the mother they will know. This calm, happy version. She can do that. Be better. She can put herself to the side for those periods of time, knowing she has the space, the work and the meaning that fulfil her.

The boys will have the love and patience they deserve. They'll live in a happy home. She's going to do that for them.

–

When she gets back downstairs, Angus has opened a bottle of wine and started the fire. The frigid living room is warming up and, in this light, it looks cosy and appealing rather than cobwebbed and damp. She'll treasure the illusion.

She holds out her glass, the ruby liquid darker than blood, and toasts him. 'Here's to you.'

They drink and she holds his gaze.

'So, tell me,' she says. 'About your idea. Because I think it might be the same as mine.'

He raises an eyebrow. 'Great minds…'

'Exactly.'

'Well, look.' His face becomes serious and he takes her hand as she settles beside him. 'I know things haven't been easy for you since we moved. Your life has changed a lot more than mine.'

The resistance she's built up to him inside her is crumpling. A log cracks loudly on the fire, sending a cloud of sparks up the chimney.

'Now that my salary is going to be a lot higher, we'll have some extra cash and, if we budget properly, I think we can convert the outbuilding.'

Bryony is so ready to agree – poised to confirm that, yes, she would like to hire a nanny – that she doesn't understand the words she hears.

'The outbuilding?' She's still smiling and curious, drifting on the wave of affection that's built up between them this evening. 'What do you mean?'

Angus is beaming at her, delighted with his idea. Bryony realises the wave is about to crash and all of the happiness drains out of her.

'We can create a two-bed annex, maybe three. This is the perfect area for a bed and breakfast. Now that the boys are at school, you can use the time to build a business.'

Her mouth drops open. This is not what she had in mind at all. More cooking and cleaning? More people to care for?

She lets out a shocked laugh. 'You're kidding.'

Angus frowns. 'No. I thought you'd welcome the challenge.'

'But why would I want to do that? I've never said anything about running a bed and breakfast.'

Her voice is high and wavery, like the boys' get when they're going to cry. She thinks this should be enough of a clue and Angus should heed the warning, but he keeps going, doubling down on madness.

'It would be all yours – something to build and be proud of. I know how important independence is to you.'

She shakes her head, trying to get the words out of her ears, because they are buzzing like flies at her brain.

'What did you think I was going to say?' Angus sits back, his voice betraying the hurt he feels at his wonderful idea meeting a lacklustre reception.

'I thought you were going to say we could get a nanny.'

'A nanny?!' He spits the words. 'For the boys?'

'Yes, for the boys. What do you mean, for the boys?' She wants to stot her head off the wall. Who else would they need a fucking nanny for?

'But. This isn't what we wanted. It isn't what we moved all the way out here for. What I'm working so hard for. For someone else to take care of our children.'

Bryony feels all the resolve inside her liquifying. The little glimpses of contentment she had this evening are vanishing. 'Angus.' She tries to be patient, reaching for his hand, though the emotion is making her voice rise to the beams of the old farmhouse. 'I don't want to run a bed and breakfast. I want to be a lawyer. I *am* a lawyer.'

'You were a lawyer,' he says. 'But…'

'I'm still a lawyer. This work I'm doing for the community is making me remember how much I love being a lawyer.'

'Writing a couple of letters is hardly being a lawyer,' he says. 'Come on, Bryony, be realistic. We chose this life and certain things had to change; we had to make sacrifices.'

'I didn't choose this. I didn't want to give up work forever.'

'Then you should have said something before we left Glasgow and it was too late,' he says, throwing back the blanket covering their knees and rising to his feet. The sound his wine glass makes as he sets it on the coffee table makes Bryony think it will shatter, but it holds, slopping red wine onto the wood.

She watches the liquid soak into the gaps. When she looks up at her husband, he's looking at her with such dislike that it takes her breath away. Immediately, her mind leaps to Duncan, to the clearing in the woods, the shooting lessons and the sense of power she felt then. Not like now, weak and helpless.

'Why do you have to ruin everything?' He hisses the words from above her, running his hand through his hair as if she's driving him mad. She tries to stand, intent on leaving the room, but he shoves her back on the sofa and something inside her clams up in warning and fear. 'Wait. God, Bryony, I'm so sorry. We need to talk about this.

This was a big day for me and I thought the idea was something you'd welcome. It feels like you have to keep making everything about you and what you don't have.'

His voice is pleading and the more he speaks, the more incensed and trapped she feels.

'You run a fucking bed and breakfast, then,' she snarls, throwing up her hands.

Angus' face contorts and before she knows what he is doing, he thumps the sofa arm beside her so hard that it must be agony. She feels the reverberations run the length of her body, sees the intent and the desire in his face: he wishes it was her he was striking instead. She gasps a breath and holds still, afraid to move, not wanting to trigger more anger from this man she thought she knew. This isn't Angus. It's a total stranger. And this isn't her life. It's a nightmare.

He makes an anguished noise then echoes her thoughts, as he backs away from her to the door. 'I don't think I know you at all.'

Her head feels woolly. She's capable of arguing her case, making him see, using reason, isn't she? Why do their conversations always degenerate these days?

He spins and vanishes from the room, then she hears the front door slam and the sound of the car accelerating hard down the driveway. Angus never drives fast along the drive. It makes the potholes worse.

Bryony sits perfectly still. Then the thoughts rush in, bringing the terrible reality of the destroyed evening with them, and she starts to shake. A moment later, she hears movement and a cry above.

'Mummy!' The sharp little sound of Robbie waking from a nightmare.

She lifts the glass to her lips, only now noticing that it has sloshed onto her clothes, the couch, the blankets. Staining everything. She drains what little is left and then she reaches for Angus' glass and knocks that back too, grabbing for the bottle before she is even done with it.

The cries rise higher above her. She forces her neck back and drinks the wine. She drinks and she waits, and she does not go to him. The cries lessen after some time. Bryony remains transfixed – split in two. The kinder, mothering version of her watches in horror as the lost and anxious side wins, pinning her to the couch with its misery.

Which one is real? She doesn't know.

CHAPTER TWENTY-NINE

In the morning, Cal clutches the memory of his call with Shona tight to his chest, amazed when she texts him that it wasn't just a magical dream.

But on the walk to Robbie's house, he tucks thoughts of her to one side and ponders the glimpses of the past that Morag and Duncan have offered: one sliding between then and now, the other clamming up at the difficult questions. One of the problems with reporting on cold cases is that memory dulls and shifts the facts and recollections. Sometimes this works in his favour and people are more willing to reveal information and secrets than they were at the time of an original investigation, but at other times stories become entrenched: an individual's version of the truth reinforced over the years.

The road curves steeply up from sea level and he leans into the incline, feeling the muscles he developed in his hill walks with Shona coming to life once more. There's a cold wind coming off the sea but the exercise warms him, leaving a sheen of sweat on his temples and under his T-shirt.

He'll need to talk to Angus about Duncan. Today, though, the conversation has to be about Robbie and his erratic behaviour in the pub. He's called ahead and Katherine said that she and Angus will be there, but Robbie is working and Sean at school. It's the perfect opportunity to talk to them. He won't continue, he's decided, if it's going to make everything worse for Robbie.

As he turns down the drive flanked with rhododendrons, he sees the step in the distance, remembers Hamish's description of that day. He tries to ignore the voice in his head that tells him it's too late to back out. The boy's distress is so acute that he could be a suicide risk — it's irresponsible to carry on if that's the case.

Katherine told him to go round the back, so he traipses round the side of the house, lifting the latch and ducking to avoid the branches of a sprouting hedge that needs cutting back and is stretching out its arms to touch the walls of the farmhouse. Something rustles inside as he passes — a bird or a rodent perhaps.

He knocks on the back door and Katherine appears, her face pinched with strain. Maybe raising fears about Robbie is unnecessary — she already looks like the weight of the world is on her. Angus rises from the table, looking like he has aged a decade.

'How can we help you?'

Katherine throws her husband a look. 'Cal, come in, would you like a cup of tea?'

'Thanks, that would be great.' He shuts the door behind him, feeling the expectation in the air. 'I wanted to see you without Robbie because I'm a bit worried about him.'

'I told you,' Katherine says to Angus, setting the kettle down. 'He isn't right.'

Cal watches a mixture of worry and impatience cross the man's face.

'He's had these episodes for years. How Tom puts up with it at the pub, I don't know.'

'This feels different, though,' Katherine says. 'Maybe the podcast is too much for him.'

'I don't understand why. This whole thing is his idea. He's got what he wanted. Raking over everything. Bryony's been gone a long time and the rest of us are trying to get on with our lives but he's dragging it all up again.'

Katherine puts a hand on his arm, but Angus shakes her off, crossing the kitchen to the sink, where he fills a glass with water and drains it. She looks crestfallen.

The realisation smacks Cal in the face. He shouldn't be here. This isn't right for anyone. He's going to have to tell Sarah that this series isn't going to work. Despite the element of disappointment he feels, there is relief too. He can walk away: leave the cottage, the sabotage and the dead fish. He could take a detour to see Shona before he drives home, which is where he should be. He'll face Barr and his slick misinformation team, fight Margot's corner with the truth.

'Look,' he says. 'This is not how I normally do things. When I met Robbie, I was led to believe everyone was on board with this. Maybe it's not the best thing to continue with the podcast. We don't have to go ahead. We can stop.'

As he speaks, he sees the relief crossing Angus' and Katherine's faces too – the air in the kitchen seems to lighten. But before anyone can speak, there is a cry from behind them.

'You can't!'

They pivot as one to see Robbie in the doorway. He must have moved like a ghost through the creaking house for them not to have heard him coming. He looks like one too – even paler than when Cal saw him yesterday, the dark shadows beneath his eyes now hollows. As they watch, tears run down his face and he wipes at them with the sleeve of his oversized black jumper.

'You're back early,' Katherine says.

'You can't give up. You can't,' Robbie pleads, looking at Cal. His breathing accelerates.

'He has to!' Angus thunders. 'This isn't helping you.'

Alarmed at the way the boy seems to be rapidly losing control, his breathing heightening, Cal steps forward and takes Robbie's wrists, speaking gently.

'Breathe, Robbie, just breathe. It doesn't mean we can't ever look into it, but this is causing you such distress. Maybe we should take a break for a little while.' He fixes Robbie's gaze. 'Your mental health is more important. Your mother wouldn't want this.'

Robbie shakes his head, moans. 'You don't understand.'

'Then help us,' Angus exclaims, and Cal feels Robbie flinch beneath his touch. The anguish he sees in the boy's eyes spins him backwards in time. Nine years old, his legs swinging under the table, a glass of milk in front of him and his stomach falling as he listens to the police tell his parents that his sister is gone. A moment he will never forget, which lives inside him now. He can see Robbie has it too. The investigation is bringing something out in him – you can almost see the hidden hurt surfacing, like shadows coming up through the water.

'What is it?' Cal says. 'Is there something you aren't you telling us?'

'I can't.' Robbie sobs.

Katherine and Angus remain frozen behind Cal.

'You can. It's okay.'

'It's all my fault. I should have saved her.'

'Robbie, you were only five years old, playing in the back garden.' Katherine finds her voice, though it breaks a little. 'There's nothing you could have done.'

'That's not true. It's not.'

'What do you mean?' Cal is studying Robbie, foreboding spinning inside him.

The boy shakes his head. Opens his lips, closes them.

'What is it you're trying to say?' Angus moans.

'I was there,' Robbie shouts, and the words fall like shattered glass to the floor. 'I was there and I saw her dying.'

Stunned silence hits the room.

Cal waits, horror a tornado building inside him, until the silence is broken by Angus in a hoarse whisper.

'No. You were in the garden. You and Sean didn't see anything. You didn't.'

Angus is now a strange shade of horrified grey. He claps his hand to his mouth, and it looks like he's going to be sick.

'That's not true, Dad. I saw her. And she saw me, too. I used to think it was a dream, but it wasn't; it was real.'

Cal can see the pain that has been building inside Robbie, governing his life, now spilling out. This makes sense to him. It explains why Robbie has never got over his mother's death.

Katherine steps back until she's against the sink and has no further to go, her gaze darting between her husband and stepson, seemingly lost, shock and apprehension on her face.

'But did you… did you…?' Angus flaps his hands in front of him.

'No,' Robbie says miserably. 'I didn't see who it was.' The tears streak down his cheeks.

'Oh God,' Katherine breathes.

Cal waits for Angus to embrace his son. The man lets out a tortured moan. He shakes his head like he's trying to dislodge water from his ears, and takes two steps towards Robbie. Then he stops and presses his hands to his chest.

'I'm sorry,' Angus says, his breath heaving like his son's moments earlier. 'I just need a minute.' And just when he is so close, Angus backs away, grabbing the handle of the door and wrenching it open.

Cal looks at Katherine. She seems so young in the face of this drama, ill-experienced to cope with the competing needs of husband and stepson.

'He didn't mean to,' she says, stepping forward and pulling Robbie into a hug. 'You know he doesn't mean it, Rob.'

Cal has seen this before. In the wake of tragedy not everyone is offered a life raft. Some people are forgotten and they fall through the cracks because the adults in their lives are too preoccupied or grief-stricken to do the right thing for them.

He looks at Robbie, his head resting on Katherine's shoulder. The boy who has grown around the cancer of this secret. He's missed years of therapy, understanding and support. That's the reason he looks like a broken person – he's never had the chance to be whole.

He lifts his head and looks at Cal, red-eyed and desperate.

'Please. You have to help me find out what happened to her.'

Cal's resolution to pack up and leave disintegrates like paper in the rain. How can he leave when there is so much riding on the truth?

'I'll stay, Robbie. Of course I will.'

CHAPTER THIRTY

EPISODE FOUR: WHAT ROBBIE SAW

Robbie Campbell was five years old when his mother was shot. For fourteen years, his family have believed he was safely in the back garden of the family's farmhouse when Bryony was killed on the front doorstep. The police found the boys playing, seemingly unaware that their mother had lost the fight for her life in the driveway.

The awful truth is that Robbie did witness his mother's murder. It's a secret he has kept all this time.

'Tell me about that day, Robbie.'

'Sean and I were playing. I wanted to push him on the swing but he was looking for worms and he didn't want to. Mum used to say Sean was the stubbornest person she knew and, when he'd decided, there was no persuading him. He's still like that now. She was upstairs changing the beds — she'd told us to stay out of the way.'

'It's okay, Robbie, take your time.'

'I just remember Sean singing in this funny little voice he used to do and the smell of the muck on the fields. I went on the swing and I made it go higher and higher until the chains were jerking. I shouted at Sean to look and when he did, I let go and I went flying through the air, then over and over on the grass, doing this ninja roll thing I used to do.'

'That sounds fun.'

'Yeah. It was… I don't think I ever did that, after.'

'And then what happened?'

'I was lying there all dizzy when I heard the bell. It rang for ages, like someone was holding their finger on it, and I wanted to see who it was. There was a space inside the hedge, down the side of the house, and you could crawl along inside it to the front. I… I went down the hedge.'

'Do you want to have a break, Robbie?'

'No, I need to get this out.'

'I understand.'

'Before I got to the front of the house, I heard the door open and then someone was talking but I couldn't hear who. My jumper got caught on a twig and I had to stop and unhook it – it was one Granny knitted for Christmas and it was supposed to go to Sean when I'd finished with it. And then I got it free and Mum shouted.'

'Do you remember what she said?'

'Something like, "You're not supposed to be here." I remember because I thought she meant me. I wasn't allowed in the hedge, and I was supposed to be watching Sean. So I stayed really still, and I was going to say sorry, but then there was this bang and it was so loud and all the birds flew up and I put my hands over my ears and it was so quiet. And I didn't know what it was but I knew something was wrong.'

'What happened then, Robbie?'

'I was so scared. Then there was another bang. When I looked, I could see the gravel on the driveway and it was red like paint. It didn't seem real. I… wet myself and I thought Mum was going to be even more cross with me then, so I curled up. I stayed there too long. If only I hadn't done that.'

'It's not your fault, Robbie.'

'And then I heard her. I kept thinking she was going to come and tell me off but she was just breathing funny, sort of like blowing bubbles in the bath. I didn't know what to do.'

'Robbie, did you see the person who shot your mother? Did you see anyone else there?'

'No. I was too scared to look. After ages, I peeked. I saw her foot and her toes were moving. I didn't understand. So I crawled forward and... she was lying there and it was all so... Sorry, I just...'

'I know. Take your time.'

'She saw me and she said something and I couldn't tell what she was saying and I was going to go out to her but... But then I heard Sean calling my name and he was on his own in the back and I was supposed to be looking after him, and I could hear him coming to the hedge – his wellies made this clumpy sound when he ran, and I didn't know why but I didn't want Sean to see.'

'Robbie, you understand that this wasn't your fault, don't you? That you were five years old and there was nothing you could have done to help?'

'I think I know what she was saying now. I think she was saying my name. I can hear her voice when I go to sleep. She needed me and I ran away.'

CHAPTER THIRTY-ONE

Cal makes it a condition of continuing with the podcast that Robbie seeks help. He still has misgivings but the first episodes have gone out and Robbie is so distraught at the idea of him stopping that he allows himself to be persuaded. He still hasn't mentioned the information he has about Bryony and Duncan, and the secrecy makes him uncomfortable. He arranges to meet Angus for a walk, hoping that getting out of the farmhouse will help him open up.

Cal passes Sean on his way down the drive, walking with his backpack slung over one shoulder and his hair in his eyes. The boy just scowls and grunts hello, not slowing his pace. Cal almost laughs at how surly and uncommunicative he is – he's never had a teenage boy of his own but this one seems to fit the stereotype. It makes him feel sad, though, thinking of the pictures Katherine has shown him of a chubby toddler with a beaming smile. How much of the change is down to what happened to Bryony?

Angus is waiting for him at the front of the house, wearing muddy wellingtons and a weathered coat, a stick in his hand. Far from opening up, he looks desperately uncomfortable as he gestures to a stile by the side of the property that takes them up and over a small hill. Cal's heart sinks, but he falls into step behind him.

'How is Robbie doing?'

'Not great. But he's been to the GP, as promised. They're referring him for counselling and he has some pills to take.' Angus sighs. 'I just don't understand him. Sometimes he is so like his mother that it frightens me.'

'He's been bottling up his feelings for a long time. I'm sure he'll improve now that he's let some of it out.'

The man is silent and Cal wonders if he's at all reassured. He finds it so hard to break through the armour that Angus has constructed around himself. There's no way to tell if he was always like this or has developed it in reaction to what happened to Bryony.

'I haven't asked you,' he says eventually. 'Do you have a theory about what happened that day?' Angus glances at him. 'You must have thought about it more than anyone.'

'I've always wondered about the man Bryony used to work for in Glasgow. I told the police and they said they looked into it, but…' He shrugs.

Cal remembers mention of him in the file the police shared. 'Sal Ellis? The property developer?'

'That's the one. Though property development was the respectable front for a crime franchise. I hated that Bryony worked for him. It was something we argued about before we relocated here. And after. She had this crazy idea that she could commute to Glasgow and work part-time for him.'

'Did she fall out with him over it?'

'Not that I know. But I've always thought it has to have been someone with easy access to guns. He was notorious. He'd easily be able to pull a stunt like that.'

'I'll look into it,' Cal tells him. 'But on the subject of access to guns, someone mentioned to me that Bryony was friends with a man called Duncan?'

They've reached the brow of the hill. Cal is invigorated by the climb, enjoying his new-found fitness, but Angus is sweating and breathing heavily. He wonders if the man ever enjoys the hills and countryside around him or if familiarity has made the backdrop invisible.

'Duncan? We don't know a Duncan.'

He sounds dismissive, quick to discount, like he's heard every theory under the sun.

'He's the Laird of Rillgowan,' Cal says, pointing over in the direction of the hills where the estate lies. He studies Angus' expression, watching the frown that is never far from his face re-form. 'She never mentioned him? Maybe in connection with the footpath right of way she was fighting?'

Angus shakes his head. 'Never.'

'Do you know what Bryony did while you were at work during the day?'

The man seems to prickle, his body language changing, and Cal steels himself for hostility. 'What are you saying?'

'People in the village say Bryony didn't really spend much time down there. That she was usually off walking in the hills while the boys were at school. I wondered if she met him on her walks, perhaps.'

He tries to be gentle, but he can see Angus recalibrating his relationship with his first wife, waves of anger and confusion crossing his face.

'So, are you saying...'

'I don't know,' Cal says quickly. 'I have nothing concrete. But he runs shooting holidays from the estate and has a large supply of guns. It just made me wonder. Maybe he developed a fixation of some kind.'

Angus looks at the ground. When he speaks, his voice sounds thick. 'Have you spoken to him? What did he say?'

'He wasn't very helpful. I wanted to speak to you next because I know this might raise questions about the nature of their relationship and I don't know how Robbie is going to react when we cover it on the podcast. Sean, too.'

Angus is silent for long minutes. When he looks up, Cal watches the ripples on his face as the thoughts twist inside him.

'I guess you have to feature it,' he says eventually. The words are slow, forced. 'If you're doing this properly.'

'I'm sorry. I know this is hard.'

'How do you do it?' The words burst out of him. 'With your sister? Their death always hanging over you, tarnishing everything. Sometimes I think Bryony ruined my life back then and that she keeps doing it, over and over again.'

Cal doesn't know what to say to this. He has never thought that Margot ruined his life, only that someone else ruined hers.

'Do you think it's possible,' he says, avoiding the question, 'that Bryony met him on a walk and didn't mention it to you?'

Angus takes a moment to answer, and when he speaks, his voice is heavy with resignation.

'Honestly, when it comes to Bryony, anything is possible.'

CHAPTER THIRTY-TWO

He needs to try Duncan again, Cal decides. He can't allow himself to be fobbed off. If he is going to juxtapose the suggestion that the Laird and Bryony had some sort of affair with mention of the arsenal of guns the man has on his estate, every word will have to be carefully weighed and calculated.

In the morning, he calls his mother and has a stilted two-minute conversation before she claims she has to go because she has something on the hob. The call sits heavily on him as he drives along the single-track road to Rillgowan once more, slowing for camper vans and ambling sheep. Expecting the same reception, he starts his microphone and braces himself for another unpleasant conversation.

But the man he meets today seems deflated in comparison to his previous open aggression.

'You again,' he says when he opens the door and sees Cal on the step, his air one of resignation rather than hostility. 'I told you I didn't want to speak to you.'

'I know. But her family need answers.'

'You aren't going to find them here.'

'If that's true, then what's the harm in speaking to me?'

Duncan makes a sound of frustration. Cal waits, while the man deliberates.

'Come in, then.'

Cal follows him through a neat boot room lined with wellies and jackets. It's pristine and cared for, not what he expected at all.

'No one ever brings the right gear,' Duncan says shortly when he sees him looking.

In the kitchen, copper pots hang above a vast range, and expensive handmade pottery is displayed in a large dresser. Through the door, Cal spots the dogs flopped in beds beside a vast fireplace, grand enough for four people to stand in.

'This is impressive.'

'It's all for the guests. They expect the best.' He gestures to the table. 'Please, sit.'

Cal pulls back a chair. 'Do you mind if I record this?'

'I have nothing to hide.'

'So you admit that you knew Bryony, then?'

Duncan waits for a moment, seemingly engaged in internal calculations. 'Aye. I did. But it wasn't common knowledge, far as I know. Who told you?'

'Someone saw you arguing on the shore…'

A look of annoyance crosses his face. 'Nothing goes by anyone here.'

'You didn't come forward when she died.'

The eyes that meet Cal's are edged with pain but defiant. 'I didn't think it would be helpful to the family.'

Who's to say what's right, in the end? Assuming he is innocent, Cal can see his point, but at the same time the frustration of victims' families burns through him. When people keep secrets, it's so much harder to find your way to the truth. He thinks of Andy, his sister's boyfriend – the years of deceit – and wonders if there are others keeping pieces of the jigsaw from him. The truth is more that they keep these secrets to protect themselves.

'So how did you two meet?'

Duncan sits back in his chair. 'Up on the hill one day. She was walking. We got chatting.'

'Where did you see each other when you met? How often?'

'Usually once, twice a week up on the hills between here and there. She used to go walking while the boys were at school. Rain or shine. If I was over that way we'd share a coffee, just sit together for a bit...'

'Tell me about your relationship.'

Duncan looks pissed off. 'We didn't have a *relationship*.'

'I think you know what I mean.'

Duncan's gaze fixes on a distant point. 'We were friends, that's it.'

'Nothing more?'

'No.'

'So why did the person I spoke to think it was something else?'

The man looks uncomfortable but Cal waits it out. 'I kissed her once. That day on the beach. But she shoved me away.'

'And were you upset about that?'

'Of course I bloody was,' Duncan explodes. 'But I didn't kill her, if that's what you're asking.'

This ability to switch between calm and fury is startling. He can imagine that Duncan snapped and did something rash back then, no matter what he says. Beneath it all, he thinks Duncan is cut up about Bryony's death. But he's been fooled before. Since Layla's case, and the mistakes he made, he's found it harder to trust people, and to trust his own judgement.

Cal thinks of what Morag also told him about the land dispute, and what he has learned about Bryony's role in the community pushback against footpath closure. He tries a different tack.

'There was a dispute back then, over access across your land. Was that an issue between you?'

'I think you know that it was, otherwise you wouldn't be asking.'

Duncan lapses into silence.

'Bryony isn't here to tell us, Duncan. You're the only one who can shed light on this. It matters to her son.'

He sighs. 'Yes, we argued about it. I was angry with her because I thought she hadn't been honest about helping the committee. But I was being an arse. She didn't know I was Laird, so she didn't know it was me she was fighting. I let her think I was just managing the estate.'

'Why?'

He shrugs. 'Just didn't want to be loaded with the assumptions people make when they know.'

'How did she feel when she found out?'

'She was angry with me. We argued. We didn't make up before she died.' The man's eyes are distant again and Cal can tell he's reliving it, by the way his words fade out for a moment.

'And you reopened the path? After she died?'

Duncan studies Cal. 'She was right, what she said about it.'

'What did you think when you heard about the shooting?'

He looks at his hands for a moment before speaking. 'She said things, a couple of times, that made me think she wasn't okay. I should have done something. I've always regretted not pushing her to talk about it. When I heard...' He shudders. 'At first all that was said was that a woman had died of a gunshot wound. So, I assumed...'

211

'That she'd done it to herself.'

'Yes.' He looks pale at the memory, and Cal is struck by how affected he still seems. 'I thought it was all my fault.'

'Really? Why would you think that?'

'Well, for one, I taught her to shoot.'

Cal stares. 'Bryony knew how to shoot?' This isn't something Angus or Robbie has mentioned.

'Aye, she did. She was a good shot and all.'

Cal's mind freefalls. 'Did she have access to your guns? Is that how you thought she'd hurt herself? Is that why you didn't come forward?'

Duncan looks uncomfortable at the memory. 'I went out to the gun shed that night, and checked and rechecked, and they were all there, I'm sure they were.'

'You don't sound sure.'

'She'd been here that week, that was all. I'm almost 100 per cent certain.'

Almost.

'Why didn't you come forward and tell someone?'

'I was going to, but then they said it was murder and I knew that if it was my gun I'd lose my licence, lose the income, the estate. I couldn't do it. I was lost back then, just like Bryony.'

The words burst out of him so fast that Cal can see he is giving away more than he intended.

'What do you mean?'

'She was like a shadow,' Duncan says. 'It was like she'd forgotten how to smile. I think she was ill. Struggling with the move here.'

'And you?'

He grimaces. 'You must have heard the gossip.'

Cal shakes his head.

'I moved here with my wife and son,' he says. 'We were going to run this place together.' He looks around as if only now seeing the house properly.

'And what happened?'

'They died. In a crash on the A82. He was killed instantly. She was cut from the wreckage and airlifted to Aberdeen. She was gone by the time I got there.'

'I'm sorry.'

'It was a long time ago. Twenty-six years, now.'

'Did you ever...'

'Find anyone else? No. There was only one woman who ever came close.'

From the way Duncan looks at Cal, he knows they're talking about Bryony again. He finds it hard to encapsulate the loss in his mind. The way it must have compounded, hollowed him out.

'You need to go,' Duncan tells him, standing. 'There are no answers for you here.'

Cal follows his lead, pushing back the chair. 'Before I go, do you have any theories, about what might have happened to her?'

'Only the obvious one.'

'Which is?'

Duncan shrugs. 'It's always the husband, isn't it?'

'Angus has an alibi for that day.'

'I don't know then,' he says, shortly. 'Is that all you need? I've got things to do. A load of guests are arriving tomorrow.'

'Just one more thing,' he says, watching the craggy features for a tell. 'Where were you? The day she died?'

'I was here,' he says. 'Alone.'

CHAPTER THIRTY-THREE

Cal slips out of the cottage early, dawn only just cracking the eastern sky. The hills crowd between him and the day, great hulking shadows blocking out the light. It's cold and he zips his coat to his neck, tucking his hands in his pockets as he walks to the car. He woke easily this morning, excited by the prospect of seeing Chrissie.

The roads are empty and easy to coast along. He makes it to Loch Leven and stops for a fry-up and a pot of coffee, before calling Shona to say good morning.

'Today's the day? Chrissie still coming?'

'Yes. I can't wait to see her.'

'Are you sure it's okay for me to come this weekend? I don't mind delaying to give you two more time on your own.'

'I've talked to her and she wants to see you. She has college work to do so she's going to need to get her head down. Said something about me not getting in her way.'

Shona laughs. 'Okay, well if anything changes just let me know.'

'I heard from Foulds last night as well.'

'Oh?'

'Nothing concrete, but they've cleared the rest of the scrapyard. Margot's is the only body there. Now we need to wait for forensics.'

'They'll do everything they can,' Shona reassures him. 'It might just take time.'

Time. Always time. But picturing someone like Shona working hard to find evidence helps him.

Cal makes it into Glasgow with a stream of commuters. He strolls down Buchanan Street, whiling away the time he has until he's supposed to meet his friend Mark for coffee. He's drawn by the way the city's majestic Victorian buildings jostle with modern architecture, the buzz of people in the street shopping or heading for work, the friendliness. When he pauses on a street corner, it isn't long before he gets an *are you lost, pal?* He must have tourist written all over him. He thanks his would-be saviour and, when he checks his watch, sees he's been idling too long and has to hustle to meet Mark. It's been several years since they worked on a documentary together but they've kept in touch sporadically.

'Looking good,' Mark says as they backslap and pull out stools to sit at a corner table.

'It's all the walking I've been doing,' he says. 'Though the pub meals are getting to be a bit of a bad habit.'

'You are working on the Gulduigan shooting, then? The rumours are true?'

'Yes. I was supposed to be on holiday but kind of got sucked in. Stuff wasn't great at home, so…'

'I'm sorry, mate,' Mark says, looking curiously at him. 'All that time working together and I never knew about your sister. Felt like I'd missed the memo when I saw the papers.'

'Sorry,' Cal says, knowing that many of the people he's worked with over the years have felt wrong-footed by the news that his sister was Margot Longacre, worrying about what they might have said to him that was unintentionally insensitive. 'It wasn't something I ever shared with anyone, to be honest.'

'No worries.'

'How are the kids?'

'Growing like weeds. They're ten and twelve now, would you believe?'

Cal remembers Mark turning to him for advice when they worked together – his children were babies then, younger than Chrissie by a few years.

'So, what can I help you with?' Mark says when their coffees arrive at the table. 'It's related to the investigation, I'm guessing.'

'Yeah. One of the angles I'm looking at is someone Bryony used to work for. Sal Ellis.'

Mark gives a long whistle.

'So you know the name?'

'Everyone in Glasgow knows the name. The guy's father worked with the Krays.'

'The husband seems to think she was trying to get back in with him when she died. He has this theory that Sal was someone with hired help and ready access to guns.'

'Well, he's got that right.'

'Can you help put me in touch with anyone who might talk?'

Mark sucks his teeth. 'You don't half ask for favours…' For a second, Cal thinks he'll refuse. 'I can ask around. Can't promise anything, though.'

'It would be appreciated.'

'I assume this is off the record for now.'

Cal laughs. 'Yes, but the story's yours first when the time comes.'

'Deal.'

Mark has to get back to the office, so Cal wanders the streets, curious to see where Bryony and Angus used to work. He can't find Bryony's firm but easily finds the law firm Angus used to work for, where Bryony also started her career. A gleaming golden plaque attached to the railing announcing the names of the partners. One of them – *N. J. Broadland* – sounds familiar. Then he realises it is the name of the solicitor who gave Angus his alibi all those years ago.

He glances at his watch. Still an hour until Chrissie's train comes in. Drawn by curiosity, he mounts the steps and rings the polished bell.

The secretary at the desk is nonplussed about the lack of an appointment.

'I can make you one for next week.' She starts scrolling on her computer.

'Well, the thing is, I'm only in Glasgow today, so it was just on the off chance…'

'What was this regarding?'

'I'm making a podcast.' Cal fishes for a business card. 'Have you heard of the Gulduigan shooting?'

Recognition springs to her face. 'Such a sad case. Those poor wee boys.'

'Well, Nadia worked with their father back then and I'm just following up on things. It would be so great to have a quick chat. It wouldn't take long.'

'She's very busy.'

'Could we just ask her, maybe?'

He gives the woman his most wheedling smile, and she relents and lifts the phone. He watches as she explains who he is and why he's here. She looks up at him once or twice, but he can't read from her expression which way it's going.

The secretary hangs up the phone. 'She says no.'

Cal sags. 'No chance it's worth trying again?'

The woman shakes her head.

Frustrated, he leaves the building and takes the steps slowly. Why has Nadia refused to see him? It wasn't as if she offered him a call instead, or an appointment on another day. It was just a flat no. Isn't that a little strange?

He's hovering between the last step and the pavement, pondering, when his phone beeps.

> Train held at red signal. There's something
> on the track that they're trying to clear.
> Sorry.

So he has time to kill.

There's a cafe just down the street so he orders a coffee and a croissant, then chooses one of the stools in the window. His eye is repeatedly drawn to the solicitors' office in the distance. He didn't really want to see Nadia Broadland that much before, but he does now.

Cal opens the browser on his phone and googles the practice. The *About Us* tab has little black-and-white photographs of each of the partners. He studies the image of Nadia: polished and professional, with dark gleaming curls and a pearl necklace. Then he sits and waits. Until Chrissie's train is moving again, he has nowhere else to be.

Any kind of surveillance is boring enough to make your eyes water. He spends an hour and a half staring at the steps and moving to alert every time the door opens. As it gets closer to lunchtime, the street fills up with people leaving their offices, seeking fresh air and sandwiches, so he has to pay more attention and fix his gaze past the crowds. He's worried she isn't going to take a lunch break, or he's somehow missed her, when a woman with dark curls steps from the building and clips down the steps, her camel-coloured coat swinging. When she reaches the pavement, she turns away from him, sidestepping a group of students and setting off down the street.

Cal leaps from his chair, grabbing his bag and charging down the road after her. He's terrified he's going to lose her in the crowds, but her hair is distinctive and his practice following Barr has paid off. He's soon twenty metres behind, keeping her in comfortable sight. After five minutes, Nadia pauses outside an exclusive-looking Italian delicatessen and Cal takes a breath.

'Nadia?'

She pivots and he steps back, smiling, trying to look as unthreatening as possible. She frowns, clearly trying to place him and failing.

'I recognised you from your picture online,' he says. 'I'm Cal Lovett. I popped into the office this morning.'

Her face shutters.

'I'm sorry,' he jumps in. 'I know you're busy but I wondered if I might be able to talk to you while you queue?' He gestures at the short line in front of them. 'I'll buy your sandwich, and when they've made it, you can go back to your office and I'll go on my way, and you won't have wasted any time.'

Nadia's features twist. She's clearly trying to think of a way to say no but can't come up with anything reasonable.

'I don't know...'

'I just wanted to have a quick chat, to be honest. I'm trying to help Angus and his sons…'

Her face softens at the mention of Angus. 'How is he?'

'You don't keep in touch?'

She looks younger, less sure of herself, as she shakes her head and glances down at her feet. 'Not these days, no.'

'He's doing okay. He's remarried now, of course.' Cal sees the tiniest wince of regret on her face and his senses heighten. 'His older son, Robbie, isn't doing so well.'

'I'm sorry. What happened was just… horrible.'

'I'm here in Glasgow looking into some of Bryony's work connections,' he confides, feeling his phone vibrate in his pocket, anxious at how quickly the queue is moving, cursing the deli workers for their efficiency. 'Did you ever have much to do with her work-wise?'

'No,' Nadia says. 'We never even met. She'd left our firm by the time I joined.'

'But you worked with Angus?'

They step forward another foot and he tries to make their conversation feel like innocuous small talk.

'Yes.' She smiles and, from the wistfulness, he can tell she had feelings for him. 'He was my mentor.' What is it with Angus and women, he wonders, experiencing a feeling of incredulity at the way they seem to admire the man, when to Cal he seems like a fairly normal bloke. Maybe it's the flip side of the Barr effect, he realises. Tragic widower versus dangerous convict.

'And he was with you when Bryony was shot.'

Nadia grimaces at his statement, ever so slightly, but at that exact moment, the man behind the counter interrupts by leaning across to take their order. She rattles off something containing pastrami, and Cal nods and asks for the same, his mind working away at the implication of her reaction. He takes the ticket when it's handed over. Thankfully, they now have to queue for the till.

'You *were* with him that day?'

'I told the police I was,' she says. He notes the failure to answer the real question, a lawyer's solution to the problem. Don't lie. 'We were working on a client's account – they had the auditors in and it was all a bit of a mess. Not our mess, I hasten to add, we'd taken it over from another firm…'

She's garbling, her face flushed and her body language uneasy, directing him away from his original question.

'Nadia,' he says. 'Is there something you aren't telling me?'

The buzz and clatter of the shop fades away and he focuses only on her. She looks, suddenly, as if she's going to cry.

'I'm a solicitor,' she says. 'If it were found that something I said wasn't… quite right, then I could lose my job.'

Cal knows he needs to tread carefully. 'A woman was shot. One of her sons saw her bleeding on the drive. He's nineteen now and he still isn't okay. The most important thing here is that we get to the truth. You know that. I can see you know that.'

The man at the till calls them forward and Cal scrabbles in his pocket for his bank card, taps the reader and accepts the sandwiches. He takes them outside and Nadia follows him, her head drooping, her hands twisting together. He holds out one of the packages.

'Are you going to expose me?'

He shakes his head. 'Not if I can avoid it.' She chews her lip, fighting a losing battle with tears. 'Maybe it isn't important, but maybe it is.'

'I've told myself for years that it didn't matter,' she says. 'That no one would ever know anyway. I was just making things easier for Angus, and he was grieving and I felt so sorry for him. And… well, I looked up to him, you know? A lot.'

She meets Cal's eyes and he knows what she's confessing, what she's trying to tell him without humiliating herself. So he nods.

'I understand. Honestly, I do.'

'I wasn't with him,' she says in a rush. 'He looked awful, said he wasn't feeling well and he needed to get some air, and would I mind not telling anyone he'd gone early.'

'And so he left at what time?'

'It was early, not long after we arrived.'

Cal feels a spark of thought bursting inside his skull. Bryony was shot dead in the morning. He needs to check the exact details of the journey from the client's office to the farmhouse, but he has the horrible feeling that this puts Angus in the unlikely, rather than impossible, category. Everything inside him switches.

'Nadia,' he asks, unsure why it's so important for him to know. 'Did anything ever happen between you and Angus? I'm sorry to ask.'

She flushes and looks away from him, down the street in the direction of her office so that he thinks he's about to lose her.

'A kiss,' she says. 'Just once, when we were working late. He regretted it. Said we had to be careful it never happened again. He'd just been made partner and…' She makes a noise of frustration in the back of her throat. 'Look, I have to go. Angus couldn't have done this. There's no way.'

'Thank you, Nadia. I appreciate you telling me.'

Cal feels desperately sorry for her. If this ends up mattering, he's going to have to tell the police and Nadia may no longer have a career.

She fades from view in the crowds, which are parting around him like he's a rock in a stream. Angus. Could he have killed his wife? All this time, have the grief and confusion been nothing more than an elaborate charade? How would Robbie and Sean ever cope if they lost their father too? What has he got himself into?

He dimly registers that his phone is ringing in his pocket again. Chrissie. He fumbles with the handset in his eagerness to answer.

'Chris, so sorry.'

Her voice is both patient and unamused. 'Dad, where are you? I've been at Glasgow Central for ten minutes now. Did you go to the wrong station?'

'Shit, I'm so sorry. I'll explain it all in a minute, coming now,' he tells her, setting off at a run in the direction of the station. 'Meet you out front.'

Cal sprints up the road, ducking around cars and people, his heart thudding in his chest. The lunchtime rush is not the best time for speed, but he pelts as fast as he can to the station's gleaming glass frontage, where his daughter is standing with a bag slung over her shoulder and another on the floor by her feet, her red curls instantly recognisable, marking her out as his own.

He speeds towards her, and she looks up and bursts out laughing as he hams up the desperate run and throws his arms wide.

'Chrissie.'

She's in his arms, and she feels well and healthy – he can tell from the way she's no longer skin and bones, like she was last year. He squeezes her tight.

'Oh my God, Dad,' she says, her cheeks pink. 'You are such an embarrassment.'

CHAPTER THIRTY-FOUR

'I forgive you.'

'You do?'

'If there is cake. I forgive you only if there is cake.'

He grabs her bag and holds his arm out for her to take. 'Come on. I'll buy you the biggest, stickiest bit of cake we can find.'

Over cups of tea and massive wedges of coffee and walnut cake, Cal marvels at how much more grown-up Chrissie seems since she's started sixth-form college. She used to try and tame her curls, making her red hair smaller and flatter, as if trying to minimise herself or apologise for the space she was taking up. Now it's piled extravagantly on the top of her head, her eyes are bright and she's sitting taller. She's found her tribe and her wings – and what's even more astounding to him is that it doesn't hurt like he thought it might.

She arches a brow as she registers him watching her. 'What?'

'Nothing! Just glad you're here. I've missed you.'

'Thanks, Dad. I've missed you too.'

'How's Mum?'

She darts a look at him, worry seeping into her expression.

'Don't look so worried – genuinely asking with no agenda.'

'She's good. She's…'

'What?'

'I don't know if I should tell you, but it feels weird not to.'

He waits, not wanting to tell her what to do.

'She's seeing someone.'

Cal makes sure the smile on his face stays in place. 'That's okay. It's better than okay.' He wonders if it's the man whom he saw her kissing all those months ago.

Chrissie tilts her head. 'Really?'

'Yes, she deserves to be happy.'

Underneath the facade, he examines his reactions and finds that he actually means it. It's like pressing on an old wound and checking whether it stings. It doesn't still hurt, does it? He doesn't think it does, or at least not in a life-threatening way; it's more bittersweet and aching.

'Are *you* okay about it, though?'

She nods. 'I think so. She's sort of keeping him separate. For now. It's weird, though.'

'It *is* weird. I think it's normal that it is.'

'Yeah. I sort of wanted to ask you…'

'About Shona?'

'Yes. It's more than friendship, isn't it?'

'It is now,' he says. 'But it wasn't then, not before Mum and I split up. Honestly.'

She nods, toys with her fork, shredding bits of the cake into crumbs.

'If you'd rather she didn't come and stay this weekend, she won't,' he tells her. 'My priority is seeing you.'

'I think I'd like to see her again. After Aberdeen. If she hadn't done what she did, I wouldn't be here.'

They're both silent a moment and Cal reaches for her hand. That day was the worst of his life.

He clears his throat. 'On the subject of relationships…'

Chrissie rolls her eyes. 'Dad, you aren't allowed to ask.'

'Why not? I'm curious. I just kind of got the impression there was a… someone on the scene? Is he… or she still around?'

She shakes her head and sighs. '*He* was becoming a bit full-on. I'm just not really up for anything serious, so I've told him it's better if we're friends.'

Cal studies her face, knowing the last boy she rejected acted despicably in the aftermath. 'And how's he taken that?'

'Pretty well.' She stabs her cake with her fork. 'It's not like before.'

'Well, that's good.'

'Change the subject,' she says, through a mouthful of cake.

He laughs. 'We'd better get on the road. I'll fill you in on the way.'

They drive out of the city and into the hills, skirting Loch Lomond's shining waters as they head north. Cal talks Chrissie through the progress he's made. Summarising it for her helps him take stock: the secret Robbie kept, the hidden relationship Bryony had with the Laird, her work for a notorious gangster, her husband's alibi, her mental state.

'So the gun could have come from the Laird's store, or he could even be the shooter?'

'Yes.'

'Or it's a hit ordered by a Glasgow kingpin?'

'That's a theory. Or maybe she was never the intended victim at all.'

'Or it was the husband.'

'Yes,' he agrees, his heart heavy at the thought. 'Or it was the husband.'

'So, not many options then…'

He sighs. 'Just a few.'

They lapse into silence and Cal finds himself running through next moves, frustrated that everything he does just seems to open, rather than narrow, the options. Despite his dislike for the man, he is desperate for it not to be Angus, because he doesn't want to lob that grenade into the family. But maybe deep down Robbie knows that the culprit is his father, and that's the source of his distress.

They stop briefly to stretch their legs and take photographs, arriving in the village at the end of the day. It's cold, but the sun is shining as it sinks, and the tide is in, wavelets kissing the shore. Chrissie runs down to the water's edge and he watches her skimming stones, contentment spreading through him.

'It's beautiful,' she says, laughing as she scrambles back up to him, her jeans spattered with sea water and her cheeks flushed.

'Come on, I'll show you where we're staying.'

Chrissie coos over the mint-coloured cottage, with its thick walls and salt-stained windows. They set her up in the twin back bedroom, where a desk overlooks the hills.

Cal leaves her to unpack. As he waits for the kettle to boil, his phone beeps. Mark has worked quickly.

I have someone who will talk to you. An intermediary. Shall I set it up?

He fires off a reply.

> Yes! Thanks, Mark. I owe you.

> You really do.

All he can do, he realises, standing at the window, watching the waves and listening to his daughter humming upstairs as she arranges her sketchbooks, is follow the trail where it leads. It isn't up to him to make the facts anything other than they are. Deep down, he knows that. It's just that when you are alone in an investigation, you start to feel like you are one of the subjects.

An hour later, he extracts Chrissie from the deep windowsill in the living room, where she is sitting cross-legged, sketching the motion of the waves. He guides her to the pub, relishing her effervescence in what is usually a quiet and lonely time of his day.

The blast of heat knocks him sideways as they shuffle into an unusually packed bar. Down one end of the room are crowded tables. He pushes a path through.

'Quiz night,' Tom shouts to his bemused face. 'We do it once a month.'

Cal gives him a thumbs up.

'I've got my daughter here – Chrissie, this is Tom.'

'Good to meet you.' Tom waves and then pours Cal a pint and Chrissie a lime and soda. 'It's quiet in the back bar. You eating?'

'Yes.' Cal grabs a menu for Chrissie's benefit. He knows it by heart now.

'Go through; we'll come and take your order in a bit.'

They settle at a table, listening to the quizmaster calling out questions, accompanied by a mixture of general grumbling and intense heckling.

'I was wondering something,' Chrissie says as he sips his pint. 'About Auntie Margot.'

Cal stills. He's been trying not to think about her. Not to look at what the trolls online say: the ridiculous conspiracy theories and abuse.

'I know things aren't good now, Dad. But they found her. After all this time. And that's something.'

He tries to smile at her and she carries on. 'I think it's worth marking somehow.'

'We aren't allowed a funeral yet, love.' The words come out sounding wooden, all of the emotion leached out of them.

'What about a memorial, then? In the meantime.'

They are interrupted by Tom dashing over to take their order and Cal thinks maybe he's escaped this grilling for now. He does want a memorial, but he wants it to be fitting, to be well attended – for love to sweep through it, not division and hatred, which is all that seems to have landed since Margot's bones were taken from the earth. He wants to celebrate his sister, yes, but any tribute needs to be perfect. He has had most of his life to prepare for this but he still isn't ready.

Chrissie is looking at him expectantly. He swallows. 'I don't know. I like the idea but… it's a bit overwhelming, if I'm honest. Your gran and I aren't really speaking at the moment, and her friends…' Here he has to bite back tears. 'I wouldn't know where to begin finding them.'

'That's what I'm trying to suggest, though, Dad. Why don't you leave it to me? I could arrange something.'

Cal's instinct is to laugh off the suggestion but he sees that she is utterly serious. 'How would you…'

She shrugs, enveloped in an oversized jumper. With her hair up and her glasses on, she looks so confident and calm. 'Don't worry about that. That's my problem.'

'I couldn't ask you to do this.'

'You're not asking. I'm asking, and I'd love to do it. I never met her and this would be my way of doing that, sort of. That doesn't make sense. Maybe I'm not explaining it well.'

'No, you are.'

'It would mean a lot if you trusted me to do this, Dad.'

'Of course I trust you, that's not my reservation at all.' What is the hesitation? Cal can't even properly articulate it to himself. 'Can I think about it?'

'I guess so.' She rolls her eyes at him and they are saved from further conversation by the simultaneous arrival of their food and some loud boos from the front bar. Tom sighs as he sets down the ketchup and a box with cutlery.

'The Mad-eyed Dancers have won again. It's going to be a bad night.'

'They win a lot?' Chrissie bites into a hot chip and the steam spirals from it.

'That's three years now. Undefeated. We keep hoping, but they take it very seriously.'

–

The bar is bustling and they fall into comfortable chatter about the work Chrissie has to do and her friends at college. Cal feels the squeeze around his heart that accompanies discussion of Margot loosening, his anxiety unwinding a little as he drinks a second pint and Chrissie tackles a chocolate brownie dripping with sticky toffee sauce.

He's just about to suggest that they leave, when a familiar face appears to clear the table.

'Robbie!' Cal is pleased to see the kid looking a little better than the last time he saw him. His face is still pinched but no longer grey; his eyes are tired but not bloodshot.

'Are you finished?' Robbie's eyes dart to Chrissie and then back to Cal.

'Yes, but let me introduce you to my daughter, Chrissie.' He touches her arm. 'Chris, this is Robbie. His mum is the lady I'm making the podcast about.'

Robbie's eyes widen at the mention of Bryony and Cal feels bad for being so bold in his introduction, but Chrissie doesn't let a beat pass.

'I'm so sorry about your mum,' she says. He ducks his head, blushing, but Cal is surprised to see that he raises his eyes and thanks her. He's sure the Robbie of a few weeks ago would have scuttled away. Maybe he's not giving him enough credit.

'Chrissie's here for her half-term and reading week,' he says, moving the conversation on. 'She's going to be studying hard.'

'Not all the time, Dad,' she groans. 'I need to find some good places to draw the sea while I'm here, too. I have an idea for a project.' She looks up at Robbie. 'Are there any sandy coves nearby, or are they all rocky?'

'There's a mixture,' he stammers, astounding Cal when he adds: 'I could show you around sometime if you like?'

She grins. 'Thanks, I'd like that.'

Robbie heads back to the kitchen with their plates and a spring in his step.

Cal looks suspiciously at his daughter.

'What? He seems to be the only other person under forty in this place.'

'That's not quite true.'

'He looks sad,' Chrissie says, more seriously, her gaze straying to where Robbie is stacking glasses. 'Does he always look that sad?'

'Yes,' Cal says. 'This is one of his good days.'

CHAPTER THIRTY-FIVE

WESTER ROSS, SCOTTISH HIGHLANDS

BRYONY, 2007

The street looks a little dingier and the heels pinch her feet so that she wonders how she ever strutted about in them, but as she ducks into the alley that leads to the back door of the building Sal uses as his office, Bryony feels closer to her old self than she has in ages. A disloyal shot of euphoria at being away from Angus and the boys.

She mounts three steep steps to the door, green paint peeling in strips like she remembers. The door to the nightclub is at the front of the building, with red ropes and hefty bouncers. In fact, the glossier of the two is the tradesmen's entrance and this unlikely portal is the main door.

The legend of Sal tells that he refused to move to a corporate office when he moved into commercial property development, that he wanted to honour his roots by keeping the places and people he'd grown up with close. For Bryony, it's always seemed less about that humility than the fact that the man will not bend.

Journalists have interviewed him at the huge scratched desk he's always used, building designs strewn across it, Sal poring over them in an expensive suit with fat gold cuff-links, his thick neck straining beneath collar and expensive tie, the flicker of a scantily clad dancer in the background. The press love the murk that comes along with him and Sal knows it: the colour, the spice of sex and the sniff of violence. But above all, the power. The intoxicating alchemy of it all.

He makes them come to him: bouncers, investors and lawyers alike. They come to pay tribute, to be made to feel uncomfortable, forced to drink tea from chipped mugs instead of the clean cups in their offices on Bath Street. Gangster tourism. Bryony has watched Sal enjoy others' discomfort many times.

But now, as she knocks, she realises she is no longer on the inside. The joke could be turned on her. It's too late to go back. The door swings open and a man with a gold tooth and a week's stubble leers down at her.

'I'm here to see Sal,' she says, swallowing. 'If he's got a minute?'

The man looks her up and down. 'Who's asking?'

'Bryony Campbell. I used to be his lawyer,' she adds, shifting her bag on her shoulder.

The man shrugs. 'Gie us a minute, hen.'

The door is shut in her face.

It's far longer than a minute. Bryony paces in the alley, half-hoping Sal will refuse to see her. This is madness. What does she expect, that he's going to offer her a job on the spot? If Angus could see her now, what would he say? She isn't sure how she managed to fall from being his equal to someone he looks down on. Perhaps the illusion is that they were ever on a par.

She's just decided she'll give it another two minutes, when the door swings back and gold tooth gestures inside, forcing her to squeeze past him. 'You'll have to wait.'

'No problem.'

Of course she will. There's no way Sal is going to admit an unexpected visitor immediately. The man leaves her on a chair in a hallway that smells of smoke and disinfectant, the walls a pallid hangover green that's a lighter shade of the door. Pass through to front of house and it turns to rose, blush, rouge. She can feel her own heartbeat.

All of a sudden, a door slams in another part of the building and she jumps, hearing the sort of sobbing that sends chills through you. She stands, dithering over whether to go and help for long enough that another door closes and the sound mutes, then vanishes.

Half an hour later, she's checking her watch and calculating how much longer she can wait, if she's to get back and get the boys from the babysitter, when the man comes back to fetch her.

'You've nay long, mind,' he says as she hobbles after him, blood flowing painfully back into her foot. 'He's a lunch to get to.'

Bryony has a sudden vision of the past – dark corners of old-school Glasgow restaurants, thick pieces of steak and bottles of red wine, or Sal's florid face above a pint of ale with a flaky pie and mash. She'd watched him sink pint after pint, the only sign of inebriation the deepening red of his nose and cheeks, while his sparring partners wobbled opposite.

Sal always got his way. He'd lean on his point, reiterating it until the other side wore down, or couldn't drink another drop. If they held out against him, he'd be tightly polite but obviously seething as they left the restaurant, everyone trying to placate him, and Bryony left to pick up the bill and persuade it through expenses at the office. Sal was a character to be feared, but he was also good business, and if you looked after him, he looked after you.

She'd lost track of the number of times it seemed things weren't going his way, but then magically, between meetings, the landscape would alter. A previously cocky opponent would end up quailing. She wasn't stupid. Sal had people working for him who would do the dirty work, lean where they needed to lean and grease the palms that got in the way. If the palms wouldn't be greased, there were rumours that less palatable means of persuasion were deployed.

Bryony found herself increasingly drawn into his orbit back then, something Angus – with his straight-laced by-the-book job – hated, especially when word got out that a rival had threatened 'Sal's lawyer'. He could never see the glamour that Bryony saw, the excitement and the thrusting hard work of it all. Making something from nothing, taking derelict blocks and raising gleaming towers in their place. Sal's topping-out parties and completion dinners were legendary, even though he himself never seemed to reach the top, always striving for more.

Sal meets her now, taking the few steps round his desk.

'Look what the cat dragged in,' he booms as he bears towards her, his voice like smoke and cracked glass.

Bryony thrusts out a hand to shake his because she's suddenly afraid that he's going to hug her. She sees a glint in his eye that makes her think he knows that. He holds her hand in his meaty paw for longer than is needed, examining her face, like reading tea leaves or a betting card. Nothing gets by Sal.

'I'm sorry for dropping in on you,' she says.

'Nay bother. What can we do you for?'

Sal retreats to his big leather chair and Bryony waits for gold tooth to pull over a wooden one so she can perch in front of the desk. She feels the divide acutely – no longer part of the team.

'I was wondering how you were doing. I used to like working for you and I'm thinking of doing some part-time work...' Is she? The words just spring to her lips and become truth. '...So I just thought I'd see if there's anything I can help with.' It sounds lame but she's here now.

'Did you now?' Sal steeples his fingers in front of his face. The silence is heavy and uncomfortable, and she reminds herself to keep it nipped. He's waiting her out. She lifts her chin and looks right at him.

'You're all right,' he says, after a moment, more to himself than her. Then: 'Do you no have wee ones now?'

'Two boys,' she says. 'They're both at school.'

'So why don't you go back to your old firm? Won't they have you now they've gone respectable?' Bryony had heard they no longer represented Sal, wonders how it shook down, given the curl of his lip and the tone of disgust.

'I always liked the work I did for you the best,' she says, feeling her way through the swamp of their conversation. 'And I probably can't do full hours. Not yet, anyway. But I could help with due diligence, look over some contracts...'

Bryony waits while Sal assesses her. She resists the urge to recross her legs, tries to convince herself that she isn't doing a deal with the devil himself. 'Aye, maybe you could. What do you think, Mickey?' Sal addresses gold tooth but keeps his eyes on Bryony.

'Ah, well. I guess, it would be... like, ah dinnae ken, Boss, what were you thinking... I mean, she could...'

Mickey doesn't want to come down on a side of the fence until he knows which way Sal's swaying.

'Quit your havering.' Sal frowns and slips into a genteel Glaswegian, sending Bryony up, she realises, but good-naturedly. 'Do you have a card on you?'

'No. They're at the printer's,' Bryony lies, enjoying Sal's smirk – the first sight of the conspiratorial humour she's sure they once shared. 'But I can write down my details for you.'

'You do that.' Sal nods at Mickey, who slides a pad of paper across the desk. 'We'll be in touch.'

Bryony scribbles her details and retreats to the door, followed closely by her metal-mouthed escort. She pauses on the threshold, wondering if she'll ever be back here or if it's all blow.

'Thanks, Sal,' she says. 'It was good to see you.'

As she turns down the corridor to the back door, she hears raised voices in the club to her right, startles at what sounds like furniture being thrown, a heavy grunt and a glass smashing. She knows better than to slow her pace or ask Mickey for an explanation. Music thumps suddenly out, masking the noise, and in seconds she is out in the street, eyes blinking furiously at the light.

The door slams behind her and she wobbles on her feet, casting a hand to the wall for support, just for a moment. Then she draws herself tall. She's been in the building less than an hour. But in all that time she hasn't once thought about Angus or the children. She hasn't been a mother or a wife. She's been herself, and for better or worse, her whole soul rings with it.

CHAPTER THIRTY-SIX

WESTER ROSS, SCOTTISH HIGHLANDS

BRYONY, 2007

The meeting with Sal took longer than Bryony had planned but she still has time to get back to give the boys their tea. Just. When she rounds the end of the alley, she starts to jog in the direction of the station, twisting around the office workers emerging for sandwiches or heading to the pub for a sit-down lunch.

Maybe it was foolish to show Sal her hand, but there was no other way. She's going to have to hope he needs her enough to work around her time restrictions. Bryony knows she's good at what she does – on more than one occasion she'd spotted terms in contracts that everyone else had missed. One of her spots saved Sal £2 million in fees and got someone at a rival firm fired.

She'll get the work first, she's decided. Then she'll broach it with Angus – one day a week in the city for meetings. If he drops the boys off, she'll make it in early enough to make it worthwhile. The babysitter can pick them up – the girl's mum is keen for her to earn a bit of cash and she reckons that means Sue will bridge the gap and do the pick-up until her daughter is back from school. It makes financial sense, and that's the line she's going to have to take. The money will come in handy. There are things they need to do to the house, which has turned out to be a maintenance money pit. Angus will see the sense of it.

Bryony is so focused on catching her train and rehearsing her arguments that she doesn't take her phone out of her bag until she's flopped into the seat. Three minutes to spare and the train is leaving on time. Her heart is thudding after the jog across the city and the thrill of having pulled it all off, so it takes a moment for her to register the slew of missed calls. Her racing heart skips several beats and her limbs run cold with dread.

Angus. She listens to the messages. Robbie's sick and needs picking up. *Where are you?* Mild irritation becomes concern and then anger with each of the three messages. She stares at the handset in horror as the train slides from the station, taking her back to her real world, away from a day of being the person she used to be. She feels sick. But she has to call him back.

He picks up on the first ring.

'Bryony! Where are you?'

'I'm sorry,' she says and her voice sounds small in the empty carriage. 'I had my phone on silent.'

'Where the fuck are you, though? You're not at home. I called Hamish from along the road and asked him to check. Robbie's been puking his guts up; the school are going crazy. I had to leave the office. I'm almost back.'

'I'm on a train back now. I didn't know Robbie was going to get sick. I'm sorry.'

'A train? Where have you been?'

'Glasgow.'

'Glasgow? What? I've had to run out of work because you've been shopping and hadn't turned your bloody phone on?'

'I wasn't shopping.' She tries to sound confident. 'I had a meeting.'

There's a silence while Angus digests this. Bryony wishes he would react and fill it, because the calm before the storm is the worst bit of all. He'd have been happier if she had been shopping, spending money on a lunch with the girls. She isn't one of the girls anymore, though. She's fallen between everything.

'A meeting? Who with?' He sounds utterly confused.

'Sal,' she says. 'I was meeting Sal.'

'But how were you going to get back in time for the boys?'

'Sue's daughter was going to watch them for me if I didn't make it back in time. Just for an hour.'

Angus goes really quiet when he's mad. He shuts down and pulls away from her. She can almost feel it as a physical reaction, even down the end of a phone line.

When he speaks, his voice is cold. Frozen over. 'I need to get our son. We can talk about this later.'

'Angus, wait…'

Bryony takes long breaths, trying to stop the tears from coming. There are one or two passengers sitting further down the carriage. They could be people from the village. Her feet are throbbing, even in the low heels, and her skirt feels tight and uncomfortable. It doesn't fit anymore. She's the same weight she always was, but she's changed shape since she had the boys. She gets everything wrong. All the time.

Miserable, she watches the landscape change as they leave the city and head north. What if she just doesn't go back? She could get off this train at the next stop. Walk away from her life. Never look behind her. The boys would be better off without her, let's face it. She's a disaster of a mother. She thinks of those rosy-cheeked women in the coffee shop, effortlessly juggling children and drudgery, while she feels like an aberration.

She and Angus used to laugh together. He used to look at her as if stars were shining out of her skin. Now his gaze, when it deigns to land, exudes disgust.

The journey back is agonising. She texts Angus an apology, asks him to let her know when he's picked up Robbie and whether he's getting Sean, too, or if she should. But he doesn't reply. She knows she deserves it, but as the miles elapse, shame, guilt and anger swirl inside her. If Angus had been more supportive, she wouldn't have had to lie by omission. If he'd listened to her, none of this would have happened.

She knows the gossip will be round the village already. That Bryony Campbell was nowhere to be found; that poor, long-suffering Angus Campbell was forced to come back from work, while she was off gallivanting. She knows the mix of fascination and iciness those women can put into their stares.

The silence from Angus means she will have to call school to check if Sean needs picking up. But she finds she can't. It's too humiliating to admit that she doesn't know. She'll just turn up at the door. If Sean's been collected long ago, she'll pretend she forgot Angus was doing it, she decides.

It feels like there's a hush as she walks into the playground and stations herself near the classroom door. She keeps her eyes on the ground, her phone gripped tightly in her hand. It's cold now: the wind tearing off the sea is bitter, whipping her hair in her eyes as she clutches her work coat around her. She's determined not to look at the other mothers, isn't going to even try to make an effort with them today. She hates them for their own failings and hers. It feels like the teacher is deliberately prolonging the end of the day but then she sees Sean's little face in a line and she feels a bolt of relief that she's in the right place doing the right thing for once.

Sean bursts out of the door and throws his arms around her. He's so perfectly uncomplicated. A tiny shaft of sunlight. She lifts him up and squeezes him tight, trying to get comfort from the person she should be comforting.

'Can't breathe,' he squeaks and so she sets him down. 'Robbie was sick, Mummy,' he says, his eyes round and shining with drama. 'Everywhere! It smelled horrible. Daddy had to come and get him.'

She takes his hand in hers and they set off together. 'But Daddy didn't get you?'

'No. I had story time.'

Is she being paranoid to think the real reason Angus left Sean was to set a trap for her? So that when she rushed home without stopping for Sean, he'd have another example of her feckless mothering? She experiences a frisson of triumph that immediately dissipates. Aren't they supposed to be on the same team?

Bryony wishes she could prolong the walk forever. The closer they get to the farmhouse, the slower she moves. A couple of cars pass them but then they're out of the village and through the herds of free-ranging sheep that drift across the roads, the verges and into gardens when people forget to close their gates. Sean calls to them, holds his hand out, but they never come close. They're about as friendly as everyone else in this place.

She knows some of it is her fault. That she got off to a bad start, and felt superior and wrong-footed, and she's never recovered. She tries too hard or not enough. Doesn't know how to break down barriers and make amends with these people who've decided they dislike her.

They go round to the back door. Angus is working at the kitchen table, on his laptop. He looks up when they come in and breaks into a huge smile that is solely directed at Sean. Bryony is invisible. He doesn't look at her. Just goes back to his work, the message clear: he is important, and he has better things to do than speak to his errant wife.

She sets down her bag as Sean kicks off his shoes and runs down the hall. 'I'm really sorry I wasn't contactable earlier. I didn't know he was going to be ill...' Angus doesn't lift his head, keeps typing. She waits. 'Angus, I'm trying to apologise. Could you look at me?'

When he meets her eyes, she's stunned by the dislike in his glare.

'Aren't you going to go and see your sick son?'

Bryony swallows back tears. Slides her feet from her shoes. The tiles are cold and her tights slip on them as she pads through to the living room, where Robbie, swathed in towels, sits watching cartoons, a bucket perched next to him. His face turns to hers, pale and anxious. He's a weathervane for anxiety, instantly alert to shifts in mood and disturbances in their equilibrium.

'Were you sick?'

He nods as she slides in next to him.

'Rob-Rob – you were sick everywhere,' Sean tells his big brother in wonder, looking at him like he's a museum exhibit. Bryony shoos him off to the other sofa, as Robbie buries his head in her stomach. She stifles the urge to recoil, push him away so she can have her own space for a moment. He's all elbows and he reeks of the sharp sour smell of sick. Opposite them, Sean starts making a warm burrow in the blankets, writhing around until he is lying on his tummy and sticking his head out to watch the TV. Bryony feels the plunging despair of home settle back over her.

'Have you had a bath?'

Robbie shakes his head. 'Daddy said you would do it.'

She sighs. 'I'll go run one.'

Robbie's arms tighten around her, but she can't sit here; she needs a minute on her own, because there are lumps in her throat and they can't see her cry.

'I need the toilet,' she tells him. 'Time to let go.'

She prises his arms away and he looks so forlorn, so small, as she leaves him. She trots up the stairs, a burning feeling beneath her skin. She can't give anyone what they need. She is light years from the woman who sat in front of a Glasgow hardman today and stated her case. It's like she's two different people. One is capable, interesting and valued; the other is a constant disaster zone.

–

When the boys are in bed, she picks the argument that they need to have. Angus is still ignoring her, eating his dinner silently and so self-righteously that she wants to scream. But the boys have just gone down and the last thing she wants is to rouse them, so she swallows her petulance, trying to meet him halfway.

'This is childish,' she tells him. 'The silent treatment. I thought you'd be above that.'

Angus affects a rational tiredness and patience that strips the sense from her, makes it seem that she's the unreasonable one. 'I just don't know what to say to you. Everything seems like such an effort.' He lifts a forkful of pasta to his mouth and chews.

She clenches her fingers on her knife and fork. 'What do you mean?'

A sigh. 'You make everything so hard, Bryony. We have this wonderful life and you're always thinking about what you don't have.'

The unfairness of it takes her breath away. 'Maybe we don't have the same experience of life, Angus. Everything is the same for you as it ever was.' She hisses the words across the table, setting down her cutlery because the desire to throw it at him is too strong. 'You have no idea what things are like for me. How they've changed.'

He shakes his head. 'I don't know what you expect me to do, Bryony. I have to work. This house costs money. Is swanning off to Glasgow to have coffee with a criminal going to pay the mortgage?'

His tone inflames the sense of helpless anger that's flowing inside her. 'Stop speaking to me like I'm stupid.'

Angus sighs again. 'I'm tired. It's been a busy day. Do we have to do this now?'

'Do what now? Talk about our problems? I'm terribly sorry if this is inconvenient for you, Angus, with your big important job. Perhaps I can call your secretary and schedule it in at a time that would be convenient?'

Her words bite the air – she can hear herself, shrill and out of control, and she hates that it's come to this. When did this imbalance kick in?

Angus pushes back his chair, the pasta half-finished. He takes it to the bin and scrapes in the remainder. She watches, stunned, as the sauce she slaved over, the meatballs she hand-formed, slide into the squalid mess inside the bin, and tears come to her eyes. She'd envisaged an intimate evening, a proper discussion, impressing him with her solution to what she had thought were joint problems. Stupid Bryony. They aren't joint problems at all – they're hers and hers alone.

She looks at the man she's been with since she was twenty-one. Remembers their wedding on the shores of Loch Lomond, the promises they made and the over-whelming sense of being a team that could take on anything together. She doesn't recognise him anymore. His face is thinner and harder. Objectively, he's better looking, but she misses that sweet, chubbier version. The man she knew would never have been this cruel.

Maybe this is just the heat of the moment. This isn't her Angus. Any second, he's going to turn and apologise, start a proper conversation. He's just cross about not knowing, that's all. She's blindsided him.

But instead of coming back to the table, he sets the plate down on the surface above the dishwasher and walks from the room. She stares at the plate, stained red by the sauce, sitting so close to the place where it's supposed to be. On top of the dishwasher but not fucking in it. She scrapes the last mouthful of her supper into her mouth, chews slowly, barely feeling the pain that she knows is inside her, waiting to strike.

She pushes back her own chair, walks to the countertop and picks up his plate. She studies it for a moment. Then she hurls it at the wall.

The china shatters. The noise is piercing. Her ears ring and her blood thrills, but gradually Bryony comes back to herself, shaking, scanning the damage, assessing the time it will take to clear up the spatters of sauce and the decimated plate. She stares at her trembling hand and waits for Angus to appear, tears flowing down her cheeks, afraid of herself and what she has begun. For a moment she was outside herself, unaware. She honestly didn't mean to do it.

Then, into the silence, there is the sound of the front door closing.

She rushes to the hallway, picking her way over the mess, panicked. From the window she sees her husband striding down to the end of the drive, his shoulders hunched and furious. He turns towards the sea, heading in the direction of the pub. She presses her head against the glass, stricken, trying to breathe.

The boys are upstairs. She can't go after him. She is trapped in the house.

Abandoned, she sits on the bottom stair. She puts her fist in her mouth and screams.

CHAPTER THIRTY-SEVEN

EPISODE FIVE: GLASGOW GANGSTER

The quest to discover who shot Bryony Campbell on the doorstep of her Highlands home fourteen years ago has taken me down some unusual alleyways. Bryony's husband, Angus, has always wondered if Bryony fell foul of a man she worked for as a solicitor. Or if she was killed as a revenge attack against him.

The one person who can help us is not someone who is easy to track down. Luckily, we've been aided by some local Glasgow contacts, who have put forward our request for information.

We've agreed not to name this man, who is notorious in the world of organised crime, in return for his openness about Bryony and the case. Suffice to say, he has a significant property empire in Glasgow and across the UK, extending to Ireland, Spain and beyond. The business, which Bryony advised in her time as a solicitor in the city, is widely believed to be the legitimate front for a very different kind of empire – there are rumours of drugs, organised crime and violent repercussions, none of which we have investigated or attempted to substantiate. All we're interested in is what happened to Bryony.

Today I'm meeting an intermediary who has agreed to talk off the record about Bryony's case on this man's behalf. We are allowed to record audio only and have agreed not to disclose the location we are taken to. The only description I will give is that we are in an ordinary house on the edge of Glasgow, in a nondescript housing estate. The place is nicely furnished but seems not to be lived in – there is nothing in the fridge, the water is off and the smell is stale.

A journalist friend and I have been instructed to wait here and we sit for an hour, wondering if anyone is going to show.

Eventually, the front door opens and the intermediary enters, accompanied by an older man. He is bald, short and stocky, and he brings both an air of authority and a sense of menace with him. We can tell immediately that we've been granted a more significant audience than we imagined. Right now, we aren't sure what we've got ourselves into.

The man takes a seat at the table, opposite us. He's wearing an expensive suit, and his hands are thick and scarred. Part of his face is disfigured, reputedly from a revenge attack seven years ago, since which he goes nowhere without protection. We clearly aren't seen to be a threat, as his minders wait in the hallway while we talk.

'You know who I am?'

'Yes. Thank you for seeing us.'

'And you're looking into the shooting? Of Bryony.'

'That's right. I'm hoping you can help us. Do you remember much about her?'

'Aye. She was a right good lawyer. She kept her head down and her mouth shut when needed. And she could hold her own when it came to the drink. Bad business that was, what happened to her.'

'Her husband seems to think she was working for you when she died.'

'She came asking for work.'

'And did you employ her?'

'I offered her a job. Part-time, like she asked. I had a few builds that needed taking care of so I thought on her proposal *and I said yes. Flexible working. Wasn't quite the thing it is now, back then. We were ahead of the game.'*

[Laughter and the sound of a hand slapping the table.]

'And how did the work go?'

'It didn't.'

'What do you mean?'

'She turned me down. Never took the job after all. Bit of a time-waster.'

'Did she say why?'

'Just that it wasn't going to work after all.'

'And were you angry about that?'

'You need to be careful with the questions you're asking. You agreed to be respectful.'

'My apologies. I'm just trying to find out the truth about what happened to her.'

'I'll tell you now that it wasn't me or anyone working for me. I'll tell you that for free.'

'Could it have been someone who wanted to get to you?'

'That's what I thought. Right away. But I tell you, I've had my ear to the ground a long time now and I've asked the right questions of the people you need to ask in these cases, and I've put on the pressure, if you know what I mean.'

Here, the man twists his hands in a way that tells us exactly what he means.

'I can't have people taking those liberties. Not with my people. How would that look?'

'And what did you find?'

'Nothing. Whoever did it wasn't of the street. Believe me. I've rattled the cages and I'd know.'

The man never ever grants an audience. So, it's not a surprise when he stands to go. He's been here less than ten minutes. As he pushes back his chair, I take a risk and ask one more question.

'Why did you come here today? It seems a bit unusual, if you don't mind me saying.'

He looks angry, and I worry I've pushed too far. But there's something else there, too. Sadness? Regret? Guilt?

'She didn't deserve it. Whoever it was needs dealing with. There's a bullet with their name on it.'

Whoever it was better hope this man doesn't find them.

CHAPTER THIRTY-EIGHT

CAL

Cal knows he should confront Angus, but he's putting it off. The time would be so tight for him to get back from the client site that he's pretty sure the alibi still holds; he's just confused over why Angus would lie. The weather has been fine and, since he got back from his second trip to Glasgow, he's been enjoying showing Chrissie the coast too much to want to ruin the peaceful interlude. The week has flown past and he can't believe they are halfway through her trip. She and Robbie have been for a couple of coffees, as well as him showing her some of the more interesting and secretive coves. The boy is losing his haunted look.

Today Cal has been collating his notes and going through everything again, walking the road that leads from the farmhouse to the village and exploring in the other direction, wondering where you could park a car unseen, how you would flee the scene of the crime without a soul spotting you. He's looked into the neighbour, Hamish, who found Bryony gasping on the step. There is nothing in his past or present that suggests he could be responsible. He's been researching all the other neighbours too – searching for a plausible target. There must be something he is missing, something obvious.

He trails back towards the cottage, hands in his pockets, turning the problem over in his mind. If this continues, the podcast will have to end with a speculative guess rather than a concrete solution. It's frustrating, but not every case can be a Layla – not everyone gets justice. He knows that all too well. Cal kicks at a loose rock on the tarmac and sends it spinning along the road.

Shona is arriving tonight and he can't wait to see her. He'll take the weekend, he decides, toeing the rock into the future once more, and then he'll tackle the difficult conversations. He's lingering on the bend, admiring the view, when the roar of a four-wheel drive startles him out of his freewheeling thoughts. The driver can't have seen him, because he feels the breath of air by his shoulder as he's almost clipped by the car's wing mirror.

He falls backwards onto the grassy bank by the road, more shocked than hurt. He's conscious of the car lurching a little on the tarmac and hopes it won't hit the opposite wall when it brakes, but as he scrambles up, he hears the whine of the engine change and realises it is accelerating again, speeding away from him.

Shaking, he stands on the high bank, craning to see into the distance, but there's only a flash of dirty white on the far bend, and the car is gone. He grips the stone of the wall, feeling the damp moss under his palm. It was a near miss and a panicking driver, that's all, but the close call has left worst-case scenarios cascading through his overactive imagination.

He should be paying more attention. Just because he's in the middle of nowhere, it doesn't mean there won't be traffic. He strides down the right-hand side of the road, keeping his ears and eyes alert, reaching the village without incident, now more annoyed with himself than frightened.

He thinks he might go to the cafe for a pot of tea and a slice of cake to recover, but as he reaches the door, he sees Chrissie and Robbie in there, deep in conversation, his dark head and her red curls bent together. As he watches, Robbie lifts his head and laughs at something Chrissie says and his expression is so clear of the clouds he seems to wear most of the time that Cal can't bear to interrupt them. He steps backwards, retreating to the cottage.

–

Chrissie has announced that she's going to watch a film with Robbie, so Cal and Shona are on their own for a booking he's made for a restaurant further inland, on the edge of a long sea loch. The glass-fronted lodge has had write-ups in the national papers for its seafood, as well as its setting.

'Are you sure you don't want to come?' Cal asks Chrissie for the millionth time.

'Yes, Dad. I'm sure it would be lovely, but you guys should have some time together and I want to see Robbie tonight, if that's okay?'

'Are you and Robbie…'

'We're friends, Dad. I've only known him a week, remember?'

'I know, it's just that he's a couple of years older than you and…'

Chrissie rolls her eyes so hard that they almost end up in the back of her head, and Shona laughs and takes his arm.

'Come on, Grandad. The kids will be fine.'

'Thank you!' Chrissie grins and waves as they leave the cottage.

Cal feels the natural worry that has lived inside him, since Margot disappeared, rearing up.

'They'll be fine,' Shona says, watching him. 'Chrissie is one of the most sensible teenagers there is. You know that.'

'It's my trademark worry,' he says, pulling her close and kissing her. 'It's a very attractive quality.'

'You just keep telling yourself that.' Shona laughs.

When they reach the glassy loch and see the lights from the restaurant reflected in its dark waters, Cal is glad he made the effort to book this place. Shona seems pale and tired from all the extra hours she and Cliff have been doing. He needs to take her mind off it for a little while and the glen they've driven to is like something out of a Highlands fairytale.

They have a table on the first floor, overlooking the water. He drinks one glass of champagne, conscious that he will be driving in a few hours, and they order the house special seafood platter, which arrives dripping with lobster, langoustines, mussels, stuffed crab and scallops. They take their time feasting on the fresh shellfish, accompanied by hunks of bread and creamy coleslaw.

She's been listening to the podcast, but Cal talks Shona through his progress – or lack of it – behind the scenes. He watches her cheeks go pink in the heat, enjoying the fact that they are cocooned in the lofty space with the roar of other diners and voices around them.

By the time they are ready to leave, it is late and Chrissie has texted to say that she's home. He tells her to lock up, that he has his key and they won't be long. He can see that he was wound up and overreacting earlier, and the tension has been loosened by the good food and relaxing atmosphere. They step outside into the cold and Shona presses her lips to his, wrapping her arms around him beneath his coat.

'Thank you, that was a lovely evening,' she says.

'It's just a shame we have a forty-five-minute drive back.'

'Do you want me to drive?'

'No, I'm fine, you rest. You drove all the way over here earlier.'

They set music playing and Cal sinks into the rhythm of the empty roads in the utter darkness, his bright beams creating a small pool of light that punctures the wilderness. He's getting to know these roads well now, but they do look different in the night. At one point what looks like a pine marten scurries across their path and he brakes, not wanting to hit it.

'Sorry,' he tells Shona, who is drowsing.

They're only five minutes out of the village, on a long piece of narrow road, when it happens. His phone beeps and he's thinking that it must be Chrissie, when there's a screech and a whirl of light as a vehicle pulls out from a passing place, hidden behind a jutting rock face, and falls into place behind them, its beams dazzling.

Blinded by the headlights, Cal raises a hand to protect his eyes, squinting to see. The car accelerates until it's right on their tail. Instinctively, he brakes, but the other car doesn't pull back and there is a jolt of impact, the scream of metal scraping metal. He grips the wheel so tightly that his fingers seize.

'Oh my God.' Shona has bolted awake and her frame is rigid, her hands flying out to hold the dash. 'What's…'

Cal hears a rushing in his ears, everything slowing as he fights to regain control, but then the vehicle behind pushes forward again and bumps them hard. The world spins out of control: all he sees are stark, illuminated snatches of countryside in their headlights as the car shunts to the side. They're being forced off the road. Cal tries to steady their course, but before he can recover, there's another impact from behind. Shona shouts out and his gut freezes as the car mounts the verge and tilts. It seems to hover for the tiniest fraction of a second and he thinks maybe it will be okay, but they are rammed again, and it tips up and over the edge.

He can hear screaming. The airbag explodes in his face, and then inhuman crunching, crashing and grinding noises fill his ears, glass cracking and spraying around them. Everything is moving, tumbling. How far are they going to fall?

And then the car rocks up and over one last time, and everything falls into stillness. There is only the sound of hot metal groaning and settling, the shock of cold night pressing in on him through the broken windows. Somewhere on the road above, the other car revs its engine – tyres squeal on the tarmac, lights vanish into the darkness.

Cal's thoughts ooze. He thinks of Bryony, of the blood pooling on the doorstep. He can see it in front of him. So red and sticky and bright. But he can also hear the birdsong and feel the touch of the sun on his skin. The very realness of it all.

He must slide from consciousness. When he opens his eyes, it seems only a second has passed and the world as it is comes spinning back in again. Shona. Cal tries to turn his head but everything hurts and the pressure in his skull is intense. They are upside down, protected by the car's roll cage but trapped. The car has come to rest on its roof, wheels spinning and airbags deflated, a stranded hot metal insect. He can see the shape of Shona next to him. She isn't moving.

'Shona.' His voice sounds far away. 'Shona, can you hear me?' There is no reply. He tries yelling into the void beyond the car. 'Help! Help us!'

But his voice fades into nothing and he realises how pointless it is – that there is no one there. He is all they have. Whimpering, he tries moving his limbs, exhaling tears when he finds that he can, though they hurt like he's been beaten with a metal bar. Cal reaches up and fumbles for the plug of his seatbelt, which is holding him fast. Bracing against the ceiling with his other hand, he jabs at the button several times.

'Come on, please, come on.'

Frustrated tears run backwards to his hairline, but then the plug releases. Grunting in pain, he bumps down onto the roof then twists round in the small space so he can see Shona. But her head is turned the other way. He stretches out a hand towards her motionless figure and then pulls it back: he mustn't touch her, until he sees what injuries she has. Why isn't she moving? More sobs escape the back of his throat.

The door beside him is mangled and caught in the dirt – it won't open. Lifting his feet, Cal kicks at what remains of the shattered windscreen, clearing a path that he can crawl through.

His hands are stinging and tacky with something. Stumbling to his feet on the soft damp hillside, he looks up and sees they aren't that far from the road, after all. Maybe the car has only rolled two or three times on the incline. They are lucky – a hundred metres further on and it would have plummeted over a drop. There is the sound of a stream close by, the noise of sheep calling to each other, but nothing feels real.

The headlights are still blazing, allowing him to pick his way to the passenger side. Dropping to his knees, Cal can see her shape behind fractured glass. The door is buckled and won't open but the window is broken, so he pulls off his jacket and wraps his hands in it, using them to lever the glass out, ignoring the pain.

Her face is streaked with blood, skin white in the gloom and hair matted. It's hard to keep looking. As he leans in, Cal's teeth start to chatter violently, the clashing sound reverberating in his head.

'Shona, it's Cal, can you hear me? Shona? Please. Come on, wake up, Shona, please.'

He touches her cheek but she doesn't move.

'Shona. Open your eyes, come on, love. I'm here.'

Frantic, he pulls himself up on the car and scans the horizon, but there is only darkness outside their pool of light. No one to help them. The moaning sound must be coming from his lips.

Get a grip. The small voice inside seems to come from somewhere else. It sounds like Margot. He drops back to his knees and takes long breaths of air, forcing himself to keep calm.

'Shona. I'm here. It's okay, love, I've got you.'

He reaches into the wreckage of the car again, pulling her hair aside to check for a pulse. His thoughts spring to Duncan, the Laird who lost his wife and son in a car crash, but he pushes them away. Cal's fingers shake. He can't feel anything so moves his two fingers across, nestling them further back. A flicker of life threads beneath his fingertips, he's sure.

'Come on, Shona, come on. It's me. I'm here. Come on.'

Cal keeps pressing, desperate. Only a weak beat, though that could be his imagination. He can't let go of her. Not now. Not alone on the hillside, with only the creaking of the wounded car for company.

'Shona!' He leans close, shouting into the car. 'Can you hear me? Wake up, come on. Stay here. Stay with me, damn it.'

He ducks his head in, close to her, the smell of blood and hot metal making him nauseous. It's so tight but he fights down the claustrophobia, holding still, his heartbeat a staccato. Then he feels the whisper of breath on his face. She's alive and she's breathing. Relief is a flood rushing through, but it lasts only a moment. He mustn't move her, he thinks, is that right? But the engine is hissing and ticking – what if there's a fire?

Think, Cal. Think.

His jacket lies discarded a few feet away, so he scoots over to it, praying his phone is still in there, swearing when he pulls it free. The screen is shattered but it lights up. He peers at the brightness but there is no reception.

'Fuck.' His wail pierces the mountainside. There is just the text from Chrissie sitting on the screen, sent in another universe. *Night, Dad xx.* He slumps forward at the memory of the evening. Of the time before.

Wait. The text came in, he realises, his brain still working like sludge, just before they were hit. That means there was reception up on the road. There has to be. He turns, stares up the slope into the darkness.

Then Shona groans and he ducks his head down into the car again.

'Shona. Can you hear me? It's Cal. Stay still, love, you have to stay still a moment. We've had an accident but it's okay. I'm going to call for help. I just have to walk to the road. I'll be right back. I promise.'

She's quiet again and he thinks she's fallen unconscious. He sinks down, checking for pulse and breath once more. Is it his imagination, or is her breathing shallower?

He can't waste time. Leaving her feels like the worst thing he's ever done in his life, but he has to get help; he can't get her out on his own, as he doesn't know how badly injured she is. She needs professionals.

So he makes himself stand and climb upward, away from the car, the phone gripped so tightly in his hand that he can feel the splinters of glass digging into his palm. He's dizzy and his body is racked with shooting pains as he forces himself towards the road, step by step. It feels so far away. Above him, the stars are perfectly clear; the night is cold.

Eventually, Cal pulls himself over the lip of the verge, onto the tarmac. Bent double, he stares at the handset in despair. Nothing. Fighting the lumps of panic in his throat, he starts to trot along the way they came in the pitch dark, too sore to run. To his left and down the slope, the headlights of their crashed vehicle seem as far away as the stars. Then. So brief he almost doesn't see it. A flicker of a bar of reception.

'Yes. Oh, thank God.'

He dials 999 with shaking hands.

As soon as it connects, he starts to talk but his words trip over each other.

'Calm down,' the voice says, a lifeline solidifying. 'We're going to help you, but I need to take some details so we can find you.'

The operator talks him through pinpointing the location on his Maps app. His fingers shake as he repeats the grid reference. The woman doesn't reply for a moment and panic clenches his chest.

'Are you still there?'

'Yes. I'm not going anywhere.'

'The car came off the road and rolled down the slope,' he says. 'Another car rammed us from behind. I've left her to find phone reception. I have to go back now. She's trapped and on her own.'

'Help is on the way.' Her smooth voice wraps itself around him. 'Stay on the line as long as you can. I'm with you.'

'How long?'

'We've dispatched a paramedic in a car and a fire engine with cutting equipment. There's a police unit closer, though. That car should be with you in eighteen minutes. Try to keep your friend calm and still until they get there.'

'I'm going back now,' he says. 'I'm going to lose you. Tell them to look off the edge for the headlights. We aren't on the road. Tell them we aren't on the road.'

'I've got your location, don't…'

But whatever she was going to say is lost.

–

Cal retraces his steps, falling as he climbs off the road and hitting his knee on a rock. Shivering, he slips and slides down the boulder-strewn moorland to reach Shona, praying to anyone that will listen that she's still alive.

He hears her before he sees her. She's crying and groaning, calling out in the night. He careers downhill. Yelling her name.

'Shona, I'm here, I'm here…'

Then he's by the side of the car again, lying on the cold ground, his head and shoulders inside the car with her. She's flailing around, her arms pinwheeling in the dark, trying to escape.

He grabs her hand. 'Shona. The ambulance is on the way. Stay still. You have to stay still.'

'It hurts.'

'I know it does. I know. Just hang on.'

Her panic is lessening, changing to heaving sobs, her hand gripping his so tightly that it burns.

'Cal. Don't. Leave. Me. Please.' She gasps the words and he wonders what damage has been done that they don't know about yet, because she sounds so odd and unlike herself.

'I'm not leaving you. I'm staying right here.'

She is shaking with shock and he so desperately wishes he could hold her in his arms. The minutes are long and lonely. He finds himself offering reassurances he can't possibly back up, soothing and promising.

Time seems to pass impossibly slowly.

'Cal?' Her words are weaker now, barely a whisper. Someone has to come soon.

'Yes?'

'I need to tell you…'

'Shhhh. It can wait.'

'We don't know that.' Each word seems to heave itself out of her.

'Shona…'

'Please, Cal. These last months…' He waits, stroking her cold hand, his eyes stinging. 'Best of my life.'

'Me too,' he whispers. 'But we're not finished, okay?'

Shona wheezes and her hand loosens in his. '…Love you.'

Something inside him drops away as he realises what she's doing. 'Don't, Shona. Don't you dare say goodbye.'

'Cal…'

'I love you. Stay with me, Shona. Please.'

But she's quiet and limp, her fingers no longer loosely entwined with his.

'No, no, no.'

There are flashing lights in the distance. Two vehicles in convoy, far away on the twisty road that leads up the hill. They're so close.

'They're coming. I can see them. Please, Shona, come on. So close. Wake up!' he shouts, rubbing her hand hard. 'Don't go to sleep.'

She briefly resurfaces, but it's no good. She's drifting away from him. The cars reach the point on the road parallel to the crash site and one turns across it, blocking the way and illuminating the path down to the shattered car. He sees someone running to the boot and grabbing a bag, hears the doors slamming and a figure from the second car joining the first.

'They're here,' he tells her, squeezing her fingers again. But her hand is so cold and she doesn't react. He rouses himself through the tide of exhaustion and stumbles up towards the approaching figures, waving his arms and trying to yell, though his voice comes out in a croaking whisper. 'Here. We're over here. Hurry.'

'All right, hold on. We've got you.'

The paramedic, a man who must be around his age, runs to the side of the car where Shona is suspended. Once he flicks a torch on, Cal sees the true horror of her trapped form. He cries out at the sight of the blood spattered over the wreckage. Within seconds, the paramedic has crawled inside the car, calling her name, taking over.

Cal feels hands on his shoulders and he is turned firmly round by the police officer who has followed. It takes a moment to register that she is asking him questions – he sees her lips moving before sound comes back. What is his full name, his age, where was he going tonight? She's shaking free a foil blanket and wrapping it around him. 'Okay, Cal, we've got you.'

'Please,' he cries. 'Please help Shona.'

'We're doing everything we can, I promise.'

The paramedic shouts something and Cal stands help-less as the officer lunges forward, sinking to the ground and thrusting her arm into the car while the medic rifles in his box. Is this it? Is this when he loses her? A flash of memory: Shona on a peak only a few miles from this spot – the wind whipping her hair as she turns away from him.

Then there is a sound from the sky that fills the night and his senses. He's watching the officer and the medic, but he can't hear the words and there are bright lights overhead, looking like the headlights. Cal flinches away. Blasts of air send the heather and the grasses rippling like the ocean. He is adrift.

The helicopter lands on the road and then there are more cars and lights, and there is cutting equipment and sparks, and they're trying to get him to go and sit in the warmth of a police car but he can't, he won't. He has to stay near her. He promised.

They have her on a board and they're all working in concert – all these arms and these voices together. He's swaying with tiredness just watching it all. There's a collar around her neck and blood on her face, and they're taping her down, hooking her up to drips, and then their faces are grey and they're carrying her fast, fast, fast, up the hill and away from him. He can't keep up. And he knows that means she's still clinging on and he wants to call out to her. *Stay with them. Don't leave.* But they're gone and he finds he can't speak.

He hears his name again. He hears the word *shock* and thinks how perfectly that describes everything. The shock of the impact, the lights and the sound. The shock of the blood and the fear and the cold. The shock that anyone would do this to them.

By the time Cal manages to get up to the road, his arm in the safety of the police officer's grip, his feet moving of their own accord, the helicopter has lifted off the ground, buffeting them with the downdraught. It drifts at a strange angle, away and over the hills, only a series of blinking lights in the distance and then not even that.

The officer takes him to an ambulance that he didn't see arriving. He hears her talking to the paramedics.

'He's stopped talking and he's cold. We haven't had time to assess his injuries properly.' And he realises, distantly, that they are talking about him. And he wants to tell them that he's okay, that it's Shona they need to worry about, but then he's being made to lie down and there are blocks holding him still, tape across his head, and his eyes are closing and it's better, safer, to take refuge in the blackness where none of this ever happened or ever could.

CHAPTER THIRTY-NINE

Cal wakes in the ambulance en route to Raigmore Hospital in Inverness. Immediately, the image of Shona in the car, unconscious and broken, flashes across his vision. He tries to breathe normally, but he can't help picturing her as they spirited her away, strapped to the board, small and pale, the smears of her own blood hiding the features he loves but needs more time to get to know.

But then he tries to move, struggling against the constraints of the stretcher he is on.

'Wait. You need to stay lying down.'

'I'm fine. I was walking around.'

He fights to raise his chest and shoulders, but firm hands push him down and Cal finds he is woozier than he expected.

'How is Shona? The woman I was with. Do you know?'

The medic keeps gloved hands on him, gently pressing him still. 'We'll be able to find out as soon as we get there. Right now we need to focus on you. Is there anyone we can call?'

Chrissie. Cal's mind crashes into focus and he curses himself. What if she's in danger too? What if the person who ran them off the road tries to hurt her? New waves of panic crest.

'I'm going to have to sedate you if you can't stay still. I really don't want to do that.'

'Please. My daughter. She's on her own. She's seventeen but she was expecting us back around eleven. What time is it now?'

'It's two a.m.'

Cal feels cold. Chrissie is alone in the village on the coast, while he speeds away from her.

'Do you have my phone?'

The paramedic holds up his shattered phone, entering the code for him. Through the crystals of glass, Cal can just read the slew of text messages.

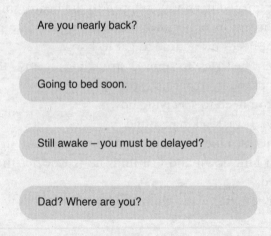

Are you nearly back?

Going to bed soon.

Still awake – you must be delayed?

Dad? Where are you?

'I need to send a message. I don't want to call, in case she's asleep.'

'I'll do it for you, just stay calm.'

Cal dictates a message. His own fingers tremble, useless, by his sides as the paramedic types.

> Chrissie, I'm okay but we were in a car accident. Shona is hurt and I'm on my way to the hospital. Are you okay?

The events of the previous evening ricochet inside his head. If someone has targeted him, the car was likely the same one from his near miss. Is it related to the podcast? Or Shona's ex-boyfriend? Or is this all about Jason Barr and the raging media coverage around Margot's discovery, the grotesque support he has inspired in a certain community? If they think they've got him, they won't go for Chrissie, surely?

His phone starts to ring. The medic holds it to his ear.

'Chrissie? Are you okay?'

'Yes, but oh my God, Dad, what happened?'

'I'm not sure, love. We had a car accident and Shona was trapped. They had to cut her free and she's been airlifted to hospital in Inverness.' He tries to keep his voice calm, but as he relates the events, he feels his composure wobbling. He feels trapped, desperate to move and prove to himself that he's fine.

'Where are you?'

'I'm in an ambulance.'

'What?'

'I'm okay. I promise you. Just a bit wobbly, and some cuts and bruises.' Cal crosses his fingers. 'They just need to check me out and I need to see how Shona is doing.'

'Is she all right?'

Flash. Blonde hair matted with blood.

'I'm not sure,' he says, trying not to let his fear leak into his words. 'She was unconscious when they took her away.'

'What should I do?' Her voice sounds small and he wishes he could hold her in his arms, as much for his comfort as for hers. She needs a parent.

'Hold tight. I'm going to call Mum now and then I'll call you back.'

The paramedic hangs up. 'You need to rest.'

'Please, just one more call. To her mum.'

'One more.'

As Cal listens to the rings, he wonders how he is going to explain, but knows he is calling the only person who will drop everything in the same way that he would. When she answers, her voice is thick with sleep.

'It's me, Al. Chrissie is fine,' he says quickly.

'Cal, it's two in the morning. Why are you calling?'

He explains the events of the evening as quickly as he can, struck by how impossible it all sounds. When he tells her he thinks it was deliberate, she gasps. 'Chrissie wasn't there,' he says. 'She decided not to come for dinner last night. But I'm worried about her now.'

'Oh my God.'

'I'm on my way to the hospital, Allie. I don't know how long it will be until I can get back there and' – he sucks in a breath – 'Shona isn't in a good way. I don't know what to do.'

Allie falls silent. They both know they owe Shona everything after what happened in Aberdeenshire. Chrissie wouldn't be here if it wasn't for her. But they haven't ever talked about their new relationships and now is not a good time to broach that. Cal's ears are ringing, his eyes gritty.

'Right. I'm getting in the car now and I'm going to drive up to Chrissie. I'll call her and make sure she doesn't go out anywhere until I get there. Is there somewhere she can go to if she needs help?'

'Yes. Tom in the pub. The landlord. She knows how to get to him.'

'I'll tell her.'

Allie sounds galvanised and in control. Cal feels himself relax into the narrow stretcher and a tear traces its way down his cheek. 'Thank you, Allie. Thank you so much.'

'It's fine,' she says, and he can hear the sound of her feet on the stairs in his old home, already on the move. 'It's going to be fine.' When she has gone, her words play in his head over and over. He wishes they were true.

—

At the hospital, he is wheeled to a cubicle where the paramedics hand him over to a tired but friendly-looking accident and emergency doctor. All Cal sees are flashes of ceiling, the edge of faces. As he bids the paramedics goodbye, he feels like he's losing the people who understand, the ones who had a glimpse of the accident and the bleak aloneness away from this warm, bright hospital packed with equipment and experts.

He immediately starts begging for news. 'I need information on my friend Shona. She was brought in by air ambulance from the crash. Please, can you tell me how she is? Is she alive?'

'I can find out for you in a moment, but first I need to just check you over. I understand you were walking around after the accident but we need to do a scan, just to be sure.'

'No.' Cal groans. 'Please. I need to know how she is.'

He can feel the distress rising, his limbs moving almost involuntarily. If he were able to fight his way up and run through these corridors, could he find her?

The doctor's face floats above him. Her eyes narrow. 'Hey, calm down. It's not unusual for adrenaline to mask serious injuries. You may feel okay but not be okay. If I send someone to get a status update, do you promise to co-operate with my checks?'

'Yes.' He grasps the olive branch with both hands and makes himself still. 'Anything.'

Waiting for the scan seems to take forever. The hospital shifts around him – the hushed night conversations, sounds of feet on the linoleum, the beep of machinery and the rolling of beds. At one point, the sound of sobbing makes crystals of ice form inside him. But then the nurse is back, peering over him, her face grave.

Cal feels his stomach dipping away from him. He clenches his fists tight.

'She's in surgery,' the woman says, and the blurring world comes into focus again. 'She has a lot of internal bleeding. We won't know anything for several hours.'

'She's alive?'

'Yes. She's alive. The police have contacted her next of kin. A brother – Graham? He's on his way.'

Shona has mentioned Graham but they aren't close, not since their parents died. These are not the circumstances in which he'd hoped to meet her family. *Please let her pull through*, he thinks, *please*.

He lies inside the CT machine, moving backwards and forwards, all the while thinking of her, praying to whoever is listening to let her wake up. The minutes he waits tick by agonisingly. Now that he knows Shona is alive, he notices pain across his body, how it hurts to breathe. Exhaustion is making the world spin, even from his prone position. His eyes close; sounds fade.

'Right.' Cal's eyes jerk open. A nurse is gently pulling the tape from his head. 'Good news.' He turns to find the doctor's voice. 'Amazingly, you have no serious internal injuries, though one of your ribs is cracked and you have bruising. But that's not surprising, given what you've been through.'

Propped up, Cal submits to an examination: poking and prodding, checks of his skull for bumps, the gentle pressing of his torso, the light shining in his eyes, and the requests to move his arms and legs.

'The nurse will clean up these cuts, though they seem to be superficial,' the doctor murmurs. 'Tell me, do you remember hitting your head as you fell?'

'The airbag went,' Cal tells her. 'But then we went down the hill. I just remember going over as the car rolled. It's all a blur.'

'You've been very lucky, though these bruises are really going to hurt so if you need some pain relief, we can give you something for that.'

Someone lets Cal plug his devastated phone into a charger and he is able to update Chrissie and Allie, gingerly working around the broken screen and the cuts on his hands. After they have cleaned all of the wounds, he is left to rest for a little while, checked at regular intervals. Now that the adrenaline has left his body, the injuries are throbbing and he is stiffening up, even with the strong painkillers they give him.

Shona is still in surgery. The looks on the faces of the nursing staff when they update him make Cal feel sick. They give him the facts and neutral reassurances, but he can see it in their eyes. It's been hours now.

Eventually, they allow him to leave the bed and he walks to the waiting area.

A policeman is there, apologetic but determined.

'I'm sorry to have to do this now,' the man says. 'But I'll need a statement while it's fresh in your mind.'

'I understand,' Cal tells him, though the look of scepticism in the man's eyes as he recounts the events on the dark road makes him feel hollow. The only person who can back him up is fighting for her life – what does it matter if the officer believes him or not?

'So you're saying this vehicle was waiting for you?'

'I don't know. It appeared that way – it pulled out from a hidden lay-by rather than coming up behind us.'

'And you think it was the same car that almost hit you yesterday?'

'I can't be sure, but they were both light-coloured 4x4s.'

'But you didn't report that.'

'No. At the time I thought it was an accident. Someone taking the corner too fast.'

Cal's head is thumping, his mind woolly. His ribs hurt. He keeps thinking about Shona. She's been in surgery for so long now. Surely, they must almost be done. *Please make it, Shona.*

'Can you think of anyone who would want to hurt you?' Cal doesn't blame him for sounding disbelieving. He can't focus – every time a nurse comes into sight, his whole body tenses – and his voice keeps tailing away, but he does his best to explain about the latest podcast and about Barr. The officer jerks to attention when he realises that the man beneath the bruises is the one with the dead sister plastered over the papers. He also mentions Shona's ex – just in case it's nothing to do with him at all.

'And what's this man's name?'

'I'm sorry, I don't know.'

He is saved from more sceptical interrogation when the officer's phone rings. The man listens intently and Cal tunes out, distracted by more footsteps in the corridor. 'That fits with what I'm being told,' he says, glancing up at Cal in a different way, as if taking the measure of him.

'The road traffic investigators have found skid marks and evidence on your vehicle that back up what you've told me,' he says when he hangs up. The rest of the statement is taken more diligently and Cal feels the band of suspicion loosen around him a little.

'We've got your contact details and we'll be in touch. I'll give that DI Foulds you mentioned a call to verify some of these details. You're free to go now; we won't need to talk to you again today.'

Cal has no intention of going anywhere and mounts a vigil in the waiting room. He is trapped in a nightmare. Everything as slow and oozing as treacle. He texts Chrissie every half hour and only breathes properly when she replies. That relief lasts minutes before he is gripped by anxiety all over again.

–

Late morning, a man hurries up to the desk and Cal hears Shona's name, so he forces himself to sit up and face him, realising this must be her brother. The woman behind the desk points to Cal and the man turns to look. He stands in preparation, unsure of what to do or say, wondering if her brother knows who he is.

'Graham?' he asks, when the man leaves the desk and approaches him.

'Aye. Who are you?' The question isn't unfriendly, but Cal can see the hesitation on his face. He understands it.

'My name is Cal, Cal Lovett. I'm a friend of Shona's. We were on a weekend away on the west coast together when the accident happened.'

'They say she's in surgery?'

'It's been seven or eight hours now. I've been waiting for news. The doctors will come and talk to us as soon as she's out.'

Cal can see the resemblance to Shona as the man runs his hand through his hair. It's a jolt of shock and then the similarity melts away. He rubs his eyes, trying to stay alert.

'What happened? All I know is there was an accident. Was she driving? Were you?'

The man stiffens as he takes in Cal's visible injuries. Cal swallows and realises how dry his mouth feels, how his hands have gone clammy. If only they hadn't gone to that restaurant for dinner, if he had been going more slowly or had somehow managed to dodge the impact. He sways a little under the exhaustion.

'Shall we get a coffee and you can explain what happened?' Graham sighs. 'I've had a long drive. They've said they'll come and get us when there's news.'

Cal is reluctant to leave the waiting room but Graham is already speaking to the receptionist and guiding him along the corridor. He lets himself be steered, though his movements are stiff and painful.

'I can't take this in,' Graham says when they have drinks in front of them.

'I was there and I can't either,' Cal says quietly, unsure whether to launch into an explanation or give Shona's brother time to catch his breath. His eyes are gritty and the world shimmers around them.

'What happened?'

'We'd been out to dinner and were run off the road by another car when we were driving across a mountain pass on the way back.'

Graham makes a noise of disbelief in his throat.

'In a way we were lucky it happened where it did. There was a slope down to a plain by a stream, and the car rolled down and stopped. Shona was trapped. Her side of the car suffered the most damage.'

Cal has to clear his throat before he can go on: all of a sudden, the isolation and the dark crowd back in around him. He has to anchor himself in the bright noisy hospital.

'They had to cut her out.' He puts his head on his hands to hide the tears. 'She spoke to me after the accident but she was unconscious by the time they got there. They airlifted her here. I haven't seen her since the crash.'

'I just don't understand,' Graham says, shaking his head. 'Why would someone drive off after causing an accident like that? Even if you were scared at what you'd done, you'd stop. Surely?'

Cal just shakes his head, his eyes swimming. How can he begin to explain to Shona's brother that it wasn't an accident at all? He can't get his thoughts in order – it will have to wait. All that matters now is Shona.

Coffees finished, they walk back to the waiting room together and sit awkwardly in silence. After a while, Graham goes outside with his phone – Cal can see him pacing, talking to someone, and he notes the similarities to Shona in the way he moves. He checks his own phone repeatedly and is just wondering if he should call Allie, when it buzzes in his hand.

'I've got her,' Allie says. 'She's fine.'

'Oh, thank God.'

'Are you okay? Have you been checked out?'

'All fine. Cuts, bruises and I need to watch out for concussion. One cracked rib. That's all.' He shudders at the memory of the turning, falling car. 'I was very lucky.'

'Is there any news of Shona?'

'She's still in surgery. Her brother is here.'

'So long?' There's a pause as Allie waits for him to speak but he has no words. 'Okay, well, let us know. I'm going to sleep for a bit but we'll stay by the phone. Chrissie's friend – Robbie – is going to come and see her.' He hears a bark. 'Oh, and that's Rocket. He likes the beach.'

Cal tries to smile at the thought of the old Labrador trundling through the waves by the holiday cottage, but then he thinks of his and Shona's things scattered across one of the bedrooms and his ex-wife dealing with everything, and his mind buries itself beneath the horror of the crash. It should never have been like this. Allie should be hundreds of miles away; Chrissie should be safe. He should be on that beach with Shona. He closes his eyes and he's there, waiting for her, in a parallel world.

–

It's another hour before the doctors have news. Cal has been slumped in an uncomfortable plastic chair, drifting under and then jerking awake again. When he closes his eyes, the slaloming countryside he saw illuminated in the headlights as he fought to keep the car on the road appears, along with the scrape of metal and the scream of tyres.

'Graham?'

An older woman, salt-and-pepper hair, clean scrubs. Both men leap to their feet. Cal's leg twinges; pain shoots through him.

'I'm Ms Chaudhury. I operated on your sister.'

The surgeon isn't smiling. Cal's skin goes cold.

'How is she?'

'She had some internal bleeding and I'm afraid we've had to remove her spleen.'

Cal stands mute, uncomprehending.

'But is she going to be okay?' Graham's voice echoes in his head.

'I'm afraid it's touch-and-go. We've moved her to intensive care but a lot is going to depend on how she does in the next few hours.' The doctor's face has tiredness and sympathy etched into the lines. 'I'm sorry, but I think you need to prepare yourselves that it may be bad news.'

'What?' Graham clutches Cal's arm.

'We're doing all we can. It's a case of waiting now. Your sister was very badly injured. You are welcome to stay here as long as you like. There's a family room you can use, or we can recommend a place to stay locally if you need a hotel.'

'Can I see her?' Graham asks.

The doctor nods. 'You can, but only very briefly.'

Cal wants to ask the same thing, but he isn't family. He opens and closes his mouth, his eyes pricking with heat. He can't lose her. Please, this can't be happening. It's not real. They're still on the hills, in the clouds. But Ms Chaudhury is leading Graham away and this is it, his chance to say goodbye... His dry lips part and the words croak out.

'Can I...'

The doctor looks at him, sympathetic. 'That's really up to the family.'

Graham turns back and all Cal can do is stand there, praying this man who has control will take pity on him.

'Please…'

Shona's brother frowns and then nods once.

'Thank you,' Cal whispers, but Graham has turned away.

They are led through the hospital to the intensive care unit, where they have to sterilise their hands and put masks on. Cal struggles to move his stiff and bruised arms so a nurse helps him to hook the mask strap.

'Do you want me to wait out here while you go in?' He feels so guilty being here, and yet desperate to see Shona. He needs to tell her he's sorry.

Graham's face is chalk white and his hands are shaking as he fiddles with the edge of his mask. 'I've not been a very good brother. We haven't spoken in a while. I don't know what to say.'

'You're here,' Cal says. 'That's all that matters.'

'I wish that was true.'

But then they're following the doctor and they're in the hush of the ward, the quiet chilling. When they reach the bay, Cal has to press his hand to his mouth to keep the sound inside. He barely recognises Shona beneath the ventilator, the wires and the tubes. Her skin is pale and the bruises stark, the gash on her chin angry. She looks so much smaller than normal.

The wheeze and hum of the machines monitoring her, and the drips hanging above her bed, bring it all home. He's going to lose her, and there is nothing he can do. He can't go back to that mountain pass and do it all over. At the doctor's urging, Graham steps forward. He has barely taken Shona's hand and mumbled that he's there, when he backs away, looking at Cal, panicked and apologetic.

'I can't, I just need some air…'

The doctor follows Graham. Cal looks at the nurse for permission.

'Go on,' she says as she notes something on a chart. 'But just for a minute.'

'Can she hear me?'

'We're not sure. But it's possible.'

Cal steps forward and perches on the chair beside Shona's head, realising he will fall if he doesn't sit. He reaches for her hand and holds it carefully around the wires taped to it, slotting his first two fingers into her palm. She is warm. Tears start to fall.

He leans in. 'Shona, it's me, Cal. I'm here. You're in hospital. You're going to be okay. You are. You have to be.' He presses his forehead on the sheets and takes a juddering breath. 'I'm sorry,' he says. 'So sorry.' He closes his eyes, and wishes them back in the restaurant by the loch, the dark glassy waters and the smell of pines.

'Okay.' After a few minutes, the nurse touches his back.

It's all been too brief. There isn't the time to say the million things he needs to tell her. All that she's done for him. She's brought him back to life and laughter in a way he didn't think was possible.

His legs shake as he stands and kisses her forehead. It seems clammy; her skin tastes different to normal, and it feels like it leaves a residue on him.

'Thank you,' he whispers.

–

He barely makes it downstairs. Seeing Shona has made everything hurt – but his heart most of all. This is all his fault. He can't live without her. He can't but he's going to have to. He saw, then, what the doctor was allowing them to do – he sees it on the faces of the nurses around them – she was letting them say goodbye.

Graham doesn't come back. After another hour sitting in the waiting room, one of the nurses approaches Cal. She has a coat on, a bag slung over her arm. He thinks she treated him but his mind is now playing tricks, images sliding in and out.

'Are you still here?'

'I'm just waiting for…'

'You won't be able to help your friend if you collapse,' she says. 'You need to have some rest.'

'I can't.'

'You have to. Wait there.'

He sits, compliant, while she asks the receptionist to call the nearest hotel.

'You can almost see it from here,' she says. 'They have your number. You'll be moments away and they will call if there's any change. Come on. It's on my way. I'll point you in the right direction.'

Mute, Cal follows her out of the door. His feet drag as he listens to her chatter but hears none of it. When she deposits him in front of the hotel, his thanks seem inadequate – the words stutter from his lips. He steps into the foyer and when he looks back, she has gone.

It's getting dark. He's grateful for the no-frills hotel chain, with its fast check-in and lack of questions. He has nothing with him, is starving but too tired to eat.

As he enters his room, his phone buzzes and he yanks it from his pocket, thinking it must be the hospital, but it's Foulds.

He studies it for a moment, unsure if he wants to talk to anyone, but she's probably just checking on him after hearing from the police officer who took his statement. It's easier to take it.

'Cal?'

'Hi?' His voice dries up and his mind is tired so he just waits. Not the time for small talk.

'This wasn't something we were aware of, and I'm assuming that's the case for you too?'

'I'm sorry?'

'The picture.' She sounds rushed, annoyed. Cal can't wrap his head around her words. What is going on? What is she talking about? 'Of Margot.'

His body stills. 'What picture?'

'Haven't you checked the news today?'

'No, I've…'

'I'm sending it to you now,' she says. 'It would really have been good to know about this before.' And then she's gone. Like Cal has done something to displease her.

Robotically, he slides open his emails on the broken phone. His hands are shaking, eyes swimming.

The image loads slowly but even so, Cal can't take it in.

It's Margot. His sister is instantly recognisable with her red curls and impish expression. Her face is pressed next to someone else's and his arms are wrapped around her. They're grinning at the camera, cheek to cheek, clearly on a night out, having fun. The expression on her face makes her look like a stranger. He can't work out what is going on. None of it makes sense.

The man she is out with is Jason Barr.

CHAPTER FORTY

WESTER ROSS, SCOTTISH HIGHLANDS

BRYONY, 2007

'We can't go on like this.'

Bryony is astounded that Angus has bothered to come and talk to her. She thought he'd just ignore her again and go to bed. Icy cold, she's been staring into the ashes of the fire, too exhausted and upset to light it. It took her an hour to clean up the pasta sauce and the shards of plate that were spattered across the kitchen. She's had time to reflect on her anger; time for that anger to turn to self-hatred and despair.

Angus moves from the doorway to the end of the sofa. He perches far from her, as if approaching a dangerous animal. 'Bryony?'

'I know,' she says softly. 'We can't.'

'I don't want us to break up.'

There are tears in his voice and it is this that shocks her into raising her head, afraid to look at him but compelled. His eyes are red and she can smell beer on his breath, so he has been to the pub. Does everyone in the village know how unhappy they are?

She feels numb, prodding at her thoughts to try and elicit some sort of feeling. Does *she* want them to split up? She thinks briefly of a Glasgow flat, a job, freedom. It's tantalising. But it is also her past. Thoughts of the boys spring forward, pushing the old version of herself to the side. In her own imperfect, impatient way she loves them. She does. She is desperately unhappy, but she cannot go back to how things were before.

'Tell me what I can do,' Angus pleads.

Her instinct is to retract, close up and protect herself from him. But something inside her says this is rock bottom and she needs to reach up soon and grasp any help offered, because if she doesn't, she's going to drown.

'I don't know.' The words are like glue on her tongue. 'I feel so miserable and so angry, Angus. All the time.'

'Do you… do you wish…'

'What?'

He breaks down and she can barely hear the words through the sobs. 'Do you wish we'd never had them?'

The thought that flies into her head is *yes*. She wishes that. But it's more complicated than that. She cannot fathom a world in which Robbie and Sean don't exist, but she is not cut out to be a mother. She is simply not good enough. She shakes her head.

'I can't imagine not having them.'

And that has to be enough. Angus falls forward, crying. She reaches for him in a mechanical way, going through the motions of what she should be doing, while feeling appalled and afraid. After a moment, he lifts his head and pulls her onto his chest, fixing strong arms around her. He is warm, and she leans into the heat and the comfort.

'What can we do?' he says, when his breathing slows. 'Practically, what can we do to make it easier?'

He isn't offering to move; she knows that without asking. But maybe she needs to set her sights below happiness for a while. Perhaps that will be enough.

They talk long into the night and they agree that Angus will reduce his Glasgow nights to two a week. They will spend more money on a babysitter and go out together every weekend, and they'll make sure Bryony has a day to herself at least.

As they draw up the plan, she wonders if it will last long, or if things will slip back to the way they were. But she thinks they both know that they're at the end if they do.

When they finally switch off the lights and go to bed, it is two in the morning. Outside, an early frost is glittering on the lawn. Bryony brushes her teeth and crawls under the covers. Normally, she and Angus roll as far away from each other as they can, but tonight he slides over to her side and pulls her into his arms. She tucks her back against his chest and listens to the clock ticking and the house creaking around them.

CHAPTER FORTY-ONE

Cal can't process what he is seeing. Horror races through him, together with confusion. He can't look online, not yet. He knows already what the comments will be, what this will do to the case against Barr, the impression of Margot. He sinks onto the bed, tempted to hurl his phone at the wall, but his cracked rib screams and he stops, arm raised, when he sees himself in the mirror. His bruised face and the dark circles around his eyes make him unrecognisable. It reminds him of Shona, lying on her hospital bed. The phone is his only connection with the hospital. And with Chrissie and Allie. Besides, he loathes the image he sees, the twist of violence in his expression. His arm drops.

Easing off his shoes, he fires off a holding message to Allie and then crawls up the bed, unable to cope with anything more than sleep. He can't even bring himself to cross the room and shut the curtains, just pulls back the tightly tucked covers and contorts himself until he is underneath them, making sure his phone is in reach. He is dimly aware that everything aches but it doesn't matter: nothing will keep him from sleep. Not the bright room, the pain, the grief for Shona or even the gnawing sense that his world has tilted up and fallen out from under him.

Margot, he thinks as he fades to sleep.

The picture looked like that of a boyfriend and girl-friend together, faces flushed and eyes shining. The strands of hair stuck to her forehead with heat – had she been dancing? With him? What does this mean? What does any of it mean? His last thought before unconsciousness claims him is that he was a child back then. Margot vanished when he was nine years old. Maybe he's wrong about her. Maybe the truth is that he never really knew his sister at all.

He sleeps without dreaming, feeling the urge to slide right back underneath when he wakes. But then he remembers where he is and wrenches back the cover to grab his phone. There's nothing. He lies back, heart pumping. His eyes just want to close, but his mouth is parched and he's starving and weak. He dials the hospital but can't get through to the right person. Is no news good or bad? It's better just to go over there.

Cal pushes himself off the bed and lurches to the bathroom. His body buckles with the effort of moving – he's almost crippled with stiffness. Frustrated, he runs a shower, letting the hot water ease some movement back into his limbs. He doesn't have any spare clothes, so he dresses in the same ones and leaves the room.

The message from Foulds – the picture of Margot – flickers into his head briefly but he pushes it away. None of that matters. Not now.

When he reaches the hospital, there is still no news on Shona's status.

'Is that normal?' he asks the nurse.

'She made it through the night,' the man says, giving his arm a squeeze. 'She's not giving up, so we won't either.'

They won't let him see her, so he heads to the canteen and eats as much of a cooked breakfast as he can manage.

The food isn't anything to write home about but he feels less shaky than he did: warmer and more real. His phone is glitching in and out so he decides to walk into Inverness and see if he can get it fixed or replaced. At the hospital they told him to check back in a couple of hours, when the doctors have done their rounds.

Everything seems upside down. He can barely think about the basics of feeding and clothing himself, of contacting Chrissie and Allie – much less the intricacies of the podcast and the investigation, or Margot and Jason Barr. But, sitting in a cafe across the road from the kiosk that has fixed his phone, he needs a distraction. Steeling himself, he dials Foulds' number.

'I was in an accident,' he tells her. 'A friend and I were run off the road. You're going to get a call from Police Scotland, if you haven't already had one.'

'What?'

'The other car drove off. I'm not sure they believed there was one to start with, but they've found evidence that backs my story.'

'How on earth did that happen?'

'I have no idea if it was a targeted attack or an idiot. Could it be Barr or one of his psycho supporters?'

'Barr's not left the area, Cal; we're keeping tabs.'

'I passed on your details, just in case, but I'm working on a podcast so maybe it's related to that. I don't know.'

'Are you okay?'

'Bit bashed up but I'll live. My friend is in intensive care. She still hasn't woken up.'

The words come out in a robotic way. Cal can't let himself go back there right now. Not to the squeal of brakes and the terrible falling that felt as though it would never end. Not to the implications.

'I'm sorry,' Foulds says. 'This isn't the time to talk about Jason Barr. We don't have to do it now.'

'I saw the picture,' he says, ignoring her. The door to the cafe swings open and a group of teenagers head for the counter. Chrissie's age. 'Is it real?'

'Yes. As far as we can ascertain, it is.'

'And what's he saying?'

'He's been to the papers. The angle he and his legal team seem to be pursuing is that he and Margot were romantically involved and he did see her the night she vanished. He claims he loved her...' Cal lets out an involuntary sound. 'I know. But he's saying her disappearance screwed him up and she's the reason he attacked those other women – crimes for which he is deeply sorry and has paid his dues.'

'You're kidding.'

'No. I'm sorry.'

'But I don't understand.' Cal reaches for a sugar packet on his table and turns it over in his fingers. 'What's his game?'

'Well. Either it's the truth...'

Foulds lets the silence grow and Cal feels his mind falling into it.

'Or?'

'Or he's worried we'll find his DNA on her remains and he's getting out in front with a cover story.'

His fingers tighten around the sugar, tearing the paper. 'But is he smart enough for that?'

'No, but the people around him are.'

'He won't get away with it, will he?'

Foulds sighs. 'Look, I have to be honest with you. At the moment, the CPS aren't minded to pursue on the basis of the limited evidence we have.'

'What?' Little grains of sugar are now scattered over the table. He sweeps them into a pile.

'We're still hopeful we'll find something. It may come down to the DNA. Hang in there.'

Cal's phone beeps before he can respond. He takes the handset away from his ear and sees that another call is coming in from an Inverness number. The hospital.

'I've got to go.'

Cal hits the button to cut Foulds off and accepts the other call, already on his feet and heading for the door. He's spent his whole life seeking justice for Margot, but right now he would give it all up, every last chance, just for Shona to be okay.

CHAPTER FORTY-TWO

CAL

She's awake. He has to wait to see her, as Graham is visiting, but eventually the nurse comes to the corridor where he is pacing and says Shona has asked for him. Asking for things has to be a good sign, doesn't it?

But when he reaches her bedside, it is still a shock. She's half-propped up on the pillows and seems small and shrinking against them; her skin has a white-grey hue, apart from the stark bruising and the cut that bled so heavily when she was in the car, and is now crossed with butterfly plasters. He swallows at the memory. She's still wearing an oxygen mask but when she sees him, her fingers flutter a little so he approaches the bedside and takes her hand, afraid to hurt her.

'Hey,' he says, a bubble forming in his throat. 'It's good to see you.'

Shona pulls at her mask and he shakes his head but she insists, managing to lift it away from her face.

'How are you?' She mouths the words, her eyes flicking to his sling, and his heart swells.

'Never mind me. I'm fine. It's you we're worried about.'

He can't take his eyes off her face but his attention is drawn repeatedly to the machines around them, afraid that something will happen to wrench her away again.

294

'Did they catch them?' Her words are barely a whisper. 'You remember?'

She nods. Waggles her hand to indicate not everything.

'The other car drove off. They haven't found them yet.'

Shona sinks back further into the pillows and though she looks beaten and knackered, her eyes flash with anger. A million things pass between them. He didn't know what a relief it would be to spend time with the only other person in the world who understands the horror of that night, who remembers the moment they toppled.

The nurse approaches them and Cal nods. 'You have to rest,' he says, squeezing her hand. 'I'll come back later.'

He leans over and kisses her head, picking a place without bruises. Her skin feels normal to the touch again, the waxy cold feeling that it had before gone; he almost wonders if he imagined it. As he backs away, her eyes are closing. She's slipped into sleep before he's at the end of the bed.

'She's exhausted,' the nurse tells him, crossing to the machine and checking the drips hanging above her. 'But she's passed the first hurdle.'

–

Cal stays on in the hotel, visiting Shona for increasing snippets of time over the week. He sees Graham occasionally, but most of his time is occupied with checking on Allie and Chrissie, and making trips into town for things Shona needs. Neither of them has anything beyond what was in their pockets. Cal has managed to contact Cliff and he is holding the fort at work for Shona.

The tasks leave time to think. Too much time. Cal spends it obsessing about Barr and his wealthy wife. She has the money and the clout. Did she pay someone to take care of Cal? It sounds like the plot of an implausible film.

Now that Shona is out of immediate danger, he needs to go back to the west coast and say goodbye to Chrissie and Allie. He doesn't know what he's going to do about Bryony and the stalled mystery of her death, though. When he set out on the investigation, he felt compelled by the trauma Robbie had suffered – this overwhelming desire to make it right and repair some of the damage. It is obvious, even to Cal, that Robbie isn't the only person he was trying to help.

But what he's coming to realise is that you can't take it back. All of the pain and the grief and confusion. The damage is done. And even if Jason Barr did kill Margot and he is put behind bars, it's too late. Margot has been gone so long and so many people have forgotten her. Even if he finds the person who pulled the trigger and left Bryony to die, the pathways in Robbie's brain have formed; loss has carved channels through him that can never be undone.

Cal tries to heal and distract himself by walking. In the long hours while he cannot be at the hospital, he finds it impossible to concentrate. Even if he had his laptop and his notes, he doesn't think he could bring himself to sit still. Instead, he discovers Ness Islands: he hobbles at all hours along the river to the footbridge and crosses into a green haven, where carved wooden sculptures and an earthen amphitheatre lie beneath the trees. Sometimes, he sees slick seal heads bobbing in the water as he walks from the town centre, their whiskery watchfulness creating an ethereal atmosphere, broken only by the occasional jogger or dog walker.

He feels the weight of failure lying heavily on him, along with a strange sort of malaise. He honestly doesn't feel he has the energy to continue investigating Bryony's death.

Graham is obviously anxious to get home. He hovers by Shona's bed when he visits, looking uncomfortable and helpless. He and Cal usually visit at different times, but today when Cal arrives at his allotted time, Graham is still there, shifting from foot to foot. Cal sets down the bag of dough rings that he has brought on the side of the bed. They are a favourite of Shona's and he's hoping the fact that she's asked for them – the fact that her appetite is returning – is a very good sign.

'Now, boys,' she says, reaching for the bag. 'Hang on, give me one of those, would you?' Cal rolls his eyes and fishes one out for her, then offers the bag to Graham, who shakes his head.

'She asked me to stay,' he says. 'Till you got here.'

'Yes.' She grins, through a mouthful of pastry and icing. 'She did.' Cal gets a flash of Shona as she usually is. Endearingly bossy and fizzing with energy. He wants to laugh at the perfection of it, this coming back to herself. Instead, he perches on the visitor chair and waits.

'I need to get out of here.'

'Now wait—' Graham says.

'I need to be at home,' Shona interrupts, 'and they're saying I can maybe go in a few days if all goes well. But I'm a bit weak and pathetic, so...'

'I'll come and stay,' Cal says – the words speed from him automatically. 'If you want me to, that is. Until you're back on your feet.'

Shona looks at him in surprise. 'I was just going to ask for a lift and some more dough rings. What about Chrissie... and the podcast?'

'I do need to go back over there first,' he says. He knows, as soon as he speaks, what he has to do. 'Allie is going to take her back this weekend. I have one or two interviews to do and then I think I'm going to wrap up over there, for now, anyway.'

'Really?' Her blue eyes pierce the surface of his reasoning. 'What about Robbie?'

'It's not doing anyone any good.'

As he says this, Cal realises why he's putting it all off. Angus. The truth is that, deep down, he thinks he knows what must have happened to Bryony – the process of elimination is leaving only one plausible avenue, but it's just not one he wants to pursue. He's been grasping at straws, chasing organised crime links, and the Laird and his gun supply, the footpath dispute. Wouldn't it all be so much easier if the whole thing was a horrible mistake, a twist of fate?

But more and more, he is coming to believe it is deeply personal. You don't stumble across a place like Gulduigan by accident. Its remoteness and the strength of community there make that almost impossible. You come from within. If that's the case, can he do it? Can he blow it all apart? The man has moved forward with his life. He thinks of Katherine, Robbie and Sean. What if the truth will be harder than not knowing? But these thoughts run counter to all he has ever believed.

Shona is gazing at him in assessment.

'I'd really like to be there for you,' he says.

'You don't have to do that… become my nursemaid because you feel guilty. It isn't your fault.' Her face is creased into a frown.

Blunt as ever. Cal can't help but laugh.

'I want to come,' he says. 'It's your sunny disposition. I just can't get enough of it.'

She swipes at him and Graham clears his throat.

'Well,' Shona says, apparently stumped for words. 'That pretty much lets you and Mary off the hook, Graham.'

'You know we'd love to have you…' he starts, tailing off at the look she gives him. 'Aye, well, maybe at Christmas, then.'

CHAPTER FORTY-THREE

WESTER ROSS, SCOTTISH HIGHLANDS

BRYONY, 2007

On Monday morning, instead of rushing off to beat the Glasgow traffic, Angus makes breakfast and clears up while Bryony showers.

'Won't you be late?' She doesn't want this to come back and bite her later.

'They'll understand,' he says.

When she comes back downstairs, she pauses on the bottom step, hearing him chivvying the boys. The three of them ineptly packing school bags.

'What do you need, Robbie? Where's your reading book?'

'Maybe we should ask Mum?'

'No, let's try and do this for ourselves, shall we?'

She should feel better, shouldn't she? This should be a relief? Instead, she feels even more tired than she did before, only realising now how much she has been doing and how much more there always is to do.

As she enters the kitchen, the phone rings. Angus reaches for the handset on the wall.

'Hello?' She watches as he frowns, then sighs in exasperation. 'Hello? Is anyone there?'

He hangs up and looks at her. 'There must be something wrong with the line.'

–

'Will you be okay?' Angus asks when he drives them down to the village. 'Walking back, I mean?' His face is so anxious, it makes her want to smile and also to hit him.

'I do this every day. I'll be fine.' She leans in and he kisses her cheek. After a few days of intense scrutiny, it's a relief that he is going for a bit. She needs to gather her thoughts.

They've agreed to visit a local fair at the weekend, even though the forecast is turning wintry. Then Sue and Kevin's daughter will be babysitting so they can have a meal at the pub when the boys are in bed. There is something on the horizon to break the monotony at least.

'Bye, Daddy!' Sean waves until the car is out of sight.

Bryony takes his hand in hers and reaches out for Robbie. They stroll along the lane to the school, not late for once, mixing in with the other parents. Robbie slips his grip from hers and races to catch up with a girl from his class. She watches as he chatters, a warm relief curling inside her. The mother in front turns in surprise.

'Morning,' she says to Bryony. 'Cold night.'

And she smiles and agrees, and something shifts infinitesimally inside her, like the promise of a thaw.

–

She's still avoiding the hills after her confrontation with Duncan, so Bryony scuffs along the shore and up onto a cliff path, exploring a new route out of the village that weaves through the trees and affords her a view of the pewter sea below. When she turns back, she finds herself tempted into the village store. Morag is at the till, and she buys herself a pack of iced buns and chats to the older woman.

'Still no news from the Laird,' Morag tells her.

'He'll have to talk to his agents and his solicitors, I guess,' she says, trying to hide the sadness she feels. 'I hope I didn't make things worse.'

'Not at all. John was singing your praises. I think he's going to ask if you'd make your committee membership a permanent thing. Would you be up for that?'

She has the sense that Morag has been asked to sound her out; the older woman is watching her expression closely.

'I'd need to talk to Angus,' she says. 'But I'd like that.' And she would. The chance to use her brain, to feel wanted and needed. More than a mother.

As she leaves the shop, Bryony feels another twist of warmth inside, a slight lessening of the loneliness that has been her constant companion.

It starts to sleet on the way back up the hill. When she unlocks the back door and tumbles in on the mat, she is shivery and cold, her skin smarting from the wet needles of icy water driving into her face as she walked along to the farmhouse. The phone is ringing and she dashes across the kitchen to grab it, in case Angus is calling. He said that he might.

'Hello?'

There is only the static sound of silence for a moment and she's about to slam the receiver down on the anonymous caller, when a familiar voice sounds in her ear.

'That you, Bryony?'

'Yes. Is that… Sal?'

'Aye. I've been thinking on your proposal.' Bryony's gut freezes. 'If you'd like to do a few days a week I'm sure we can find some legal and other administrative tasks. If you're willing to be discreet. But that goes without saying.'

She stares at the water dripping from her boots onto the tiles, forming a cold, wet puddle. The possibility is close enough to touch – the thing she's been longing for. But what will be the cost?

She pauses so long that he chivvies her on. 'Well?'

'I really appreciate it,' she hears herself replying. 'I'm so sorry to mess you around. But I don't think I can manage to do it after all.'

A bark of annoyance. 'You're joking me.'

'I'm sorry, Sal,' she whispers. He isn't used to people refusing him.

'Aye, right. Well, I won't be offering again, you know.'

'I understand. I'm really, really…' But he is gone, and with him the last trace of her old life. She stands very still, clutching the receiver, staring out into the garden, where the leaves have covered the lawn. Angus had raked them into decaying piles, but the wind has undone all of his work. He's going to have to start again.

CHAPTER FORTY-FOUR

CAL

Early the next morning, Cal takes a last walk along the river, to the islands. The air is cool but the skies are clear and the water glassy. They have settled on the plan that Graham and his wife will stay in Inverness and visit Shona in hospital, giving Cal time to say goodbye to Chrissie and wrap up the things he needs to with the podcast.

Allie offers to pick him up, but conscious of the long drive she has ahead of her, he takes the train from Inverness station, with his handful of purchases in a plastic bag. It's strange having so little to tether him. Maybe when he is back at the cottage, he will lose this floating feeling he's had since the accident. Occasionally, emotions puncture the sensation of being adrift from it all, but then he finds he separates from the world again.

Cal hardly notices the time passing as the train skirts numerous lochs on its journey to the coast. After a couple of hours, he recognises features in the landscape: the great bulk of Loch Carron, with its smattering of islands. He feels the tightness in his shoulders ease, though really that is counter-intuitive, given all that has happened since he first came here weeks ago.

He walks down through the village and stands above the beach, looking out at the water. A breeze is up, and choppy wavelets are dancing around, bobbing boats and buoys. He hears a shout and turns to see Chrissie running along the shore, Rocket on her heels and Allie behind. He holds a hand out, before she barrels into his cracked rib, then leans into a gentle hug, his arms wrapped tight around her.

'You're here!'

'I got an earlier train. Thought I'd surprise you.'

'We were just out buying biscuits. We've run out.' She brandishes a pack of dark chocolate Digestives and squints up at him, holding her hair out of her eyes with the other hand. The wind teases tendrils of red in front of her face. 'You look thin, Dad.' His daughter's eyes are filled with the kind of worry that should be the other way round – parent to child.

'It was a bit scary, Chris. But I'm doing fine.'

'Do the police know who it was?'

'No, not yet. I'm not sure they'll find the car now. It vanished into the night. But you never know.'

They fall into step, walking into the wind towards Allie, a waiting wraith on the sand.

'Do you think someone targeted you?' Chrissie's voice is small as he wraps an arm around her shoulder.

'I doubt it. Someone probably just got fed up of my slow driving and tried to give me a scare.' He's lying, but where's the benefit in telling the truth?

'I'm so glad Shona's going to be okay.'

'Me too. I'm really sorry I haven't been here.'

'Don't worry – I never would have got as much done with you interrupting me all the time.' She nudges him with her elbow.

'Hey!'

'Wait till you see. And Tom's been giving me and Mum free brownies in the pub.'

'I'm glad you've survived without me.'

They reach Allie and he hugs her, struck by the strangeness of them being here together and the realisation that they are always a family, no matter what.

'Thank you,' he says as Chrissie runs ahead with the dog.

Allie shakes her head and he sees all his own thoughts reflected in her eyes. 'Always.' She lets a moment pass and then says, more lightly: 'Wait till you see what your daughter has been doing.'

At the cottage, Chrissie slots her key into the door, an action that makes Cal remember his is lost somewhere in the twisted heap of metal that was the car. His nostrils fill with the smell of hot metal and then the hallucination vanishes.

They step into the kitchen. Cal halts and then pivots on the spot. 'Wow.'

Chrissie's eyes sparkle as she watches his reaction.

Every surface is covered in paintings and sketches of the coastline. He sees starfish and driftwood, piles of shells and the outline of the cliffs. Tears come to his eyes. She's created something so beautiful.

'This is incredible.'

'Robbie spoke to Angie in the teashop. She's going to put some on the walls. My first exhibition.'

Cal looks at Allie and sees the pride he feels mirrored in her. It's the first time since the crash that the crushing feeling has lifted.

'And there's this,' Chrissie says. 'Through here.'

Cal follows her into the living room, while Allie fills Rocket's water bowl. Laid on the long, low coffee table are a series of sketches, taken from photographs that sit next to them. It takes him a second to realise what he's looking at. Two small boys poking at the ground with sticks.

'That's Robbie! And Sean.'

'Yes. And this is Bryony.'

Cal looks at the drawing Chrissie has done of Bryony. She's somehow managed to capture the sense of restlessness he is told she had, as well as her beauty. The more he finds out about her, the more he realises how lost and lonely she was. The feelings spill out of the picture so clearly.

'And Robbie gave you these pictures?'

'We worked on it together. We got talking and he doesn't really have mementos of his early childhood. It all vanished when she died – his dad put things away – and they never really talk about his mum and what the boys were like when they were little. I think it's helping him a bit.'

Cal hugs Chrissie to his side. 'That's really kind of you, love.'

'I enjoy his company,' she says. 'He's different to the boys at college. A lot more thoughtful. Deeper.'

Cal feels a twinge of nostalgia for his own youth as he looks at her. She seems so full of possibility, so open to everything.

'What about Sean?' He peers at a sketch of the brothers on a bench. 'Is he helping?'

'No. Robbie and Sean don't really get on. Sean's closer to his dad.'

He picks up the final set of sketches, surprised to see Katherine in them. Pictures of the family they became.

'These too?'

'Yes. He wanted to make sure she was included. She's been there for them. That's one of the things we've been talking about – that loving her doesn't mean he's being disloyal to his mum.'

Cal's eyes fall on a photograph of Katherine and Angus from years ago. He's astounded at how young she looks. Not much older than Chrissie is now. His arm is round her shoulder and she's looking up at him with such adoration. But it's the expression in Angus' face that makes Cal feel chilled. He's facing the camera and his eyes are hollows, the emotion off-kilter, more akin to pain. There's something about it that makes him shudder.

–

Cal sleeps for an hour, comforted by the sound of Chrissie humming downstairs as she works. He's still exhausted by the aftermath of the crash, assailed by occasional flashbacks and little spirals of panic, like dust devils pirouetting through his mind. He wakes as it is getting dark, making him feel dislocated, but when he stands at the window and drinks in the view, he feels calm coming over him. For all that's happened here, he still loves this place.

Allie tactfully decides to stay in, but he and Chrissie walk along to the pub. He's greeted like a hero by Tom, given his first pint for free.

'It's a relief to see you in one piece.'

'Thanks, Tom – and for looking out for this one.'

'She's done a lot of good,' Tom says, gesturing to where Chrissie is chatting to Robbie as he clears dishes from an empty table. The youth's hair looks cleaner, his skin clearer. There's a lightness about him that seems to have come from unburdening himself over the past weeks.

Now, with distance, Cal can see it. Maybe the podcast hasn't been such a failure after all.

Robbie follows Chrissie to the bar.

'Hi.' He smiles at Cal. 'Good to see you back. Are you okay?' His eyes fix on Cal's face and he is reminded that it is a palette of bruises.

'I'm fine, Robbie, thank you. Can you join us for food?'

'I'm working and then going to practise with my band, so I can't. Thanks, though. See you later.'

He raises a hand and Chrissie catches his fingers. Cal averts his eyes at the contact between them. He'd suspected that they both had feelings for each other. Chrissie glows as they take their seats at their favourite table.

'I've been doing something else while you've been away,' Chrissie says when he's been to the bar and ordered their food. 'I've been speaking to people about Margot's memorial.'

He startles, surprised that she's been pursuing it. Maybe he never really expects anyone to pay more than lip service to Margot's loss, he realises. Not even his own daughter.

'Have you?'

It strikes him that this conversation was planned, and is the real reason Allie has left them to it.

'Yes. I called Andy, Dad, I'm sorry.'

His heart stills at the memory of his sister's boyfriend. For so long, Andy was a source of solace for him, so to discover the truth – that he left her alone that night and lied for years to protect himself – was a brutal blow. Cal feels it has undermined his trust in himself, his good judgement.

'Oh.'

'I know. But he's been a good source of information. I've been able to get the names of some friends and I managed to track one down on Facebook – Diane – because she is still using her maiden name. She's connected with other people who knew Margot and they'd really like to come to a memorial.'

'I think I remember Diane,' he says. The sound of laughter and a bedroom door shutting on him as a cheeky eavesdropping child sends thrills of memory along his arms. 'She was fun.'

'She's been brilliant,' Chrissie says. 'She'd love to talk to you.'

He meets his daughter's gaze and swallows down the fear that's rising unaccountably. 'Maybe that would be nice.'

'I'll give you her number.'

'Okay, thanks.' He's afraid, he realises. Of what he might discover.

They are silent for long minutes. He can feel that Chrissie is waiting for him to talk but he can't find the words to express himself.

'We haven't talked about the picture, Dad,' she says softly.

If it was anyone else, he would shut them down, but Chrissie holds the key to him. The light in the bar is warm and low. He feels safe here, with the sea outside and his daughter in front of him. He should be protected from the cold, hard feelings that flood him when she mentions it.

'I know. I just can't get my head around it,' he says.

It's so wrong to feel Margot has betrayed him. He knows that's unreasonable in the extreme, but that is the dark unfairness he lives with. Chrissie is watching him, so he tries to make his face neutral.

'Pictures don't always tell the truth. That "picture tells a thousand words" thing is rubbish. They're just a tiny moment. You can be looking at one thing, but really seeing another.'

'Thanks, Chris.' He reaches for her hand and squeezes it. 'I appreciate what you're saying. I guess the thing is that we can't go back and ask her for her side of the story. He gets to tell it. And he seems to be wiggling out of trouble in front of our eyes.'

'I hate him,' she says. He doesn't like seeing that look in her eyes.

'Don't,' he tells her. 'Don't let him in, Chrissie; you'll never get him out again. Let me hate him for us.'

She shakes her head, but at that moment Tom puts their food on the table and he takes the opportunity to change the subject.

–

They walk back to the cottage and Chrissie gets ready for bed – she and Allie are sharing the twin room. They're leaving early the next morning for home. Cal moves through the house, turning off the lights and checking the locks. His hand on the living-room switch, he pauses, drawn in by the photographs and sketches on the table. He enters the room and scans them all once more, his gaze landing on the one of Angus and Katherine. It is a moment before he notices a shoebox on the floor, filled with others.

Feeling slightly guilty at the intrusion, but fairly sure Robbie wouldn't mind, he sits on the sofa and leafs through them: they're all jumbled but he can see how they trace the time before Bryony died. Most of them do, at least. He's not sure why the one of Katherine is in there. But then he finds others from the set and sees they were taken at a market or fair. There's more of the boys, looking at sheep, Katherine wearing the same jeans and top.

And then he stops. Because now someone else is in the picture. And it's the same day, with the same clothes and people, a pirate plaster at a jaunty angle on Sean's knee.

Cal stares at the images. How is this possible? He shakes his head to ward off the fuzzy tiredness that must be distorting his reasoning. A headache is creeping in at the edges; he needs to take paracetamol. He sorts through and finds the images from that set, and then lines them up on the coffee table. He checks and double-checks, sure now of what he is seeing but mystified as to what it means. Katherine is there beside Angus, her future husband. But Bryony is there too. These photos were taken before she died.

He sits and stares at the images until his head is drooping and his body screams for sleep. What does it mean and why is it making him so uneasy? There's something wrong here, and Cal can't put his finger on it. As much as he wants to stay here and puzzle it out, Cal's body is rebelling, his thoughts closing in, his mind refusing to co-operate.

Reluctantly, he takes some photographs on his phone, then flicks out the lights, pausing to stare at the rushing waves outside and the ghostly reflection the moon makes on the surf. He has to use the bannister to haul himself up the steep stairs. As he does, his thoughts stutter and collide. But as he lies in bed, in the last seconds before sleep claims him, Cal knows he has been wrong about one thing. He is not doing damage. Robbie is better for the light they're shining on the past and it is cowardly to avoid taking this investigation to its conclusion. Tomorrow, he decides, folding into darkness – tomorrow he will speak to Angus.

CHAPTER FORTY-FIVE

Allie and Chrissie are ready to leave early, Rocket curled in the boot, his fur salty and sand in his paws. Cal helps them load their things into the car and waves them off. He hugs Chrissie tight before she slides into the passenger seat, and then he and Allie stand in front of each other, the distance back between them now that the crisis is over.

'Be careful,' she says.

'I will. I'm going to wrap things up today and head over to Aberdeen.' He casts a look along the shore, already leaving in his mind. 'I'm done here.'

She nods and he holds his arms out for a quick hug before she ducks into the car. When it rounds the corner, he feels a sense of loss, something slipping away forever as he and Allie forge a new way. He wishes he could follow them but he knows he can't.

More than Cal's physical body was battered when the car left the road and spun down the hillside: his sense of himself and the world have also taken a beating. Or maybe it's the picture of Barr and Margot, and the national consensus that they were once a couple, that is playing with his view of the past, present and future. How can he seek justice with this uncertainty resting over everything?

Today he can try for justice of a different kind. He's going to confront Angus with the lies about his alibi and see where it goes from there – no concrete interview plan, just riding on instinct. After lunch, he makes the walk out of the village and up the hill, his steps slow and faltering. At the gate to the long driveway, he waits to catch his breath for a moment, the sea a reassuring blue below. He's more tired than he would like to be, sheened in sweat and breathing heavily.

After a rest, he walks to the now-familiar door, with its sunken step, and rings the bell. There's a sense of finality for him, though the chance of a resolution is slim. He hears the sound echoing in the house, but no one appears; after a few long minutes, he tries again but with the same result. Half-irritated and half-relieved, he makes his way round the side, calling out a greeting. Though rain is forecast, the day is unseasonably warm so perhaps they are outside.

The garden is deserted; the old swing is rusting and the grass long. Cal skirts the edge of the paddock and heads for the outbuildings, unnerved at the silence.

'Angus? Katherine?'

At the back, an old garage-cum-shed leans against the barn and the smell of long-gone animals still lingers. The door is ajar so he pushes it open, peering into the dark and waiting for his eyes to adjust to the low light. What he sees makes his heart jump.

A vehicle. A dirty white Land Rover, by the looks of the back of it – all that is visible from this vantage point. He grips the doorway with his free hand.

After a moment, Cal's breathing steadies and he moves into the shed. It smells musty and oily, the air close. He touches the car's chassis, trailing his fingers along the side as he approaches the front in a dream. There it is: the horrible truth. Dark scrapes of paint from the back of a red car, a busted headlight and an impact dent. The lights are in his mirror again, Shona's screams in his head.

Cal feels sick, suddenly aware of his isolation and vulnerability, of the obviousness of it all, which he has been in denial about. Was there ever really going to be any other outcome? He presses a hand to his chest, thoughts pelting about, sadness for Robbie and Sean. Then he takes a long shaky breath and forces himself to focus. He pulls his phone from his pocket and starts taking pictures of the damage to the car.

Sending the images to Sarah in a WhatsApp message doesn't work; the dial spools and no tick appears. Swearing under his breath, he heads back to the door, holding his phone out in front of him, hoping to get reception when he is outside. Focused on the screen, he steps into the sunlight, momentarily blinded.

'What are you doing?'

Cal startles and almost drops the phone. A few feet away, Sean is peering at him, his face in its trademark scowl. He stutters a moment, caught off guard.

'Oh, Sean. I was just looking for your dad?'

'Why?'

'I wanted to have a chat, that's all.'

'He was filling the wood store. He's in the kitchen now.'

'Great, thanks, I'll go and find him.'

As he passes, words leap from the boy's mouth in a sort of whine. 'Why won't you just leave him alone?'

Cal is taken aback by the animosity on the teenager's face.

'I'm just trying to work out what happened, Sean,' he says. 'So you can all move on.' The words stick in his throat a little.

'We had moved on!' Sean clenches his fists then turns and strides away from Cal, disappearing into a line of trees that skirt the other side of the property.

He waits for a moment, shaken by the confrontation. But he makes himself think of Robbie and what he wants, of Shona and Bryony – the justice they deserve. He could go for help – he should do – but there's a boiling impatience inside him. He needs to do this now. He takes a breath, starts his microphone and walks to the kitchen.

Angus comes to the door long moments after he knocks, a frown on his face. 'Robbie's out.'

Cal swallows the angry words rising in his throat, the red-hot desire to confront. He makes his tone calm. 'Actually, it was you I came to see. I have a few questions.'

For a moment it looks like he's going to be turned away, but then Angus steps back and lets him into the kitchen. As he passes over the threshold, Cal shivers involuntarily. His fingers curl into his palms.

'I'm sorry about what happened,' Angus says. 'I hope your friend is recovering. Those roads can be very treacherous if you're not used to them.'

Cal forces himself to stay calm, not to rise to the bait. 'She's doing well,' he says, lightly. 'She's made of strong stuff.'

They stand in silence for a moment. He lets the discomfort swell, forcing Angus to fill the quiet.

'Katherine is doing a bit of shopping in the village. She'll be back soon.'

Steadying his breathing, Cal draws back a seat at the table without waiting to be asked. His senses are wired and his mind alert, no trace of the exhaustion he felt walking up the hill. There's a hum in the air, the certainty that he is on the right track.

'So, what did you want to ask me?' Angus stays back from the table, leaning against the counter, his arms folded, barriers raised.

'I wanted to ask you about your alibi.'

'What do you mean? We covered that.'

'I spoke to Nadia. You haven't been telling the truth.'

Angus' face ripples with pain, but before he can answer, there is an anguished shout from the doorway.

'No! Leave him alone! Why can't you leave us alone!'

As Cal spins around to look, he sees the other man's face contort in horror, is aware of his hands flying up in shock. It takes his mind long seconds to catch up with what his eyes are seeing. Sean is there behind him, his face red and tear-streaked, his eyes wild with grief and anger, a shotgun in his hands. He's pointing it at Cal, shaking so much that the dark circles of the barrel dip and rise before their eyes.

The suspended moment gives Cal time to look into his own death. It's Chrissie he pictures – standing, looking out to sea – clear and strong, and worth fighting for more than anything. *No.* He tells himself. *No, no, no.*

'Oh my God. Sean!' Angus cries out and the pain in his voice cuts into Cal. 'What are you doing?'

'I have to, Dad.' Tears and snot run down the boy's face. He takes one hand from the gun to wipe his nose. Cal thinks about springing but hesitates too long. 'He's going to take you away from me.'

'Where did you get the gun?' Angus sounds shell-shocked and as confused as Cal. 'I don't understand. What are you doing?'

'I found it.' Sean sobs, looking at his father. Cal sees the desperate sense of betrayal mingling with love and need. 'In the hiding place.'

'The hiding place?'

Christ, Cal thinks, staring at the gun. Sean's known the truth. All this time.

'The one in the fireplace in your bedroom.' Sean sobs. 'I was just sitting there. I didn't mean to look. The stone moved and there it was.'

Scrambling backwards, Cal manages to get to his feet, backing into a corner of the kitchen. He scans the room but there is no clear path to the exit.

'I won't let him take you away,' Sean wails, swinging the gun towards Cal again. 'I keep trying to warn him off but he doesn't listen.'

'That was you?' Cal's voice is thin, threaded with confusion as he recalibrates. Some of it fits. The childish fish on the doorstep, the keyed car and the slashed tyres. Not Barr, or Shona's abusive ex-boyfriend, but the acts of an angry teen protecting his father.

'What?' Angus turns to Cal for an explanation, his eyes wide. 'What are you talking about?'

'Someone's been trying to scare me off for a while.' It dawns on Cal what this means. It seems unfathomable. He stares at Sean. 'You ran us off the road. You nearly killed us.'

'What? Sean? What is he saying?'

It seems impossible that a boy could channel that much hate and desperation, but Cal can see it all there in Sean's face.

'The car in your shed is damaged,' he says. 'I'm pretty sure the paint will match the one of the car we were in. I've texted the pictures to my producer.' He prays that the message has gone.

Angus makes a noise of uncomprehending distress. 'What? Sean would never…' But his voice tails off as he stares at his son, at the reality.

'I can't let you take my dad.' Sean's fingers tighten on the trigger and fear washes through Cal as he sees the boy trembling. 'No matter what he's done.'

'What do you mean *no matter what I've done*?' Angus's voice trembles.

'I *know*, Dad. I found this.' Sean lifts the barrel of the gun slightly and Cal braces against the fridge. 'I've known for a while.'

'This isn't possible,' Angus says faintly. 'I don't understand.'

'Your alibi doesn't check out, Angus,' Cal reminds him. 'It's time for the truth.'

Angus glares at him.

'I went for a drive, that day,' he spits. 'I was upset. I was thinking about leaving her.'

At that moment, there is a noise from the hallway – the sound of the front door opening and someone dumping plastic bags on the mat. Sean startles and swings the barrel of the gun as he turns to look. Cal ducks and puts his hands to his head.

'Thanks, Robbie.' Katherine's voice floats through the house, followed by the rustling of coats and boots. Cal lunges forward, but Sean jerks the gun back towards him.

'Don't move!' The boy's scream silences the laughter from the hall.

'Sean?'

Quiet follows Katherine's words. Because of the way Sean is standing, she won't be able to see the gun.

'Katherine.' Cal finds his voice. 'It might be better if you both come back later. We're just having a chat.'

Sean's face creases in pain and Cal feels a terrible churning in his stomach. A sense of inevitability about it all. Why won't his mind work more quickly? He is stupid and slow, weakened by the crash.

'Sean? What's going on? Why are you crying?'

The boy stumbles further into the kitchen, backing into the corner opposite Cal. Katherine reaches the doorway, Robbie close behind, his face tight with confusion.

When she sees the gun, Katherine freezes and the shopping bag she is carrying crashes to the floor. In a single second, all of the colour drains from her face and she twists to look at Angus. Cal is struck by the intensity of anguish and dread.

'No,' she whispers, shaking her head. 'Please, no.'

He watches Katherine press her hand to her mouth, as if she can physically hold in the shock and emotion, stop it all pouring out into the room.

Robbie is trying to get past her, twisting his hands, staring at his brother. 'What's happening? Sean, what are you doing?'

'Robbie,' Cal calls. 'Get out of here, please.'

'No!' Sean screams again, arcing the gun across the kitchen, clearly terrified. 'No one leaves.'

'Sean, it's okay,' Katherine says, her voice so much calmer than Cal feels. 'We're all here.'

'I can't lose Dad.'

'I know, I know,' she croons. 'You won't.'

'Katherine,' Angus says, his voice breaking. 'You have to believe me. I don't know where this gun came from. Sean, please, put it down so we can talk.'

Angus takes a step towards his son. The boy moans and shakes his head.

But Cal is still watching Katherine. Tears have started to leak from the corners of her eyes. She makes no attempt to brush them away. There's something so still and strange about her, like she's made of glass. He thinks back for a moment. To the pictures on his coffee table in the cottage. Chrissie's words about Margot fly into his mind. *Pictures don't always mean what you think, Dad.*

Except maybe they do. Maybe you just need to know what to look for. That image of Katherine gazing up at her future husband, his first wife by his side. He'd focused so much on Angus that he forgot to look beyond.

He remembers now. The devotion on Katherine's face, mixed with something else: a sort of determination.

CHAPTER FORTY-SIX

WESTER ROSS, SCOTTISH HIGHLANDS

BRYONY, 2007

The small hand shaking her awake doesn't register at first, and when it does, Bryony rolls away towards the cold, empty, Angus side of the bed, trying to escape. She needs more sleep. Just another half an hour.

'Mum.' The whisper and the small hand on her again. She feels exhausted and irritated as she opens her eyes and looks into the worried face.

Even before she smells it, she knows that Robbie has wet the bed. Despair rushes through her, waking her fully.

'For God's sake, Robbie, not again?'

'Sorry,' he whispers. 'I tried to make it in time.'

She throws back the covers and brushes roughly past him, her whole body filled with an energy that feels like bile. When she opens the door to his room, she sees that the sheets are sopping and tangled, soft toys caught in the stinking mess. There is a trail of drips across the carpet and into the hallway, to the bathroom. Three rugs and the bedroom carpet are going to need cleaning. She wants to scream.

Sean is asleep in the bunk beneath so she has to leave it for now, because she can't take him being awake too. She can't take any more of this.

As she stands, fuming, on the landing, the sight of Robbie shivering in his wet pyjamas only incenses her more.

'Can't you go and sort yourself out? You're supposed to be a big boy now, Robbie. This has to stop.'

He nods, hanging his head and trailing to the bathroom. She turns away from the sight of him peeling off his sopping Superman pants and reaching for a flannel.

Why is Angus never here for any of this shit? Why is it always down to her? All these new promises mean nothing. She thinks of the job with Sal that she's just turned down and she wants to hit something.

'Mum.' The small voice again. 'Where shall I put these?'

He's holding the reeking clothes in his arms, his face pinched with worry.

'Just leave them in the bath,' she says, hating herself even as she hears the tone of her voice.

'Mouse got wet.' His voice trembles.

'Whose fault is that? Go and get some clean things on. Leave him there.'

'Sorry,' he whispers again.

She knows she should reach out and comfort him. 'I'm going to have to spend all morning cleaning everything,' she says, seeing his face drop even more. 'We won't be able to go swimming.'

Bryony thinks of the bag, packed and ready by the door. It's a school inset day and after the cold snap, the weather is unseasonably warm. She'd decided to try to make plans, to turn over a new leaf and be the mother she should be. That idea seems laughable now.

When they are all awake, she slams around the kitchen, unfairness spilling out of her, while the boys eat their breakfast. Then she goes upstairs to strip the beds, and gathers up all the wet soft toys and rugs. It will take three loads to get all this clean – she'll be washing and hanging washing all morning. Nothing ever dries here. Not properly. Angus still hasn't fixed the tumble dryer like he promised.

When she's opened the bedroom windows, she starts to tidy the toys scattered across the room, hurling them into the box. She lobs a purple dinosaur in and dislodges the mechanism, so it starts roaring, legs cycling. Swearing, she crosses the room and lifts it out, fumbling for the switch, half-tempted to throw it at the wall instead.

But then she looks up and she catches sight of her face in the mirror, contorted with self-pity and grief. And it's shocking. Seeing herself through another lens. She's a monster. Something in her breaks. She sways a little at the sight and then lowers herself to the edge of the bottom bunk.

Look – she wants to shake that woman – *look at the sight of you, how scary you are.*

She runs her hands down her face, almost shaking with the cold, hard truth of herself. This is not what she resolved to be. This is awful. The boys, Angus, would be better off without her. She should leave.

But then another thought makes its way through the despair. It's a clear thought in what is usually the fog of her mind and she holds it carefully, in case it breaks or dissolves. She doesn't *have* to be the monster.

Bryony strokes the plastic object in her hands – something her sons love – and feels resolve filling her. *Enough.* She takes a long, deep breath and sets the creature on the shelf, its ugly face pointing at the bunk.

She's going to have to be better. To be stronger. She's going to have to change. None of this is their fault. Standing, she walks to the top of the stairs. Mouse is on top of the pile of washing and she lifts his damp body.

'Robbie,' she calls, making her voice soft. 'Rob-Rob.'

His little face appears at the foot of the stairs so quickly that she knows he must have been waiting there, and her heart contracts. She lowers herself to the top step and holds the mouse next to her as if it were alive. She clears her throat and when she tries to sing, her voice is rusty and awful, but she carries on anyway because he won't care.

'I saw a mouse. Where? There on the stair. Where on the stair? Right there.'

As she sings, she makes the mouse dance, watching Robbie's face for a reaction. It's humbling how quickly his anxiety transforms to a sort of awe-struck curiosity.

'A little mouse with clogs on, well I declare, going clip-clippity-clop on the stair.'

As she sings, Robbie's mouth twitches into a smile. A second later, Sean's cheeky little face appears, peeking out from behind his brother. She carries on, warbling terribly, amazed by their delight. She's never had a moment like this with them, not ever. This is not something her parents would have considered doing either, she realises.

Bryony comes to the end of the song. She pauses and the boys remain totally still at the bottom of the stairs.

It's Robbie who speaks first – something as out of character for him as singing is for her. One tiny word. 'Again.'

'Again?'

He nods.

So she makes the mouse sing and dance, and this time the boys dance in time with it. She can barely finish the song for laughing. They do it three more times.

When she finishes, she slides down to the bottom step and takes a breath, holding her arms out to her sons and plunging into new territory as she squeezes them tight.

'I'm sorry. Mummy lost her temper. That was wrong. It's okay, Robbie, accidents happen. We can go swimming, okay? There's still lots of time.'

And there is, she realises, time to make things right.

'Really?' Sean squeaks. 'Yes!' He leaps from her arms and does a little sprint down the hallway to the swimming bag.

'Not this second, Seanie. Soon, though.' She looks at Robbie. 'First, we need to wash this guy, don't we?' She holds the damp mouse out and he flings his arms around them both. 'Why don't I put him in the washing machine for his bath and then we can hang him up to dry. You two can play in the garden until then if you like? Does that sound like a plan?'

'Yes!' They both shout and a warm revelation sweeps through her. They're suddenly all on the same team.

She helps them on with their coats and boots, and then goes back upstairs to gather the other wet cuddly toys. She pauses at the bedroom window and looks out. The boys are both bent over a hole they've dug right down the bottom of the garden, near the barns, prodding at the earth with sticks. She can hear their little voices on the breeze and she thinks about calling out to them. She wants to tell them, *I love you. I do love you*.

Bryony feels a sort of power rise up in her. A realisation that she has the ability to make this different. She's both less and more than she thought she was.

She leaves the window and walks to the landing, stepping over the pile of cleaning products she's been using to scrub the floors. None of this matters. Angus is coming back tonight – they can sort it out then. But before she reaches the stairs, the doorbell goes. A long, hard press that drills into her head.

Who could it be? No one ever comes to the door. She thinks of the anonymous calls they've been getting and her mind goes to Duncan, to the way things were left. The dread of a confrontation stalls her for a moment, making her pause halfway down the stairs, gripping the bannister. She wants to go to the boys, wants to start making things right, right now.

But then whoever it is leans on the bell again and she feels a surge of determination. If she has to tell him once and for all to leave her alone then she will. Things are going to be different now. No more stupid silent calls. She's taking her boys out. As she sets down the toys and takes purposeful steps, she has a sudden and unaccountable longing to feel Robbie's little arms around her, for him to press his worried face into her neck. She has so much making up to do.

Bryony pulls open the door, steeled. Ready to be decisive and firm. She is going to be the person she wants to be. But it isn't Duncan standing there.

'Oh. I didn't think you were coming today.' She forces a smile to move the corners of her mouth. 'Have we made a mistake? Or did Angus book you?'

Maybe, she thinks for a split second, he's surprising her.

And then she looks down and she sees the gun.

'What?' She half-laughs. 'What are you doing?'

'Angus said he wanted to learn to shoot. I thought maybe today…'

Does this girl really think Angus has time for that? That he'd even be here?

Pieces fall into place.

'He's not here,' she says, folding her arms. 'And I really don't think you're his type, you know. Have you been calling the house?'

The schoolgirl's face turns red and she screws her eyes up tight as if she's concentrating on her homework, blurting out the words, 'You don't deserve him.' She steps backwards, the gun rising in her hands.

'Kitty. What on earth are you talking about?'

'You should leave him alone. And Robbie and Sean. They'd be better off without you. All of them.'

The echo of her own thoughts in the girl's words stuns Bryony. The words are true. They were true. But she's going to change. She is.

'What are you going to do? Steal my husband?'

It's preposterous, being warned off her own husband by a schoolgirl. She gestures at the gun. 'Does your dad even know you've got that?' Bryony steps down onto the long slab of stone, feels it cold beneath her feet. 'Go home, Kitty.'

'Angus needs someone better. So do Robbie and Sean.'

A bubble of hysteria travels up Bryony's throat and breaks free: another strangled laugh – disbelief rather than amusement. Honestly, she's going to have to talk to Sue and Kevin. They can't have her here again. Ever.

'Don't laugh at me!'

'I'm not!' Bryony holds her hands up.

'You're so mean to them.'

A protective anger wells inside her. How dare this schoolgirl threaten her like this? But then, she's telling the truth.

The truth as it was. Not anymore.

'We won't need your help anymore, Kitty. You need to go home. You're not supposed to be here.'

'You make me sick!'

Kitty's face twists and she lurches, and then there's the loudest sound. So loud that it jerks Bryony backwards and she hits the door frame. She sees the shock on the girl's face, reaches out a hand to her, confused and wondering why she feels so odd. Bryony stumbles and then the gun goes off a second time, and a chunk of stone falls from the wall by her head.

She slides down the door jamb until she's sitting on the step. Her thoughts start to jumble and contort.

Today was going to be different. They were going to go out. From here, she can see down the driveway, almost all the way to the sea.

Kitty is crying – approaching then retreating, her hands shaking. Bryony closes her eyes. She doesn't want to look at her. The girl keeps crying, louder now. 'Sorry, I'm sorry, I'm sorry...'

A hand touches her, pulls back.

Footsteps, stepping over her and running into the house.

Then returning. Another desperate sob. Feet crunching on gravel, round the side of the house, towards the hill. Only then does Bryony open her eyes. Her foot twitches without her permission.

Help, she thinks, vaguely. *Robbie. Sean.*

CHAPTER FORTY-SEVEN

Katherine steps towards Sean.

'Don't.' He sobs, but she keeps moving steadily across the floor, hands held out, and it dissolves some of the boy's false bravado.

She's been his mother – the thought stabs Cal. All this time, she's been his mother. She puts her hands over his, gently unclenching his fingers, so careful it hurts to watch. He should move, do something, but he is frozen to the spot.

'It's okay, Sean. You can let go,' Katherine croons.

'I found it,' he tells her, sounding like a child again. 'There's a loose stone in the hearth upstairs. The one in your room.'

'I know,' she says. 'I know there is.'

She lifts the shotgun from his grip and sets it carefully on the table behind her. Sean falls into her arms.

And all the pieces tumble into place.

Katherine. Kitty. The daughter of the farmer who sold the house to Angus and Bryony. The one who volunteered to babysit and take some of the strain. Who knows this house like the back of her hand.

'You grew up here.'

She looks over Sean's shoulder at Cal, grief wearing away the youth on her face. 'That's right.'

'You've left it there. All this time?'

'What?' Angus looks like a man whose world has spun on its axis. His voice trembles. He cannot hear what he is being told, because it is going to destroy everything.

Cal has time to see the resignation in Katherine's eyes, the dark secret festering at the heart of it all, before she moves her gaze to Angus. Regret and desire intertwined.

'I didn't know what to do,' she whispers. 'I had no way of getting back into the house. For years. And then... I thought maybe it was all a bad dream. I wished it was. So I left it there. I didn't look.'

'No.' Angus sways in shock and for a moment Cal thinks he might fall. Sean steps back, his face pale and disbelieving. She's the one who held them all together. She patched them up and made them strong.

'I thought' – Katherine swallows tears, looking round at them all – 'that if I could be the best wife and the best stepmother then it would make up for it. That one stupid, stupid thing I did. The worst thing I ever did and can never take back. I thought that maybe it was meant to be, that we were meant to be...'

She looks anxiously at Angus but Cal can see the man's usual tenderness towards her is morphing in the face of this new reality.

'You killed Bryony?'

The words are barely a breath but Katherine's body starts to shake. 'It was an accident. I didn't mean to do it. I loved you, Angus. I loved you even then and I couldn't bear the way she was with the boys and with you and... she laughed at me and I just didn't think. I didn't know the gun was already loaded.'

Cal can feel the tension in the room rising again, the way they all bristle at the mention of Bryony – difficult or unwell, depending who you asked, but wronged, either

332

way. He is also intensely aware of the weapon lying on the table, seemingly forgotten. Is it loaded now? There's no way to tell, but it certainly won't have been maintained over the past fourteen years it's spent languishing, a rotten secret at the core of their home. Could it go off without warning?

'Whose gun was it?' Angus whispers. 'How did you get a gun?'

'My father's. From the farm.'

'So… does he *know*?' Angus looks terrible, his skin chalky. 'He must know it went missing.'

'I don't know.' Katherine shakes her head and a tear runs down her cheek.

'He stays away, though,' Angus says slowly. 'Doesn't he?' He looks at Cal. 'I've always known he disapproves of us. He won't look at me. I thought it was the age gap. All this time. That's what I thought.'

Cal glances at Robbie – his eyes are filled with tears but he is completely still, watching.

Katherine reaches out for Angus, whether seeking or offering comfort, it's not clear, but he recoils and she cries out. A sound so piercing, Cal wishes he could put his hands over his ears and cower under the table until it all goes away.

He's about to step forward and take the gun, move it somewhere safe, when an ear-splitting sound starts up, a shrill and piercing beeping. Startled, Cal jerks his head to look up: the smoke alarms must be connected – they are all going off.

'The fire. I was lighting the fire.' Angus darts past and down the hallway. Cal chases after him in time to see him throw open the living room door to billows of noxious smoke. The hearthrug is completely alight, flames snaking towards the heavy curtains. His throat feels tight; his lungs protest.

Angus speeds back past him into the hallway and grabs a fire extinguisher from a cupboard. Cal has never seen the man move this quickly. 'There's a fire blanket by the oven,' he shouts.

'Robbie, get the others out,' Cal calls to the boy. 'Out the back. Go, now.'

He runs to the kitchen and grabs the red box on the wall by the oven. The clean air at the back door smells so sweet. He's vaguely aware of Robbie guiding Sean, who seems mute with shock, no longer a dangerous teenager but a small boy again.

He rushes back to Angus, who is spraying foam on the curtains. Cal throws the blanket onto the blazing rug, smothering the flames. Then they work together, stamping on the sparks that have spread around the room.

They're both coughing and it's hard to see, but then Robbie is there behind them, with a bucket of sand. He hands it to Angus, who uses it to douse the flames. Angus is a man possessed – maybe the urgent need to save his home is staving off the terrible truth he's going to have to face. Cal feels pinpricks of guilt at the thoughts he's had about Angus. Duped for so long.

The three of them stand, panting for a second, scouring the room for evidence that the fire is still burning, but all they see is a mess of smoke and soot, foam and sand. Angus crosses to the windows and throws them open, bending over the sill and dragging clean air into his lungs. The fire alarms are still shrieking, and they waft the smoke out, trying to clear the house.

'Where's Sean?' Cal feels a spear of worry that the boy has been left alone.

'He's outside.'

Robbie joins him as he runs through the house to the back door. Standing a few feet away, Sean is pale and shuttered, no more a threat than the ashes in the living room. Cal feels a toxic mixture of revulsion and pity kindling inside him.

But then his heart stutters.

Where is Katherine?

He spins on the spot. The kitchen table is empty. The gun is gone.

'Where is she?' he yells to Sean.

'I don't know. She didn't come out. She said she needed to help. To fix things. I thought she meant the fire…'

'She's taken the gun. Robbie, can you get Sean somewhere safe?'

Cal grabs Robbie's arm. 'Get him away from here.' He pushes him from the doorway, frightened for them, alarmed at how fast things are slipping out of control. 'Call 999.'

Then he runs to the living room, where Angus is emerging, his soot-covered face tracked by tears. Mercifully, the alarms cease their protest.

'Katherine's missing,' he tells him. 'She's got the gun. She didn't go out the back.'

Angus strides to the front door while Cal checks the dining room, knowing it's unlikely she's there, and finds it cold and empty. Then they hear the creak of footsteps on old floorboards above them. Angus turns to the stairs.

'Katherine!'

'Angus, wait…'

Cal tries to grab him, but trips, still weakened by the accident. He hits the floor and lies stunned for a moment, the world advancing and receding. It would be so easy just to stay here.

But then, from the corner of his eye, he sees the flare of flame in the living room: the fire persisting despite their efforts at suffocation. The open window is giving the obsessive creature more oxygen.

Move, Cal, you have to move. He forces himself into action. He has to get the others out. But as he rolls onto his side, he hears a shout from Angus.

'Katherine! No!'

There's the sound of furniture flying, a struggle happening above him. Cal crawls forward, rising to his knees and grabbing the newel post to pull himself upwards. He can guess why Katherine took the gun and vanished, can only pray Angus will stop her. But as he rises to his feet, the gun goes off.

Silence for a split second. And then a terrible keening. Katherine.

Cal inches forward up the stairs. The wind has been knocked out of him by the fall.

'Katherine,' he whispers. He follows the sound down the hall. His senses are coming back to him, his pace is quicker, the hairs on his arms are standing in fear.

As he turns into the bedroom, the scene that greets him is one of destruction. In the centre of the chaos, Angus is crumpled on the floor, blood soaking into the rug beneath him. Katherine is cowering in the corner, trembling, the gun by her side.

Wide fearful eyes meet his. 'It was an accident,' she howls. 'I tried to do it and he jumped in the way.'

Cal feels sick. He steps forward carefully, keeping his eyes on her. She stays crouched in the corner, rocking back and forth, her head in her hands. He drops to his knees beside Angus and rolls him over. The man has suffered a glancing blow, his shoulder a bloody mess. As Cal applies pressure, he groans and writhes at the pain.

'Katherine,' he yells. 'Listen to me. He's alive. I need you to help me.'

But Katherine is lost. She keeps up her rocking and wailing, making a kind of sing-song noise of distress. He rushes to her and shakes her arm but she wrenches it away. 'Katherine, we need to get out. The fire has restarted.'

Cal's mind feels like it's going to explode. The smoke alarms are blaring again and Angus is bleeding. He can't stay up here; it isn't safe.

He'll have to take him down and come back for Katherine. Or pray that she comes to her senses and follows.

He shouts to her what he's doing, while he hoists Angus to a standing position, looping the man's good arm over his back and finding reserves of strength he never imagined were in him. The pain from his rib is blinding. As he staggers to the doorway, he tries to turn and see if she is coming but she's still crying in the corner. He roars with the effort of holding Angus upright, using the sound to find more energy, then grits his teeth and half-carries, half-drags him down the hall towards the stairs.

At the top, he sees the smoke, once again swirling from the living room, hears the crackle and dance of persistent flame, and he pauses and looks back. She still isn't following.

'Katherine! Come on!'

He slides Angus to the floor – the man isn't properly awake – but at the moment he turns to go back, there is a crash of debris in the living room. It sounds like parts of the ceiling have caved in. The flames have reached the hallway and if he doesn't get Angus down there now, they're going to be cut off.

Cal dithers for one impossible second. What's the right thing to do? His mouth and nose are clogged with smoke and the infernal screeching of the alarms. He turns to go back to the bedroom. There must be time to save them both. But then another noise halts him in his tracks. The crack of gunshot – the sound of a decision being made for him.

–

Cal drags Angus down the stairs, cradling his head as best he can as they slide down into clouds of smoke. Inch by inch, he pulls him towards the front door, reaching up to find the latch and to wrench it open. He tugs him out onto the wide, warped stone, and lies there coughing and gasping in the fresh air. As soon as he can move, Cal pulls off his jumper and presses it to Angus's shoulder, holding tight against the wound. The man is weak and pale, drifting from consciousness as he lies on the great slab of stone.

Behind them, the living room burns, the reignited flames consuming the furnishings and sending smoke pouring from the windows in a great, grey funnel that must be visible for miles. Cal urges Angus to hold on, tells him to stay for his sons, but he isn't sure the man can hear him. The world feels lonely.

Then, feet on the gravel. He looks up to see the neighbour, Hamish, sprinting down the driveway, fourteen years after he found Bryony.

'The boys,' he shouts to him. 'They're round the back. Can you get them?'

Hamish dashes away.

A few moments later, Robbie appears down the side of the house, his blue eyes wide. When he sees his father, he recoils in shock.

'It's okay, Robbie,' Cal shouts when he sees the boy's horror, the way he is transported back through the years. 'He's alive.'

He reaches out a hand and beckons him closer, keeping the other pressed on Angus' shoulder. 'Come on, Robbie, come.'

Eyes glassy, the boy edges closer. He crouches down and Cal grips his hand in his.

'Talk to him, Robbie. He can hear you.'

The step is cold beneath them. From here you can see the sea in the distance. A siren sounds and the house burns.

CHAPTER FORTY-EIGHT

EPISODE SIX: ON THE DOORSTEP

When you can't find the answer, sometimes that's because the answer is too close for comfort.

Bryony Campbell's grave is on a small rise that overlooks the sea. In the summer, the slush and swill of the waves makes it a peaceful spot. In the winter, the fury of the salt and spray is a different kind of tribute to the way her life ended.

This podcast has raked through the details of her life, seeking answers to the mystery of who had motivation to shoot her on the doorstep of her home fourteen years ago. The crime broke her family apart and, struck by the effect Bryony's death still had on her eldest son, Robbie, we wanted to try and find a resolution that would allow him to move forward with his life.

Only, it turns out that it wasn't Bryony's life we should have been looking at.

Angus married his second wife, Katherine, four years after Bryony died. But Katherine, then known as Kitty, was close to the family before that. The daughter of farmers Sue and Kevin, she had actually been brought up in the house Angus and Bryony bought when her parents relocated the family to a modern property a few fields away.

When Bryony was struggling with her mental health and the care of her two boys, it was suggested that a babysitter would allow her and Angus to spend some time repairing their relationship, as well as taking a little of the strain that Bryony was feeling from motherhood. A local teenager with time on her hands and in need of cash, Kitty was an ideal choice to help out.

What grew from there was Kitty's obsession with Angus and her conviction that Bryony didn't deserve the family she had, that Kitty was far more deserving of it. We cannot ask Katherine what happened that day on the doorstep, but we know she went there with a shotgun from her father's farm, we know she took Bryony's life, and we know that, in a panic, she hid the weapon in an upstairs hearth before fleeing the farmhouse.

The missing gun lay hidden for years, until one of Bryony's sons found it and assumed it meant their father had killed their mother. Terrified of losing both parents, he kept the knowledge secret until he believed Angus was about to be accused. Once the gun was found, Katherine turned it on herself and took her own life.

Before she died, she made her confession. Today we will play you recordings of that moment.

It's my personal belief that Katherine was no longer the same person she had been as a teenager, and that she spent her adult life paying for the horrific act she had committed. As stepmother to Bryony's children, the more she grew to love them, the greater her shame became and the deeper the secret had to be buried to protect them.

There are no winners in this tale. The fallout of the crime continues. Angus, widowed for the second time, was injured in his attempt to wrestle the gun from Katherine, and the farmhouse has been destroyed by fire. His son Sean is now in a secure institution, awaiting treatment for crimes he committed to protect his father. I'm Cal Lovett, and this is the final episode of this series of Finding Justice.

EPILOGUE

CAL, THREE MONTHS LATER

He's dreading this day. It's a mistake, he knows it is. No one will come or, worse, protesters will show up and turn the whole thing into a circus. But he can hear the whispering outside the door and he knows he can't hide in the bedroom much longer. Looking in the mirror, Cal straightens his tie and tries to mentally adjust to the lines on his face and the fact that he looks way older than he feels.

'Is he coming?'

'You ask him… or shall I?'

Despite the nerves, he can't help but smile as he creeps over to the closed bedroom door. His new flat is a two-bed rental a few streets from his mother's place. They both agreed that living together was a failed experiment. Though things between them are still strained and she isn't coming today, they are trying. He knows he will never live in his childhood home again. It was a huge mistake to go back there, to believe that the ghosts would be manageable rather than overwhelming.

Here, he has no history. Just a fresh start. There are shells lined on his windowsills that Robbie sends Chrissie whenever he goes home for a weekend from Edinburgh, where he is starting a work placement while he applies to study engineering. Cal loves that Chrissie has made the flat her own space too. She has her own room – he wanted her to have the brighter, bigger of the two so she can paint in the best light – and he loves that Shona and Rocket can come and visit without seeking his mother's permission.

He does not love the fact that they're now ganging up on him.

Easing down the handle, he flings back the door so that Chrissie and Shona almost tumble into the room in surprise. He chuckles.

'Dad!'

'I can hear every word, you know.'

'Well,' Chrissie says, and he can see by the way her hand hovers at her throat how nervous she is. '*Are* you coming?'

He has to get over this. It matters to her and he agreed to it. He plants a smile on his face.

'Yes. I'm ready. How do I look?'

'Beautiful, Dad,' she says, her back already turned. 'Robbie's meeting us there. Come on, let's go.'

Shona hangs back while Chrissie grabs her coat. Cal notices that she's steadying herself against the wall – still not at full strength. He reaches for her, twisting his fingers through hers and leaning in for a kiss, giving her support as subtly as he can. Not that he can hide much from her. He can tell that she sees his reluctance about today. He pats his pocket, checking that the brief speech he has written is still in there.

'You've got this,' she whispers, and he feels the strength flowing from her to him.

More than three months on from the accident, she is only just back at work on reduced hours and with additional nagging from Cliff. He can't believe how close he came to losing her, but she's here and every moment they spend together seems to weave her more tightly into his life.

The memorial for Margot isn't at the river, or at the bench in the park. Those are places infused with sadness, and Chrissie is adamant that today is a celebration of her aunt's life. She hasn't told Cal the full guest list but he knows she's spent hours tracking down old friends and asking them about Margot.

It's something he's wanted for so long – this memorial to his sister – and his daughter's dedication to it is the most precious gift. But the fact that the world turned against Margot changed Cal. It makes him want to hide her memory and protect it from the ridiculous victim-blaming judgement.

Is that how his mother feels? he wonders, glancing at Chrissie as they stroll along the pavement in the sunshine. That bringing Margot into the light is exposing her? It's the first time he's come close to some reasoning around her behaviour and it startles him that he can almost see a way to understanding. But then Chrissie grins at him and links arms, and again he cannot fathom how his mother can bear to stay away.

It doesn't matter, he decides. If it's just the three of them and DI Foulds there, then so be it. They will get through the service, remember Margot and he will grill Foulds on how she's going to put that fucker Barr away. The thought makes his pace lighten. Forensics have matched Barr's hair to one found with Margot's remains but the CPS have been vacillating on the decision of whether or not to prosecute.

When they reach it, the churchyard is deserted: grave-stones slump in the shade, and it is cool and inviting under the yew trees on this warm day. This is where Margot's ashes will be interred when the police have finished with her remains. It is his mother's wish and Chrissie has chosen the location in the hope she can bring them together.

'Where is everyone?' Chrissie frowns, and Cal feels a beat of sympathy for her. She's worked so hard. But then Robbie appears from the entrance to the small chapel, looking sharp in a suit and tie, and her face breaks into sunlight. Once she's greeted him, Cal strides forward and takes Robbie's outstretched hand, pulling him into a tight hug. It's such a relief and a reward to see him looking whole and healthy, no longer a wraith.

'How are you doing? How is your dad getting on? And Sean?'

Angus has refused to speak to Cal since that day at the farmhouse.

Robbie's face clouds for a second and he shrugs. 'Dad's okay. He's staying in the village, but in one of the cottages on the seafront. He's selling the land. Sean's still angry. I think he might be that way for a long time.' He turns to Shona. 'I can't believe what he did to you – I'm so sorry.'

'You have nothing to be sorry for.' She touches his arm and Cal sees the tension in Robbie's frame dissipate.

'Come on,' he says. 'Everyone's here.'

Cal follows, relieved that one or two people have made the effort – not bad, considering more than thirty-six years have elapsed since she vanished.

He is completely unprepared for the scene that greets him inside. The church isn't large, but every pew is packed with people wearing bright colours. Their heads swivel to him as he enters, and he finds he is overcome with emotion as he scans the room. Andy is here, hair slicked back and tugging at his sleeves, and he also recognises police officers, old teachers and friends of his from school. Cal pauses on the threshold, trying to take it all in. There are flowers everywhere. There are children sitting on parents' knees. The whole room is bursting with life. It strikes him full in the face: people care.

The revelation leaves him paralysed. His face is frozen and his throat clogged.

Chrissie hands him a programme and he looks down to see an elegant pen-line sketch of Margot on the cover, alongside photographs of his sister as she was: smiling and beautiful. He doesn't recognise all of the pictures – where has Chrissie found them? He must ask her later, but right now his hands are shaking and a million questions swirl around in his head.

Shona takes his arm and leads him down the aisle to the front row. He puts one hand to his mouth, his eyes smarting. As they sit, he feels Shona and Chrissie pressed tight to his sides, holding him in place. It feels as if they are the only things stopping him from drifting away. The vicar steps forward to shake his hand and then turns to the congregation.

Cal hardly hears a word of the sermon. He is lost in memory and emotion. It's as if Margot is in the room with him, spinning in the motes of dust that dance in stained-glass light. This is everything he ever dreamed and more.

When it comes to the time for him to say his few words, he can't stand. The lump in his throat won't let him speak and he feels a blinding flash of panic that he's going to let them all down. But then Chrissie gently takes the notes from his hand and steps up to the pulpit. Her red curls catch the sunlight as he watches her, taking the burden for him.

'I don't know if I can read my dad's writing,' she says, and he exhales as the congregation laughs at her joke, the atmosphere saturated with kindness. 'But he's feeling a little overwhelmed. It's been so long since Auntie Margot was taken that he didn't think anyone would remember. He didn't think anyone would come.'

A sympathetic murmur ripples round the church. He hasn't said this to her, but of course she knows, his sensitive, thoughtful girl. She can see into him, after all.

She reads about his memories of his sister, and the void she left, so lightly and with such love that he doesn't notice the tears streaming down his cheeks until Shona hands him a tissue. Looking around, he sees he's not the only one in the room crying.

'I also wanted to add a few words of my own to Dad's,' Chrissie says, when she reaches the end. Her smile wobbles and Cal feels a matching lurch inside himself. 'I never met my aunt. But I feel as if she's walked beside me my whole life.' One side of her mouth lifts. 'Dad's over there panicking now that it means I've been damaged by the family trauma.' They laugh and he marvels at the way she holds the room so effortlessly. 'But that couldn't be further from the truth. From everything I've been told, Margot was bold and fun and brave. The terrible thing is that she didn't get to live her life, but her memory is so strong and those qualities so definite that it feels like they've guided Dad's parenting of me and created this belief that I can do anything. I love the fact that I look like her; it makes me feel that we have a special bond, even if we never got to meet in person.'

347

As Chrissie ducks her head and crosses to their pew, someone at the back starts to clap and the sound spreads so rapidly that by the time she sits down the air is filled with applause and her face is crimson. Cal hugs her to him.

'Thank you.'

'Was it okay?'

'It was perfect.'

The vicar waits for the applause to die down. 'Before we move into the hall for some refreshments, would anyone else like to say a few words?'

Cal can't imagine anyone is going to volunteer and, sure enough, there's a moment's silence into which someone coughs. He waits for the vicar to wrap things up but then a woman sitting a few pews back on the other side raises her hand.

Curious, Cal swivels to watch as she squeezes out of the pew. Her greying hair is elegantly pinned to her head and her lips are a slash of scarlet that jolts a memory. She smiles at him as she moves past and a twist of recognition turns inside him.

'I'm Diane,' she says when she reaches the front. 'Some of you know me.' She looks at Cal: 'But I haven't seen *you* since you were nine years old.'

Diane. He remembers her now – she and Margot locked in his sister's room, screeching with laughter. His mother always thought Diane was a bad influence.

'Your sister would be so proud of you. She doted on you.'

He nods, welling at the acknowledgement. He knows this, really, but to have someone else validate it is wonderful. All of the negative media attention has had him questioning everything he thought he knew. He settles back and listens to Diane's memories, her tribute to her friend, and Margot swells and becomes real once more.

Then more people put up their hands to speak and for the next twenty minutes he hears their memories and stories, collecting them to add to his own. When everyone has spoken, he stands at the entrance to the hall, shaking the hands of the people who have come to pay tribute, a blurry onslaught of condolences and kindness. He can't quite work out what he feels about it all.

When he moves into the body of the hall, he is again surprised, this time to see tables laden with sandwiches, cakes and drinks. He turns to Chrissie. 'How did you manage this?'

'It was Diane's idea,' she says. 'She organised everyone to bring it all. I didn't have to do anything.'

Cal sees Foulds and another couple of officers with full plates of food, mingling among the mix of people. Andy is hanging back, trying to keep out of their way, and when Cal catches his eye, he seems to panic, scanning for an exit. He is shocked at how old and stooped the man seems these days. He has the feeling Andy is punishing himself enough. He nods at him and then his elbow is caught by an old friend of Margot's who wants to say hello. When he turns back, Andy has gone.

The afternoon passes in a whirl. After a couple of hours, the room has thinned out. Diane approaches – she's been busy corralling people and they haven't had a chance to say more than hello.

'I remember you,' he tells her now, as they embrace.

'I've never forgotten her,' Diane says fiercely. He can see a deep sadness in her eyes: a different kind of loss. It's overwhelming to see the ripples of one cast stone. 'Maybe now isn't the time, but I wanted to ask what's happening about her case…'

'I'm not sure,' he says, sighing. 'There's DNA evidence they had contact but his line is that they were in a relationship so that's to be expected. I'm not sure the CPS will go ahead, to be honest.'

He realises how tired he feels and wishes he could lie down and sleep. He looks over the room at Shona, conscious that she must be exhausted, but she is sitting, chatting to Robbie.

'But that's nonsense,' Diane says with the kind of blazing anger he is too worn down to summon. 'Margot was never interested in him. Never.'

'You remember him?'

'He was a bouncer at a club we used to go to.' She glances around, then reaches into the inside pocket of her bright purple blazer and pulls out an envelope. 'Look, I brought this in case you wanted to share it with the papers to stop them printing the nonsense they have been. I can't bear it.' Cal's heart rate ratchets up: he's not sure he can take this today. It has been too beautiful and perfect, but he's also curious and cannot turn away.

He slides the photos out.

'You don't have to do that here,' Diane says, but it is too late.

It's a photograph of a wall. He frowns, confused.

'It was his thing,' Diane says in disgust.

'I don't understand.'

Diane stabs the photo with a manicured nail. 'We snuck into the staffroom one night and took a picture of the pinboard. I've been looking for this ever since they published that picture of him and her.'

Cal looks more closely. There is the occasional poster for a music night or happy hour and some staff announcements tacked up, but the board is basically papered in photographs. Cal peers at it. It's hard to tell, but he thinks the images are of Barr. Other bouncers too, but mainly Barr. In each shot he has his arms round a different woman. Some of them are smiling, but most look uncomfortable, and in several they are being assaulted. In one, Barr has his hand on the exposed breast of a clearly drunk girl, her top wrenched down to allow him access. He's leering at the camera. Cal feels bewildered and sick.

'What am I looking at? I don't understand.'

'It was his thing,' Diane says again in a low voice, as one of her grandchildren toddles past them, a sausage roll in her chubby hand. 'To allow you into the club they – usually he – would make you take a picture and if you didn't smile then they'd turn you away. You can see some of them were worse than others. They put their favourites on that bloody wall. We snuck in to try and get back one showing our friend.'

'You're kidding.'

'No. And the thing that blows my mind is that we all hated it but we thought we had to put up with that shit. That's why she was smiling – because they gave you a hard time if you didn't look like you were enjoying it. It was easier to get it right the first time.' She stares at where her granddaughters are spinning, dresses flying out around them, laughing. 'I really hope it's different for them.'

Cal has to make a conscious effort to stop himself swaying.

'But this…' *This changes everything.* He looks up at Diane, hope kindling inside him. 'Can I keep this?'

She nods. 'Have it.'

Cal looks around for Foulds but she must have left; he vaguely remembers her waving across the room at him. He puts the photograph back in the envelope, tucking it into his pocket. 'Would you be willing to talk to the police about this?'

'Hell, yes. I'll stand up in court and testify if it helps put that piece of shit away. I'll find others to back me up.'

'You think it was him.'

Diane's lips form a tight, thin line. She nods. Barr's publicity machine hasn't got everyone fooled. She wraps her arms around him in a hug. He feels for a second like he has an older sister looking out for him. In that second he loses Margot all over again. He doesn't have an older sister. Not anymore.

–

When Diane has gone to mastermind the cleaning up, he leans back against the wall and watches the chaos of the room dwindle to peace again: the last children scooped up, the final plates covered and the floor swept by Robbie, while Chrissie stops Shona trying to do the washing-up and makes her sit down. He should help, he knows he should, but he's too tired to move. It's such a bitter-sweet experience. Finding this community of memory and loss, but also seeing Diane and her family, and truly understanding the life Margot lost. They should have been grandmothers together.

By the time they leave the church, there are long shadows in the orange light of the graveyard. Chrissie and Robbie are walking hand in hand, so comfortable together, and it warms him to see it. After a moment, she drops back to where he and Shona are walking and links her arm in his. Shona moves forward to speak to Robbie and he is relieved to see she is walking better than she has been recently. Maybe her energy levels are coming back.

'You okay, Dad?'

He looks down at Chrissie, overwhelmed by what she's done.

'Thank you, love,' he says. And though the words seem inadequate, as it is impossible to truly measure the gift she has given him, she seems to understand. 'It was perfect. I just wish your grandmother could have heard those stories.'

'Robbie was filming it so you can listen to it again. Gran can too.'

Cal finds himself unable to speak for a moment. All of those memories have been captured for him. 'That's incredibly thoughtful,' he says finally.

'It was his idea, Dad. I think he understands how you feel.'

He watches Robbie ahead of them, chatting to Shona, the two of them laughing at something she has said. He has such mixed feelings about the podcast. It broke as many things as it fixed. But, ultimately, everything that came crashing down was founded on lies. Bryony didn't deserve it, and the truth has helped Robbie to step out of the shadows. For that, Cal is glad.

As they reach the road, Cal turns and looks back at the church.

It could be his imagination, but he thinks there is the silhouette of a man in the distance. A man with a thick neck and the curl of cigarette smoke around him, a man who could not bear to stay away. He doesn't want Chrissie to see him – the day has been perfect and he won't have it ruined. But when she catches up with Robbie and Shona, he stops and turns again, his stance making it clear that he knows, fixing his gaze on the dark blot. He hopes the gesture makes it clear that he's not afraid. That he can see it all and he's coming for him. Soon.

The figure peels away from the wall. It melts into the dusk as if it was never there at all.

Acknowledgements

A huge thank you to the people who've supported me in writing the next in the Cal Lovett series – and to all of the incredible booksellers, bloggers, readers and reviewers who were kind enough to read, review and promote *Unsolved*, helping it find a wider audience. Your enthusiasm, both for Cal and for books in general, has propelled me. I am so grateful to you all.

Working with the team at Canelo continues to be a dream. Thank you to my editors Louise Cullen, Katy Loftus and especially to the lovely Alicia Pountney for keeping everything running like clockwork. Thanks to Victoria Hughes-Williams for her insightful structural edit, Miranda Ward for a wonderfully thorough line edit and Daniela Nava for her copy-editing expertise (and especially the GIFs). Huge thanks to the rest of the Canelo team, including Kate Shepherd, Thanhmai Bui-Van and Nicola Piggott – you've worked so hard to get Cal in front of readers. And thank you to Andrew Davis for another stunning cover.

Thank you to my agent Charlotte Seymour for continuing to guide me through the publishing world and for being endlessly kind and supportive of even my craziest ideas. Thanks also to Hélène Butler, Anna Dawson and the rest of the Johnson & Alcock team.

A very big thank you to Ali Schwind for her shooting expertise, Genevieve Loveland for keeping me right on the legal terminology, Adrian Marsh and Tim Trebble for medical expertise, and Jon Bates for sense checking RTA details. Any errors that remain are mine alone!

I'm so lucky to have incredible writing friends who are so generous with their time. Thank you, Sam Holland and Rachael Blok, for early reads of *Unburied* and for suggestions that drastically improved the text. Thank you, Jo Furniss, for helping track down the expertise I needed. Thank you as always to Tammye, Chris, Gillian and Eugenia for monthly writing support and for reading the full manuscript at very short notice.

To the fabulous Criminal Minds – Adam Southward, Rachael Blok, Clare Empson, Dom Nolan, Elle Croft, Fliss Chester, James Delargy, Jo Furniss, Tim Kinsey, Susie Lynes, Niki Mackay, Simon Masters, Polly Phillips, Eleanor Ray, Kate Simants, Rob Scragg, Louisa Scarr and Victoria Selman – thank you for daily wit and wisdom. And badgers.

Huge thanks to all of the authors who read and blurbed *Unsolved*. It means the world. And to all of the lovely people I've met at events and online – thank you too. Your company and community transforms the archetypal solitary writing life.

To all of my friends and family – thank you for being so enthusiastic and supportive in my debut year. It's been wonderful celebrating with you and you've blown me away with your excitement. A special mention to my Mum, June, for being my bookshop tour buddy on more than one occasion.

And finally, the team that keeps me going every day: Will, Rachel and Adam. Thank you for being such stars. I'm sorry two of you can't read it yet…

ⓒ **CANELO**CRIME

Do you love crime fiction and are always on the lookout for brilliant authors?

Canelo Crime is home to some of the most exciting novels around. Thousands of readers are already enjoying our compulsive stories. Are you ready to find your new favourite writer?

Find out more and sign up to our newsletter at canelocrime.com